The Harlow Hoyden

Lynn Messina

D0707387

potatoworks press
greenwich village

CHAPTER ONE

Miss Emma Harlow was so intent on her task that she did not notice the gentleman in the leather armchair. She didn't see him lower his book, cock his head to the side and examine her with interest.

"I say, is that the best way to do that?" the gentleman asked after a moment.

Emma, whose feathers were never the sort to ruffle easily, even when she was behaving improperly in a place she didn't belong—in this case, with her fingers around the stem of a prize *Rhyncholaelia digbyana* in the Duke of Trent's conservatory—calmly turned around. Her blue-eyed gaze, steady and sometimes intimidating, met with an amused brown one. "Excuse me?"

The gentleman closed the leather-bound edition, taking care to mark the page, and stood up. "Snapping the stem will ill serve your purpose," he said, approaching.

Emma watched him stride across the room, taking in his handsome features—the long, straight nose, the chiseled jawline, the full lips—and neat appearance. The unknown gentleman was tall, lean and given to easy grace. She liked the way he was dressed, simply and without affectation in buckskin breeches, shiny Hessians and white lawn. His shirt points were without starch and his shoulders without padding. Of course, she readily noted,

1

his broad shoulders precluded the necessity of such foppish enhancements. His hair, a deep rich brown color that well suited his dark complexion, was cut short in the fashionable mode. "My purpose?" she asked when he was within a few inches of her.

"Given the situation, I can only assume that you were overcome with admiration for this lovely and rare flower and sought to take it home with you to show off to all your friends in the Horticultural Society." He didn't wait for her to confirm or deny his theory but continued in the same conversational tone. "Surely as a member of that esteemed institution, you know that the only way to ensure that the flower lives is to cut it at the bulb through the rhizome."

At these words, Emma dissolved into delighted, unguarded laughter, and several seconds passed before she could respond intelligibly. "You must be the visiting country cousin the duchess spoke of!"

A faint curve touched the gentleman's lips. "I must?"

"Yes, of course," she insisted. "Who else in town would bandy about the word *rhizome?*"

"Your logic is irrefutable. Indeed I must be the visiting country cousin. And who are you?"

"Nobody."

"Come! You are standing here in the conservatory with me, as corporeal as I am. You're hardly a ghost. Surely you wouldn't have me believe such a whisker."

"No, not that sort of nobody," she explained. "I'm nobody of importance. You needn't bother asking my name because you will only forget it in a minute or so and then I will have to remind you, which will be a dreadful embarrassment for the both of us. Now do show me where the rhizome is so I may return to the party. I told Mama I would be gone only a minute and now it has stretched into five. Mama brought me here as a favor—she and I rarely socialize together—and I'd hate to do anything that would distress her."

Unaccustomed to orders and amused by the novelty, the gentleman complied. "The rhizome, my dear, is the stem usually under the—"

"Sir, you are very kind to try to edify me on the topic of rhizomes, but I assure you I have little interest in learning about plants."

Feigning a look of disappointment, he said, "Very well. We will need a knife for the operation. I don't suppose you brought one with you?"

Emma laughed, a pleasant trilling sound that made the gentleman smile in appreciation. "Sir, I did consider smuggling a knife out of the kitchens, but a gently bred lady cannot wander the streets of London with a knife in her reticule. It's just as well, of course, since my sister-in-law keeps very close watch over the family silver and I couldn't bear it if a scullery maid was turned off because of my lack of resourcefulness." Emma examined the room, considering the situation. Her gaze settled on the desk. "Perhaps you should search the drawers for a letter opener. Yes, that would be just the thing!"

"Rifling through my host's drawers is a very sad sack way of repaying his hospitality," he observed.

Emma stared at him for a moment before saying, "You make an excellent point, sir, and far be it for me to corrupt the newly arrived country cousin. Since I'm the one lacking in any sense of propriety, it's best that I do my own dirty work." The drawer was unlocked and glided easily open. "There," she said, taking the long silver object in hand, "now we shall cut the rhizome and return to our separate occupations. No doubt Mama is wondering what happened to me."

The gentleman accepted the letter opener and was about to apply it to the plant when his hand halted in midair. "You know, Miss Nobody, I am suddenly struck with a vulgar bout of curiosity. What *do* you plan to do with this lovely flower after I finish cutting it?"

"I will stick it in my reticule and return to the party," she answered.

The gentleman smiled. "And then?"

Emma stared at the gentleman's hand and tried to think of a convincing fiction. However, even as she closed her eyes and told herself to concentrate, nothing came to mind. "Then I will hand it over to my sister, who's a great cultivator of orchids."

"If your sister is so great a cultivator of orchids, I wonder why she sent her sister to steal one of the Duke of Trent's *Rhyncholaelia digbyana*."

Emma laughed at the thought of Lavinia sending anyone to do her evil bidding. It was almost too ridiculous. "You misunderstand the situation, sir. My sister has no idea I'm here. Indeed, if she did, I imagine she'd be quite horrified."

"Then why are you here?"

"It is a sordid tale of malice and spite, which I think I had best keep to myself. We are new acquaintances, and I would loath to earn your disgust so quickly. It usually takes me a day or two to offend a man of your stature."

"Now you must tell me. I'm a curious fellow, and your speech has whet my appetite for the truth. We will not leave this room until I know the whole of it."

Miss Harlow sighed deeply and said, "The truth of it is that my sister is engaged to marry a man who does not approve of her pastime of raising orchids. Why not, I cannot fathom, since it is a genteel hobby and not at all down in the dirt like raising horses or chickens. If that were the case, then perhaps I could sympathize with his aversion. However, the wretched man is trying to make her withdraw from the Horticultural Society's annual orchid show. My sister earned honorable mention in last year's show, and she's sure to win the blue ribbon this year. Alas, I fear her resolve is slipping under Sir—" Emma broke off her speech abruptly. It would not do to muddy the waters with names. "Under her betrothed's constant disapproval. I merely wished to supply her with such an excellent example of an orchid that she

4

won't be able to resist participating. Everyone knows that the Duke of Trent grows the finest orchids in all of England."

"I suspect the duke would be much gratified by the compliment."

"I do not know. I've never met the duke. I know only his mother, the lovely and good-hearted dowager duchess. She was at school with my mother and was kind enough not to mind my coming today." She looked toward the doorway, where the sound of chattering ladies could be heard drifting in. "Now, sir, can we please get on with it? It would be an awful embarrassment if anyone else were to find me in the conservatory with an ill-gotten letter opener in my hand. Mama would no doubt ring a peal over my head and send me to bed without supper. Then I would be tossed back to Derbyshire in disgrace."

"We can't have that," he said, before applying the sharp instrument to the root. It took him only a moment to slice cleanly through. "There, do be careful not to get soil on your dress. It would be a waste to ruin such a lovely picture."

"Bah, lovely pictures are the least of my concern. I will take caution because a patch of dirt would rather give up the game and reveal my true nature to the ladies at the tea party." Emma opened her reticule and let the dowager duchess of Trent's country cousin help her place the orchid within. It was a delicate procedure, and she was relieved that he handled the flower tenderly and with skilled fingers. If left to her own devices, she would've no doubt crushed it thoroughly. "I am reminded of my nephew Richard, who claimed with frightful vigor that he didn't finish the last chocolate tart while incriminating evidence spotted his cheeks."

"No reason to worry, my dear. We've covered up your profligacy nicely. You look as though butter wouldn't melt in your mouth and not at all the degenerate you have proven yourself to be."

"Thank you, sir," she said, pleased to have succeeded with her plan despite the unexpected hitch of discovery. "I'm in your debt for not calling the Runners on me."

"Excellent. I trust you'll be at the Bennington ball?" At her nod, he continued. "You can pay me back then with a set. Save a place for me on your dance card."

Emma laughed. "That would be just the thing, sir. I don't often have the opportunity to dance with anyone other than my brother and shall relish the opportunity. Perhaps it will be a waltz? I love the waltz, but one simply cannot do it with one's brother."

"Fustian!" the gentleman said.

"Really, I assure you, sir, I have danced the waltz with Roger and it's awful. He's light on his feet, of course, and is well familiar with the steps, but even I, who am not a romantical silly miss, knows the waltz should be performed with a beau."

"I meant, my dear girl, that I cannot credit your lack of dancing partners. I might be from the country, where we do things differently, but even in London, the hands of beautiful ladies are always sought. It's the way of things."

Emma laughed, pleased with the comment. "That's such a lovely compliment and so prettily done that I begin to doubt your rural origins. Despite the way you toss around words like *rhizome*, you have town bronze. But you will soon learn that here in London beauty aligned with too much personality isn't very attractive at all," she explained. "I'm afraid I am very much a quiz as far as society is concerned. I chatter too much and I'm too free in my manners, and I have all of society turning their heads away in disgust. Fortunately, I don't have a large enough portion to whet the interest of men like your cousin the duke. If I did, I'm afraid I would be forced to behave, which would be dreadful dull."

"Come, you're a gently bred woman and a rather young one at that. What can you have possibly done to set society on its ear?"

Emma looked around the room just to make sure they were alone before leaning in and saying very quietly into his ear, "I raced from London to Newmarket in my curricle and broke Sir Leopold's record."

The gentleman's brow furrowed and then cleared. "I know of you. You're the Harlow Hoyden."

"*C'est moi*," she said.

"You are notorious." An interested smile hovered over his lips.

She shrugged. "Only a little and I do not mind much. It keeps the serious suitors away and leaves me to my freedom."

"The Harlow Hoyden," he said under his breath. "Sir Leopold's record stood untouched for three years and you broke it by two minutes."

"Two minutes and seven seconds," she said, identical dimples revealing themselves in both her cheeks. "I'm an excellent whipster and would have done better if Roger hadn't been with me. I had to take him along for propriety's sake. Sometimes propriety is the very devil, is it not, sir?"

He nodded. "Speaking of propriety, you should return to the party. Surely your absence has been remarked on."

Emma knew it was true—she herself had said the same thing several times—but now that the moment had arrived, she was reluctant to end this delightful interlude. "You are right. Thank you for your help, sir." She turned and walked away.

She was almost at the door when he called her name. "Miss Harlow, I believe you said a waltz." She nodded. "Until tomorrow then, my dear."

A few moments later, Emma returned to her mother's side, very pleased with that afternoon's work.

Miss Lavinia Harlow stared at the ill-gotten specimen with greedy eyes. "Why, it's beautiful, Emma," she said, holding the flower gently in her experienced hands. "I've never beheld such a perfect flower in all my life. That shade of yellow is uncommonly bright, almost like the sun itself, and the shape of the petals— Do you see how the edges are almost like an antique lace veil?

That's a characteristic of the *dighyana*, but these petals have a touch of the *fuertesii* about them. Notice how perfectly round it is and how no light travels in the spaces between the petals? That's highly unusual. And look at the habit of spike, so thick and strong." With a delicate finger, she illustrated all the excellent points of the orchid.

Her sister, whose interest in orchids had ended the second she handed the flower to Lavinia, yawned. What she'd told the helpful gentleman this afternoon was true. She had no interest in learning about plants.

"The texture is sublime. Run your hand over the petal. Go on." Emma complied absently. "See how it's soft and fleshy? And how there's no droop or flop? These things are the bane of my existence. Try as I might to get it right, my flowers are dull-colored and droopy."

"Don't be silly, Vinnie," her sister dismissed with a wave of her hand. "You won honorable mention at last year's Horticultural Society exhibition, and this year you shall take home first prize. I just know it. Your skill with plants is remarkable. Now do pay attention. I need your help in choosing my dress for the Bennington ball. I want to look dashing." She pulled a gown out of her closet and held it up. "What do you think of this one?"

Lavinia was not prepared for the subject change, and she examined her sister with quizzical eyes before shaking her head. "I might have some luck and a true devotion to the pastime, but whoever grew this flower has skill and—" Miss Lavinia Harlow broke off her speech and stared at her younger sister suspiciously. "Emma, darling, from whence did you get this flower?"

With her head deep in the closet and comfortably buried under muslin and crepe, Emma did not hear her sister. "Did you say something, dear?" she asked, pulling out another confection, this time a pink dress decorated with rosettes.

"I asked you where you got this flower."

Emma stuck her head in the closet and mumbled a reply.

"What's that?" asked her sister, recognizing a weak ploy when she witnessed one. "Step away from the closet. Your voice is muffled, and I can't hear a word you say."

Coming out of the closet, Emma affected her innocent look and said, "Nowhere in particular."

"Nowhere in particular?" her sister repeated. "You found a diamond-of-the-first-water *Rhyncholaelia digbyana* nowhere in particular? Really, Emma, after all these years, I'd think you'd know me better than to expect me to accept that banbury tale. Where did you find it?"

Emma sighed and said, "You know very well subterfuge does not come easily to me and I would think as my sister you would love me enough to let me lie upon occasion."

"Emma," she said threateningly. It was the tone she always used seconds before seeking out their sister-in-law and chaperone.

"All right. It might have been the Duke of Trent's conservatory," she confessed.

Lavinia took exception to her choice of words. "It *might* have been?"

"Well, I can't be sure, can I? I thought it was the conservatory, but there was a man in a large leather armchair reading, so it *may* have been the study."

There were so many disturbing things about her sister's behavior that Lavinia didn't know where to start. "A man saw you steal the Duke of Trent's prize *Rhyncholaelia digbyana?*" She closed her eyes as if in pain. "There are witnesses to your crime?"

"Dear, don't be such a melodramatic miss. There was only one witness, and he was a lovely man. Indeed, we're going to dance the waltz together tomorrow night at the Bennington ball. There's no cause for alarm."

"You can't dance with the man who saw you steal the orchid. What if he tells the duke?"

Emma shrugged. "Let him. I don't see why the duke should care who his cousin dances with."

"No, what if the cousin tells the duke you stole his *Rhyncholaelia digbyana*? What a fine pickle that would be. Sir Waldo would be horrified by the scandal, and I can't say that I'd blame him."

The mention of her sister's awful fiancé caused Emma to answer more harshly than she intended. "Well, if Sir Waldo Windbag doesn't—"

"Wind*bourne*."

"—like it, then I suggest he align himself with another family. The Harlows of Derbyshire cannot spend their lives worrying about what little thing might set him off. You need someone with less delicate sensibilities, who doesn't take a pet every time a lady says 'devil' in his presence."

Lavinia, who knew her sister's passions intimately, gave fair attention to this speech but was unswayed by it. "Your language could stand an improvement, my dear."

Emma made an inelegant grunt that sounded like something one would hear from a horse.

"You know that Sir Waldo comes from one of the oldest families in England. His people are very proud and correct, and they do not do things the Harlow way. But I believe he's a good man."

"Too good," Emma muttered.

"What dear?"

"Nothing."

"I know you're upset that I'm marrying, but it won't change anything, my darling. You shall see. Sir Waldo is not quite the ogre you think he is. I expect we'll both be changed by our marriage. He'll become a little more free in his ways, and I'll become a little less so. Compromise. That's what marriage is about."

Emma's experience with Sir Waldo had convinced her that he was a man incapable of compromise, especially when dealing with a woman. But she held her tongue, unwilling to fight anymore with her sister. "Please, let's not tease ourselves over this. The important thing is that you have a flower to show at the Horticultural Society exhibition next month. Now do help me select a dress for tomorrow night's ball. Imagine! Me *finally* dancing the waltz with a man who's not a relation."

"I cannot use this flower," Lavinia said.

"Why ever not?" Emma asked, beginning to despair of ever finding a dress. When had her wardrobe become so bland and missish?

"It's not mine. I haven't raised it. Using it would be a violation of the society's rules. Besides, think of the scandal if the duke was to recognize it. What if he entered the very same flower? They would toss me out of the society on my ear."

This was the last thing Emma wanted. "Of course it wouldn't do to pass the duke's orchid off as your own. I meant for you to use it with another one of your plants to make a new plant."

"Cross-fertilize it to make a hybrid?" Lavinia's eyes lit up. "That would be just the thing. I have an excellent *Altensteinia nubigena*. No, not excellent like the duke's is excellent, but the colors are vibrant and the stem fine and erect. Yes, it would go very nicely with this orchid, assuming the cross-fertilization worked. Oh, wouldn't that be marvelous. I could call the new hybrid the Stolen Trent or something like that."

"Wonderful. I look forward to seeing it at the exhibition."

Lavinia laughed. "My dear, how silly you are. You can't grow a new orchid in six weeks. It might be ready for showing next year but even that's doubtful. It usually takes two or three years to get a show-quality flower."

"Oh," said Miss Harlow. The thought of waiting two or three years to get results seemed intolerable to her. "Well, in the meantime, what do you think of this gown?" She held up a high-waisted cerulean blue silk dress.

Lavinia barely glanced at it. "Very becoming, I'm

sure. But I can't spare much time. I must plant this before the bulb dries out. You're the best of good sisters to give me such a thoughtful present." She kissed her sister on the cheek before flying out of the room and leaving Emma to her unsatisfying wardrobe.

Emma craned her neck but couldn't see above the awful crush at Lord Bennington's ball.

"Really, Emma, do cease twitching in that ghastly manner," Sarah Harlow said sternly. "You are making me terribly nervous."

With effort, Emma stopped her fidgeting and glanced at her sister-in-law. Her brother's wife was a tall, slim woman with excellent posture and a refined manner. She never twitched or squirmed or chafed, and she could always be relied upon for useful, sensible advice. She and Emma were opposites in many respects, but they rubbed together very well indeed. "I'm sorry, Sarah. I'll try to behave."

"I don't know what your problem is today. You're never a pattern card of correct behavior, but you usually have enough sense not to stand on your tippy-toes and teeter about. You look like an oak tree about to fall over."

"I am sorry, dear. It's just that I am very excited to be here."

Sarah snorted. It was an unladylike sound and one not often heard emanating from her elegant person. "You're never excited to be anywhere this crowded."

"Pooh," she dismissed, trying to stretch her neck in a covert way that would not reveal her true intentions. Alas, all she spied were the jeweled curls of the lady in front of her. "I often enjoy social outings of this stripe."

"You can't hoodwink me, my dear. You loathe packed drawing rooms and overstuffed balls. If you enjoyed social outings, then your poor mama would not despair of marrying you off."

Emma momentarily abandoned her ineffectual search and looked her sister-in-law in the eye. "Now you are telling fibs, Sarah. You know very well Mama would despair of me whatever I should do. As long as I'm unmarried and ostensibly still her responsibility, she will continue to despair," she said without the heat of resentment. "You'll note that I say *ostensibly*, since she dumped me and Vinnie on you and my brother without a second thought. I'm not complaining, of course. I'd much rather stay with you than with my mother anyway."

Sarah knew Emma's assessment was correct—Margaret Harlow's maternal instinct was sadly lacking—but she didn't want to admit that to Emma. She would rather that the girl had some illusions left. "Surely *dump* isn't quite the right word."

Emma laughed, said no more on the subject and strained her neck again. If only she were just a little bit taller...

"Really, my dear, tell me what has you in this tizzy," Sarah ordered.

"I'm going to dance the waltz for the first time," answered Emma, a becoming blush instantly staining her peach cheeks.

Sarah witnessed the flood of color and marveled at its cause. "Rubbish, you know very well that Roger has danced the waltz with both you and Lavinia. You make a handsome pair with your blond heads so close together."

Not caring to explain yet again the difference between dancing the waltz with a relation and every other man in the world, she simply said, "Well, it will be like the first time."

Sarah stared at her with a familiar quizzical look. "You're a strange child."

At three and twenty, Emma was certainly no longer a child, but she did not take offense at this appellation. She'd been called a strange child ever since she had put her hair up.

The orchestra began a second waltz, and Emma began to fear that the duke's cousin was not going to show after all. She really wasn't surprised, of course. Town life offered many delights and distractions to the unencumbered male, especially those just arrived from the wilds of Yorkshire, and a tedious ball with warm lemonade could not compare. Perhaps she should seek out the duchess and strike up a conversation. Surely the duchess would know if he was coming or not. Now, if she could just see over this blasted crowd…

"Well, now," said Sarah in a contemplative tone, "this is an unexpected development."

Emma wasn't interested in Sarah's unexpected developments but was well bred enough not to show it. "What's unexpected?" she asked, her eyes straining to see something above the fluffy blond head in front of her.

"Your sister," answered Sarah.

"My sister?" Emma was unable to conceive of Lavinia doing anything unexpected.

"Yes, your sister is dancing with a duke, one with whom I didn't know she was acquainted."

Emma gasped with surprise and clapped her white-gloved hands. "Lavinia is waltzing with a real live duke? But that's marvelous!" Instantly she was back on her tippy-toes, trying to get a clear view of the dance floor. Oh, why couldn't she be tall like Sarah? "Tell me. I can't see. Is he handsome? Of course he is. All dukes are handsome in their finery," she said before a thought struck her. "Oooh, is Sir Windbag here? Do tell me you see him! Wouldn't that be above all things wonderful if she were to jilt Sir Windbag for a duke! Very proud of his heritage, is he? He doesn't have anything on a duchy."

Sarah sent her a quelling look. "Emma, my dear, you must learn to be discreet and not quite so childish. Sir Waldo Windbourne is an excellent catch and a very nice feather in your sister's cap."

"Bah! One does not marry feathers." Emma dismissed.

She would not listen to a favorable word said on his behalf. "Just tell me if he's here."

Sarah used her height to advantage. "Yes, I can see him. He's standing on the other side of the dance floor and he looks none too pleased."

Emma giggled. "Of course not. So much for his consequence." Her balance was precarious, and when she felt herself begin to fall, she clutched Sarah's arm—and accidentally elbowed the lady in front of her. Although Emma apologized charmingly, the woman took offense and haughtily walked away, leaving a clear view of the dance floor in her wake. Greedily, Emma's eye drank in the scene until she caught sight of her sister's dancing partner. Then she paled.

"But, Sarah," she said, her voice almost a whisper, "that's not a duke."

"I assure you, dear, that is a duke."

She refused to accept this. "No, you must be mistaken."

"Really, Emma, I've been out for almost ten years. Surely I know the Duke of Trent when I see him."

CHAPTER TWO

Alexander Keswick, the seventh Duke of Trent, watched the last guest of his mother's tea party climb into her carriage before seeking out the duchess. He found her in the front parlor with note cards on her lap and wire frames perched charmingly on her nose. He sat down on the settee across and helped himself to a leftover scone.

"Don't pick," admonished his mother, putting the pen down and removing her spectacles. "That has been sitting out for an age. If you're famished, I'll have Stuart prepare you a plate." She pulled the bell and waited patiently for a servant to appear. "Stuart, a small morsel for the duke and a fresh pot of tea for me."

Trent's hunger was far from acute and the much-criticized scone served the situation very well, but he knew better than to try to derail a plan of his mother's. Once she got an idea in her head, it lodged itself firmly there. As the order of tea clearly demonstrated, she was about to embark yet again on her favorite topic: the marriage of her only son. The duke sighed and began thinking of ways to extricate himself from another long, fruitless coze with his single-minded mother. It would take more than a pot of tea to convince him to get leg-shackled.

"How was your party?" he asked, picking at the scone despite his mother's exhortations.

Although the dowager duchess could not be distracted, she didn't mind a short-lived diversion. "Delightful. Mrs. Parker is redecorating her town house in the latest style, and she brought swatches of fabric with her in order to get my opinion. I was very flattered by her consideration and did my best to steer her in the right direction."

"Nonsense, madam. As the prevailing arbiter of style, you thought it was no less than her duty to ask your opinion. What did you tell her?"

"That the oriental fashion is just a passing fancy and the lavish splendor of the pavilion in Brighton is a poor example for a drawing room in London. She was a bit surprised by my fervor—although how one can defend the charms of good old-fashioned English furniture without passion escapes me—but I'm confident that in the end she will be guided by my wisdom."

Familiar with his mother's vehemence, he could only assume that Mrs. Parker was even now ordering Gillow, Druce, and Cubit for her drawing room. "Excellent," he said, as Stuart entered with a tray. He set a plate of fresh scones and jam in front of the duke, then placed the pot of tea in front of the duchess. The duke watched her pour the tea. "I say, did I see the Harlow Hoyden leaving with her mother?" he asked with calculated casualness and her grace noticed nothing amiss.

"Yes, Margaret Harlow came with her younger daughter in tow. We've never met before and I must admit I was a bit cross at the notion of having the Hoyden in my parlor, but she was everything that was well mannered and proper." The duchess put the teapot down and spooned a small amount of sugar into her cup. "She sat so quietly in the corner that at times I could have sworn she wasn't even here."

At this statement, the duke smiled, but fortunately his usually observant mother did not notice. She was too busy stirring her tea.

"She was so well behaved that I begin to suspect that the tales of her exploits have been greatly exaggerated. Surely it is not possible for a gently bred young lady to drive four horses at breakneck speed along the Newmarket road." Jane Keswick took a delicate sip of her tea and began shaking her head. "Now that I think upon it, I'm convinced it did not happen. If I recall the story correctly, her brother was with her. I can only assume that he was the whipster and scandalmongers put her in the driver's seat because it made a much better story. You know how people can be. The plain truth is never interesting enough."

Having met the lady in question, Trent doubted very much that the widespread tale had done its subject a disservice. He had no trouble believing Miss Emma Harlow was in the driver's seat, and he could well imagine her taking offense at his mother's conclusions. "Her mother is a great friend of yours?"

"Not a great friend, no, but certainly a good one. We went to school together an age ago, and she's just recently returned to town." The dowager duchess helped herself to a scone and generously applied strawberry jam. "She's been rusticating in Derbyshire, although I believe her husband remained in town. I can't recall where the family seat is, but I trust it's somewhere very provincial and dull. Nevertheless, her older daughter—I think her name is Lucy—managed to nab Windbourne. They are to be married early next year."

"And the other daughter?"

"Emma? Oh, I would be very surprised if she had any eligible *partis* sniffing about. She's very beautiful, of course, and most likely unfairly maligned by society, but no man wants a hoyden for a wife."

Recalling his encounter this afternoon, Trent thought that there were a great many things worse than finding oneself wed to the Harlow Hoyden.

"Since we are speaking of wives," his mother said, causing the duke's heart to sink in his chest. The topic of Miss

Emma Harlow had so thoroughly distracted him that he'd momentarily forgotten the disagreeable point of this coze. "Your sister and I are very concerned about you, Trent dear. You are not a boy any longer. You are, in fact, thirty and must start thinking of the succession. You know that it was your father's dearest wish to see you happily wed to an amiable woman of upstanding birth equal to our own."

The duke knew nothing of the sort. His father's wishes and desires were a complete mystery to him. Although a kind enough man, the previous duke was rarely at home, and the only contact he had with his son were the infrequent occasions when he bumped into him at the club. And then he'd only apologize for his clumsiness and walk away. It was his mother's habit, when either backed into a corner or short on logic, to drag his father into the discussion.

"The previous duke enjoyed the company of a certain type of woman, and it's obvious to me that you are following close in his footsteps. That is fine. You're men and you will behave as men have always done. However, it should not stand in the way of your forming a suitable connection." The dowager duchess of Trent was nothing if not practical, and the finer emotions had little or nothing to do with the decisions she made. "Your father thought highly of Portia Hedgley and believed the two of you would rub together very well. Miss Hedgley is a biddable girl, soft-spoken and well bred, and would make an excellent duchess. I have spoken to her mother and she's assured me that her daughter would welcome your attentions. It was your father's one regret, my dear," she said, introducing a well-placed note of tragedy into her voice, "that he couldn't see you comfortably settled with Portia."

The duke knew this was patently false. Portia Hedgley was a green miss just out of the schoolroom and could not have been above ten years old when his father died. He doubted very much that his father had been aware of her existence.

"I would love to linger, Mama, but I must leave you to

finish your tea alone," he said, deciding it was time to make his escape. He was an agreeable and patient man who dealt with most situations with good-natured acceptance, but he would not marry to please his mother. "I have an appointment with Cousin Philip at my club, and I'm loathe to leave the boy waiting for too long. He is new to town and still wet behind the ears and seems game for all sort of trouble. Please accept my apologies."

His mother squinted her eyes in suspicion, but she didn't try to detain him. She knew what it was like with willful men. His father had been the same way. "This is not over, Trent," she said warningly, a hint of steel in her otherwise charming voice. "I will get my way."

The duke left the front parlor quite determined that she would not.

Alex Keswick arrived at the Bennington ball with Cousin Philip firmly in tow. The young cawker, a slim, gangly awkward boy who had yet to grow accustomed to his sudden height, didn't take well to the constrictions of formal wear.

"Stop tugging at your cravat," said the duke. "It took Stebbens a half hour to get it right, and I will not have you upsetting his work before the first waltz is played."

"Devil take it, sir, the damned thing is itchy," the boy whined before giving the cravat a final pull and lowering his hand.

Morgan Pearson, an intimate of the duke's for these ten years, listened to the exchange and smiled. He was not accustomed to seeing the Duke of Trent squiring around clumsy hayseeds and found the whole experience to be enlightening. As far as Morgan was concerned, the duke had the patience of a saint. The entire carriage ride had been given over to Philip's complaints. He didn't want to go to the ball. He wanted to seek more manly pursuits like gaming and boxing. It was only after the duke promised to introduce his young cousin to Gentleman Jackson that they had any peace.

Although Philip was new in town and didn't have many friends, he instantly spied an acquaintance and excused himself. The duke watched him wander off with a faint smile. "The young cawker can't even lie with any skill."

Morgan, who had been examining the room for familiar faces, looked at his friend. "How so?"

"He doesn't know anyone here," Alex explained. "He just said that to get away from me."

"What a novel experience for you, your grace. It's usually the Duke of Trent who's trying to get away from the admiring young lads—and admiring women of all ages, for that matter." Morgan nodded at a beautiful widow his friend was currently pursuing.

"It's understandable, of course," the duke said reasonably. "I suppose if I were nineteen, I wouldn't want an old man telling me what to do." Since his father never took an interest, he had no idea what it was like.

"Old man, Alex? Doing it a bit brown. Thirty is hardly the age of senility. Surely you have three or four good years left."

"Try convincing the dowager of that. She's terribly afraid that I'll expire before producing an heir. Luckily, I find it infinitely preferable to be valued for one's potential lineage instead of for oneself," he said, accepting a glass of wine.

"I wouldn't know," answered Pearson. "No one's concerned about my descendants. It comes, I suppose, from my not having a title."

The duke nodded and tried not to feel envy for his friend. Although Morgan would scarcely credit it, the duke often wished his title to Jericho. Most usually when his mother was talking marriage.

Thinking of his mother, the duke surveyed the room, searching for that estimable woman. He found her chatting happily among biddies her own age. No doubt she was telling them of Mrs. Parker's proposed oriental drawing room. He also saw his sister, Louisa. She was talking to Portia Hedgley, and Trent made a mental note to avoid his dear sibling. From her easy familiarity with his prospective bride, he concluded that she was in league with their mother. He walked in the opposite direction and found himself standing two feet away from the Harlow Hoyden. What a lovely circumstance.

"Miss Harlow," he said, bowing in a cursory manner, "it's a pleasure to see you again."

Miss Harlow looked taken aback by this familiarity, but she smiled in response.

She was more subdued than yesterday, and Trent marveled at the change. Her cheeks were not so rosy and her eyes didn't quite sparkle, but it was unmistakably she. One could not forget those golden curls or those ravishing pink lips. He put her reserved behavior down to the fact that she must have learned the truth. No doubt she was embarrassed to have stolen the Duke of Trent's prize *Rhyncholaelia digbyana* under the Duke of Trent's nose. He was about to introduce himself to her companion—a short, round man with no neck—when the orchestra struck up a waltz. "A waltz, you said?" He smiled and offered his hand. Miss Harlow accepted it and went out on the dance floor, leaving her attendant to look on with disgruntled annoyance.

After they had settled into a comfortable rhythm, Miss Harlow looked him in the eye and said, "You're not the country cousin."

His lips twitched. "No, I am not."

"You do not mind the stolen flower?"

"No, not when the thief is so charming. Tell me, how did your sister like the flower?"

"She adores it and she thanks you."

"Please tell her it was my pleasure."

The duke saw the sparkle return to her eyes. "You just did, your grace."

"Excuse me?"

"She did not mention that we were twins?"

The duke started laughing, and several couples turned

to see what was amiss. "No, she did not mention that," he said, genuine amusement shining in his eyes. "But it seems like just the sort of thing the Harlow Hoyden would not mention." He felt the other Miss Harlow stiffen in his arms, and he rushed to apologize. "I mean no disrespect. Please believe me when I say that I have nothing but the utmost admiration for your sister. She's enchanting."

Lavinia relaxed slightly. Seeking to put her further at ease, the duke asked, "What sort of potting soil did you use for the *Rhyncholaelia digbyana*? I hope it has a good deal of magnesium in it." It was an unsuitable topic for a London ballroom, but his partner did not notice.

"Oh, yes, your grace. And iron, as well."

The rest of the dance was given over to a lively discussion of potting techniques, and when the musicians finished, he brought Miss Harlow back to her fiancé.

"Thank you, your grace, for an enlightening dance."

"No, thank you, my dear," he said. Before taking his leave, he discreetly looked around the ballroom.

"She is, I assume, tucked away in some corner with my sister-in-law, Sarah," Lavinia said, easily reading the duke. "She doesn't like crowded places overmuch."

He was only momentarily surprised. "No, I don't imagine she would." The duke took her hand and laid a gentle kiss on it. "Thank you."

"Not at all, your grace."

Trent left her there and went in search of the real Emma Harlow but not before hearing Sir Waldo Windbourne take his fiancée to task for being too familiar with a duke.

By the time Trent found her, Emma was reconciled to the fact that he was a duke and not the country cousin she had previously supposed. Indeed, a plotting miss who always had one scheme or another percolating in her lively mind, she'd already figured out a way to use this information to her advantage.

"My lord duke," said Sarah when he approached, "it's lovely to see you again. It's been a long time."

"Sarah." Taking her hand and bowing over it, he behaved just as a gentleman ought, but his eyes couldn't help straying toward Emma. Up close, he could see that she was everything he remembered: the peaches-and-cream complexion, the rosy cheeks, the sparkling eyes, the delightful smile that revealed all her secrets. It seemed inconceivable now that he could ever have mistaken someone else for her.

"I don't believe you know my sister-in-law Emma," Sarah said by way of introduction. "You were dancing with her sister earlier, but no doubt you've already drawn that conclusion, given that they're mirror images of each other."

"Actually, I've already had the pleasure." He laid a kiss—a shade more lingering than proper—on her hand, and Sarah, noticing the familiarity, sent a quizzical look Emma's way. Her young in-law responded with a slight shrug.

"You have?" asked Sarah archly. She found this development rather curious. The Duke of Trent rarely showed interest in green misses.

"Yes, we have," he answered Sarah but kept his gaze on Emma. "Yesterday at my mother's tea party. Miss Harlow was a guest. I believe she was very taken with my orchids."

Emma dimpled. "What he means to say, Sarah, is that his orchids were taken with me."

The duke sketched a bow. "I stand corrected."

Sarah watched this exchange with a growing sense of unease. The Duke of Trent was flirting with Emma! Out and out flirting! Sarah had known the duke for years—her brother and he had been at Oxford together—but she had never seen him flirt with an inexperienced chit before. Although his behavior with her had always been circumspect, she knew that his reputation as a rakehell was well earned. There were few peers more handsome—or wealthy—than the duke, and he had been pressing his advantage with widows and courtesans for years. Sarah thought she could trust him not to play fast and loose with her sister-in-law but, nevertheless, Emma would do well to stay out of his way. There was no point in playing with fire. She looked at Emma's shining face. Now, if only she could convince her feckless charge of that.

"Sarah," said the duke, remembering his duty, "tell me, how is Andrew?"

"He's very well, sir. Much to my surprise, he's taken to the country like to the vicarage born, which he was, I suppose." Sarah smiled fondly as she recalled her townish brother tramping around country fields talking about crop rotation.

"And Martha?"

"The proud mama of another boy, named Oliver after my father."

"He must be pleased."

"Both my parents are very happy with how well Andrew turned out. I think they were both worried that he would gamble away the fortune before he was four and twenty."

Emma listened to these pleasantries impatiently. She wanted to talk to the duke—alone. She had a plan to put into action.

"Your grace," she said, forestalling whatever reply he had been about to make, "don't I hear the first strains of a waltz?"

The duke cocked his ear. "No, that is a minuet."

"I believe, then, that you promised me a minuet. I left it empty on my dance card specifically for you." Of course, much was left empty on the Harlow Hoyden's dance card.

"I am positive it was a waltz and am happy to wait."

Emma made a moue of annoyance and was about to insist on a minuet when Sarah intervened. "Your grace, I'm feeling parched. Perhaps you could get us something to drink?"

There was no way for Trent to refuse, and he graciously went off in search of refreshments. When he had disappeared amid the crowd, Sarah said, "Explain yourself."

Emma pressed her lips together and tried to look innocent. "Explain what?"

"You know very well. How familiar you are with the duke. What has passed between you?"

"It's nothing of note, Sarah dear. Do not tease yourself over it."

"He is not a suitable *parti* for a woman your age."

Although Emma was not interested in the duke for herself, she took exception to these words. "Really, Sarah, you speak as though I'm still in leading strings. I'm three and twenty, you know. I do have a little experience."

That was what disturbed Sarah the most. A little experience was a dangerous thing. "My dear, you are ill prepared to deal with someone like Trent. He's a rake."

"I know. That is why he's perfect."

Sarah's alarm escalated. "Perfect for what?"

"For what I have in mind."

"And that is?" There was something like fear in her voice.

Emma looked at Sarah and realized for the first time that her sister-in-law was indeed worried. She laughed. "Sarah, whatever are you imagining? Whatever I have in my mind, I assure you, it's not nearly as bad as what you have in yours. Trust me, all will be well."

"It's hard to trust you when you have that look in your eye."

"What look?"

"That look. That Harlow Hoyden look, the one you got in your eyes just before you went tearing down Bond Street in your tilbury."

"Don't be ridiculous, dear. Only a ninny would go tearing down Bond Street in a tilbury. It was a stanhope, of course."

Sarah rolled her eyes. "That's very beside the point, Emma. I do wish you would tell me what you're up to."

"I cannot tell you because you will get all disapproving of me and that would only serve to make me cross with you. I don't feel like being cross tonight."

Having dealt with Emma for more than three years, Sarah knew further discussion would bear little fruit. Emma would reveal her plan only when she felt she must, which was usually ten minutes or so before the gossipmongers got ahold of it. "Just promise me you won't do anything to disgrace the family."

"Disgrace the family. The way you talk you'd think I had no sense of propriety whatsoever."

"You don't, my dear."

Emma chose to ignore the slight. It was not that she didn't have a sense of propriety; it was simply that she so rarely heeded it. Doing things the proper way was dreadful dull. "Don't worry about it. You've done your duty and warned me off. You can go home to Roger with a clear conscience."

Sarah knew better than to protest. Her concern for Emma was indeed tied to her concern for her husband. "It's just that we care about you, dear, and want to see you happy. That's all anybody wants, dear."

Emma seriously doubted that. Her mother, Margaret, never concerned herself with her daughters' happiness. She was too selfish for that. All she wanted was to get her progeny out of her hair, and if the match happened to lead to happiness, well, she hoped her daughters weren't ninnyhammers enough to believe that it would last. Her own marriage had been a disaster, and for some reason she held everyone but herself responsible. "I am happy," Emma said, smiling as the duke approached with glasses of ratafia. At least she was now that she had a plan for extricating her sister from that awful Sir Windbag.

A blond boy with long limbs accompanied Lord Trent and instantly annoyed Emma with his very presence. They seemed embroiled in a conversation and despite the duke's frequent head shakes, the boy persisted in the unwelcomed topic. *Excellent,* thought Miss Harlow, *now when I get him alone and present my scheme he will be too cross to listen.* She sent the young boy a scathing look, but he misinterpreted it as friendly and introduced himself.

"Miss Harlow, I cannot tell you what an honor it is to meet you. Surely it is," he said, standing a shade too close and talking loudly into her ear. "I am Philip Keswick, Trent's cousin." He didn't bow or kiss her hand or do anything ingratiating. "I'm from Yorkshire, but I know who you are. You are famous, after all. Three hours and fifty-seven minutes! There is nothing like it and from a woman, no less. I heard Sir Leopold didn't go out into society for a whole year. Is that true, do you think? "

Unable to remember just how long Sir Leopold had sequestered himself—it was more than six months but certainly not as long as a whole year—Emma looked from the duke to young Philip and raised an eyebrow. She was hard pressed not to laugh. To think that she had mistaken the duke for this cawker. One could not compliment this country cousin on his town bronze.

"I say, Philip, it's rude not to wait for an introduction," the duke observed before handing Emma her ratafia.

"Introduction, bah!" he dismissed. "An out-and-outer like Miss Harlow don't stand on ceremony."

"She may not but I do."

His voice was strict, and Emma observed a blush creeping up the boy's neck. She instantly felt sorry for him. "A thing easily remedied, your grace. Mr. Keswick, allow me to introduce my sister-in-law to you, Sarah Harlow."

Philip fell in line reluctantly. "It's a pleasure to meet you," he muttered before performing a less than graceful bow over her hand. "How d'you do?"

Sarah's lips twitched. "I'm well, sir, and yourself?"

It was clear from the look in the boy's eyes that there were many answers to that question, but he reined himself in in time and said only, "Enjoying my first season, ma'am."

"Are you?" asked Emma, some imp urging her on. "Then you're very lucky, Mr. Keswick. I found my first season to be dreadful dull."

"Did you? This is my very first ball, and I have to say that it isn't at all what I was expecting." He tugged again at his cravat. "To be completely honest, I have found doing the society rounds very constr—" He seemed in the verge of giving spleen to a great many complaints, but the duke interceded.

"Isn't that a waltz I hear?" he asked, interrupting his charge.

"Is it?" Philip cocked an ear. He didn't know the difference between the tempo of a waltz and a minuet, but he did know that the former was very scandalous and not at all the thing in the wilds of Yorkshire. He turned to Emma. "Miss Harlow, would you do me the honor of this dance?"

Despite the urgency with which she longed to speak with Trent, she didn't have the heart to turn down this enthusiastic young cub. "I would be—"

But before she could get the sentence out, the duke interrupted. "Sorry, old fellow, but I've already claimed Miss Harlow for the next waltz." A devilish light suddenly glinted in his eye. "Perhaps Mrs. Harlow could be convinced."

Mrs. Harlow was amused but did not accept Philip's offer, which was fast in coming following his cousin's words. "I would much rather stand here and drink my ratafia. Perhaps you could tell me about your London adventures while they dance."

Laughing, Emma let the duke lead her out to the dance floor. "How dare you mistake me for that ill-mannered urchin!" he said, sounding very much like an offended duke.

Emma waved him off. "Really, what was I supposed to think? You were reading in the conservatory."

They were on the dance floor now, and the duke took her into his arms. Emma felt a shiver run up her spine at his touch and savored the feeling. No one had ever made her shiver before. She closed her eyes, threw herself into the experience and let him twirl her around. It was breathtaking.

"What does my reading in the conservatory have to do with it?" he asked.

"What doesn't it?" she asked teasingly, opening her eyes and watching the room spin around her. The feelings were so exhilarating, it was a wonder she could talk, let alone form coherent sentences. She should have danced the waltz with a handsome duke years ago. "Everyone knows that a town-bred gentleman would not be caught dead reading in his own conservatory. His paramour's, certainly, while she peels a fig for his pleasure, but not his own conservatory. That's what the clubs are for, your grace. I'm not so green that I don't know that."

"You do yourself a disservice, Miss Harlow. Perhaps you're more green than you realize. After all, I was reading in my own conservatory. Practice has disproved your theory."

"It's a good theory and I'm determined to stick to it, no matter how unconventionally—and, dare I say, inconveniently—you behave. Surely you're the only gentleman in all of London reading in his conservatory. Indeed, I would go so far as to say you are the only gentleman in all of London reading at all. It's little wonder I didn't mistake you for the butler, your grace."

The Duke of Trent laughed and didn't notice the curious stares of people around him. "I think you greatly overestimate the illiteracy of my fellow peers."

"I think you greatly underestimate it," she said, "but that's neither here nor there." She paused for a moment and contemplated how to word her next thought. "Your grace, I have a project with which I would greatly welcome your help."

"If it is stealing dahlias from Lord Beverly's garden, I must warn you, I do not climb fences."

"Calm yourself. The dahlia appeals little to my sister, and if it did, I would be quite capable of fetching it on my own. I don't need an accomplice."

The duke cocked his head to one side and looked at her consideringly. "Are you sure, Miss Harlow? I distinctly recall your being about to snap the stem of the *Rhyncholaelia digbyana*. Certainly you would have succeeded in stealing the bud but in vain: By the time you arrived home, it would've been dead."

Emma knew this was true, but she still resented the implication that she wasn't a competent flower thief.

Nevertheless, she wanted the duke's assistance and saw no point in contradicting his statement. It would lead only to an argument and quite possibly alienation. She had a better plan. "I saw you dancing with my sister. Did you have a chance to talk with her?"

"After I realized she was not you, we had a lively discussion of potting soil."

"Potting soil, your grace?"

"Yes, your sister prefers a liberal amount of volcanic pumice to aerate and loosen the soil whilst I favor forest humus."

Emma marveled at this. Her sister danced with the Duke of Trent and spent the entire time discussing compost. And the family thought she was the odd one! Really, at least Emma knew better than to discuss dirt with a duke. "And how did you find her?"

"Very charming, once I realized she was not you. She thanked me for the orchid. I understand she's going to cross it with her *Altensteinia nubigena* and nourishes hopes of showing it in next year's Horticultural Society's exhibition. I wished her well."

"She's a very good woman, my sister, and a prodigiously talented horticulturalist."

The duke nodded. "I do not doubt it."

"And she deserves happiness, no?"

"My dear Miss Harlow, I should imagine we all deserve happiness."

Miss Harlow could think of a few exceptions. Sir Windbag, for one, and perhaps her mother. "Then you will help?" she asked.

"I cannot say. Help with what?"

"Help my sister attain happiness."

"I'm afraid that is beyond my talents. Indeed, I suspect that it's even beyond yours, my dear. You cannot help people find happiness. They must do it on their own."

Emma thought the duke sounded very wise—and very off the mark. "Perhaps that is often so, but I assure you this is not one of those cases. All we have to do is end her engagement with Sir Windbourne, and she will be very happy indeed."

Trent was silent for a moment. "Is she being coerced? Does she not want this marriage? I'm surprised. Sir Windbourne has always seemed like a proper fellow, too well bred, certainly, to terrorize over females."

"I've found no evidence of terrorism—yet," she admitted. "But he's a villain, nonetheless."

"But your sister welcomes the union?"

"Yes, she does. But she doesn't know what she's doing. She's getting married only because she fears that if she doesn't marry Windbourne she'll never marry anyone. She wants children, of course, but this is not the way to go about it."

"On the contrary, Miss Harlow, that's exactly the way to go about it."

"No, I meant—" Emma broke off. It wasn't that the conversation was becoming very inappropriate, it was just that the waltz would surely end soon and she had yet to state her proposal. "I need your help in splitting them up," she said, returning to the point. "Do I have it, your grace?"

"I cannot in all good conscience agree to help you, although what I could do, I have no idea. I don't know Windbourne, and he would hardly listen to me if I brought up the topic of his engagement."

"Pooh, that would be a waste of time indeed."

"Well, then, Miss Harlow, I suggest we talk about the weather."

Emma sighed. "Really, your grace, I begin to suspect that you are going to be a sad disappointment to me."

The duke was unaccustomed to being a disappointment to anyone, let alone a sad one to an improper miss who didn't know how to behave. Ordinarily he'd give the speaker a good setdown, but because Miss Harlow sounded so disappointed, he found himself intrigued despite himself. "How so?"

"Well, I was counting on you to seduce my sister away from Windbourne," she said, laying all her cards on the table.

The proposal was so preposterous, so utterly ridiculous, so completely beyond the bounds of anything respectable, Trent missed a step and stumbled. His misstep threw off Emma's balance, and for a split second she thought she was going to fall. Luckily, the duke recovered his composure in time to intercede. His arms tightened around her and held her steady as they twirled gracefully around the room once again.

Emma looked at the duke, waiting for him to say something. He did not. "Your grace," she began, "it's not as bad as you think. You see, Lavinia is a—"

"Miss Harlow," said Trent in a surprisingly cold voice, "I suggest we do not discuss this further until the dance is over."

Emma failed to see why they couldn't discuss it right then and there on the dance floor—the congeniality of the topic would not alter depending on the location—but she held her tongue. If the duke needed a moment to think about her proposal, then she would obligingly give him all the time he needed—as long as he decided by the end of the evening. If he didn't see the wisdom of her scheme, she would have to proposition someone else. She didn't know very many libertines, but they couldn't be so hard to come by. Otherwise, Sarah and her brother wouldn't worry so much about her virtue.

They finished the dance in silence, and when Emma moved to return to Sarah's side, the duke interceded with a strong grip on her arm. He had other things on his mind and led her to a quiet corner where they could discuss them. There was nothing improper about their situation— they were in plain sight of everyone—but the corner afforded them some privacy.

In a low voice, the duke demanded, "Explain yourself!"

Usually Emma didn't take well to orders, but she understood the duke's anger, although it was scarcely a fair reaction to her suggestion, and explained herself. "Your grace, it's very simple. You are to use your considerable charms to woo Lavinia away from Sir Windbourne. It shouldn't be very difficult. He's hardly a fair match for you."

"And then what, Miss Harlow?"

Miss Harlow blinked at him. "Excuse me, your grace?"

"What happens after I've wooed your sister away from Windbourne?"

"That depends on you. Go on with your regular life, I suppose. I don't see what that has to do with anything."

"But what about your sister?"

"Lavinia? She'll go on with her life, too."

"So I'm to win her affections and then callously drop her after I succeed?"

"Well, yes."

The duke's face suddenly turned a faint red color. "Miss Harlow," he said in his most intimidating sneer that he used on only the worst toadies, "I do not toy with the affections of innocent misses."

Emma was far from intimidated. "Of course you do. You're a libertine."

Inconceivably, the duke laughed. He tossed his head back, closed his eyes and laughed for several minutes. Indeed, it was only after a single tear ran down his cheek that he managed to get ahold of himself. He took a deep breath as his color returned to normal and said, "Miss Harlow, you are an original."

Her originality was beside the point. "So you'll do it?"

"Absolutely not."

"But my sister's happiness depends on you."

"Your sister's happiness depends on your sister. What you're suggesting would be abhorrent to any gentleman."

Emma looked at him crossly. "Oh, what good is a libertine if he won't toy with your sister's affections and then ruthlessly drop her!"

"Miss Harlow, I don't know who provides you with your information, but they're wrong. I'm not the man you think I am."

"Bah, you're the sort of man mamas warn their daughters about."

This was news to Trent. "On the contrary, I'm the sort of man mamas point their matchmaking bows at and shoot," he explained. "I'm the sort who's the object of countless schemes. I'm a bachelor, not a libertine."

"But you have many mistresses," protested Emma. "And the latest *on dit* concerns your tryst with Mrs. Waring."

"Miss Harlow, I will not discuss this with you."

"Why? Because I am an innocent miss? Really, your grace, just because I'm unmarried doesn't mean I'm unobservant. I know how men behave. They do not try to hide it from us, so much as forbid that we speak about it. My own father is reported to keep a stable of fashionable impures on Wardour Street."

"I do not like having my behavior bandied about by gossipmongers."

"Then perhaps you yourself should not bandy about with widows."

The duke stared at her for several seconds, the humor completely gone from his demeanor. He seemed to be struggling to rein in his temper. Emma was not concerned. She was well used to anger. For some reason, she aroused it in many a person's breast. "Miss Harlow," he said agreeably, changing tactics midbattle, "surely this discussion is unnecessary. Although I don't know Windbourne personally, I have never heard a thing said against him. Your dislike of him is unfounded."

This argument was nothing new to Emma. Sarah, Roger and even Lavinia herself had been saying the same thing to her for weeks now. But they were wrong. "Bah, you do not know Windbourne as I know him. Nobody does."

The duke tried to be patient. "How do you know him then?"

"As an awful man, a tyrant who would seek to dominate his wife," she said in tragic tones, "who would isolate her from her family and not let her indulge in her most beloved pastime, raising orchids."

"If your sister has told you this, I wonder why she still wants to marry him."

"Lavinia would never be so indiscreet. Windbourne himself told me when he thought I was Lavinia. He said that my, or rather her, willful ways—which, I might add, is a ridiculous statement to begin with, since dear Lavinia has never done a willful thing in her life—would be tempered once she stopped spending so much time with her hoyden of a sister," she said, outrage shining from her eyes. Recalling the scene brought back the anger of the moment. How dare he criticize Lavinia's behavior! Lavinia, who had never done a wrong thing in her entire life! "And that's not all. He also said that he hoped she would forget 'this silly hobby' of hers. Silly hobby! Growing flowers is not a silly hobby. It's her passion. At home in Cromford, she spends hours in the nursery and she's very happy there. Her skill with flowers is unparalleled. Perhaps if I could make such beautiful things come to life I wouldn't get into trouble quite so much. But now Sir Windbag has decided that it isn't proper for his wife to dither around in the dirt. Dither around in the dirt!" Emma knew that she was raising her voice, but she was unable to help it. "I swear to you, Trent, those were his exact words. That pompous twit would dare call my sister's talent dithering. You should have seen him, puffed up with his own conceit, telling her—*me*—that she mustn't worry about raising anything but his children. Really, your grace, if that isn't a villain, then I don't know what is."

During this impassioned speech, the duke's gaze had softened and in a gentle voice he said, "My dear girl, that doesn't make him a villain. It makes him a husband."

Miss Harlow was taken aback by this intelligence and stared at the duke for long moments in silence. "Well, then," she said quietly, with little of the usual spirit, "husbands are very wretched things, and I should wonder why anyone would want one."

"Come, my dear, it's not all bad," he insisted, fearing that he might have done more damage than he intended with his offhand comment. "There are some advantages to marriage."

"Advantages?" she scoffed. "What advantages are there to losing one's freedom, for having someone else tell you what you may or may not do?"

As a devoted eluder of the parson's mousetrap, the duke saw little advantage to marriage, but he was a man. It was different for women. "Children, for one."

"Bah," said Emma.

"Bah?" Trent echoed, unsure what to make of this response.

"Yes, bah."

"Children are a treasure and a joy."

"To a man, maybe, who would stick his head into the schoolroom once a sennight to flirt with the pretty governess. It's the woman's responsibility to see to their educations and their health and their care—and her unfair burden." Emma thought of her parents' marriage. "A man's life continues in the same vein, as if nothing out of the ordinary has happened, while a woman's is altered irrevocably. I'm not sure that's an advantage."

"Miss Harlow, you are being ridiculous."

"Am I, your grace?" She raised an eyebrow and gave him a very disgusted look. Emma Harlow was used to being called ridiculous—by society, by her family—but for some reason his saying it was different. She had been so looking forward to their dance, and he had ruined all her lovely plans by being a duke. And now he was ruining them again by being intractable. "Or perhaps you just insult that which you don't understand. You are a man, after all, and will one day be a husband. You are all villains in my book. Now excuse me. I shall remove my ridiculous self from your presence."

She was several feet way when she heard the duke say, "What about this plan of yours? You will give it up, I trust."

Emma had no intentions of giving it up. "That, your grace, is none of your business."

What a willful girl, he thought, as he watched her disappear among the glittering crowd of dancers. Yesterday afternoon when he had met her in the conservatory, he had been charmed by her frank demeanor. He had been looking very forward to their dance this evening and had even been thinking to set up a mild flirtation. Nothing that her mama—or his—could take exception to but a light dalliance that would distract him from the tedium of yet another season. Emma seemed like an interesting little imp—being where she didn't belong, taking flowers that weren't hers—but now he knew the truth. Emma Harlow's epithet was well earned. Only a hoyden would think such scandalous thoughts about children and a husband, much less utter them in the presence of such an esteemed personage. The duke admired her honesty and the way she thought for herself, even though they revealed a naiveté he had not thought possible in a young woman of today. She would learn in time that marriage was a woman's only option. There was nothing worse than dwindling into an old maid. She would realize one day that it was a far better thing to be in the nursery than on the shelf. It would be an unpleasant discovery for her, but she would adapt. All ladies did in the end.

But in the meantime he would stay out of her way. She would learn these lessons someday, but he was certainly not the man to teach them to her. The Duke of Trent was not interested in green misses. He didn't have the patience for their flights of fancy. Seduce her sister! He'd never heard such an outrageous proposal in his entire life. How dare she think that he would do something so infamous. And to call him a libertine! The duke was not a libertine. Perhaps he had too much of a free and easy way with fashionable impures and ladies of easy virtue—could he help it if women found him irresistible?—but he had never played fast and loose with an innocent. And he wouldn't now. No matter how much the Harlow Hoyden fluttered her lashes at him.

Returning to the ballroom, the duke saw Philip still at the side of Sarah Harlow. He was looking at the older woman with something akin to worship on his face. The duke felt a flicker of concern. Whatever could Andrew's sister be saying to put such a face on his hayseed cousin?

"…and then I tried reeling him in, but the boat was unequally balanced because my brother didn't believe that I had enough strength to do it myself. Of course the boat tipped over and the trout got away. I was very cross with Andrew for days. Not only had he ruined my chances of catching the largest trout in Lake Muir—and I haven't completely dismissed the notion that it was intentional; poor Andrew could barely stand it if I hunted *and* fished better than he—but the unexpected dip in the frigid waters left me with an awful case of the sniffles," Sarah finished with a laugh that was echoed by her companion.

"That is very similar to what happened to me and my brother," said Philip eagerly, "only the water was more muddy than frigid and I ruined my best pair of Hessians before I was able to extricate myself from the pond."

"Well, cub, that's what you deserve for fishing in your Hessians," said the duke to his cousin before devoting his attention elsewhere. "Tell me, Sarah, how did this scamp of a cousin manage to turn the conversation from drawing rooms to unpleasant things like muddy ponds?"

Philip took offense at this. "Dash it, sir, just 'cause Mrs. Harlow and I were talking about fishing don't mean that I *made* her talk about unpleasant things. I was just saying—"

"Philip, I believe Lord Sanderson is gesturing to you. See what he wants."

The young cousin turned in the indicated direction and looked in vain for Lord Sanderson. "Don't know what you're talking about, sir. Lord Sanderson isn't there," he said.

"Nevertheless, you're wanted over there." Trent's tone would brook no arguments.

Looking confused and a little bit disappointed, the

young man took his leave of Lady Sarah. "It was a pleasure, ma'am, a real pleasure." He then tried to sketch a bow as he had often seen his sophisticated cousin do. Alas, it was a poor imitation and he wound up bumping into a curmudgeonly dowager who had no patience for the queer starts of callow youths. Amid a cavalcade of exhortations to behave himself, a red-faced Philip slinked away.

Sarah held her laughter until he was out of earshot.

The duke said, "Sarah, please accept my apologies. If I had known you'd be subjected to a horde of rural tales the whole while, I would never have left you alone with him."

"Pooh, your grace. I brought the horde of rural tales down on my own head," she said in defense of the awkward young man. "Upon discovering that Mr. Keswick was from Yorkshire, I mentioned that I'd been up there once. That led to a lively discussion of fishing."

The duke didn't look convinced. "Nevertheless, he's an exuberant youth and needs to learn some manners."

Sarah agreed. "That is true, but I wouldn't be too harsh with him. He means well and he looks up to you. Before we embarked on our rural discussion, we devoted ten minutes to your skill as a pugilist."

An amused smile lit his face. "I am well aware of my cousin's love of pugilism. I had to make him a bargain along those lines to get him to come tonight."

"Well, your grace?" Sarah said, after a moment.

"Well?" he asked.

"Yes, you certainly didn't send Mr. Keswick away on a fool's errand for no particular reason. What do you wish to talk about?"

The duke wasn't at all surprised by her reasoning. Andrew's sister had always been clever. "It's about Miss Harlow."

Sarah didn't have to ask which Miss Harlow. People rarely wanted to talk to her about Vinnie. "Yes?"

"You must watch her carefully," he cautioned, his eyes sweeping the room in search of the lady in question.

"I believe she's headed for trouble."

Although she was much distressed to hear this from the duke, she didn't show a reaction. She would not discuss family matters with nonfamily members. Still, she was curious. "Oh?" she asked, hoping that alone would convince him to tell more of what he knew.

"Yes, she made the most infam—" The duke broke off. Suddenly it seemed wrong to share privileged information. He had no desire to get Emma into trouble with her family. He just wanted to keep her from tumbling into another scrape. "Miss Harlow seems unsettled by her sister's forthcoming nuptials."

Sarah wondered what the duke had been about to say, but she knew better than to pursue it. "Yes, she is. *Unsettled* is exactly the word."

"I fear her…unsettledness might lead her into trouble."

"You needn't worry yourself, your grace. Emma is just having a hard time adjusting to the change, which is understandable," she said with a good deal of the common sense she was known for. "I suspect she's worried about losing her sister. They're twins and have been very close their entire lives. There's no denying that Lavinia's marriage will alter their relationship some. But once she realizes that these changes are for the better, Emma will calm down and accept it."

This reasoned explanation did not reassure the duke at all. "In the meantime, keep a close eye on her. She might do something"—Trent tried to think of a harmless word to describe asking a libertine to seduce her sister—"impetuous."

He said this in a tone that caused Sarah to look at him sharply. "Your grace, is there something you're not telling me?"

The duke had no intention of getting drawn into some other family's dramas. He had enough of that with his mother and his cousin Philip. "Just watch her," he said with unusual abruptness before taking his leave.

He walked away knowing full well that Sarah was puzzled by his words and unsatisfied with their talk. He had meant to wash his hands of the whole affair, but when it came time to tell Sarah of Miss Harlow's scheme, he couldn't do it. For some reason, telling had seemed like a betrayal of Miss Harlow's trust.

In a dark mood, Trent went in search of Pearson. It was time to leave this suffocating place and breathe freely in the smoky room of a gambling hell. What he saw instead was Miss Emma Harlow in the arms of Sir Everett Carson. Now *there* was a libertine, he thought, with disgust. He recalled her intention to find someone else to help her and marveled at how fast she worked. Not a half hour had gone by and already she had found a suitable candidate, made his acquaintance and charmed him into dancing with her. This from a woman who said her dance card was always empty! The duke watched her with glowering eyes for several minutes, assuring himself that it was not his problem if the silly chit got herself ruined. He looked around for Sarah. Sarah should be there to warn Emma off a rakehell like Carson. Where was that woman? Why wasn't she keeping a better eye on her charge? Clearly her own family could not be relied on to keep her out of trouble.

Devil take it, he thought, his brow blacker than it had ever been, *I'll keep an eye on her myself.*

CHAPTER THREE

Having decided on a course of action and having been so thoroughly disappointed by the Duke of Trent, Emma decided that the best thing to do was to make up a list of eligible seducers. In order to do that, she needed help. Emma was no more knowledgeable of society rakes than she was of society matrons. Therefore, she called on her friend Kate, an estimable young woman who not only had entrée to the best drawing rooms but who also had an encyclopedic knowledge of went on in them as well. It was usually Kate who kept Emma abreast of the Harlow Hoyden's latest exploit.

"Really," Emma said, when she discovered that she was supposed to be in the midst of a torrid flirtation with the Duke of Trent, "I've never heard of anything so ridiculous. We had one dance."

"A waltz," said Kate, ringing the bell for tea and pushing an errant red curl behind her ear. It was early—visiting hours wouldn't begin for a long while yet—and she was still in her morning gown of white cotton. She hadn't expected her friend but wasn't surprised. Emma rarely stuck to schedules—either her own or anybody else's. Kate didn't mind. She enjoyed the hours she spent with Emma, even if it left her little time to do her hair properly before gentlemen callers arrived. Kate Kennington was a natural beauty, and if every strand was not perfectly in place, her beaux never seemed to notice. They were too busy gazing into her unusual green eyes or admiring her milk-white complexion or staring at her perfect nose and full red lips.

"Bah, it was just one waltz," insisted Emma, taking to her feet. She had too much energy this morning to sit tamely on the settee in the front parlor.

"But you disappeared together afterward," her friend remarked.

"You make it sound like some sort of parlor trick. We didn't disappear at all. We walked to a quiet corner, in plain sight of everyone, I might add, to distance ourselves from the crowd. The ballroom was stifling, and you know I cannot stand overly packed spaces."

Kate smiled. "You don't have to explain yourself to me, dear. *I* do not believe that there's anything between you and the Duke of Trent. I was merely informing you of what the biddies were saying last night. You know how the *ton* is. They only talk about what is right in front of them. It's of the least consequence, I'm sure. Tonight we'll go to Lady Beverly's route and they'll see Trent talking to Portia Hedgley and forget all about you."

Emma stopped her pacing. "Portia Hedgley?"

"Yes, the dowager and her daughter are trying very hard indeed to bring about the match." Just then the doors opened and the Kennington butler stepped within. He laid the silver tray in front of Kate before asking if there was anything else. Kate assured him that they had everything they needed. When he was gone, she continued. "It would be a very suitable match, of course. Both families are well connected, wealthy and respected. There's much talk about the duke falling in line this time. He's advancing in years and does need to think of the succession. I would be surprised if he could withstand the persuasion of his mother and sister. The duchess is known to be quite ruthless and single-minded in pursuit of her objective. I wager he'll have the chit just to get some peace."

For some reason the thought of the duke with Miss Hedgley disturbed Emma. Because they'd spent time together at a weekend party in Dorset last year, she was familiar with Portia Hedgley. But in all their time together she had discovered very little to recommend her. The young lady in question had a tendency to speak in one-word sentences—it was impossible to get her to elaborate no matter how many questions one asked her, unless one were a man. No, not a man, Emma corrected herself, recalling the smitten Mr. Uxbridge, who couldn't get a useful utterance out of her either. The truth was that in order to get Miss Portia Hedgley to bestir herself on your behalf you had to be a peer, preferably a viscount or a marquis. Of course, a duke would do.

Up until the point when he had demonstrated himself to be most unreasonable, Emma had liked the duke. She'd found him good humored and kind and after leaving him in the conservatory had thought he might make a nice friend. Yes, Emma had very much liked the duke, but if he wanted to throw his life away on a pinched-face climber that was his prerogative. She would not be disturbed by it. She would not be disturbed by him, certainly when he showed himself to be so unreasonably unhelpful. They deserved each other, she thought, although she couldn't quite convince herself of the truth of the statement.

"He could do worse," Emma said now in an attempt to be polite.

Kate laughed. It was more of a cackling sound than the ladylike trill she used in mixed company. "Really, my dear, after the way you railed against the pinched-faced Miss Hedgley after spending three days with her in Dorset, I'm surprised you think that there's worse."

Emma smiled. "True. Perhaps I meant to say that the duke does not deserve better."

Pouring tea into a porcelain cup, Kate raised an

eyebrow at her friend. "I'm surprised by your harshness, Em. What has the duke done to earn your ire?"

"He refused to seduce Lavinia," she said, glad that they were finally on the topic she'd come there to discuss.

Miss Kennington looked up. "Well, I should hope so," she said, as if nothing were amiss. Indeed, there really wasn't. She was well accustomed to her friend's outrageous statements.

"Oh, I didn't mean for him to *seduce* seduce her," she said with a dismissive wave of her hand. "I just wanted him to flirt and arouse her interest enough that she would dump that horrible Sir Windbag."

"And the duke said no?"

Emma rolled her eyes. "The duke not only said no, he lectured me about the joys of marriage and seemed quite horrified when I showed an unfeminine lack of interest."

"I can't say I'm surprised." She handed Emma a cup of tea and poured one for herself. "He's never toyed with the affections of unmarried ladies."

"Yes, yes, he devotes all his energy toward toying with the affections of bored married ladies and widows. I'm well aware of his reputation." Emma sat down with a *whoosh*, spilling tea in the process. "That man vexes me so. Really, what good is a libertine who won't seduce an innocent? He's an aberration of nature!"

"I trust you didn't say that to the duke?"

"No, not quite, although I did take him to task for being a libertine with morals. It's simply not fair. One should be able to rely on rakehells to behave badly. Is nothing dependable anymore?"

Her friend sounded so despondent that Kate had to hide her smile. Sometimes she was amazed by Emma's inexperience. Although she had been among the *ton* for more than five years, Emma had never immersed herself in its ways. She had always stood separate, partly because she feared she wouldn't be accepted but also because it bored her. She had too much energy and too many interests to sit comfortably in a drawing room dissecting *on dits*. "Perhaps the Duke of Trent is not a proper libertine."

"Exactly!" said Emma, jumping up again and spilling even more tea on her periwinkle walking dress. "That's why I have come. I knew you would be able to help me."

Kate was sure she could help, but something about her friend's demeanor made her uneasy. What was the Harlow Hoyden up to now? "Stop pacing back and forth like a fenced-in horse—you're making me dizzy—and tell me how I can help you."

Emma stopped pacing, although she hardly felt like a fenced-in horse. "It's very simple, my dear. All you have to do is help me compose a list of all the proper libertines in town this season, so that I might find one who's willing to seduce Vinnie. I'm sure it shouldn't take you above five minutes. I'll just sit here silently while you draw up the list. Do you have a quill?" Emma reached over to ring the bell. Kate forestalled her.

"I will draw up this list for you, of course, but first we must discuss the qualifications. What *exactly* are you looking for in a libertine?" In truth, Miss Kennington had no intention of indulging her friend's whim. As far as she was concerned, there were few things more irresponsible than sending the Harlow Hoyden out into the world with a list of rakehells. She might as well instruct Emma to dance naked in the street. Both would ensure her ruin, but somehow, Kate felt, the list would do it faster—and more thoroughly.

"Qualifications?" Emma seemed incapable of digesting the notion. "What sort of qualifications does one look for in a rake?"

"Well, we must be discriminating, my dear. I cannot write down the name of every libertine in the country." Kate took a sip of tea to hide her smile. The look of confusion on Emma's face was priceless.

"He must be adept at seducing women. That is all," Miss Harlow said, sitting down once again on the settee.

"But surely Lord Danforth would not do. I believe he

just passed his sixtieth year. Is that the sort of man you're thinking of?"

"No, he must be young and handsome."

Kate indulged a pleased smile. "See? We are making progress already. The field is considerably narrowed. Now, about his other credentials…"

Young, handsome and adept. Emma could think of none others. "Whoever you have in mind I'm sure is qualified enough."

"No, dear, we have much still to talk about. Needless to say we need someone who's an excellent seducer, but he mustn't be too good. I trust the point of this exercise is not to see your sister ruined."

"Of course not," she said, much offended by the notion. "I love my sister and would never want anything bad to happen to her."

"*I* know that, darling, but we must make sure that our libertine knows it as well. He mustn't seduce her for real."

"You mustn't tease yourself on that front, dear Kate. Lavinia could no more be seduced by a libertine than I. She could, however, have her head turned. That's our objective."

These words had the exact opposite effect on Kate than their author's intention. Rather than leave off worrying about Lavinia's seduction, she began to worry about Emma's as well. Despite her worldly experience—and Kate was not convinced that racing at breakneck speed down the Newmarket road made one either worldly or experienced—Emma knew nothing of men and was poorly matched against one bent on seduction. In her mind's eye, she could easily see Emma approaching a Lord Bancock about her sister's virtue and walking away with a little less of her own.

"All right," Kate agreed, keeping this disturbing thought to herself. "But we must find a rake we can trust. We don't want the tale spreading through drawing rooms. The scandal would destroy your whole family. And I daresay your mother would not thank you if you all had to retire to Derbyshire in disgrace."

Emma realized that this was a very real concern. Oh, she would think nothing of it if they had to bury themselves in the country, but if the story got out then surely Lord Windbag would hear of it. Nothing would be served if he knew of her scheme. "You make an excellent point. Young, handsome, adept and trustworthy. Just jot down a few names and I'll be on my way."

Of course Kate recognized this for the paradox it was. Young, handsome, adept and trustworthy—these were the qualities of an eligible *parti*. Few of the most sought-after bachelors in the realm had this much to recommend them. Only Trent, and he had already shown his mettle. That was the caliber of gentleman they were looking for. Kate needed time to reflect on this problem. "I would love for you to leave with the list right now, my dear, but I must give it some thought. I have some ideas in my head, but I want to make sure that I choose the right gentleman. The wrong gentleman and the results could be disastrous."

Emma knew this was true, but still she was impatient. Now that she had a plan for breaking up her sister's engagement, she wanted to go forward with it as soon as possible. She wasn't made for things like *waiting*. "I guess you're right," she said sulkily.

"Take heart, Em, the engagement was announced not a fortnight ago. The wedding itself is months away. Plenty of time to do mischief."

"I'm well aware of that, but it comforts me little. Every second she spends with him she falls deeper under his evil spell. Soon she may even love him. Then we'll be in a pickle."

"If she loves him, then perhaps she should marry him," Kate said logically, although she knew logic had nothing to do with the way Emma felt about Sir Waldo Windbourne.

"It is not a real sort of love," Emma scoffed. "It is just the familiarity one mistakes for liking. Lavinia fears becoming a spinster. She doesn't want to play maiden aunt to Roger's monsters. She wants her own children. I cannot question the sentiment, but I can take exception to her solution. She's marrying Sir Windbag because he's the only man who has asked. She's settling for a man she won't be able to stand in a few years. His charm, such as it is, will pall, and she will be left with a hollow sham of a marriage. Her interests will have been taken away—I told you how he does not like her 'hobby' of raising orchids—and she will have nothing left to make her happy. I do not want that sort of life for my sister. She deserves better."

"Her children will make her happy."

Emma doubted that very much. Her parents' marriage was very similar to the one she'd just described, and nothing she or Lavinia or Roger had done had ever made her parents happy. "No, they will just remind her of the rash choices she made when she was too young to know better."

Not for the first time Kate's heart went out to her dear friend. She knew Emma didn't have a happy childhood and was still much affected by it, but she didn't realize how deeply the hurt went. *No wonder she is afraid of marriage,* Kate thought. "Each person must take responsibility for her own decisions. I cannot believe that dear Vinnie would take her disappointment out on her children as your mother did. If she has had no other offers of marriage, then perhaps this is the best thing for her," she added gently.

"Lavinia would have offers if she were more lively. She is very pretty."

"Yes, I think so."

"It's just that she's so practical, isn't it? She never has adventures like other women. She'd rather stay at home and read horticultural texts. And she reads more now that she's engaged to Sir Windbag. Wouldn't she read less if she were really in love?"

"Emma darling, other women don't have adventures. Only you do."

"Well, then, doesn't that just demonstrate all that's wrong with the world?" she asked with a wave of a distressed hand.

Miss Kennington wasn't inclined to agree, but she said nothing more on the topic. "I will think carefully on this project and get back to you as soon as I've compiled a list of agreeable candidates. Will I be seeing you tonight at Lady Sizemore's musicale?"

"Good gracious, no!" answered Emma, horrified at the thought of spending even a minute listening to Sonia Sizemore's off-key alto. "Sarah has promised to escort Lavinia and me to the theater. We are going to see the very excellent production of a *Midsummer Night's Dream* at Drury Lane Theater."

"Is Roger not back from the Continent yet?" Kate asked, examining the clock on the mantelpiece. The hour was growing late, and she needed yet to change her gown.

"No, though we expect him any day. I do not think it's right that Mama send him to France to do business for her. Surely there are unmarried men without families she could hire to do her bidding. Must it be Roger?" Emma noticed her friend's glance and stood up. "No need to say it, dear. I'm leaving. No doubt you are eagerly awaiting a call from Lord Hastings. I expect any day now to hear word of your engagement."

"Don't be so sure," cautioned the lady. "I haven't decided if I want him or not. Mr. Roth has been very charming of late."

Emma didn't know who Mr. Roth was and knew better than to ask. Even if he had been charming of late, he would not last. Kate's affections were fixed on Lord Hastings whether she admitted to it or not.

They were approaching the door and finishing their good-byes when a thought struck Emma. "Tell me, Kate, what do you think of Lord Everett Carson?"

"A cad."

"Just as I thought!"

Kate didn't like the look in her friend's eye. "What are you thinking?"

"I might have a possible solution. Carson would think

nothing of courting a betrothed female. Perhaps I shall endeavor to engage his affections."

"Why should you engage his affections? I can't imagine what good that would serve."

"No, my engaging his affections would serve no good, but if he thought I were Lavinia…" She trailed off as she considered her scheme. If she pretended to be Lavinia for a little while and if she flirted mercilessly with Carson, then maybe he would fix his attentions on the real Lavinia. It was a known fact that men liked women who liked them. The idea had merit. She looked up to find Kate staring at her, and she laughed at the expression on her friend's face. "Don't look so horrified, my dear. Lavinia and I are twins. What good is an adventure about twins without a case of mistaken identity?" She gave her dear friend a kiss on the cheek, promised to see her soon and went outside into the chilly March air. Miss Emma Harlow was much satisfied with this morning's work. She might not have settled on the details yet, but she expected that within a month she'll have extracted Sir Waldo Windbag from their lives. It was a lovely prospect.

When Emma arrived home, she found Sarah in the parlor, staring blankly into the fireplace. Her needlework lay untouched on her lap and her eyes were red from tears.

"Sarah darling," Emma said, flying to her sister-in-law's side and kneeling at her feet, "how distressed look you. Whatever is the matter?"

"It's Roger," she said, faintly, turning her eyes away from the flame.

Emma gasped. "He isn't…"

"No, dear, he isn't. But he has been hurt just the same." Fresh tears began to trickle down Sarah's face. "They had to amputate—his left arm. My dear, darling Roger."

"Come here, darling," Emma said, pulling Sarah into her arms and murmuring words of comfort. "He's alive, dearest, that's all that matters. He doesn't need both arms."

"I know that, Emma. I'm not crying because he lost an arm. Really, I'm not such a ninny as that. He can hold me tight enough with one arm." Sarah sat back in her chair and straightened her hair. "I'm crying because of all the pain he must have suffered, all the pain he must be suffering still. It's unbearable. I should be with him. It should be my hand he holds on to for comfort."

Never one for inaction, the Harlow Hoyden considered this problem and arrived instantly at a workable solution. "Very well, we'll leave this instant. I'll throw a few things into a bag and have Dobson pack one for you as well. We will be in France by nightfall."

For the first time since getting the dreadful news an hour before, Sarah laughed. "France is many miles away. We cannot reach it by dark."

"Well, Dover then," she said reasonably. "We will take a boat across the Channel first thing in the morning. I better tell Dobson not to prepare dinner for us. And I must leave a note for Lavinia. Where's my sister anyway? She should have been here to comfort you when the news came. Is she in the conservatory? Really, Sarah, all you had to do is send Ludlow to fetch her. She would have gladly abandoned the *Rhyncholaelia digbyana* for you."

"Emma, we cannot reach Dover before nightfall."

"Yes, we can," she answered, distractedly. She was trying to compile a list of things she would need for the journey. She would leave Ellen here, of course. An abigail would just slow them down, and Sarah was all the companion she needed to put the stamp of respectability on it.

"No, we can't, my dear. It is too far away."

Emma smiled. "Not the way I drive."

"No, dear, it's very sweet of you, of course, but I must insist that you stop in your wild notion. We will not go tearing off after Roger in a curricle," she said, thinking of all the things that could go wrong with such a plan.

"All right," said Emma with that faraway calculating look in her eye, "*we* won't go tearing off after Roger."

Sarah knew her sister-in-law too well to accept this statement without further caveats. "And you will not go on your own. You will sit here and comfort me and not move from my side. I don't want you sneaking off under the cover of darkness, either, as soon as my back is turned. I'll have your word on this matter."

Since this was exactly what Emma had planned to do, she gave her word with a petulant look. She knew she shouldn't burden Sarah with her bad temper, but sitting around waiting for news was not her style. She preferred to chase after things, rather than let them come to her. "All right, dearest, I give my word, but only because you look so worried. Really, Sarah, you needn't worry so much about me. I'm no longer a child and am well adept at taking care of myself."

"Yes, it's your reputation you don't have a care for."

"Well, which is more important—my person or my reputation?"

Sarah looked at her with considering eyes. "Honestly, my dear, I don't know the answer to that one."

"Well, I do, and that's all that matters. Now let's get some tea into you and then you can tell me all about it." She stood up, stuck her head out of the parlor doors and called for the housekeeper. "Dobson, Dobson, where is that woma— Oh, there you are. Can we get some tea in here? And some sandwiches. My sister-in-law is in need of sustenance." Sarah tried to demur, but Miss Harlow ran roughshod over her. "Yes, you do. Dobson, also bring some of my brother's brandy. I've always found it very reviving." She closed the door.

"Emma, I do wish you'd use the pull cord like everyone else. You can't go around yelling your head off. The servants find it off-putting."

"Pooh, certainly it's less off-putting than being called with a bell like a dog."

Sarah could not bestir herself to argue. "Very well. But I don't think we should have the brandy. It's the middle of the day."

"Bad news doesn't defer to the time of day—why should we?" Emma made herself comfortable on a footstool across from her friend. "All right, tell me everything. I know naught other than he lost his arm. How did it happen? *Where* did it happen? Who is taking care of him?"

"It was a riding accident," explained Sarah. "His horse took a spill and landed on top of his arm. We are very lucky that he did. A few inches to the right and Roger's chest would have been crushed. The doctor says that he's very fortunate to have survived such an accident."

"But there must be some mistake!" exclaimed Emma. "Roger is an excellent rider. He's never taken a spill in his life. 'Twas he who taught me how to hold a seat, and a horse has never fallen on my arm."

"I assure you it's no mistake. The roads in France must be different than the roads in England. Perhaps there are more potholes. Perhaps he was riding at night. I do not have all the details. I only know that it happened four days ago in Calais and that he is alive. I don't need to know more."

Emma saw the look of calm on Sarah's face and restrained her impatience. Because she didn't have Sarah's inner serenity, she was unable to accept this information without further questions. She wanted to know more, and she cursed the promise she had given. Really, if she left right now, she would be in Dover before dark and in Calais by luncheon tomorrow. It was so much more preferable to just sitting here waiting for news. "Does the missive say when Roger will be well enough for travel?" she asked.

"The doctor hopes within a week, barring infection."

Emma nodded. Surely she could wait a week to get the details from Roger. She was much interested in hearing about this spill. Something very treacherous indeed must have crossed his path to make such an accomplished rider as he lose control of his steed. She allowed that on a moonless night a large animal like a deer might be able to do her some mischief. "We'll have to prepare the house for his arrival. Shall I instruct Dobson or would you rather do that?"

"I shall take care of everything. Thank goodness the

children are at Ridgeview House. I wouldn't want them to see their father when he's unwell. In a few months, I daresay, he'll be used to his condition and will be able to put them at ease. When adults are awkward or uncomfortable, children sense it and react accordingly."

"Yes, that's exactly how it is." The door opened and in stepped a footman with a tray of food. "Ah, here is Ludlow. Please leave it on the table and we will take care of it, my good man. And here's the tea. I don't see the brandy. I trust that's forthcoming? Excellent. Sarah, why don't you sit back and let me serve. You've done enough for the day. Why don't you give me that sampler? You've got better things to do than drag a needle through a piece of fabric."

All thoughts of going to the theater were instantly abandoned upon hearing the news about Roger. The Harlows were content to pass the evening quietly in their drawing room, taking comfort from each other. Even Lady Harlow changed her plans, telling her cronies to play whist without her. She sat now by the fire, anxiously shuffling a pack of playing cards. Emma was surprised and pleased by the concern their mama demonstrated. It had always seemed as if she didn't care.

Emma's scheme to break up Lavinia and Sir Waldo would have also been forgotten had Sir Windbag himself not come to sit with the family. He put himself on the couch, right next to Sarah, effectively squeezing out Lavinia, who had been quietly talking to her, and began asking questions. He had a morbid interest in accidents and seemed determined to get the details out of Sarah. Although told more than once that Sarah knew very little, Sir Waldo persisted in this useless line of questioning.

"You say the horse fell on his arm. Did it fall on his whole arm, up to his shoulder, or just the lower portion, to the elbow?" he asked, completely oblivious to her discomfort.

"I don't know, Sir Windbourne."

"What part of Calais was he in when it happened? I'm somewhat familiar with the geography of France. I wonder if he was near the Chapeau Triste. Did it happen near the Chapeau Triste?"

"I don't know, Sir Windbourne."

"This doctor. What was his name? I knew a family in those parts once, named Deveraux, I think. Was the doctor a tall man with a very thin—"

"Waldo, Mama and I were just about to start a hand of piquet. Won't you join us?" said Lavinia, putting an end to the awkward exchange.

Emma hid a smile when she saw the expression on Mama's face. "Piquet? Why, I haven't played piquet in years. I don't think I recall how. Why would you say such a thing, child?"

"How lovely. We'll all be evenly matched," said Lavinia as she accepted a seat from her fiancé.

Taking the recently vacated cushion next to her sister-in-law, Emma said, "I'm sorry that you had to go through that, but if his ill-bred treatment of you revealed one-tenth of his coarse nature to my sister, then I can't think it such an awful thing."

"Emma, you are too harsh in your judgment of him. Some people are uncomfortable in the company of tragedy and don't know what to say. They don't mean to behave badly."

"And you, my dear, are too soft in your judgment. But not to worry, I'm on the case and will soon have this whole problem fixed."

"What are you planning?" Sarah asked suspiciously. For the first time that day she recalled the Duke of Trent's odd behavior the night before. He'd seemed on the verge of a confession.

"Nothing to furl your pretty brow over. Just concentrate on Roger's getting well and returning home to us soon. I'll worry about everything else."

"That's exactly what worries me."

Emma merely laughed.

With the piquet game occupying her hands, Lady Harlow found her mind wandering. "The thing I don't understand is why Roger had to go to France in the first place. It's so dangerous."

"The war is over, Mama, and Napoléon has been safely ensconced on St. Helena for these many months,"

Lavinia said reasonably. "France is as safe as England."

"Ha!" said the lady. "Roger never tumbled off his horse on English soil. Traveling is foolhardy and dangerous. I myself have never done it and look at the long life I've had."

"Then perhaps you should not send him to France to do your bidding, " said Emma, reminding her mother just why Roger had been on foreign soil.

"I, send him to France? What an absurd notion."

"But what about your investments?"

"The only investments I have are English. I'd never send my money to France, where any old foreigner could steal it. Why, look at what happened to Roger. I'm not altogether convinced that this accident wasn't intentional. Surely some thieves set upon him in the night, causing him to take a fall."

Emma thought this disavowal of French investments odd but didn't refine too much on it. Her mother was a careless, absentminded woman and forgetting that she'd sent her firstborn on a financial errand was exactly the sort of thing she'd do.

"That is neither here nor there," said Sarah, fearing that Emma wouldn't let the matter rest. "What's important is Roger's health. We must all keep that in mind. And when he returns to our hearth, we must be sure to treat him as we always have. We mustn't let him think we're treating him differently because of his missing arm. His state of mind is as important as his physical health."

Everyone agreed that this was the best course of action, and the room fell silent once more.

CHAPTER FOUR

Much to his disgust, the Duke of Trent found himself looking for the Harlow chit everywhere he went. He expected to see her at the Sizemore musicale, which was the only reason he let his mama drag him there. Two hours of listening to what sounded like a hen caterwauling and not a glimpse of golden curls. He left the event in a huff and went to his club, where he passed the evening losing fifty pounds to the Earl of Tumbridge.

The exercise was repeated the next evening, at Lady Weston's route. His delighted mama watched him make conversation with Miss Portia Hedgley under the very pleased eye of that lady's father. The talk was desultory and bored the duke to flinders. If he had to hear another word about ostrich-plumed hats, he was going to scream. At the first possible moment, he offered to fetch the lady wine and disappeared into the crowd. He cornered Philip and made him deliver the refreshment to Miss Hedgley.

"What should I tell her?" asked Philip when charged with this task. "She's going to ask what happened to you, and I'm going to look like a queer fellow if I don't know."

Trent was too bored to think of a creative excuse. "Tell her whatever you want."

Philip tried to think of something. "Nope, my head's empty. You better give me an excuse to pass along."

"All right, tell her I've got the headache," he said, thinking it wasn't very far from the truth.

"Can't do that," protested Philip. "Only girls get headaches. Don't worry. I'll think of something. Not very good at lying but clearly I am better than you. A headache! Might as well tell her you had a fainting spell." Philip left in disgust.

As he watched his cousin walk away, Trent decided it was time he got going. The hour was still early, early enough to salvage something from this evening. He got into his carriage and told the coachman to take him to a gambling hell along St. James. There was a young widow he was flirting with, one he hoped to set up a liaison with, and he knew she was a fan of the baize. Perhaps tonight he would press his suit. He could think of nothing else of interest to do.

Upon entering the hell, he found the widow Enderling at the faro table, just as he'd expected. His entrance did not pass unnoticed, and he saw the lady in question casting lures at him out of the corner of her eye. *Yes*, he thought, *she's ripe for the plucking*. Somehow the prospect didn't please him as it ought. Perhaps it was because the challenge had gone out of the game.

He was making his way over to the widow when he caught sight of Everett Carson at the poker table. Without thinking, Trent changed directions and laid out his counters next to the peer. "Deal me in," he said, taking out his snuffbox.

"Trent, this is a surprise," said Carson. "From the look of it, you seemed determined in your pursuit of the lovely Mrs. Enderling. I did not expect you to be playing poker when there were other…games to be played. What does this mean?"

Although Carson had said nothing less than the truth, the duke's lip curled in disgust. "That things are seldom what they seem."

"Wise words," answered Carson before looking at his cards. "Very wise words indeed. Why, just take the Harlow Hoyden, for example."

In the process of taking a pinch of snuff, the duke halted his movement for a split second. "Yes?" he asked with deceptive indifference.

"When you meet her, she *seems* like a gently bred, butter-wouldn't-melt-in-her-mouth young lady, the sort you want your sister to be, but we all know the truth."

"The truth?" asked Trent.

"The truth. That she's wild and fast."

He was almost positive that the man was merely speculating, but it wouldn't do to lose his temper before confirming it. "I take it you've sampled the lady's charms?" he asked, dampening down the bile that rose in his throat. How dare this bounder call Emma fast!

Carson smirked. "No, not yet. We've only had one dance, but I expect it is only a matter of time. She has a passionate nature, and I, like you, enjoy other…games."

At this intelligence, Trent couldn't find an acceptable course of action. As much as he wanted to, he could not very well plant a facer on the scoundrel. To do so would be to bring scandal down on them all, for surely such behavior would only lead to a duel. Trent could think of nothing more pleasant than running Sir Everett Carson through, but he would resist the impulse. The last thing the Harlow Hoyden needed was a duel fought over her honor.

With no satisfying recourse available to him, the duke finished out the hand in dark, brooding silence and left the hell.

First thing the next morning, Alexander Keswick, Duke of Trent, presented himself at 21 Grosvenor Square. Momentarily disconcerted by the hour of the call and the consequence of the visitor, Ludlow belatedly showed him to the drawing room. A few minutes later, Emma walked in.

"Your grace," she said, "this is an unexpected surprise."

The duke bowed stiffly in welcome. "Miss Harlow, there's some matter of considerable importance that I would like to discuss with you."

Emma waved her hand in response. "Don't say it. I know what's going on. You've had a change of heart and want your flower back. I'm sorry to report that it's too late. It has been successfully cross-bred with one of my sister's *Altensteinia nubigena*. But I'm sure she'll let you have one of the blossoms when they're ready."

The duke, distracted, looked behind her toward the door. "Are you here alone?" he asked.

"Excuse me?"

"Will no one else be joining us?"

"You did ask to speak with me, did you not?"

"Yes, but I assumed you'd have the sense to bring along Sarah or at least an abigail. You should not be meeting alone with men. It's not proper."

"Pooh," she dismissed, "we're perfectly safe from wagging tongues here. No one else is home."

"It's not your reputation that you should be concerned with when you meet a man alone but your virtue."

Emma laughed. "My virtue is safe from you, is it not, your grace. Surely you have no designs on it."

A wry smile played along his lips. "I'm not speaking of myself but of other men."

"But I'm not meeting with other men," she said, taking a seat and indicating that he should follow suit. "I'm meeting with you."

Somewhat appeased by this communication, the duke sat down. "I want to talk about your scheme, Miss Harlow. You must cease and desist right now. Everett Carson is not a boy to be toyed with. He is in fact a very dangerous man."

Emma pictured the handsome man she had danced with a few nights before. Although a libertine who fit the bill in many ways, he was not to be trusted. Emma had already decided he wouldn't do, but she nevertheless resented the duke's interference. "Really, your grace, that's not very sporting of you. You have the right to refuse to help me—that's your prerogative and I respect that—but that you should come in here and insist that I not consider a perfectly good libertine is insupportable. I wouldn't have expected such dog-in-the-manger behavior from you."

"Miss Harlow, I fear you do not understand the danger you court," he said, ignoring her ridiculous speech in an attempt to remain reasonable. "Carson is not a gentleman. He'll give you cause to regret your actions."

This grave warning did not perturb her. "I seriously doubt that, but if what you say is true, then I will just have to accept that. There are no rewards without risks."

"As someone who knows more about this than you," he said waspishly, feeling the first threads of his temper getting away from him, "I must most strongly urge you to forget this rash plan. The risks are too great."

Because Trent seemed so genuinely worried about her, Miss Harlow sought to put him at ease. "Really, your grace, you have no cause to worry. I have not decided on Carson and indeed it seems now that I will not use him. I have other prospects."

The relief Trent felt at the beginning of the speech evaporated by the end of it. "Other prospects?" he echoed.

"Yes, so there's no cause for alarm."

The duke could not agree. "Who are these other prospects?"

"I do not know yet, but I'm sure they will be infinitely more satisfying than Mr. Carson."

"What do you mean by you do not know yet?"

"A dear friend is drawing up a list of possible candidates," she explained. "She has promised to provide me with at least five. I'm confident that one will meet all my requirements."

"No," said the duke in his sternest ducal voice, the one he used to quiet his interfering mother and sister.

"No?" she repeated, puzzled.

"No, you will not do this, drawing up a list of libertines and selecting one as though you were choosing a book at the lending library," he commanded, expecting to be obeyed. Nobody defied the Duke of Trent when he made a command. "It's unacceptable."

Emma didn't recognize these words as the dictate they were and protested. "Really, your grace, I cannot see what it has to do with you. You're not my father or brother to be telling me what is and isn't acceptable."

"It seems that I must be the one to tell you since neither has seen fit to do his duty," he said with more vehemence than he intended. He was now struggling to hold on to his temper. He hadn't planned on discussing this with Miss Harlow. He expected her to obey his order and leave the matter alone. That he had to pursue it further angered him. "If either had, we would not be having this discussion. You would know that it's not the thing to go around drawing up lists of libertines with the expectation of interviewing them to find the one most suitable for seducing your sister." Trent realized that Emma was not listening to him and jumped to his feet. He stood over her, looking his most intimidating with his dark eyebrows drawn in a harsh line. It was a stance that had not only quelled his mother and schoolfellows but members of Parliament as well. "Never in my life have I seen such ramshack—"

"Would you like some tea, your grace?" she asked calmly, seemingly oblivious to his intimidation tactic.

"Tea?" the Duke of Trent echoed, his brows dropping.

"Yes, tea. I have been remiss in my duties as hostess. I should have offered you some the minute I entered the room. Do have a seat and let me rectify my oversight."

The duke didn't appreciate the interruption. He had more to say on the topic of her conduct and refused to let the wind be taken out of his sails. "As I was saying, never in my life—"

"Well, I'm quite parched. Do hold that thought." She got up, stuck her head out the door and began calling for Dobson.

The duke watched this odd behavior with wry amusement. Little wonder the mindless chit was tumbling headlong into scandal and ruin; she had no sense of decorum at all.

Emma returned to the sofa and smiled encouragingly at the duke. "You were saying…" Trent straightened his shoulders and tried to recall where he left off. Seeing this, she said, "Never in your life…"

The duke's sense of humor got the best of him. "Very good, Miss Harlow. I see now why your papa has never managed to teach you manners. Do you always confuse and fluster your opponents like this?"

Shaking her head, she leaned forward on the cushion. "It was not my intention to confuse you, your grace, and I doubt very much that the Duke of Trent is ever flustered. 'Twas only that you had worked yourself into such a temper I thought surely you must be thirsty. I myself am always thirsty when riled up."

"No matter," he said, not convinced but abandoning the point anyway. "Let me be clear on this, Miss Harlow. You will not approach another libertine and ask him to seduce your sister. It's not how ladies behave."

Emma realized that the duke was not going to leave until he got what he wanted. Rather than lose a whole day to argument, she gave it to him. "All right, your grace, I'll cease and desist at once. Oh, lovely. Tea is here. Set it on the table. Very good. Thank you, Dobson."

This answer no more pleased the duke. His brows drew together again in a dark line. "That is it? You agree? Just like that?"

"Yes, the force of your arguments has quite done me in. One lump or two?"

Busy trying to make sense of the girl's sudden capitulation, the duke didn't hear the question. "Excuse me?"

"I asked if you wanted sugar in your tea. One lump or two?"

"One is fine." He took a deep breath and considered his hostess with suspicion. "Why have you suddenly agreed with me?"

"As I said, I'm quite overcome by the force of your logic," Emma said, not a hint of condescension in her tone. "Clearly no one has ever explained things to me quite as plainly as you have. I'm in wholehearted agreement. Drawing up lists and propositioning libertines is not how ladies behave."

Although they'd met less than a week before, he knew better than to accept her words at face value. "You're only telling me what I want to hear."

Emma smiled, dimples in prominence. "And it's a wonder that you're no more happy getting what you want than not getting it. Tell me, your grace, what should I do to satisfy you?"

"Say what you mean."

"I tried that approach, but it only seemed to anger you more."

He began to understand her tactic. "Then you have no intention of abandoning your scheme?"

Her eyes were as wide and innocent as a newborn kitten's. "But why should I? I respect you and sincerely appreciate the concern you seem to feel for me and my family, but my sister's happiness cannot rest on your autocratic and unreasonable demands."

Angry words flitted through Trent's head, but he held his tongue. A wise man always knew when he had been beaten by a skillful opponent. Miss Harlow had maneuvered him nicely. If his mother or sister knew how to handle him half so well, he would have been married to that Hedgley chit with a brat on the way by now. "Very well, I accept," he said, not as disturbed by the forthcoming task as he ought to be.

Emma looked at him in surprise. "Accept what, your grace?"

"Your offer of employment. I will play the part of seducer."

"But you won't do at all," she exclaimed.

His expression turned black. "*I* won't do?"

Fearful that she might have hurt his feelings, she added, "It was very kind of you to offer, but you're not suited to the task. Of course, I'm well aware the honor you do me, as you're extremely handsome and a fine figure of a man and would turn the head of *any* sensible girl."

"*I* won't do?" he asked again, seemingly incapable

of understanding the prospect that he was unsuitable for any project.

"The scheme calls for a libertine," she said gently.

"I'm a libertine."

The Harlow Hoyden laughed.

The duke took offense at her easy dismissal of him. "I am a libertine. You said so yourself."

"That was a week ago," she explained, taking a sip of tea. "I have since learned the truth."

"What truth?"

"That you're a true gentleman."

"The devil you say!" he cried out, much offended by this claim.

"Look at the evidence," said Miss Harlow and listed his finer points on her fingers. "You refused to help me. You take me to task for meeting with you alone. You offer to help me with my scheme when you realize you cannot deter me from my path. These are not the actions of a libertine."

"I keep a dancer in Chelsea."

"So does my father."

"I'm in pursuit of a lovely widow."

"Lady Enderling is old enough to make her own decisions."

"I bet one hundred pounds at my club that I could seduce the wife of a viscount."

"That is the way gentlemen behave."

"The Savoy keeps a supply of garnet broaches on hand for me so that I may give one to whichever lady I am dining with."

"Pooh. You are a sheep in wolf's clothing, your grace." She held up the pot. "More tea?"

Trent didn't want more tea, and almost seething with anger, he regarded the Harlow Hoyden. As he'd listened to her defend his character, he'd grown more and more enraged. The way she dismissed his transgressions out of hand was intolerable. The way gentlemen behave! A sheep in wolf's clothing!

He sat down on the couch next to her, so close he could feel her breathing. Then he grabbed the teapot from her fingers and placed it on the table with so much force that the silver rattled. He pulled her toward him. "I am a hardened rake!" he insisted, before his lips covered her.

It was a rough kiss at first, and Emma didn't know how to respond. She'd never been kissed before, and although she had many times imagined what the pastime would be like, she'd never expected it to be anything like this, with Trent's lips pressed so hard against hers that she could scarcely move. But then everything changed. Trent's lips relaxed and became gentle. He laid soft kisses on the side of her mouth, and his tongue delicately traced her lips until she opened them in response. Before she knew what she was about, Emma was wrapping her arms around his neck and pulling him toward her.

At one point, the duke sought to end the embrace, but Emma moaned in distress and pulled him closer, leaning back on the cushions and taking him with her. She ran her fingers through his hair, along his neck and down his back. The sensations he was creating with his lips were so overwhelming and unexpected and lovely that she couldn't think of anything but creating more of them. His hand trailed a slow path down her cheek to her shoulder. Then she felt his hand slip under the soft lawn of her morning gown. She sighed in response and pressed her lips harder against his. What else she wanted she didn't know, but she was eager for more. She suddenly realized there was a whole host of wonderful sensations waiting to be discovered and could barely wait to start the adventure.

The Duke of Trent freed himself from her embrace, pulled away and stood up. He walked toward the fireplace and rested one arm on the mantle. "There, I believe that should put an end to the debate."

For the first time in her life, the Harlow Hoyden was at a loss for words. She stared at the duke in wonder.

"I will begin my seduction of your sister right away. The

sooner we start, the sooner we finish," he said, thinking, *And the sooner my life will return to normal!* "I trust the Harlow sisters will be at the Kenelm ball?"

Emma could barely think over the loud beating of her heart, but she tried anyway to pull herself together. What a ninnyhammer she was to be so affected by a kiss. The duke seemed unmoved by the experience, and she sought to emulate his indifference. She took a deep breath and focused on his question. Oh, what was it that he'd asked? Something about the Kenelm ball. "I do not know if we will be in attendance. My brother, Roger, has had a mishap, and Sarah has not been herself ever since. We'll only go if she is up to chaperoning us."

"I hope your brother's mishap wasn't too serious," the duke said, marveling at how fast she'd recovered from that kiss. It seemed unlikely that he, the experienced one, would ever recover from it. Who knew that a lady with so much innocence could be capable of so much passion? Just thinking about it sent his blood soaring again.

"He's alive and rapidly returning to health," she explained. "It happened whilst he was abroad, in France. He should be returned to us within the week. We all take comfort in that."

"That sounds very serious indeed. Do tell Sarah to let me know if there's anything I can do," he said, making polite drawing room conversation, although polite drawing room conversation was the last thing he wanted to make.

"Of course," she said, reaching for a teacup but putting it down when she realized her hand was unsteady. She folded both hands together in her lap and hoped the duke hadn't noticed.

If he did, he gave no indication of it. "Since Sarah will most likely not be up to attending the ball, why don't I escort you and Miss Harlow? I shall bring my mother along. It will all be very respectable."

"That is a very gracious offer, your grace, and I gladly accept, assuming your mother has plans to attend. I wouldn't want to inconvenience her."

"Don't tease yourself on that point," he said, with his charming smile. "Mama hasn't missed a *ton* event in more than thirty years."

Emma, staring almost transfixed at his beautiful, skilled lips, had to shake herself free of a daydream before responding. "Excellent. I shall look forward to it. We've stayed very close to home these last few days, and it will be good to get out."

Suddenly the duke felt as awkward as a schoolboy at his first social function. Several matters had been resolved, and it was clearly time for him to take his leave. But he didn't want to go just yet. He felt something should be said about what happened—one didn't just molest innocent maidens in the front parlor and then retire from the room—but he didn't know what. His smooth tongue deserted him now that he needed it the most.

Miss Harlow, who was eager to be alone so that she could still her shaking hands in private, stood up. "Your grace, it has been a most interesting morning. Thank you for your call and for your generous offer of help. With your aid, I'm positive we will have Sir Windbourne routed in no time. No doubt one day my sister will thank you for the service you do her."

Trent bowed and resisted the urge to kiss her hand. Contact now would be the undoing of him. "Let us proceed with caution and leave your sister's thanks in the far-off future. I am not as confident as you that what we're doing is right."

"Of course you're not." She dimpled. "As I said, you are a gentleman."

Not wanting to get into *that* again, the duke bid her good day and stepped outside into the brisk March air.

What a relief to be out of there, he thought, climbing into the coach. Despite his vehement protests to the contrary, Alexander Keswick, the seventh Duke of Trent, was not a libertine. Playing fast and loose with the affections of an innocent did not sit well with him. And he didn't mean Lavinia Harlow. He was confident that a few conversations about raising orchids and a couple of his melting looks that had ensnared so many women before would have her easily under his spell. He didn't think winning her affections would require any physical contact.

No, Trent was worried about the other Miss Harlow. His behavior today had been quite out of the ordinary for him. He had never before kissed a well-bred unmarried woman, but the experience had been intoxicating—and quite possibly addictive. It was Emma herself, of course, who made the encounter so heady. He would have to take care in the future. It would not do to lead her on. The Duke of Trent had no intention of marrying just yet, and he didn't want an innocent mooning embarrassingly over him.

CHAPTER FIVE

Sarah had no intention of going to the Kenelms' ball—until she heard that the girls would be going in Trent's coach.

"Really, Sarah, there's no reason to examine me with that look on your face. I assure you the whole enterprise is one hundred percent respectable," Emma said when questioned on the subject by her sister-in-law. "He and his mama were going to the ball themselves and are only swinging by here to pick us up. It's nothing in the least."

"But I don't understand why he is 'swinging by here,' as you so coarsely put it. We're several blocks out of his way. Whatever could he be thinking?" she said, tossing her bonnet on the chair beside her. She had barely returned from her daily walk in the square when she learned that the Duke of Trent had been closeted with her younger charge for more than a half hour.

"Well, if the truth were known," said Emma in conspirational tones, deciding it was time to put her plan into action. "I think he has developed a *tendre* for dear Lavinia."

Sarah laughed. "Emma, what a child you are. The duke is not wearing the willow for your sister. While I love her dearly, I know for a fact that she isn't at all the sort of girl who attracts Trent. He likes them lively, with a bit of color in their cheeks. Vinnie's cheeks are pallid."

"But she is lively when she talks to the duke," protested Emma.

"What can she possibly have to talk about with him?"

"Orchids, of course. They are both extremely interested in cultivating orchids. Yes, the duke was closeted in here with me this morning, but all we talked about were Lavinia and her flowers. The duke is interested in her, Sarah. I know it for a fact. He even told me so himself," she added, as a clincher.

It was then that Sarah realized that Emma was up to some havey-cavey business. Try as she might, she simply could not believe Trent was interested in Lavinia. Emma—now that was another story completely. Yes, the duke usually stayed away from misses of marriageable age, but there was no telling with someone as quixotic as he. Perhaps he was interested in Emma. But why then would he pretend an interest in Lavinia? The entire story made no sense, and Sarah decided to watch the situation closely. "Very well, I shall go the ball, but we will be taking our own carriage. Write a letter to Trent and thank him for his kind offer. It wouldn't do for us to arrive in a carriage with the duke and his mother. We're not connected to his family, and it would no doubt raise eyebrows, especially with Lavinia engaged to Sir Waldo. If we should be arriving in any man's coach, it should be his. Do you know if he'll be attending the ball tonight?"

Emma had no idea, though it was her solemn wish that he not be there. She wanted Trent to have some time to get to work winning the affections of her sister, without Sir Windbag's very annoying presence. Lavinia was hardly a widgeon, but even the most levelheaded girls found jealous fits to be romantic. She didn't want her scheme to push Lavinia deeper into that villain's embrace. Speaking of embraces...

"Sarah," she said, in quite a different tone than her earlier statements, "can I ask you something and will you promise to answer without getting all stiff and matronly on me?"

Still puzzling over the matter of Trent, Sarah agreed without paying attention to the question. "Of course, dear, what is it?"

"Is kissing the same with all gentleman or does it depend on the beau?" she asked.

Sarah paled and straightened up in her seat, looking at Emma as if she'd never seen her before. "What happened in this room between you and the duke?" she asked, her voice severe.

Miss Harlow frowned petulantly. "There, you're getting all stiff. And after promising you wouldn't."

"Emma, you will tell me what occurred between you and the duke," ordered Sarah, in no mood for games.

"Nothing of note," she said, while silently acknowledging that that kiss had been very notable indeed. "As I said, we mostly talked about Vinnie." Realizing that she had to appease Sarah or she wouldn't get a useful word out of her, she said, "I'll admit that all this talk of engagements has me wondering about things that an unengaged girl shouldn't wonder about. I cannot help but think that if Lavinia kissed someone else, she would lose all interest in the horrid Sir Windbag."

"Well-bred ladies of good standing do not hunt around looking for the best kisser. That is not how you choose a husband," Sarah instructed, hoping that would be the end of the discussion.

"Ah, so some men are better than others?"

Sarah looked much vexed at Emma's astute observation. "I didn't say that, you horrible child."

Emma laughed, delighted with the way the conversation was going. In a minute she would have the truth out of her. "You better just tell me, my dear, before I take it into my head to find out the answer myself."

"Very well, the answer is yes." She surrendered to the inevitable with a sigh. "Yes, some men kiss better than others. And, no, it isn't the same with all gentlemen. It depends on a great many things."

Emma threw herself onto the cushion next to Sarah, her knees pressing against her sister-in-law's side. "Have you kissed a great many men, other than Roger?"

"How many times do I have to tell you that ladies do not sit on their knees in that ramshackle fashion?" Sarah said, exasperation clearly etched in every line of her face. "Now place your feet on the floor like a normal person."

She grunted in irritation—how could Sarah be thinking of such mundane things at a time like this?—and obeyed. "There, now tell me. How many men have you kissed?"

"Only two others besides your brother, if you must know, and the first one was an unpleasant experience."

Recalling her kiss with Trent, Emma found it impossible to believe that kissing could ever be unpleasant. "Why?"

"Why what?" asked Sarah.

"What was it unpleasant?"

"I've told you enough already, you impertinent brat. Now leave me in peace," she said, shooing her charge out of the room. "I've had enough of your nonsense. And don't forget to write that note to the duke."

Emma left, more eager than ever to give kissing a second try.

The Kenelm ball was a glittering affair, and Emma could barely contain her excitement. *Finally* something was to be done about that dreadful Sir Waldo Windbag. She had yet to catch sight of Trent but felt positive that he would be there. He had seemed very eager to get this ordeal over with, although he himself had sought out the responsibility. She had not been teasing him that afternoon or purposefully manipulating. As far as she was concerned, he *was* most unsuitable. Only a libertine should do a libertine's work.

Emma looked at her dance card, which was predictably free of names. Although she was in usually good looks in her blue silk dress, due to a knowing sparkle in her eye and a becoming blush in her cheeks, the respectable gentlemen of the *ton* kept their distance. No one ever knew what to expect from the Harlow Hoyden, and few were brave enough to take the risk. That was fine with Emma. She had little interest in the respectable gentlemen of the *ton*.

Where was Trent?

"Ah, there you are, my dear." Emma turned at the sound of her friend Kate's voice. "I've been looking for you everywhere. Why are you hanging back in a corner with the chaperones, like a wallflower?"

"Is this where the chaperones gather?" she asked with a laugh. "I hadn't realized. Its major appeal for me was the three inches of unoccupied space it offered. The ballroom is so crowded."

"I suppose it's a good thing," Kate said, "since I was hoping to have a private moment to talk about the list."

"Ah, yes, the list. What sort of progress have you made?" Emma asked.

"I'm afraid it's rather slow going," Miss Kennington admitted. "There are many rakes and scoundrels running tame in the best drawing rooms this season, but I've come across none so far that I'd stake your sister's reputation on. But don't give up hope. Perhaps in a few weeks," she explained, hoping that in a few weeks her friend will have moved on to some new, less volatile mischief. Kate had actually come up with a name or two, and should Emma persist in her plan, they would do well enough.

"Don't worry, darling. There's no longer need for the list."

This was exactly what Kate wanted to hear. "That is a relief."

"Yes, Trent has kindly offered to do the deed for me. I am even now awaiting his arrival. He promised to begin courting Lavinia tonight. I suspect by tomorrow morning, he'll have wormed his way a good deal into her heart," she said with conviction.

Kate gave her a long look. "Either you are overestimating Trent's charms or underestimating your sister's devotion. I am not sure which."

Emma laughed. "Surely underestimating Lavinia's devotion, for I don't think it is possible to overestimate Trent's charms."

This was by far the most intriguing thing Kate had ever heard the Harlow Hoyden say. Although she wanted very much to ask Emma what exactly she knew of Trent's charm, she restrained herself. Emma could be prickly and defensive, and she didn't want to get her hackles up, not when there were so many details to be learned. "That is very kind of the duke to help. What changed his mind?"

"He changed it himself. We had the most interesting scene in my drawing room today. He came in bound and determined to get me to abandon my scheme, and when he realized that I would stay the course, he insisted on helping. I don't think he trusts another gentleman to behave properly with Lavinia. I turned down his offer, of course."

"What?" asked Kate, shocked. "Why on earth would you do that?"

"Because he's not really a libertine, as you made me realize. I tried to explain that to him, but he only became more and more upset." Emma blushed as she recalled just how upset he had gotten.

Kate saw this and wondered at its cause. She could not remember the last time she had seen Emma blush. "But he convinced you in the end?"

"Yes, I suppose he did convince me."

"What did he do—"

"Dash it, there you are, Miss Harlow," said Philip, his face flushed with exertion. "Been looking for you everywhere. Hoping I could get a dance. Your card ain't filled yet, is it?"

As Emma hastened to assure him that her card was far from full, Kate sent her a quizzical look.

Emma dimpled in response. In her experience, Philip

often drew quizzical looks. "Philip, I don't believe you've met my friend Kate Kennington. This is Philip Keswick. He is the Duke of Trent's cousin."

Philip bowed at the young beauty. "It's a pleasure, ma'am. Perhaps you'd like to dance with me, as well?"

"I'm afraid my card *is* already full," she said with a smile to soften the disappointment.

"That's all right. As long as I get one in with the Harlow Hoyden." He handed Emma her card back. "I've put my name next to a minuet. Would have chosen a waltz but Trent told me not to," he said enigmatically before disappearing into the crowd.

"Now what do you suppose he meant by that?" wondered Kate.

Emma was scarcely paying attention. "Nothing, I'm sure. If Philip is here, that means that Trent must be nearby. Do you see him? Come, we mustn't hide in the corner like this. We'll miss all the fun."

Before excusing herself, Kate followed her friend to the other side of the ballroom, where they found Sarah talking to some friends. "But we will talk about this more," she assured Emma.

"Talk about what more?" Emma asked, her eyes searching the room for a glimpse of Trent.

Her friend just smiled in response and walked away.

"It is the strangest thing," said Sarah, upon seeing Emma beside her.

"What, dear?"

"The way Trent is indeed pursuing Lavinia." She gestured to the punch table, where Trent was in the process of handing Vinnie a glass. "He has been here for a half hour and has not left her side. Whatever can he be about?" she asked, almost under her breath.

"I don't know why you marvel so. A man such as he is probably tired of all those jaded flirts who crowd around him like bees to honey. No doubt he appreciates Lavinia's quiet charms and her intelligent conversation." This statement made so much sense to Emma that she found herself half believing it. She looked at the two of them drinking punch across the room, and the idea took root. Really, why shouldn't the two of them make a match of it? Lavinia wanted a family, and it was time the duke settled down. With their horticultural bent, they had much in common. Who was to say that the two wouldn't fall in love? And what was love anyway? Emma didn't know, but it seemed to her a flimsy thing indeed if Lavinia could feel it for such a blackguard as Sir Windbag.

"I suppose there could be some truth in that," conceded Sarah. "Many a young man has sown his wild oats with highfliers, only to set up his nursery with an artless lady like your sister."

"I'm confident that Vinnie will have him wrapped around her finger by the end of the month."

Sarah turned to face her. "Oh, Emma darling, don't say such things. You know very well that your sister is engaged to Sir Waldo, and she's far too honorable to jilt him just because a superior prospect has presented itself. She will marry him, no matter what she feels for Trent. Better that she go to the altar with a whole heart than with half. It must be an awful thing to marry one man while you pine for another."

"Sarah, you speak with such passion," said Miss Harlow, amazed. "Is there something you are not telling me about your own past?"

"Silly child." She laughed. "I assure you that Roger has my heart whole and complete, but I'm not so old that I cannot remember what it was like to be your age. I myself was a very romantical miss and knew I'd rather go into a decline than marry any man but Roger, my beloved. I made a perfectly ridiculous picture, considering there was nothing to thwart our happiness."

This glimpse of a younger Sarah intrigued her, but before she could delve deeper, her hand was sought by Sir Everett Carson.

"They're striking up a waltz," he said, kissing her hand. "Would you do me the honor?"

Emma's opinion of Carson, formed the other night after a solitary dance, had been of a harmless scoundrel. She had found his conversation to be light but charming and had thoroughly enjoyed their dance. Accepting his invitation now, she felt oddly discomforted by the man. Something in his demeanor had changed in the last week, and it didn't sit well with her. Perhaps it was the way he was eyeing her décolletage, as if it were a lamb chop and he a very hungry diner.

"Miss Harlow," he said, taking her in his arms, "may I say that you look stunning this evening? I don't believe I've ever seen that shade of blue before. What do you call it?"

"*I* call it blue," she answered, as she began to feel the rhythm of the music. Although Carson was as graceful and skilled as the duke, dancing with him wasn't quite as exhilarating. Still, a not-so-good waltz was always better than a very excellent minuet. "I do not know what others call it. Perhaps periwinkle or sapphire or even ocean. The nuances of the particular shades escape me. As far as I am concerned there is only pretty blue and ugly blue."

Carson laughed. "Very well said, ma'am. I often feel the same way. I cannot tell you what I admire about a lady, I only know that some are beautiful and others are merely pretty."

"A very clever remark, sir," said Emma, smiling with dimples.

"How so?" he asked, feigning innocence.

"You seek to win favor with me by complimenting my sex to me. You have completely ignored the category of ugly, as if there are no unattractive women."

He pulled back and looked her in the eyes. "Indeed there aren't. All women are beautiful, only some are more beautiful than others. Like yourself, for instance."

Emma returned his steady gaze. "You're very charming, Mr. Carson, but I suspect you are already aware of that."

"It might have been remarked upon once or twice before, but I pay no attention to such inconsequential things. Charm is very superficial, and it's depth of character that I hope to cultivate most."

Emma knew very well that it was *she* that he hoped to cultivate most, and although she found him delightful and much enjoyed having a dancing partner, she knew that nothing would develop in that quarter. Mr. Carson might have put her at ease for the moment, but with her initial discomfort in mind, she knew better than to trust him. Here was a true libertine, a genuine rake, the very sort she would never trust Lavinia's heart to.

The duke had arrived at the ball in a black mood. The entire coach ride there had been given over to his mother's complaints and Philip's enthusiasms. By the time the carriage had stopped in front of the Kenelm mansion, he was ready to go home.

He was not looking forward to this evening's adventure. The Duke of Trent was an accomplished flirt indeed and could reasonably expect to charm any woman he wanted, but there was something too calculating about Emma's plan. What if Lavinia did develop feelings for him? He did not relish breaking a young lady's heart.

Still, there was no use complaining about it, since he had only himself to blame for this mess. There had been several times during his conversation with Miss Harlow when he could have stood up and walked out. And he should have. If he had stood up and walked out like a sane man, then he wouldn't have volunteered for this business or learned what a passionate and tempting creature Miss Harlow was.

Trent saw Lavinia standing with Sarah and went over to greet the ladies. Philip followed closely on his heels and immediately began to monopolize Mrs. Harlow. He was eager to hear more of her trip to Yorkshire. That gave Trent ample opportunity to strike up a conversation with Emma's sister, and he did so posthaste, after sweeping the room thoroughly with his gaze. Where was the other Miss Harlow? Her note had said specifically that she would be there.

"Miss Harlow, tell me. How does my *Rhyncholaelia digbyana* do in your care?" he asked. Before she could answer, he added, "You'll note, I'm sure, how I'm well aware this time which Miss Harlow I am speaking with. Once one knows there are two of you, it's rather easy to tell you apart."

"You're very astute, your grace, more so than others, I'm afraid," she said. "There are people who've known us our whole lives who still cannot tell us apart."

"Come, they can't know you very well if that is true."

"My own father, for one."

"Of course," said his grace with his most engaging smile, "I can't think of any human beings who know us less well than our parents."

Lavinia laughed. "Your orchid is doing very well in my care," she said, belatedly answering his first question. "I was having some trouble with the moisture levels in my conservatory and the poor dear was wilting a little, but I've solved the problem and all is now well."

"Indeed?" said the duke, who'd been bedeviled by a great many moisture-level problems of his own. "By what method did you solve the problem? My own system has been giving me trouble."

"It is my experience that when the moisture levels are wrong it is because of improper drainage. Thus, I installed an intricate network of pipes, a very rudimentary plumbing system that I devised myself. If you'd like, I'd be happy to show it to you. I'm quite willing to share my technique, since you were so generous as to share your buds with me."

The duke caught the faint irony in her words and laughed, delighted. "Yes, I am very generous when it comes to my flowers. I hand them out left and right. Tell me, how is the new plant coming along?"

"It's doing very well, sir. Indeed, I have every expectation of winning the exhibition in a couple of years."

"I'll consider myself warned then," said the duke, "and will go straight home to start cultivating a new species of orchid myself, lest you unseat me with my own flower."

Lavinia blushed. She rarely talked with such forthrightness with anyone, let alone a duke. And it *was* his flower. Surely it wasn't right to brag about winning with a stolen orchid to the person from whom it was stolen. She began to stutter an apology.

The duke cut her off with a raised hand. "It is not necessary. Just show me how to maintain proper moisture levels and we'll call it even."

"Very well," she said, before inquiring about his other orchids. Lavinia found herself entirely at ease with the duke. There were few people among her acquaintance whom she could talk about her passion with—Sir Waldo certainly wasn't interested—and it was a lovely surprise to find a fellow enthusiast. She was so enjoying their conversation that she only reluctantly went off with Lord Dearling when he came to claim his dance.

But Lavinia needn't have worried. As soon as she was done, the duke was at her side escorting her to the punch table and asking more questions about her plumbing system. He asked her to dance and even petitioned for her company during dinner.

Lavinia was flattered by the attention, if not a little curious as to what sparked it. She had never been of interest to him before, and because she could find no good cause for it now, she was suspicious of him. What was he up to? If he sought to win Emma's favor—which seemed like the more likely explanation to Lavinia—this was a very unusual way to go about it. Surely a flirt as accomplished as the Duke of Trent realized that the best way to win a lady's heart was to court the lady, not her sister. *But perhaps I am overthinking the situation,* she thought. *It's entirely possible that he just wants someone with whom to talk about plumbing.*

However, when the orchestra struck up a waltz, her suspicions were confirmed immediately. The duke could not tear his eyes away from the spectacle of Emma in the arms of another man.

"I don't believe I know the gentleman my sister is dancing with, your grace," she said, hoping to discover just what was going on. "Do you perchance know him?"

"Yes, I do know him," he answered, his gaze unwavering as he took in Emma's smiles. How dare she flirt with that scoundrel when he had warned her off him not ten hours ago! Did she have no sense of self-preservation? If Carson had his way there would be nothing left of the Harlow Hoyden's reputation at all. "He's not the sort of man your sister should be dancing with. You should warn her off him before there's trouble."

Lavinia digested this tidbit, wondering what portion was sparked by genuine concern and what was sparked by jealousy. "I suspect you exaggerate. There's no trouble that can be caused by one dance."

He turned then and looked at her. "Miss Harlow, you're an innocent. Men like Carson are at their most charming when they have a woman in their arms. I assure you, there is nothing more troublesome than a charming man bent on mischief."

"Society might have dismissed my sister as flighty and heedless, but you'd be wise to withhold judgment, your grace," Lavinia advised. "She's capricious, certainly, but she's also intelligent and loyal and she always knows her own mind. Her head will not be turned by a few pretty words dropped from a skillful tongue. One cannot have a reputation like the Harlow Hoyden's and avoid scoundrels, but Emma does an excellent job of putting them down. I believe one gentleman still walks with a limp."

Trent took little comfort in this. It was all very well and good for Emma to be able to defend herself, but why in heaven's name did she get herself into situations where such abilities were needed? The best way to not be taken advantage of by a man alone was not to meet with men alone. He'd tried to tell her that this morning and look where that led—to a searing kiss that haunted him even now. "I'm not making an assessment of Miss Harlow when I tell you to warn her off Carson. I would do the same for any lady's sister."

Lavinia smiled, not sure that she believed him. "In that case, I will pass along your words tonight when I speak with her alone. I'm sure she'll appreciate your concern."

The duke had little doubt that Emma would appreciate his interference, but he would not stand idly by while a knave like Carson compromised her. She deserved better than a shabby marriage of convenience or total ruin. "Very good. Now shall we return to Sarah's side? Thanks to my cousin Philip's efforts, she might be the first person in the nineteenth century to actually die of boredom."

Lavinia was not the only one who noticed the duke's interest in Emma. Although ostensibly entranced by Philip's telling of a prank that involved one clueless vicar and one very large bullfrog, Sarah was in actuality reflecting on the duke's strange behavior. First to be so attentive to dear Lavinia, then to stare daggers at Emma as she danced with Carson. She had never known him to show interest in one green girl, let alone two.

Sarah was not an intimate of the duke's, but she did know him fairly well, thanks to the holidays he had spent at her family's manor in Derbyshire. Andrew and he had not ever encouraged her company, but when she'd come running after them in the meadow looking for a distraction, they never sent her away either. Still, many years had passed since then, and she did not feel comfortable asking him point blank what his game was. She would have to content herself with observing for a little while longer. Either that or get the truth out of Emma, who was clearly up to something. But getting the truth out of Emma was often an exhausting and unsatisfying endeavor. Patience and observation were the best methods at the moment.

The duke and Lavinia returned to her side just as the waltz was ending. Emma soon joined them, along with her dance partner, who was introduced to the merry crowd. He stayed for a few minutes, lavishing Sarah and Lavinia with such extravagant compliments that Trent's lip curled in disgust before taking his leave. Good riddance, thought the duke, as he glared at the departing figure.

Fearful that Carson would be back when it was time to go down to dinner, Trent excused himself and went in search of Pearson. It'd been several days since he had last seen him, but he felt certain his friend would be there. Pearson was in the petticoat line and would never pass up an opportunity to flirt with the ladies. Predictably, he found him in the middle of a coterie of pretty girls. They were all laughing at something he had said. Now, here was a libertine more suited for Miss Harlow's purposes, he thought, examining his friend's classic features and well-cut jacket. Pearson did nothing but toy with the affections of innocents, thoroughly enjoying the attention. He could probably win Lavinia over with one smile, as he did all the misses.

But then, to be fair, the duke thought, this evening wasn't going as dismally as he expected. The truth was that he liked talking to Lavinia. And if she could really solve his drainage problem, well, then, she was a rather valuable friend to have.

To Pearson's disappointment, Trent extricated him from his admirers and asked him to escort Miss Emma Harlow to dinner—as a favor, of course.

"The Harlow Hoyden?" he asked, surprised.

Trent stiffened. He didn't like hearing her described as such. "Miss Emma Harlow," he repeated, hoping he was making himself clear.

Pearson gave him a quizzical look. "Yes, of course. Miss Emma Harlow." He thought about the request. "I'm not committed to a dinner partner yet, but it will look odd. We've never met."

"No matter, I can arrange an introduction."

"Yes, but do I want to be seen eating with the Harlow"—seeing the expression on his friend's face, he reconsidered his choice of words—"er, with Miss Harlow?"

"She is very beautiful," the duke remarked, thinking that was all that mattered to Pearson.

"But she's not quite the thing."

More offended on Emma's behalf than he'd thought possible, the duke said, "I see. I didn't realize you were so easily swayed by fashion. Clearly, I have made a mistake. Excuse me." He turned and walked away.

Pearson laid a hand on his friend's shoulder. "I say, Trent, no need to be so abrupt. I'd be pleased to take Miss Emma Harlow down to dinner. Truth be known, I've always thought she was a fetching little thing."

Although Pearson sought to appease his friend with this confession, he only angered him more. "You're merely to take her down to dinner. You're not to be engaging or amusing or winning in any way. Do you understand?"

Pearson had never seen his friend behave in such an erratic fashion and was now very eager to meet Miss Harlow. "Perfectly."

Dinner progressed without incident, although Emma was much surprised to find herself partnered with a handsome gentleman who had many funny stories to tell of Trent's salad days. Pearson had only a small suspicion of what the duke was up to, but he decided there was no harm in advancing Trent's suit. And clearly the girl was interested. She plagued him for more stories until he had to make a few up.

Afterward, he signed her dance card and promised to return shortly. Emma was pleased at the novelty of having names in her dance card. When they struck up another waltz, Trent mysteriously appeared at her side.

"I believe you requested a waltz," he said, bowing.

She furrowed her brows. "I have no such recollection, your grace."

"How quickly they forget! But no matter. I recall clearly your standing in my conservatory stealing a blossom and making me promise to waltz with you."

"That was days and days ago. We already had our dance."

"Since you didn't specify a number, Miss Harlow, I assumed you meant all your future waltzes." He held out a hand.

"Very well. I suppose one more wouldn't do any harm. But you must sign my dance card first. That's the way it's done."

Trent complied, taking note of Pearson's fluid scrawl. When they were on the dance floor, he said, "You seemed to enjoy Pearson's company very well."

"He's an amusing fellow."

He had noticed them laughing together and had been very unamused by the sight. "What did you talk about?"

Thinking it wouldn't do his ego any good to know that they'd talked of little else but him, she said, "Oh, you know. This and not. What did you talk to Lavinia about?"

"Drainage systems," he answered.

"Excellent!" She smiled happily. "Nobody knows more about drainage systems than dear Vinnie. I knew the two of you would get on together. She's very interesting once you get to know her. Tell me, do you think she suspects anything?"

"I cannot know that, although it seems unlikely."

"Good. You'll take her for a drive tomorrow."

"I'm afraid I have to go to Tattersall's tomorrow," he said, although this was not the whole truth. He didn't *have* to go, he just didn't want her thinking she could order him about.

"All right. Then the next day or the next. You can also take her to the theater. Vinnie loves the theater."

"It wouldn't do for me to take her alone, but perhaps we can pull a party together."

Emma sighed. "I'm so relieved my scheme is working." She looked at him. "Tell me the truth, your grace, Vinnie isn't so awful, is she?"

"Not at all. I find her quite pleasant and very easy to

talk to. Why would you think that?"

"Because she hasn't had many beaus and is only marrying Windbag as a last resort, I am convinced. It's a horrible, horrible waste. She could do better than that villain. If he had his way, Vinnie would never install another drainage system again."

The duke laughed. "I suspect most husbands would prefer that their wives never install drainage systems."

"But you wouldn't mind, would you, your grace?"

"No, I don't think I would," he answered, softly.

Emma nodded, pleased to have her theory confirmed. The duke and Lavinia would make an excellent pair. Wouldn't her mama be shocked when one of her daughters married a duke? She'd have to take an interest then. And she could just imagine the expression on the horrid Sir Windbag's face when he learned he'd been thrown over for a nonesuch like Trent.

"I knew my plan would work," she said. "And Kate was right. You are just the man for the job."

"Who is Kate?"

"She's my dearest friend."

"And you told her about your plan?"

"Of course, one needs a confidant, no?"

Trent wasn't sure he agreed. "Is she trustworthy?"

"One hundred percent. It was she who was drawing up the list for me. I relieved her mind greatly when I told her not to worry. She was having trouble coming up with names."

Trent took comfort in this. If the woman had wanted to aid Emma in her insanity, she could have come up with a dozen names instantly. Clearly she hoped to steer the Harlow Hoyden away from calamity—a daunting task. He made a note to discover who this Kate was and seek her out.

Emma was silent for a few moments, enjoying the dance and the lovely sensation of again being in his arms. Was it only this afternoon that she had been swept away by passion in the drawing room? "Your grace, you must kiss Lavinia."

Why the duke was surprised by this statement he didn't know. She was always making outrageous suggestions. "Excuse me?"

"You must kiss Lavinia."

"Why?" he asked, thinking of their kiss earlier. He didn't want to kiss her sister. He wanted to kiss her. She was a very tempting morsel, especially when in his arms.

"Because she's only kissed Sir Windbag. He cannot know how to go about it as well as you."

"I suppose that's a compliment." There was wry amusement in his voice.

"And once she learns that there are men who kiss better than Sir Waldo, she'll drop him like a hot potato," Emma explained logically. "That's why it's very important that a lady kiss more than one man before she marries."

Trent stiffened. "No, women should only kiss the man they are to marry."

"What nonsense is this?" she asked, surprised by his conservative answer. "How is a woman to know what a good kiss is unless she's able to compare it? Surely that's why men kiss so many women before they choose the right one."

The duke knew for a fact that her theory was ridiculous. Men kissed women for a variety of reasons, the least of which was the comparison of chaste embraces. Still, he was not so much disturbed by her radical thinking as the vivid picture it brought to mind: that of Emma standing at the head of a long line of men with her lips puckered. It was unacceptable. "It's different for men."

Emma was not surprised by this answer. It was what men always said. "How so?"

"It just is."

Miss Harlow scoffed. "You're like the others—a hypocritical tyrant. You defend society's constrictive rules against women while taking full advantage of your own freedom. How nice it must be to be a man."

The duke didn't respond. He was still smarting from Miss Harlow's remarks. How could she tell him to kiss her sister when he'd kissed her only hours before? The last thing she should want was to see him in the arms of another woman. The very idea should be repellent to her. Why was she not as upset as he was? Earlier he'd wanted to plant a facer on Carson for dancing with her, and dinner had been interminable, watching her laugh with Pearson. It seemed inconceivable that she didn't feel the same way.

"Very well, I will kiss your sister," he said, hoping to make her jealous.

If they hadn't been dancing, Emma would've clapped. "Excellent, your grace. I knew you'd see the wisdom of my thinking. I can't imagine Sir Windbag is any good at it. He is always so stiff and formal and so *boring*. I don't doubt that Lavinia will be quite swept away by your technique. I don't have much experience yet, but I suspect that you're unusually good at it."

As the waltz finished and Trent led her off the dance floor, he made a silent vow that she'd never get much experience.

CHAPTER SIX

By the end of the fortnight, it was glaringly clear to Emma that her plan was working better than she could have ever imagined. The Duke of Trent hadn't called the day following the ball, as he had to go down to Tattersall's to look at horseflesh with a friend, but he came by the next day and the next and every day after that. He dropped by to take Lavinia for long drives in the park, during which they discussed the surrounding flora and fauna. Trent quickly discovered that the other Miss Harlow had a wicked sense of humor when it came to strutting fauna in ridiculous ostrich-plumed hats.

Lavinia would return from these drives laughing, her cheeks flushed. The promised theater party was another success. Sarah had been reluctant to go, as Roger was expected to return the next morning, but somehow Trent convinced her that it would be an excellent way to pass the hours. Everyone had a fun time, except Emma, who could not stand the way Trent kept whispering in Vinnie's ear.

Because she'd never experienced the emotion before, it took Emma almost a week to realize she was jealous of her sister.

When Vinnie came back from the first of these carriage rides, Emma had sat her down in the front parlor and insisted that she reveal every detail. She was eager to hear how her plan was progressing. Vinnie obliged, lingering over a particularly funny story about Lord Redkin and his hobbyhorse.

"It's fat and gray, not at all like a horse. Trent said it looked like one of those animals from Africa. And you know Lord Redkin, of course"—actually, Emma didn't—"all fat and gray himself. Well, he was riding his hobby elephant, as Trent called it, down a hill when he lost control and came tumb—" Overcome with laughter, she could not finish the story.

For the first time since they were little children, Emma found herself out of sorts with her sister. Not because she failed to finish the story or because she endlessly dropped Trent's name, but because she had made Emma feel left out. Emma, too, wanted to go to the park and have adventures and laugh at the fat, gray Lord Redkin on his hobby elephant.

After that first time, she stopped asking about their drives. She didn't have to ask, of course, for Lavinia made a point of searching her out. Vinnie noticed nothing amiss, even when she found Emma in the draughty wine basement sitting on a barrel reading Sir Walter Scott. No, she simply located an empty barrel of her own, pulled it close to her sister's and began telling anecdotes. The next day Emma went out shopping and didn't return until it was time to dress for dinner.

Emma realized she was experiencing something more than irritation when Lavinia's endless "Trents" became a trickle then a deluge of "Alexes." She wondered then if Miss Harlow had given way to Lavinia or even Vinnie. The idea was insupportable—that Lavinia should be Vinnie when she herself had never been anything but Miss Harlow.

This jealousy was an unexpected development and one she intended to ignore. She tried very hard to cling to the happiness she saw on her sister's face and chastised herself constantly for her pettiness. It was not, she convinced

herself, that she wanted Trent for herself but rather
Lavinia's happiness. She wanted to sparkle and sigh and
moon over a handsome face. Why she wanted it all of a
sudden, Emma couldn't fathom, but she was sure that it
would pass as quickly as it came. Every night she went to
bed determined to feel differently in the morning. She never
did wake up recovered. Indeed, some mornings she didn't
wake up at all, lying in bed for hours trying to figure out
exactly what her problem was.

On the tenth such morning, she was almost ready to
call the whole thing off. Because the hour was so late, she
ate breakfast alone, which was good. She needed peace and
quiet to decide what the best course of action was. Should
she make an appointment to see Trent and explain that it
was time to end the charade? He would no doubt be
relieved. But what if he wasn't? What if her plan had
actually worked? What if he was besotted? What if he
actually wanted to marry Lavinia? The thought made an
already tired Miss Harlow feel somehow more exhausted.
Trent as a brother-in-law. Handsome, charming Trent. She
didn't think she could bear it. Not because she wanted him
for herself, of course, but he would be too much of a
handful for Lavinia. Yes, why hadn't she seen it before?
He was a libertine, wasn't he? How could she stand idly by
and let her sister marry a self-proclaimed libertine? There
were those broaches at the Savoy to consider and the
dancer in Chelsea. Was it better that she marry that
pinched-faced ball of wind? She was debating precisely
that point when the pinched-faced ball of wind himself
entered the dining room. Emma cursed his return from the
country. It had been a very nice two weeks without his
stodgy presence.

"Ah, Lavinia, I am glad to have found you at home,"
he said, taking the seat at the head of the table. That he
always took the seat at the head of the table whenever
Roger was not there was just another thing he did that
annoyed her. "I feared you might be out gallivanting with

the Duke of Trent." He laughed in his high nasal way. "No, really, my dear, I make no jest. I had been told by certain members of the *ton* that you have been passing the time with him in my absence. By certain members of the *ton,* I mean acquaintances who take great pleasure in running to me with tales of your indiscretions. Though these acquaintances sound like enemies, they are the ones we need to cultivate if I am to have a career in politics." Here he talked for fifteen minutes about the exact sort of career he saw for himself. Emma watched him unblinkingly, like an owl. "Just as I always say, politics is all-consuming, which is why I am so glad that you gave up writing this horticultural book of yours. If people are going to talk about you at all, it should be about how well you serve me, not your hobby. Burning those pages was the best thing I've ever done. The wife of a member of Parliament should not have a career as an authoress." Again the horrid high-pitched nasal laugh. "Damn me, what am I saying? No wife should have a career as an authoress. Or any career at all."

As he went on in this way, explaining the importance of presentable children and a well-kept house, Emma fumed. How dare he treat Lavinia like this, coming back from two weeks away and resuming conversation as if it had never left off. No customary bidding of hello! No inquiring after one's health and the health of one's family! No fond kiss on the cheek! What an awful little man.

And to think that Lavinia was writing a book about horticulture. She'd never said a word about it. Emma wondered if Sarah knew and why Lavinia would be so closed-mouthed. *Why didn't she tell me? Didn't she realize how proud of her I'd be? Imagine, little Vinnie writing a book—a book that this evil toad burned.*

Emma could barely stand the sight of his small nose and weak chin, and she got up from the table without excusing herself. His back was toward her for the moment, as he was helping himself to a second portion of porridge, and he didn't see her depart. It wasn't until ten minutes later, after he finished outlining his new financial policy for England, that he looked up from his bowl to realize he was alone.

Unable to control her anger, she bounded up the stairs looking for Sarah. The person she most wanted to talk to, of course, was Lavinia, but she knew that she had to get ahold of her temper first. She had the urge to call out, the way she would to Dobson when she wanted tea, but she restrained herself. She didn't feel like sitting through a lecture on proper ladylike behavior, which she would have to do, if the yelling proved useful in locating Sarah. She checked Sarah's room and the study and the drawing room with no luck. Then she looked in on Roger, who was in his old room down the hall. Nurse had taken herself out of retirement to care for him and was even now guarding his door as a troll would a pot of gold.

"I am only looking for Sarah," she said, trying to keep her voice down. Earlier in the week, she had greeted Nurse in full voice and had barely escaped an ear-boxing for her trouble. "Is she in there?"

Nurse shook her head.

"Have you seen her this morning?"

Nurse nodded.

"When did she leave?" she asked, hoping to get something useful out of the woman.

Before Nurse could answer—or not answer, depending on her fancy—Roger called out from the room, "Who's there?"

"It's me, Roger—Emma," she answered, slipping past Nurse with a smug smile. "I don't want to bother you. I was looking for Sarah."

He was lying in bed, with his back against pillows. Aside from the bandaged shoulder and a chalky complexion, he looked as he always did—good-humored and robust. "Please bother me. Lay all the problems of the world at my feet and let me sort them out. I'm bored to flinders up here. I want to go outside, but my prison warden won't give me leave."

"Your body has suffered a major trauma and must have time to recuperate. Nurse wants only what's best for you." He snorted in response. "Really, you should be grateful. She's the same woman who nursed Vinnie and me, but she didn't seem to give a fig about our health. I'm sure I'd have to lose a lot more than an arm to get her attention." Having said these words, Emma realized how insensitive they sounded and gasped. "I'm sorry. That was awful of me to say."

Roger laughed weakly. "No, please don't worry about hurting my feelings. I have lost an arm but kept my life. It is a fair trade. I see that now."

"You are remarkably well adjusted to the change, Roger," she said, admiring his composure. "I think I would still be railing against fate."

"Trust me, I railed. Oh, did I rail. I'm very glad that Sarah was not there to see it. I was miserable to be with for the first few days of lucidity."

"Then it's good that she didn't take me up on my offer. I wanted to hightail it to France, you know, the second I heard."

Roger reached over and took her hand in his. "Sarah told me. You're the best of good sisters." He pulled her close and gave her a kiss on the forehead. "Now tell me what's bothering you."

She looked around, expecting Nurse to be standing over her shoulder and tapping an impatient foot. "Maybe I should…"

"No, please, I meant it. Lay every one of your problems on these shoulders—that's right, two shoulders, one arm—and give me something to worry about other than my own bedsores. You have not been looking like yourself lately."

"An astute observation from a man who hasn't seen me for more than two months."

"Please, I know what my sister looks like and you're looking more and more like her everyday."

"Ah, I see you've taken to speaking in riddles, like the Sphinx."

"Lavinia. You are looking more and more like you spend the whole day in a little room cross-breeding flowers." He patted the bed and indicated that she should sit. Emma checked to make sure Nurse wasn't watching and sat down. "Where's the customary blossom in your cheeks from too much time in the sun?"

"I have been mopey of late, but that's over now. I am much too angry to be mopey," she said, animation returning to her voice.

"What has occurred?"

"I just discovered that Vinnie was writing a book about horticulture and that repulsive worm she's engaged to burned it. Burned it! The very thought of his touching anything of Lavinia's makes the bile rise in my throat."

"How did you learn of this?"

"Sir Windbag just told me. He, too, thinks I look like Lavinia."

"You are twins."

"Yes, but the people who care about us know the difference. The Duke of Trent never mistakes me for her," she said, wondering where that thought had come from.

"Yes," said Roger, "tell me about the Duke of Trent. Sarah says he's been living in Lavinia's pocket these past two weeks. Why do you think that is?"

"Because Lavinia is beautiful and interesting and a fine catch for any man who has the sense to see it." *And because I asked him to.* "It is my dearest wish that the two of them make a match of it."

Roger digested this piece of information. He had already talked the situation over with Sarah and what puzzled him was the same thing that puzzled Sarah: Why did he spend so much time with Lavinia when it was Emma he stared at when he thought no one was looking? "But she's engaged to Windbourne."

"Pooh, what woman in her right mind wouldn't throw

him over for Trent? And it's not just that he's rich and handsome and charming but also that he respects Lavinia and wouldn't object to her queer gardening ways. He would support her in the Horticultural Society's exhibitions and be proud of her when she won and he wouldn't burn her manuscript. He would even help her get her book published." As she listed off all the reasons that Lavinia would choose Trent over Windbag, Emma began to feel better. Yes, this was what was right. So maybe she had developed a *tendre* for Trent unexpectedly—and against her will. Well, it wasn't so unexpected if one thought about it. He was everything she'd said—handsome and charming and supportive. What woman wouldn't develop a partiality toward such a man? But she wouldn't let that stand in the way of her sister's happiness. Besides, nothing could come of it anyway. Emma never wanted to marry. And Lavinia did. "I am sure that Lavinia would have no trouble jilting Windbag for Trent. He's the most perfect choice in the world, and to think that this morning I was ready to abandon the whole—" She broke off before she said too much.

Roger made a note of this odd behavior, determined to discuss it at length with Sarah. There was more here—much more here—than met the eye. He was determined to get to the bottom of it.

Noticing Roger's considering look and fearful that he might refine too much upon her slip, she quickly changed the subject. "I have yet to hear about your fall. Did Sarah tell you how suspicious I was when I first heard of it? You ride as well as I, and I would never take a spill on a pothole-ridden French road on a moonless night."

It was an arrogant boast, just the sort one expected from the Harlow Hoyden, and Roger laughed himself into a coughing fit. Nurse came in, spitting fire at Emma with her eyes until she got off the bed, and patted him on the back. Then she tucked the covers around him, in the mummy fashion, and left the room.

"I sincerely hope you never get to prove that," he

said, recalling the incident. "Actually, the experience is still fuzzy in my mind. Try as I might, I cannot recall what made the horse jump. It might have been dark, but I'd ridden that road many times and knew it like the back of my hand."

"Ridden the road many times," echoed Emma. "I did not know you were much in France."

Roger smiled. "This was only my second visit. When I say many times, I really mean three or four. It was the road from Paris to the coast. I meant to ride all night and catch the first boat out in the morning. I was eager to see Sarah again. But then this mishap." He shrugged. "The doctors were very surprised that the fall didn't kill me. In addition to the crushed arm, I had a bump on my head the size of a breakfast roll. Indeed, it lingers still. I was unconscious for the first three days. It's little wonder I can't remember the accident," he added wryly, although it was clear to Emma that he hadn't given up on trying.

"But you're home now and on the road to recovery. There's no reason to tease ourselves about something that's over and done with," she said so reasonably that her brother got suspicious.

"We mustn't?" he asked.

"No, we must instead devote our energies to stopping an evil before it happens. Now, what will you do about this awful Sir Windbag?"

Roger looked at her in surprise. "He's our sister's fiancé. There's nothing I can do about him."

"Very well," she said, standing up.

Her easy acceptance worried him. It wasn't like Emma. "Very well," he repeated.

"I'll just send Sir Waldo up to keep you company," she offered on her way out. "He has no one to talk to in the breakfast room and you did say you were bored."

"I'm not that bored," he called after her.

She stopped in the doorway and turned around. "I think this is just what you need. Fifteen minutes of Sir

Windbag's restorative conversation and you'll be begging me to let you help break them up." As she waved good-bye to Nurse, she realized that Sir Windbag had very little chance of getting past the militant caretaker. *It's not fair*, she thought, going to her room, *that we don't all have trolls stationed outside our doors to protect us from that awful little man.*

Lavinia was enjoying her flirtation with the Duke of Trent very much. When he'd first come to the house asking her to join him for a ride in the park, she'd hastened to inform him that she wasn't her sister. He'd smiled pleasantly, assured her he knew that very well, thank you, and offered her his arm. She'd stared at it for several seconds, unsure how to proceed—surely Sir Waldo wouldn't like for her to be seen in the park with another man—before accepting it graciously. She would never learn what game was afoot if she didn't play along.

The ride in the park had been extremely enlightening. Though she'd been out for five seasons, she had never actually felt like a member of the *ton*. She'd always seen herself as something of an outsider, a flower-growing misfit among beautiful people who wore flowers in their lapels and hair. She never made much of an effort to be included and had no one who encouraged her to. Sarah was usually buried with Roger in their estate in Derbyshire, and Emma never courted the good opinion of anyone.

She'd been quite surprised when Sir Waldo Windbourne started paying attention to her. There was not much to recommend him—his features were irregular and his conversation a little dull—but she could not help but think that he was a kindred spirit. She herself was considered dull by the many people who had never made the effort to draw her out. Surely Sir Windbourne had an equally sparkling inner self. That he had political ambitions only made him more appealing. Here was a man who had purpose, a desire to do something with his life more important than resting his elbow on the mantelpiece as if posing for a Gainsborough portrait.

Lavinia, who had ambitions of her own, believed she could be of use to such a man. And they could have children. How Lavinia longed to have children.

But going about with the Duke of Trent was much different from going about with Sarah or Emma or even her fiancé. He was well known and admired, everyone they passed greeted him or stopped for conversation. He knew who everyone was and what they were up to and gladly regaled her with tales of their ridiculous exploits and indiscretions. And he always knew exactly what to say and to whom. When Lord Redkin had come tumbling down the hill in his tight gray outfit, Trent had assured him that it was an excellent day for a safari. Redkin reached up to tip his hat, only then realizing he'd lost it during his travels, and scurried back up the hill to retrieve it. Vinnie could not recall the scene without breaking out into hysterics.

Despite this, Lavinia didn't count herself susceptible to his charms. She was an engaged lady—as good as married—and not at all a silly miss to have her head turned by the first charming man to pay attention to her. Besides, she had seen the languishing glances Trent sent her sister's way. Nor was she oblivious to Emma's very odd behavior. She'd realized she'd done something wrong that very first day. When she'd sat down with her in the front parlor, Vinnie had every intention of telling her sister everything, including the story of Lord Redkin. But somehow the memory got away with her, and she couldn't control her laughter. That was the point when Emma walked out of the room, which was very strange indeed. Emma had never walked out on her before.

In the days that followed, Vinnie sought Emma out and tried to discover the problem. Although Emma insisted with increasing vehemence that there wasn't anything amiss, Lavinia began to suspect jealousy. That Emma was jealous was an odd notion and one her sister had a very hard time accepting. Emma was never the sort to stand by and seethe. She always vented her emotions, and she always pursued that which she wanted. If she wanted the Duke of Trent, why wasn't she going after him? Surely she didn't think that Lavinia's interest was anything but platonic. How could it be, when she was engaged to another?

No, the whole thing was a very strange and consuming puzzle, and Lavinia might have never figured it out if she hadn't overhead a conversation between the duke and Emma's dearest friend, Kate Kennington.

"Miss Kennington," the duke said at Lady Worth's route, unaware that Miss Lavinia Harlow was standing on the other side of the blue velvet curtain that separated the music room from the drawing room, "although we have never met, I believe we have much to talk about."

"Really, your grace," the woman answered, "you intrigue me. What is it that we have in common?"

"A certain young scapegrace who would see us all ruined if we let her have her way," he said with fondness, though that was not his intention.

Kate laughed. "I should have anticipated this. It's like her to be so indiscreet."

Lavinia knew right away that they were talking about Emma. To whom else would the words *scapegrace* and *indiscreet* apply as fittingly?

"No, not *so* indiscreet," he said, in the lady's defense. "She let only your first name slip and I had to root around for the rest of the information."

"How tedious for you," she said, amused by the notion of the elegant Duke of Trent rooting around for anything.

"Not at all. It only required a few days' careful observation. Miss Harlow doesn't speak with many Kates," he explained. "In fact, you're the only one."

By now Lavinia was intensely interested in the conversation. It came as no surprise that Emma was up to something. Indeed, the real surprise was how well behaved she had been since coming to town.

"I want to thank you," he said, abruptly. "For keeping Miss Harlow out of a scrape."

"One cannot keep her out of scrapes; one can only

delay them," she said, sharing the wisdom of many years. Lavinia smiled, agreeing wholeheartedly with the sentiment.

"Perhaps, but this last one could have led to her ruin."

Kate laughed. "Your grace, they all could have led to her ruin."

From the way he said, "I see," Lavinia could tell that the duke was not amused by the information.

"Still, I'd like to thank you for not providing her with the list."

Miss Kennington pooh-poohed his gratitude. "I am not so hen-witted, your grace," she said lowering her voice to such a low level that Lavinia had to lean into the curtain to hear her, "as to hand the Harlow Hoyden a list of possible libertines to seduce her sister."

"Of course not," he agreed.

"But it was very good of you to step in and lend a hand," continued Kate. "Who knows what would have happened if you hadn't. She probably would've approached someone completely unsuitable who would have done her bidding and then published the whole deplorable episode in the dailies. Emma is like a dog with a bone when she gets an idea, and while I cannot help but feel she's irrational as far as her sister's fiancé is concerned, it's best for all concerned that she believe she's doing something to end the relationship. Nothing distresses her more than inaction. Of course, I do hope Lavinia won't get hurt in the process. She hardly seems the sort to jilt a man for anyone, no matter how eligible the *parti*."

"Yes, Miss Harlow is a sensible girl, and although I have been everything that is attentive and kind, she doesn't treat me like a lover at all. She treats me like a friend, which is very nice indeed, since she is so easy to talk with. But I do begin to fear for the success of the hoyden's scheme. Perhaps that's just as well. I hardly relish the role of cad, and the *ton* knows that I never chase after unmarried misses. The sooner Miss Harlow is shackled to her Sir Windbourne, the better for us all."

"You think so?" asked Miss Kennington in a sly tone.

"Of course," answered the duke.

"Hmm. You don't suppose that the man in question might find himself in a large crate with holes in it on his way to the West Indies?"

"Good lord," said Trent.

Lavinia smiled. It was awful of her, she knew, but the image of Waldo crushed in a box with his ankles over his ears was too much to resist. She removed herself from the blue velvet curtain and walked to the other side of the room. There, she started laughing. All of it—the whole thing, from Emma's ridiculous plan to hire a libertine to seduce her to the duke's unlikely compliance—was thoroughly preposterous. It was, she admitted when her giggles subsided, precisely the sort of scheme Emma would concoct: irresponsible, thoughtless, potentially disastrous, creative. There'd been many schemes like this when they were young and Emma didn't like the way the curate's son treated her sister or when their mama said something particularly cruel. Emma had always stood up for her when she thought she wasn't being treated well, and if Vinnie had given it any thought, she would've realized that now was one of those times.

Vinnie knew very well Emma's unfavorable opinion of her fiancé, but she, like everyone else in the family, believed it would pass once she got to know him better. But she also knew that Emma was stubborn and that her feelings stemmed from something more than simple unfamiliarity. At the root of it was an irrational fear of losing her sister. Marriage was a new phase in the life of the Harlow girls, and although they'd always done everything together, this they would do apart. Worse than that, they would do it with someone else. Lavinia knew that marriage changed one's life, but it didn't effect how one felt about one's sister. She had tried to explain this to Emma, but there was no way of getting through to her. After several failed attempts to make her understand, Lavinia gave up. She knew that Emma would soon realize that her sister's marriage wasn't the end of their relationship, but Lavinia had to get married first to prove it.

Well, at least she knew now what was going on. Her suspicions had been well justified, and although her vanity was a little piqued to discover that the Duke of Trent was only courting her as a favor to her sister, she was much gratified by the compliment he had unknowingly paid her. No gentleman of her acquaintance had ever found her easy to talk with, since, unless he had a passion for orchids, she had never talked easily. Indeed, that was the lovely thing about Sir Windbourne: He could do enough talking for the both of them.

Lavinia found a vacant chair in a quiet corner at Lord Worth's very crowded route and sat down. She needed to think about this information and develop a plan. Her first instinct was to confront Emma right away and put an end to this madness. But she controlled herself—the last thing Miss Lavinia Harlow wanted was to cause a scene—and puzzled over the situation. She knew what Emma was thinking, but it was the Duke of Trent's behavior that had her at a loss. Why would he even engage in such a prank? He was not connected to her family at all and could not feel any responsibility toward their good name. No, the only possible explanation was that he had taken an interest in Emma. But the Duke of Trent didn't chase unmarried girls; he himself had just said it not more than ten minutes before. *Perhaps the duke is chasing Emma but doesn't know it,* she thought. *Can that possibly be?* Recalling the scowl on his face when he saw Emma waltzing with Sir Everett Carson, Vinnie decided this conclusion was accurate.

But how did Emma feel about the duke? That indeed was the question. *She hasn't been herself of late and she stopped asking questions about my outings with the duke. Can she be jealous?* The idea of Emma being envious was so novel and delightful that Lavinia formed a plan to feed the jealousy. She would get a little bit of her own back, she would teach her sister a much-needed lesson, and she would perhaps arrange an excellent match in the process.

When the duke came by the following day to take her for a drive through the park, Lavinia wasted no time in putting her plan into action. She had given thought to every detail, and while the lion's share of her revenge was to be meted out to her sister, she had a little something in store for the duke.

"Your grace," she said, batting her eyelashes as she'd seen other ladies do, "these last few days have been wonderful."

The duke spared her a glance and a smile. "I'm glad to hear it."

"Truly, they have been some of the most wonderful in my life."

His smile dimmed a little, and he gave her a perplexed look. Lavinia wasn't surprised. The words sounded very odd coming from her.

"They have been so wonderful that it's my dearest wish that they never end." She was amazed by how relaxed she felt in his company. She couldn't imagine teasing Sir Windbourne like this. "Perhaps it is time for you to speak with my father?" She batted her eyelashes again.

The smile disappeared completely.

"I know you are thinking that I'm already an engaged woman, but I still have feelings, feelings that have been swayed by your marked attentions and I don't think my father would mind the change of heart. We girls are known for our flightiness, and no one will blame me for jilting Windbourne for a duke. Why don't we—"

By now the color had been completely removed from his face and Lavinia could not go on. He believed her! The poor, stricken man believed her!

She started to laugh, but it was more out of nervousness than delight. Perhaps she had gone too far. And with a duke!

"I beg your pardon," he said, his dark brows in a straight menacing line. "I cannot see what the amusement is."

"I'm sorry, your grace," she gasped, trying to contain her giggles. "I'm truly sorry. It was just a joke."

"A joke?" He stopped the carriage and looked at her. "What sort of joke?"

"I'm truly, truly sorry, your grace. Really I am. You do not have to marry me," she assured him, laying a hand over his gloved one to give comfort. However, it did quite the opposite and she removed it. "I was just playing a joke, you see, to repay you for the one you're playing on me. You should never have agreed to my sister's scheme."

Looking much more relaxed and a fair amount embarrassed, he asked, "What would you have me do? Let her approach someone like Carson, who would've relished the opportunity to seduce you and disgrace your family?"

"No, I wouldn't have liked that. But someone could have told me what she was up to."

"How did you find out?" he asked.

"A word of warning to you and Miss Kennington: The blue velvet curtains have ears."

He laughed. "I'm afraid we were indiscreet. I hope no one else was listening."

"Rest assured, the only ears the blue velvet curtain had were mine. It was a most intriguing conversation. Did Emma really ask Miss Kennington to draw up a list of libertines?"

With a smile he said, "Well, what do you think?"

"Tell me, what exactly was the plan? From your stricken expression earlier, I can assume we weren't to go all the way to the altar."

"No, it was just to be a mild flirtation. Miss Harlow was hoping that you'd fall in love with me and then jilt your fiancé. It wasn't the most logical plan, but then I begin to suspect your sister isn't a very logical person."

"Begin to suspect? What have you been about, your grace, that suspicion of her logic did not set in the second you saw her stealing an orchid in your conservatory?"

They were in the park now, and Trent nodded in greeting to an acquaintance. "You are right, of course. I'm afraid I haven't been thinking very clearly since meeting your sister. She defies logic. Her thoughts were only of getting Sir Windbourne out of the picture. What happened next was scarcely worth considering."

"Of course not. She wouldn't care if I went into a decline and wasted away as long as I didn't do it in Sir Waldo's presence." She said this with a smile, but Trent detected bitterness beneath. He hated the thought of Emma's ill-considered plan coming between the two sisters.

"If Miss Harlow behaved thoughtlessly—good lord, how can I say if? *Although* Miss Harlow behaved thoughtlessly, she only did it out of fear of losing you. She's somewhat worried about how your marriage will affect your relationship."

"I'm well aware of her irrational fear, but it is no excuse to use me—and you—so shabbily."

The duke wondered what to say next. The Harlows weren't his family and it was exceedingly improper of him to get further embroiled in their affairs, but he hated the thought of anyone being angry—no matter how justifiably—with Emma. "Her fears are not entirely irrational. I don't think I'm breaking a confidence if I tell you that your fiancé, upon mistaking Miss Harlow for you, told her that getting away from your sister should do you a world of good."

As she digested this new information, Lavinia tried to recall if Sir Waldo had ever said such a thing in her presence. Nothing came to mind, but she knew that didn't signify anything. Oftentimes when Sir Waldo talked for more than ten minutes her mind would start to wander. It was different when they were conversing—then she would focus her attention on the matter at hand and think him a very agreeable partner. But when he started to expound on a topic as though addressing Parliament, she would woolgather or ruminate on drainage systems. Had he really said that?

"When did she tell you this?" Lavinia asked, more disturbed by this information than she hoped to let on.

"Two weeks ago, when she was trying to convince me of your fiancé's unsuitability," explained Trent. He noticed a sudden withdrawn air about his companion and cursed the slick ground he had willingly trod. He had no right to insult her intended. "She didn't convince me, of course. Husbands have the right to expect certain things from their wives, like that they don't spend their days up to their elbows in mud or follow their sisters into one scrape after another. Surely that was all he meant."

Lavinia nodded, wondering what he meant about wives not being up to their elbows in mud. Sir Waldo didn't have a problem with her growing orchids, did he? She shook her head. This was all very much off the topic. "Thank you, for trying to defend Emma."

"I just don't want you to be too angry with her. She is impulsive and has some growing to do yet."

"What about me? We are the same age—three and twenty."

"I think you're already grown, but keeping in mind the trick you played earlier, I'd say there's still some impulsiveness left."

They drove around the park in silence for a while. The duke noticed how distracted she was and missed the carefree companion of only the day before. He loathed the idea of having dampened her spirits with the serious talk about her fiancé. Whom she married was her business alone—not her sister's, and certainly not his. But he knew her well enough to recognize what a shame it would be if Windbourne succeeded in ending her horticultural bent. He'd never met anyone as knowledgeable about flowers as she was.

After a while, she said, "Your grace, I'm sure you've already had enough of us Harlow women, but I have a scheme of my own that I need your help with. Do you give it to me?"

Trent laughed. "Your sister at least had the decency to tell me what it was before bullying me into compliance."

"It does not require much of you, only that you continue in the same vein," Vinnie said, knowing that she couldn't tell the duke the depth of her play. He would no doubt balk at the idea of making Emma jealous. No bachelor intent on remaining a bachelor would encourage a marriageable girl's interest. No, it was best if the duke and Emma stayed in the dark. That way they could fall in love. "I haven't settled on the details of what I'm going to do yet, but I'm not ready for Emma to discover the truth. It would serve her right if I fell madly in love with you and went into a decline," she said, imagining a deathbed scene with Emma white-faced with fright. Perhaps *that* was going too far but was there anything wrong with a small decline?

The duke thought about her request. As she herself said, he should have had his fill of the Harlow women, and yet here he was, considering entangling himself further in one of their half-baked schemes. He should get out now and leave them to their trickery. But somehow the idea didn't seem right. If he got out now, he would have no excuse to see Miss Emma Harlow, except to court her as a beau did a prospective wife. But he wasn't interested in marriage, was he? He allowed himself a moment to think about it, wondering if what he felt for the Harlow Hoyden was love. The answer was an emphatic no. That he felt lust there was no question. The duke had never wanted any woman—not the dancers he kept in Chelsea, not the widows he toyed with in their bedrooms—the way he wanted her. But he was wise enough to recognize the appeal of forbidden fruit. Miss Harlow would never be his. One had to marry respectable girls to get them into bed, and that was unacceptable. Of course, the idea of his wild, passionate Emma in another gentleman's bed was also unacceptable. He would challenge any man to a duel, even her lawfully wedded husband.

With his thoughts in a muddle, the duke agreed to Vinnie's proposal. Only one thing was clear to him: They must remain co-conspirators. It was the only way he would get to spend time with Emma, perhaps some of it alone, so that he could make her melt again in his arms. He had no intention of relinquishing his claim on Emma, at least not until he figured out what he wanted from her.

Having never schemed before, Lavinia had no inkling of how much she'd enjoy it. Now that she finally knew what was going on, it was as plain as the nose on her face that Emma was being eaten up with jealousy. Where once she could be found waiting in the parlor or study when Vinnie returned from one of her jaunts with Trent, she was now impossible to locate. On one particularly amusing occasion, Vinnie tracked her to the wine cellar and actually found her sister shivering in the basements, with two wool shawls around her shoulders. Delighted, Vinnie smiled at the ridiculous picture her sister presented and thought she and the duke would make a match of it in no time

It was obvious to everyone who knew her that something was wrong with Emma. Her usual exuberance was nowhere to be found, she seemed tired all the time, and nobody had seen her eat in more than a week. When asked if she was all right, she would grow impatient with the question and the inquisitor and storm off in a cloud of invectives.

Clearly, thought Lavinia, *the girl is besotted.*

Although she hated to see her sister suffer, Lavinia thought the whole experience was good for her. Perhaps Emma would learn once and for all that sometimes it was better to leave well enough alone. For a week, Lavinia was on pins and needles, expecting Emma to knock on her bedroom door at any moment and confess all. Vinnie was prepared to graciously forgive her and to wish her well with Trent.

But the moment never came. Indeed, something extraordinary happened. Sir Waldo returned from his country seat, where he'd gone to clear up some tenant dispute, and upon his arrival Emma returned to normal. The lethargy of the past six days disappeared, although pale cheeks remained behind as a reminder. Emma was as full of energy as she had ever been, and she resumed her efforts to throw Trent at

Vinnie's head. Once again she was willing—and even eager—to hear the details of the courtship. Nothing Vinnie said got a reaction out of Emma, aside from that happy, pleased smile she had pasted on her face. Not even when she had thrown around a few "Alexes" and even an "Allie." Nothing. It was as if someone had put a spell on her.

Three days after this remarkable change, Sarah ran Lavinia to ground in the drawing room.

"I want to know what's going on," she said, in a firm voice. She closed the door and sat down with her needlepoint on her lap. But her calm pose was deceptive. She was very angry and seriously worried about the Harlow sisters, and Lavinia wasn't leaving the room until she knew everything.

"I can't imagine what you mean," answered Lavinia, who still had a hope of getting out of the room intact. Really, why was Sarah asking her anyway? Emma was the one who started it.

"I am not in the mood for glib answers. I want to know what's going on between you and Emma. Neither one of you is behaving as you ought. Up until three days ago Emma was walking around here like a languid mummy," Sarah said, recalling Emma's sad, pale features. "Now she is bouncing around like the bird in a cuckoo clock. Something is bothering her. I want to know what it is."

"Why do you assume I know?"

Lavinia blinked innocently, but as she didn't have the experience or skill with lying that her sister did, Sarah was not taken in. "Because you are her sister. You know everything about her."

This was not exactly true, but Vinnie thought it best not to belabor the minor point just then. "It will only distress you to know. Ignorance is bliss, is it not?"

Sarah thought of the last few days. They'd been exhausting and strained—anything but blissful. "I do not agree. Tell me what's going on in this house or I will have Roger ask you. I'm sure you'd rather confess all to me than him."

This was true. While Roger wasn't a very frightening older brother, he was still an older brother. One would feel silly confessing a game of love to him. She sighed. "You must promise not to get upset. It...what Emma did was done to me and I'm no longer upset."

Sarah put down her needle. "All right. I will try to remain coolheaded."

Lavinia sat down on the couch. "As you know, Emma is not very fond of my choice in husbands and in hope of, shall we say, directing my attention elsewhere, she asked the Duke of Trent to pretend an interest in me," Vinnie said, keeping the worst of it—Emma's hunt for the right libertine—to herself.

The nature of the confession did not surprise Sarah, although the details of the scheme should have been shocking. Alas, it was just the sort of thing that Emma would think of. "I see. Continue."

"Well, I was suspicious of all the attention the duke was paying me, especially when I noticed how often his eyes followed Emma, so I investigated until I discovered the truth. Only I didn't tell her that I knew what she was up to. Instead, I confronted the duke and asked him to pretend that nothing had changed, because I wanted Emma to be jealous enough to confess her scheme *and* admit she loves the duke, so the two could be married."

Sarah thought this was a very naïve piece of work, and she marveled at Lavinia's innocence. "The duke went along with this?" Sarah asked, astonished that a man of his thirty years would play such an absurd game.

"Yes and no. I didn't tell him what I had in mind, because if he knew that Emma was wearing the willow for him, he would turn tail and run, in the way of all bachelors. But he is clearly fond of her, even if he won't admit it."

"And now?"

"Now?"

"Yes, why is Emma behaving in this erratic way? One can barely get her to sit still through dinner."

Lavinia sighed. "I have been puzzling that one myself

for many days and can arrive at no answer. Three days ago I thought she was on the verge of confessing all but something happened."

"Yes, it was three days ago. Now that I think about it, the change coincided with Sir Waldo's return," Sarah said, thoughtfully assimilating the information. She recalled Roger telling her that Emma had been looking for her on the morning of Sir Waldo's return. She also remembered Roger's report that Emma had been angry at Windbourne for burning Vinnie's manuscript. Since it had seemed inconceivable that Vinnie was writing a book—on what topic would she write?—Sarah had been inclined to dismiss this allegation. When Emma didn't make the charge again in her presence, Sarah had forgotten about it altogether. Could that be what happened? Sir Waldo Windbourne returned, giving Emma a disgust of him anew, and she, more determined than ever to thwart the match, renewed her interest in her scheme?

She heard Lavinia speaking to her and she looked up. "Excuse me, dear, I'm afraid I wasn't paying attention."

"I asked what you were thinking," explained Vinnie. "You seemed to be concentrating very hard on something."

"Yes," she said still distracted by her thoughts. "Yes, I was." She stood, leaving the needlepoint behind on the footstool, and opened the door.

"You won't tell her, will you?" Lavinia asked, running to Sarah and taking her arm.

"I think I should."

She closed the door and rested her back against it, so Sarah could not leave. She would not let her leave until she promised to keep the secret. "No, you mustn't."

"I think she has suffered enough for the trick she played you," explained Sarah, hoping that Vinnie would agree. It was not like her to hold a grudge.

"You can't believe I'm doing this to her out of revenge!" she said, alarmed at being so misjudged. "I love my sister, Sarah, and I'd never intentionally hurt her." She took a deep breath and tried to gather her thoughts. It was very important that she convince Sarah to keep the secret. "I know you must think us a daft pair of misses with our plans and schemes and you're probably sorry you ever married into our foolish family, but you must trust me on this and not tell her. You know what Emma is like, determined never to marry, to let no man rule over her. She's terrified of losing her freedom. But she's in love with the Duke of Trent—I just know it, Sarah. You should see the look on her face when I talk about him. She's in love with him, but she's too stubborn to admit it. I know him pretty well by now, and he's a good man. He would make her an excellent husband. He isn't like any man I've ever met: considerate, funny, kind, intelligent. You must let her have this chance at happiness. You must."

Sarah listened to this passionate speech and felt renewed concern. She did not doubt that Vinnie wanted the best for Emma—or that the best was indeed the Duke of Trent. No, she now worried that Vinnie, too, was in love with him. Hadn't she just described him as considerate, funny, kind and intelligent? Surely these adjectives could not be applied to Sir Waldo, whose intelligence was of the endless verbal kind.

Maybe I am making too much of this, thought Sarah. She herself had had a harmless schoolgirl crush on the duke, and she'd escaped unscathed. Why not these two? They were no more experienced with men at the age of three and twenty than she had been at eighteen. Crushes were a common— and perhaps important—part of aging. "All right," she conceded, although not without a few misgivings. "I won't say a word of this to Emma, at least not yet. But I will be keeping a close eye on her—on *both* of you."

At that, Lavinia giggled.

Exasperated, Sarah asked, "What has amused you?"

"Your saying you'll keep an eye on me. Nobody has ever kept an eye on me before," she said gaily and swept out of the room.

Watching her, Sarah had to admit that she hardly acted like a woman whose heart was broken.

CHAPTER SEVEN

After her unsatisfying meeting with Roger, Emma decided to keep private counsel. She could wait until Sarah came home and tell her what that miserable worm had done to Vinnie's horticultural manuscript, but she knew that Sarah would let her rail for ten minutes and then calmly reject her concerns as irrational and unfounded. Emma was tired of being called irrational, and she was equally tired of having her very well founded anxieties dismissed as groundless.

She decided it was time to step up the campaign. Plan A would continue to get her complete and total support, but it was no longer enough. Sir Windbag's return threatened to overturn all her hard work. Now the wretched man would be able to advance his own suit and remind Lavinia of his finer points, although it seemed inconceivable to Emma that he had any finer points. No, plan A had to be supplemented by a more aggressive plan B. She had been reluctant to implement plan B—preferring, like all unmarried misses, to stay within the bounds of the law—but tough times called for tough measures and she would not be cowered. War was not for the faint of heart.

Emma spent the day in a frenzy of planning. When Vinnie ducked her head into the study after her drive with Trent, she seemed surprised to see her.

"Oh, there you are—in plain sight. How novel," said Vinnie, making herself comfortable on the leather sofa.

"How's the duke?" she asked, hoping that he'd proposed sometime between Hyde Park and Grosvenor Square but realizing it was unlikely. "Did he have anything particularly interesting to say?"

"No, we talked about the usual trifling matters. He complimented me on my hat and I on his driving. He's an excellent whipster. Have I mentioned that?" she asked, knowing full well that she had mentioned this fact every day for the last week. She thought racing curricles was something Emma and the duke could do when they were married.

"I don't believe you have," answered Emma. "Do tell me more."

Although this wasn't the reaction she was used to, Lavinia gladly complied. Twenty minutes later, she got up to change. "I understand I missed Sir Waldo's visit. I didn't realize he'd be back in town so soon. Ludlow said he'll be returning at three, so I must go change. It's already two-thirty."

Emma did not like this display of enthusiasm on the behalf of Sir Windbag, meager as it was. To divert Vinnie's attention she asked when she expected to see the duke next.

"I believe we are to go to the theater with him tomorrow night." She paused. "You are coming, aren't you?"

Emma had no recollection of making the engagement but nodded anyway. "Of course. Will Sir Waldo?"

"I expect so," answered Lavinia, before shutting the door.

Tomorrow night was much too long to wait for a private conference with Trent. Emma wanted to put her plan into action that very minute, and she saw no reason why she shouldn't. She located her reticule, put on her pelisse and told Ludlow she was going for a walk should anyone ask for her.

Once outside, she flagged down a hackney cab and directed him to St. James. It was a short drive and minutes later she stepped down in front of the large white town house. She didn't know if the duke was at home, but she knocked on the door anyway. Realizing that it wasn't quite the thing for young ladies to visit bachelor gentlemen, she asked to see the dowager. The butler looked at her askance, of course, for she didn't have her abigail with her, but there was nothing she could do about that now. She held her head up high and stared him down. He led her to the drawing room and asked her to take a seat. Emma preferred to stand.

A few minutes later the doors opened to admit the duke.

"Miss Harlow," he said, greeting her with a slight bow, "I'm afraid my mother is indisposed. Perhaps I may be of service."

Emma had not seen the duke up close in almost a week and for a few moments she was incapable of speech. He was so handsome to look at, and so comfortingly strong and so *familiar.* She knew instantly that she had done the right thing in coming here.

"What a perfect piece of luck," she said, smiling wildly. She was so very happy to see him. "It was you I was hoping to meet with, in fact. Your mother was just a ruse. See, I do have some small sense of propriety, after all."

"*Small* being the operative word," he said, indicating with a gesture that she should take a seat. "Can I get you anything. Perhaps some tea?"

Emma recalled her mission and agreed to tea. No doubt the duke would need some convincing and the effort would make her parched. They talked of town gossip while they waited for the maid to bring the refreshment. When the tea was served and they were left alone again, the duke got down to business.

"Well, to what do I owe the honor of this visit?" he asked.

"It's about Lavinia," she said.

The duke indulged a wry smile. "Of course it is."

"Sir Windbag has returned," she stated, scrutinizing his reaction for some evidence of his feelings for Vinnie.

"The event was imminent," he said.

Emma was disappointed by this very sensible response. This would not do. "Your grace, I discovered something very disturbing today over breakfast. You see, Sir Waldo came in and mistook me once again for Lavinia."

"It's remarkable how he keeps doing that. You're nothing alike."

"I beg your pardon, your grace. We are identical."

"On the surface, perhaps."

"Anyway, he mistook me for Lavinia and talked about his plans for the future—note that I say *his* plans because I assure you they had nothing to do with what my sister might want. He lectured me for fifteen minutes. Fifteen minutes, your grace, a considerable amount of time when one has to watch him chew bacon with his mouth open. Anyway, at the end of this dissertation—and a dissertation it was, for it was nothing less than thesis, antithesis and synthesis—he tells me what a good thing it was that he burned my manuscript."

The duke, who had been fighting a smile, less the hoyden think he was trivializing her concerns, looked at her in surprise. "What manuscript?"

"That is exactly what I thought. It seems my sister was writing a book on horticultural matters." She watched him carefully and was well pleased by his reaction.

"How splendid," the duke said warmly. "She does seem to have an encyclopedic knowledge on the topic."

"Thank you, your grace," she said gratefully.

He looked at her oddly. "For what, Miss Harlow?"

"For demonstrating that all men are not beasts," she said. "Sir Windbag doesn't think that women should be authors. Or be anything, other than mothers and housekeepers."

"As I've said before, most men feel that way. And if Miss Harlow is willing to be a mother and housekeeper, who are you to scruple at her choices?" he asked reasonably.

Emma was not impervious to logic. "So you say, but *he* burned *her* manuscript. That does not sound like Lavinia is making her own choices." She decided on another tactic, one that would not allow the duke to remain so objective. "You've spent time with my sister, sir. I'd say you know her fairly well. Do you think she will be happy as a mother and housekeeper, with no orchids to care for and no drainage systems to devise? Do you think the book she might have written would have been worth your time?"

With those soulful blue eyes gazing directly into his own, he could do nothing but tell the truth. "No, I don't think she will be completely happy without her orchids. And, yes, I would have been honored to read her book."

Much relieved, Emma sighed. "Good, then we are agreed. We break into Sir Windbag's lodgings tonight and hunt for tangible proof that he's a villain."

"No," he said calmly.

Although Miss Harlow had expected this reply, she was still disappointed when it came. Why did everything have to be an argument? She decided to start with the tactic that had worked so well the last time. "All right," she said, standing up. "Thank you for the tea and please give my regards to your mother."

The duke did not stand. "Where are you going?"

"To visit a friend. I have a favor to ask her."

"If you are going to ask Miss Kate Kennington to draw up a list of possible burglary candidates, you may as well sit right down," he said, a little smugly.

"You know Kate?" she asked, surprised.

"We are recent acquaintances. She seems like a very sensible young lady. I'm sure if I asked her *not* to draw up a list of possible burglary candidates, she'd listen to me. She's just as worried about your reputation as I am."

"There is no need for you to worry about my reputation," she said, trying to settle on another approach. "And it just so happens that you are wrong. I wasn't going to visit Kate. I was going to…a…locksmith friend of mine to buy lock-picking devices."

"A locksmith friend?" he asked, amused.

"Yes, a locksmith friend."

"And what is his name?"

"That is privileged information, sir. Well, I better be on my way. I have lots to do before nightfall. I have to acquire lock-picking devices and settle on an outfit suitable for breaking and entering a villain's apartments. You will understand if I don't linger." She walked slowly to the door, expecting him to stop her at any moment. He did not. She sighed heavily and turned the knob. Well, the deed must be done, even if she must do it alone. "Good day."

The duke came up behind her and pushed the door shut. "Miss Harlow…Emma, you cannot be serious."

She looked at him with her wide blue eyes. "Can't I, your grace?"

"But what you propose is insane!" he insisted. "It would be criminally irresponsible of me to aid you. You must understand that."

"I understand that perfectly. But it would be criminally irresponsible of me to let Vinnie marry that monster. *You* must understand that. Perhaps if I had never found out about this burnt manuscript, I might have been able to accept him in the end—if I absolutely *had* to, of course—but now the game has changed. In fact, it's no longer a game and I have never been more serious about anything in my life," she concluded with a sad little smile, knowing full well that few expected earnestness from the Harlow Hoyden. "Now please let me leave."

"All right," the duke conceded with a scowl. He could not listen to such a speech and be unmoved. "I'll do it."

"I knew it!" Emma cheered and tossed herself into his arms. "You are my most trusted ally." She hugged him tightly for several long moments before she became aware of the impropriety of such behavior. She tried to pull away. The duke wouldn't let her.

"Emma," he whispered close to her ear, before his lips covered hers.

Instantly she was assaulted with an almost

overwhelming wave of sensation and had to grip his shoulders tightly to steady herself. No longer quite so inexperienced, it was she who deepened the kiss, who opened her mouth and insisted with her tongue that he do the same.

When she felt her balance return, she loosened her grip and began exploring with her fingers. She ran them along his broad chest and under his jacket, savoring the feel of him. Then she grasped the back of his head with one hand and ran her fingers through his hair. He had beautiful, soft hair.

"Enough," he groaned, pulling away from her.

Emma smiled, pleased to see that he was breathing as heavily as she. Indeed, this time he seemed very disturbed by their kiss. "Why?" she asked.

"Why?"

"Yes, why did you kiss me? Last time it was to prove you were a libertine—which you didn't do, by the way. I only pretended to agree. What was the reason this time?" She took a seat on the couch, since she was still feeling a little unsteady.

"You're very tempting, imp," he answered with some affection.

"Excellent," she said, dimples prominent. "I've never been tempting before. It's a novel experience."

The Harlow Hoyden was very beautiful, and it was hard to believe that the jaded gentlemen of the *ton* had not noticed. "I daresay you have, on many occasions."

"How interesting. Well, no one has ever given in before."

"Thank God," muttered the duke.

Emma decided that enough time had been wasted with trivialities. "Now, about the break-in, I was thinking—"

"*I* was thinking that I should go alone."

"No. You will tell me you broke in and discovered nothing, but you will not even leave your town house," she said, thinking that was what she'd do if she were in the duke's position. "I cannot agree to your underhanded plan."

"Your most trusted ally, eh?" he observed with ironic humor.

"As you are my only ally, I'm sorry to report that the bar for trust is set very low," she explained.

"What if I give you my word of honor that I will break into Sir Windbourne's apartments? Will you let me go alone then? Surely the Duke of Trent's word is to be trusted, even if the man isn't," he said with a cynical bent to her lips.

"Yes, I would trust that," she lied. The mission was too important to trust to anyone other than herself. "But I cannot in all good conscience let you take the risk. You do not live under the constant threat of Sir Waldo as your brother-in-law."

Recalling the kiss, the duke wasn't so sure about that. "But if I exonerate you of all responsibility?"

"Fine person I'd be to let you go into danger alone. Besides, you cannot exonerate a person just because you wish to. It's more complicated than that."

Yes, he was beginning to see that it was all much more complicated than he thought. "All right." Trent covered his eyes and sighed. "We'll break into Windbourne's apartments together. Tell me what your plan is."

Emma riffled through her reticule and withdrew a folded sheet of white paper. "Here is Sir Windbag's town house," she said pointing to a rough sketch of Half Moon Street. "It's located on the south side of the street, and as this is a corner, he does not have a neighbor here. This is a pantry window and the most vulnerable part of the house. It is located off the kitchens and is only used for storage of pots and pans. After ten o'clock, the kitchen servants can be found playing cards in the servants quarters, here. They will be a good distance from the pantry."

She took out another drawing. "Here we are in the pantry. From there we need to proceed to here." She indicated a room on the other side of the house. "This is

Sir Windbag's study. The most dangerous part of our mission will be getting from the kitchens to the study, for we have to go through the dining room and past the drawing room. These are the areas my source has indicated are the most likely to be occupied. However, if we time the matter precisely, we shouldn't have a problem. At eleven, Windbag's man Jamison goes upstairs to lay out his master's bedclothes. At the same hour, the butler visits the lower quarters to check on the household staff. From eleven o'clock to eleven forty-five the ground floor is completely deserted. We will make our move then."

She unfolded a third map; this time it was an illustration of the study. "I have indicated in red the areas most likely to contain secret information: the cabinet of files to the left of the desk, the top desk drawer and the wall safe hidden behind this painting of Windbag's ancestor. I have keys for the drawer and the cabinet. I could not get my hands on the combination for the safe. However, I have interviewed one of the best thieves in the country and he has demonstrated his technique for cracking safes. I am reasonably confident that I can do it."

As the duke listened to this rather remarkable speech, he went through a series of emotions. First shock, then horror, then grudging respect, then finally pride. Cousin Philip was right. Miss Emma Harlow was indeed an out-and-outer. Not one of his female acquaintance—or indeed any of his male acquaintances—could have done it more beautifully. She had compiled the details of enemy territory like a five-star field marshal and integrated the information like a first-class strategist. Trent didn't doubt that had England had the Harlow Hoyden on the front lines, Napoléon would have been ensconced on St. Helena years ago.

"Miss Harlow," he said, examining her maps, "it would seem that you've covered every aspect of the crime. I can't imagine why you need me at all."

Emma dimpled. "To watch my back, of course. I'm not such an widgeon that I'd enter a villain's apartments without backup. The first thing one must realize about a well-orchestrated plan is that nothing ever goes according to orchestration. What if the butler should hear us creeping about and discover us? I will need you to plant him a facer. I understand from Philip that you are very good at that sort of thing."

"Tell me, how long have you been planning this?" he asked, staring at the details on the maps. A skilled craftsman had made these. "Surely you didn't acquire all this information since Windbourne's return this morning?"

"No, I've had this scheme in the works from the moment Lavinia announced her engagement to Windbag eight weeks ago. At first, I merely disliked him because he was so damnably boring, but even then there was something suspicious about his manner," she explained.

"But how did you discover all this?"

"Really, your grace, there's not a bit of information in the world that can't be had from a houseboy for the price of a meat pie," she said.

"And your interview with the best thief in the country? How did that come about?"

"The docks are a veritable breeding ground for thieves. If one goes down there with enough coin in one's purse and a respectful demeanor, one can learn all sorts of useful things." She sipped her tea daintily.

The thought of Emma strolling the docks with gold in her pocket chilled Trent to the bone. "I trust you didn't go down there alone."

"No, I had the sense to bring a footman with me. Sylvester isn't very intelligent, but he's large and intimidating, and he's the perfect thing for whenever I need extra protection."

"Is that often?"

She blinked at him before answering. "No, usually I'm quite content to take my pistol. Only sometimes do I require the services of Sylvester."

This, like everything else she said, astonished the

duke. "Promise me you will not bring it tonight. The last thing we need is a mishap with a smoking gun and a winged butler. Pistols are not to be toyed with."

She laughed at his attitude. Of course she knew guns weren't to be toyed with. "I am an excellent shot. Perhaps when this is all over, we could go to a gallery and I can demonstrate my prowess."

The duke was determined to never let that happen. Women did not go to shooting galleries to show off their prowess. Indeed, women did not have prowess. "Of course," he said.

"Very good," she said, standing up and putting an end to the interview. "I should be getting home before I'm missed. I will see you tonight? I will be dropping from the second-story window on the east side of the house. Have your carriage near there at ten-fifteen." When he sought to interrupt, she forestalled him with a raised hand. "There's no need to concern yourself about my safety. There's a very durable and thick tree next to my window, and I've been climbing up and down it for years."

"You are wild, Miss Harlow, as everyone says."

"I am free, Lord Trent."

He decided not to linger over semantical points. "And Windbag," he said, voicing his last concern, "how do you know he will be away from home?"

"On that point I know nothing for certain but past behavior indicates that after visiting with Lavinia, he will visit his club and gamble. He is a devoted follower of faro, though his skill leaves a lot to be desired—as does the rest of him."

The duke made a mental note to seek out Pearson and inquire of his plans for that night. Hopefully he could be convinced to visit Windbourne's club and take up a hand or two of faro. There was no reason to leave anything to chance. He walked her to the door and helped her into her pelisse. "I've asked Harmon to bring my coach around."

"That isn't necessary, your grace," she insisted.

"I'm afraid it is. Ladies do not travel in hacks."

"Pooh, they are the safest of conveyances, and if I return home in one of yours, my family will get suspicious. Now we wouldn't want that to happen, would we?" she added.

"Miss Harlow, considering all the things you've accomplished right under their noses, I must say it's unlikely that your family will notice anything amiss."

Emma conceded the truth of this remark. If her family had been inclined to astute observation, she would have led a much duller life.

Because her recent doldrums had taken away Emma's interest, such as it was, in the social whirl, she was unaware of that evening's social commitment.

"But you must recall that we are dining at the Winchesters'," said Sarah, when she came upon Emma in the dining room devouring a collation of cold meats. "We talked about it only last evening. You were staring at your plate and insisting you couldn't finish another bite, even though you hadn't finished a first one yet, and I said that I hoped you'd get your appetite back by the time we went to the Winchesters' tomorrow. You assured me you would, but I recognized it for the bald-faced lie it was. Although, here you are eating," she said, almost as an afterthought.

Emma had no recollection of the conversation to which her dear sister-in-law referred, but she didn't refine too much upon it. "I'm sorry, Sarah, but you must pass along my regrets to Lord and Lady Winchester. I have a crushing headache and would like nothing better than to climb into bed, which I'll do as soon as I finish this snack."

Sarah's initial impulse was to argue further, as Emma was always searching for an excuse not to attend dull social functions, but she restrained herself. It was the first time she had seen food pass Emma's lips in a week and although she seemed to be recovering from whichever bug she suffered, her cheeks were still quite pale. "Very well," she said, thinking that a good night's sleep might be just the thing.

It was Emma's intention only to lie in bed and read Sir Walter Scott, but as soon as her head touched the pillow she was out cold. Four or five sleepless nights caught up with her all at once, and when she opened her eyes several hours later, it was not only dark but rapidly approaching the ten o'clock hour as well.

"My goodness," she gasped, jumping out of bed, with an awful sinking feeling that it was very late indeed. The candle on her side table had been extinguished, which meant Sarah or Lavinia or one of the upstairs maids had been in to check on her. She lit a candle and looked at the clock: nine forty-five. She only had a half hour to get ready, and she didn't know what to wear. Although she had given the details of the break-in a tremendous amount of thought, she hadn't settled on an outfit. She had only one black dress, but it was of a billowy cut that would surely interfere with her climbing in and out of windows. She pulled a storage box from the deep recess of her closet and extracted a pair of dark-brown trousers. They were homemade and roughly sewn, for the Harlow Hoyden was hardly an accomplished seamstress, but the holes were in the right places and they fit comfortably. Emma had never worn them in the city before, and she knew Sarah would be most upset to discover she'd brought them with her. They were not decent in the country, of course, but no one was ever there to notice or comment. Emma tossed on one of Roger's old shirts, which she had stolen from a laundry pile years before. Her shoes were another cast-off item of Roger's. She had managed to get her hands on them at the exact right moment, for had she waited another year, Roger's shoes would have been too big.

She finished dressing, located her safe-opening kit and glanced at the clock. It was precisely ten-fifteen. After extinguishing the candle and arranging some pillows to look like her sleeping form, Emma climbed through the window.

As she had said, the tree beside the house was a trustworthy oak, and Emma moved down among its branches with easy familiarity. Thanks to her misspent youth, there wasn't a tree whose heights Miss Emma Harlow could not scale.

As soon as she dropped to the ground, she felt a hand on her shoulder. She resisted the urge to jump, even though she felt a fleeting glimmer of fear. It was the duke, of course, not some assailant.

"All is well?" he whispered in her ear.

She nodded and indicated that she would follow. He placed his hand on the small of her back. The Duke of Trent had no intention of letting her out of his sight for the whole of the adventure. He led her to a hired cab that was stationed on the street corner.

Grosvenor Square was quiet and pretty in the late hour and Emma thought it was a shame that she wasn't allowed to take constitutionals after dark. She regretted, not for the first time, that the world was such an unsafe place for a woman.

It was only when they were in the cab and on the way to Half Moon Street that Emma felt comfortable enough to speak. "Good evening, your grace," she said, looking at him in the dim light of passing street lamps. He was dressed as plainly as she, though in clothing indicative of his sex, and she couldn't help but notice how nicely he filled out his jacket. Without any affectation or tailor's padding, he was as impressive a specimen as ever. *Really,* she thought, *he is so perfect. How could Vinnie withstand his charms?*

"Good evening, my dear, I see you're behaving as unconventionally as ever. Tell me, who is your tailor?"

Emma laughed. "You're looking at her, and since I have no illusions of my skill with a needle, you do not have to cut me down. I made them because it was necessary for them to be made."

"What's the news from home? Will Lavinia be seeing Windbourne this evening?"

"We were engaged to dine at the Winchesters' this

eve. I can only assume that as Miss Harlow's betrothed he was invited as well. Sarah did not mention it. I'm surprised she went. With Roger here, she has been inclined to stay close to home."

"How is he doing? Miss Harlow informed me of his accident. I'm very sorry," he said, talking her hand. "It must be a terrible thing to adjust to."

"Yes, but Roger is adapting marvelously. He has never been the sort to complain about anything other than boredom, and the loss of an arm is indeed terrible but it is better than the loss of a leg or one's life. Sarah could not bear it if he'd died."

The duke nodded and, still availing himself of her hand, began drawing lazy circles on her palm. While she found this distracting, she had no intention of putting an end to it. The duke's hands were soft, warm and something about his grasp made her heart beat faster.

When the carriage stopped at Windbourne's town house, the duke climbed out and spoke to their driver. He then returned to Emma. "It is ten fifty-five. I can see the south-side window hidden behind a hedge. I've told the driver to leave and circle around again in a half hour and to wait for us here. Now, are you ready?" he asked, trying to look deeply into her eyes. But it was dark and he could barely make out the features of her lovely face. "It is not too late, Emma. You can stay in the cab and wait for my return."

She gave a low laugh. "I was about to say the same to you, sir."

"Very well," he said, opening the door. "We may as well go down together."

They crept silently up the path to the side of the house. Fortunately, the lamp nearest their destination had gone out, and they worked in almost total darkness. The pantry window was six feet above the ground, just as Emma had calculated, and before she could figure out the best way to approach it from her meager height, the duke had already opened the window and given her a leg up. He then pulled himself through with complete ease, and Emma marveled at his strength. Clearly those muscles she had felt during her passionate exploration weren't merely for show.

The pantry was small and crowded and filled with so many pots that even the floor was covered, as Emma quickly discovered when she tripped over one. The sound of copper hitting concrete was indeed loud, but fortunately the duke caught her before she could fall on other loud copper pots. They both froze, expecting the door to open at any second and a large butler to come charging through. Since they were on a tight schedule, they could only spare a minute for their dread. The duke lit a candle and Emma carefully walked out of the small hazard-ridden room.

The dimensions of the kitchen were hard to discern on the strength of a single candle but they seemed to be large. She didn't have her map with her, but she knew full well which direction to take. The study lay to the north. She pointed to the doorway and Trent nodded. They walked through the dining room and past the drawing room without incident. In a flash they were in the study. Emma lit another candle and handed a key to Trent.

"It's for the desk drawer," she whispered.

He accepted the key. "What am I looking for?" he asked now, wondering how it hadn't occurred to him to inquire before now.

"Anything that appears suspicious," she said. "I don't know what we're looking for, but we'll know it when we find it. Trust me, there must be evidence of that snake's perfidy somewhere."

Since Trent believed they were on a fool's mission— an extremely organized and well-planned one, of course, but still a mission for fools—he doubted very much that he'd know "it" when he saw it. As far as he was concerned, there was nothing to know or see.

He applied the key to the drawer and reluctantly examined its contents. It was very bad form for a gentleman to rifle through another gentleman's things, and he felt extremely uncomfortable doing so. Emma, on the other hand, threw herself into the disagreeable exercise with unrestrained enthusiasm. She was a faint outline to him in the candlelight, but he could hear the energetic ruffling of papers. Every so often he heard a sound like a grumble or a groan.

The first thing the duke noticed was that Windbourne was not the most organized of peers. Stacks of papers with bent corners and weathered edges filled the desk, along with scattered note cards that were in no discernible order. He glanced at each sheet, trying to discover its business. The first batch of documents were rather commonplace correspondence with one's secretary. They made Windbourne aware of the status of his estate and informed him of repairs that needed to be made. Nothing of interest there. The second group of papers was from bankers and lawyers and spoke of investments Windbourne had here and abroad, most specifically in France. Trent perused these, looking for something uncommon, but everything seemed to be in order. Now that the war with France was over, there was nothing remarkable about owning land there. The duke checked the dates and satisfied himself that the land had been transferred to Windbourne after Napoléon's exile to St. Helena.

The third stack was a collection of gambling debts. Trent totaled up the figures, feeling like a perfect cad as he did so, and whistled softly. Windbourne was in deep with several moneylenders. Apparently Miss Harlow's assessment of his gambling skills was accurate. It seemed that Windbourne hadn't had a stroke of luck in months.

When he was done perusing the documents, Trent took a cursory look at the note cards, which were perfumed, written in French and of an amorous nature. He read one in its entirety and tossed it back into the drawer in disgust. The communication had been trite and poorly spelled. He closed the drawer. There was nothing suspicious here. Indeed, to

Trent, Windbourne seemed like the classic English gentleman, right down to his French paramour.

After locking the drawer, Trent tapped Miss Harlow on the shoulder. "Any luck?" he asked.

She handed him a document that had been puzzling her for the last several minutes. "Look at this, Trent. Windbag keeps another house in London. See, here is the deed. It's located near Covent Garden. I wonder what goes on there, for he has never mentioned owning additional London property. Perhaps this is where all his nefarious deeds take place. I think we should search it."

"Emma," he said kindly, kneeling down next to her, "that is where he keeps his mistress."

"His mistress?" she repeated, almost confused by the thought. She knew gentlemen kept mistresses—her father was a prime example—but she had never considered the possibility that Windbourne had. Perhaps because it seemed remarkable enough that he had attracted one female let alone two. "Then he's a faithless dog, no?"

"Many men have mistresses before they wed," he said, trying to treat the matter lightly.

"Many men have mistresses after they wed," she said bitterly.

Realizing now was not the time for a serious conversation but wanting to put her at ease, Trent said, "Yes, but we don't know Windbourne's intentions yet, for he and your sister are not yet married. He might cut the connection before the wedding."

"You are splitting hairs. The wedding itself is but an arbitrary date that has no bearing on one's heart. Either he loves Vinnie or he doesn't. When you love someone you do not go to a house in Covent Garden and make love to a dancer. Do not give it to me all wrapped up in society's fine linens, sir," she said angrily, fighting to keep her voice low. "I might be a woman but I am not a idiot, despite what you and your brethren think of my sex. Only unfaithful married men keep mistresses. Vinnie has the right to know about this."

Trent laid a hand on her arm. "You cannot tell her. Windbourne has the right to conduct his affairs as he sees fit."

"Not with my sister!"

"What will you do, Emma?" he asked softly. "Will you tell her that her fiancé is keeping a woman and humiliate her with the knowledge? What if she decides to go ahead with the marriage, for you yourself said she's determined to wed and have children, what will it be like for her, fearing that you think less of her for not having your strong convictions? Vinnie isn't as naïve as you, my dear. Perhaps she already knows."

"I'll consider your words," she said, knowing there was some truth in what he spoke, "but I take them with a grain of salt. You're not the gentleman to understand this, since you yourself are not faithful to one woman."

Although the duke wished with everything in his heart that he could deny this charge, if for no other reason than to prove to this darling brave girl that all men were not alike, he could not. In lieu of a defense, he changed the subject. "Have you found anything else?"

"No," she said, the disappointment strong in her voice. "There's nothing here, just files and files of financial papers and several folders of private, very boring correspondence— not one confession of an unforgivable crime."

"What is this?" asked Trent, picking up a folder that she had taken out of the drawer.

"That is their marriage contracts. I wanted to give it a careful read."

The duke didn't think that was wise. Not only was it none of her business what monies were settled where but they also didn't have much time. They had already been there for thirty minutes. "Why don't I flip through this and you open the safe?"

Since the safe was her last bastion of hope, Emma complied willingly. She took out the listening device that she had bought down on the docks. It was a cylindrical metal cup attached to rubber tubing.

"What is that?" asked the duke.

"It is a magnifying glass for the ears," she said, putting it on. "Mr. Squibb promised that I'd hear the numbers click into place. That's how I will know the combination."

Trent had little confidence in the odd device's usefulness, but he looked on in wonder as Emma opened the safe. It took less than a minute. Then he returned his attention to the marriage contracts. There was nothing out of the ordinary, except that the last three sheets in the folder were not part of the marriage agreement. They were letters to Roger.

"Hmm," he said.

"What?" asked Emma, as she looked through Windbag's sad collection of jewelry: a sapphire necklace, diamond earrings, two gold broaches and a pearl bracelet. Miss Harlow was not the sort of woman to covet precious stones, but she thought that her sister deserved better than this dismal assortment.

"There are letters of Roger's here."

"Really?" exclaimed Emma, before she remembered to keep her voice down. "Let me see." She grabbed them from Trent and read through them quickly. They were deadly dull, telling of weather conditions and coastal forecasts. "Why would anyone want to steal these?" she asked, puzzled.

"I don't think he did," answered the duke. "He must have picked them up by mistake when he gathered up the contracts. I know you'd like to lay some monstrous sin at his feet, but I don't think this is it."

As much as it killed her to admit it, Emma had to agree that the duke was probably right. Roger's private correspondence, even the ones that were not meteorologically concerned, were of little importance to the world at large. She could not imagine what Windbag would do with them, had he intended to steal them. She folded the letters and put them into her pants. She may as well return them to her brother.

"Did you find anything in the safe?" Trent asked.

"No, just some jewels."

He nodded. "Well, should we leave? It is almost eleven forty-five."

Emma knew that to remain longer was foolish, but she hated to go without evidence of his treachery. It was here, she just knew it was here, but she didn't know where to look. She sighed and closed the safe, turning the dial back to zero. "All right," she said, blowing out her candle. They would need only one to find the pantry.

Trent opened the door and looked out. The hallway was dim, lit only by a candle on the wall. He laid a hand on the small of Emma's back. "Let's go."

They stepped out the room, and Trent quietly shut the door behind them. They retraced their steps from earlier, but this time when they walked passed the drawing room doors, they opened. Hearing the turn of the knob seconds before the door opened, the duke blew out his candle and pulled Emma behind a long damask drape.

Tense and afraid the beating of her heart would broadcast their location, Emma waited in the duke's arms. As the seconds slowly ticked by, she imagined the awful scene of their discovery. No doubt the constable would be called in to haul them down to Newgate. And she could just see the smirking grin on Sir Waldo's face as he pressed charges against her. What an awful thing to have to explain to Lavinia, not to mention Sarah and Roger and her parents.

It was completely dark behind the heavy curtain and the air was hot. In a voice that was barely there, the duke whispered, "It's been a few minutes. I'm going to stick my head out and take a look. Don't move."

Don't move? thought Emma. *Fine advice. Really, to whence would I go?*

"I think it's all right," said the duke. "The candle in the hallway has been extinguished." Emma nodded. "Follow me and move silently."

More excellent advice, she thought, as she moved as quietly as possible. They returned to the pantry without further incident. Before she would step in the room, Emma insisted that the duke light a candle. "I want to hear no more clattering of copper pots," she said reasonably.

They were out the window as easily as they were in it. The hired cab was waiting for them up the street. Once they were safely ensconced in it, Emma started to laugh. She saw the duke looking at her strangely. "It's all nerves," she explained. "I was fine until that last moment, but when I heard the drawing room door open I felt fear—real fear. I don't think I've ever felt it before."

"Fear is a message, a warning that you're not doing something right. Perhaps you should heed it."

Emma dismissed this sage advice with a wave of the hand and laughed delightedly. "But fear is also exhilarating, is it not, sir? My heart is racing and I feel as though I could race to Newmarket but in two hours and fifty-seven minutes this time."

"Since I am in no mood to go barreling down a rural road at breakneck speed," he said, leaning toward her with an intent look on his face, "perhaps we should channel your energies elsewhere."

Emma knew that he was going to kiss her, and she raised herself up to meet him halfway. She had been disturbingly aware of him from the moment she'd entered the carriage. Now that they were out of danger she had time to reflect on that strength of his, that caged strength that was so out of place in polite drawing rooms and that was only unleashed in the ring at Gentleman Jackson's. Instantly she knew that she wanted to feel that strength, to have those arms crushing her to him so tightly that it was impossible to tell where she ended and he began.

"Oh, Trent," she sighed, as his heated lips moved across her neck.

"Alex," he corrected, his voice low and husky. "When you're in my arms, you will call me Alex."

Emma thought that Alex was a very nice name and said it over and over again as she unbuttoned his shirt in the dark. She kissed his chest and ran her fingers over his arms. What lovely, lovely muscles he had. "You are magnificent, Alex."

Her observation further ignited his fire, and he moved with admirable speed. Before she knew it, she was lying with her back against the carriage seat and he was revealing her breasts. Since she was wearing her men's clothes, this was an unexpectedly easy feat, and he gave thanks that her hot flesh wasn't buried under layers and layers of corsets. He raised her chin with a gentle finger and looked at her through the stygian darkness. "It's you who are magnificent."

Emma nodded and pulled his head down to hers, delighting in the feel of skin against skin, delighting in the feel of everything he did. Trent freed her lips and began blazing a trail down her neck and along her shoulders. When his lips made contact with her breast, she gasped in shock and pleasure. She did not know that this was what men and women did alone together, but it came as a wonderful surprise. She ran her hands through his hair.

"Oh, Alex," she sighed as his tongue darted across her nipple. Lying beneath him, she could feel the strength of his desire, and she wondered just how far this madness would go. She certainly didn't have the presence of mind—or the will—to stop it. Indeed, if she had her way, they'd never leave the confines of this carriage.

Trent lavished attention on her other breast, and she shuddered as he brushed her stomach with gentle fingers. Then his hand moved lower. Emma tensed for a moment—how could he touch her there?—but relaxed instantly when these new sensations proved just as delightful as the others.

Emma was on the verge of something, just what she didn't know but she felt certain that it was something magnificent, when the carriage came to a stop. It took all of a moment for understanding to penetrate her passion-filled mind, but the duke responded instantly. With disconcertingly deft fingers, he rebuttoned her shirt swiftly. He did the same with his own.

Emma didn't know what to say, so while she gathered her wits, she pretended to be focused on the listening device she brought with her. When her breathing had returned somewhat to normal, she said, "I shall be leaving now. Thank you for your help, your grace."

She would have opened the door, but the duke's arms restrained her. "Miss Harlow...Emma, we must talk about this."

"There's nothing to talk about," she said in an extraordinarily calm voice.

"You'll not dismiss my embrace so easily," he said, the anger evident.

Emma did not have the strength for this. With the absence of real, damning evidence against Windbourne in her hand, her only hope now was Trent. Emma would do nothing to disrupt plan A. "Really, I'm just saving you the trouble," she said, pulling herself free. It wasn't the whole truth, of course, but then again neither was it completely a lie. She knew enough about the Duke of Trent than to think that he'd be faithful to a woman like her—or indeed any woman. She would not go down that route. She simply would not. "Thank you again," she said, opening the door and stepping out into the cool night air.

CHAPTER EIGHT

It wasn't until a week later at the Earl of Northrup's ball that the duke managed to achieve a private moment with Emma. This finally, after a frustrating six days of trying his damnedest to talk to her and being thwarted on all fronts.

During their theater excursion the day after the break-in, she avoided his presence with single-minded perseverance, preferring to sit by Sarah's side and make dull conversation about the actors' costumes. Whenever he addressed a word to her, she either asked his opinion on the cut of Petruchio's jacket or tossed out a compliment about Lavinia. By the time the evening was through, he had agreed that Lavinia looked very lovely, that amaranth was a particularly becoming color on her, that her brow was very noble indeed, that she had the best posture of any lady of their acquaintance, that her love of the theater was inspiring to behold and that her conversation was particularly sparkling tonight.

The duke left, convinced that the Harlow Hoyden was up to her old tricks, only this time she was taking it a step further. No longer content to have her sister fall for him, she was determined to have *him* fall for her sister. This was the only conclusion to be logically drawn from that night's exercise. Having reconsidered the situation in light of Windbourne's suitability, she had decided that the only solution was for the Duke of Trent to marry her sister. Trent couldn't fault her. In many ways, it was an ideal solution—what woman would choose a windbag like the baron over an erudite lord such as he?—but he couldn't help but be repulsed by the very idea. To marry one sister while desiring the other! He could think of no circumstance less appealing or a marriage more doomed to failure. Clearly Emma had not thought it through, or she would have realized the impossibility of the arrangement. She was no more able to resist him than he was her, and if they were tossed together endlessly in family situations, their attraction would one day overcome them. The end result would be a disastrous betrayal.

Two days after the theater, the duke called at Grosvenor Square, hoping to have a private word with Emma. He wanted to dissuade her from this course, and perhaps talk about what happened in the carriage. A man of his consequence did not go around seducing innocents in his carriage—and seduction it was, for he did not know how far it would have gone had the hackney not stopped when it did. A woman with Emma's breeding should know better than to let him get away with it. There should be a price for such behavior, and although marriage to a notorious young woman too wild to recognize proper behavior had never been part of his plan, he was willing to make the sacrifice for the sake of duty. They had much to talk about, and he would not be denied.

However, it was not Emma who greeted him in the drawing room but Lavinia. "Your grace," she said, taking a seat, "I'm afraid Emma is not feeling quite the thing at the moment and she requested that I see you in her stead. I hope you're not disappointed."

The duke smiled wryly. He should have anticipated this maneuver. "Miss Harlow, it's a pleasure as always."

Lavinia laughed. "Pooh, Trent, you are too polite for your own good. Let us speak plainly with each other. It is not a pleasure at all, though I do appreciate your saying so. You had hoped to see Emma, and I am a sad substitute."

"Not quite a *sad* substitute, I assure you."

"Very good. Now you're getting the hang of it," she said, happy to see he could overcome his innate good manners to be honest for a moment. "We must do something about my sister, for she is trying with renewed vigor to bring us together. Just a few days ago it had seemed to me that she had lost interest in her scheme, but I'm afraid Sir Waldo must have said the wrong thing to her and angered her. It was Sarah who pointed out to me just this morning that Emma's reinvigorated efforts coincided with my unfortunate fiancé's return."

The duke nodded. Miss Harlow's speculation was correct, although she could not know the whole truth. For the first time, the duke regretted the gentleman's code of honor that forbid him from talking ill of a woman's fiancé. Despite his initial reservations, he was now in complete agreement with the Harlow Hoyden: Vinnie deserved much better than Sir Windbag. No man expected his wife to be accomplished in anything other than the genteel arts—sewing, painting, singing, speaking French—but Trent couldn't help but believe that he himself would've been much gratified by an authoress-wife.

"I'm at a loss as to how to proceed," said Lavinia, "and am thinking of making a clean breast of it. As you've probably guessed, I'm not adept at games of deception and should like to bring this sham courtship to an end." She closely watched the duke, trying to gauge his reaction. Did he think it was time to bring this whole matter to a close, as well? "You have been abused enough by the Harlow sisters and must be glad to be free of your ill-advised commitment." Now, thought Vinnie, he'll either run for the hills like a sane man or come up with some reason to continue the farce like a besotted suitor.

The duke considered her words carefully. What she said was true: His commitment had been ill-advised.

When he made it, he had only a small inkling of what he was agreeing to. A sham courtship, certainly, but he had no idea he'd be called upon to commit thievery—or that he'd be unable to resist the scheming imp who tempted him. The latter was an unusual circumstance for him; there had never been a woman before whom he couldn't resist.

Trent realized that he wasn't ready to let the farce end just yet. His first consideration, of course, was Emma. He relished any scheme that brought him into her company, and if she knew that her plan to throw Vinnie and him together was unsuccessful, she might have nothing more to do with him. But his second consideration was Vinnie herself. He had grown to like her very much over the past few weeks, and he respected her thoughts and opinions too much to comfortably watch her throw herself away on a wastrel like Windbourne. What he had in mind was a modified version of Emma's original plan: He would find some peer perfectly suited to Vinnie and toss them together. In order to implement his plan, he would need more time. If he agreed right then to end the sham, he'd have little opportunity to spend time with Lavinia.

"I will, of course, abide by your final decision, Miss Harlow," he said, after an extended moment of thought, "but I fear you might be giving up too easily. Your original intention to teach Miss Harlow a lesson was wise, if a little underhanded, and I think you should stay the course. I do not regret my involvement. Indeed, I wouldn't mind seeing Miss Harlow learn something, as she twisted my arm quite mercilessly to get my compliance."

This was exactly what Lavinia wanted to hear, indeed, had expected to hear. Although Emma's recent behavior indicated the opposite, Lavinia was convinced that her sister was head over heels in love with Trent. She wasn't as confident about the duke's feelings, but all evidence indicated he wasn't indifferent to Emma's charms. "Very well. If you are sure."

"Perfectly. To be honest, Miss Harlow, I haven't been so amused in years."

"I'm sure you're only being polite again, but I'll not take exception. You put my mind to ease."

"That's my intention." The duke stood up to take his leave. "In the interest of our plan, perhaps you should take a drive with me tomorrow afternoon, assuming, of course, that you do not already have plans. With the return of Sir Windbourne, I expect you're very busy."

Trent's expectation was off the mark. Lavinia had seen very little of her fiancé since his return. "Tomorrow will be lovely," she said. "I have no pressing engagements in the afternoon."

"Shall we say three then? And do make sure that Emma knows where you are going and in whose company."

"I will be sure to inform her," she said, escorting him to the door.

"Ah, one last thing, Miss Harlow," he said, "before I forget. I've been talking over your drainage ideas with Mr. Berry, the president of the horticultural society, and he was very interested. He asked me if I thought you'd be inclined to draw up a helpful pamphlet to be distributed at the next meeting and perhaps give a lecture. I told him you probably wouldn't have time with your wedding fast approaching"—fast approaching? thought the duke; her wedding was seven months away—"but it's something to think about," he said offhandedly, well satisfied with her reaction. Her face had lit up at the mere suggestion, and it was clear to the duke that she was already thinking about it. Trent left and told the coach to take him to Mr. Berry's apartments in the East End. Although Mr. Berry did not yet know it, they had drainage systems to discuss.

Trent arrived at the Northrup ball determined to speak with Emma. She had successfully evaded him the whole week through, but that was about to change. He would not be put off any longer.

"I say, Trent, you look as though someone spit on your Hessians and you're planning your revenge. I know women are rumored to prefer the forceful type, but you're doing it a bit brown," said Pearson by way of greeting.

"Good evening, Pearson," said the duke, barely sparing a glance in his search for Miss Harlow.

"It will do you no good," said Pearson.

The duke looked at him quizzically.

Pearson fought a smile. "Staring at the dance floor will do you no good. She isn't here yet. You'll want to turn your attention to the door."

Resenting the accuracy of this statement and the smug tone with which it was delivered, the duke said, "As a matter of fact, I am looking for Miss Portia Hedgley, who I saw arrive twenty minutes ago. We might make a match of it."

Pearson raised a quieting finger to his lips and looked around to see if anyone heard the duke. "You're a bloody fool to say that aloud, Alex, even to throw me off the scent. You never know who's listening. It would serve you right if you found yourself shackled to that toad-eating mushroom rather than admit you have a care for the Harlow Hoyden."

Trent was in no mood for teasing, but Pearson was correct. One never did know who was listening. "I would remind you of the same, lest you get sued by the toad-eating mushroom's family for defamation of character. They're just the sort to use the law courts to resolve their problems."

Pearson agreed to this sentiment and wandered off to fetch himself a glass of wine. When he returned he was very amused to observe that the duke had changed his position. He was now facing the door. "This is the problem with arriving on time to one of these things. As gentlemen we should linger over our toilette, so that we don't have to wait for the ladies, who always linger *longer* over theirs. It's the very devil." As he was saying this, he spied a pair of identical blond heads. "Finally your patience is—"

"Excuse me, Pearson," the duke said as soon as Emma entered the room. She was dressed simply in a dark green silk dress adorned only with delicate lace trim, but the duke thought she looked breathtaking. Her smile was wide, her dimples were out in full force, and he could hear the trickle of her laughter as he approached. He paused a moment to soak in the picture.

"Good evening, Miss Harlow," he said, taking her gloved hand and laying a soft kiss on it. "How beautiful you look in that gown."

"Pooh," said Emma dismissively, "this old thing? I've had it for years, and it's never done a thing for my complexion. But doesn't Lavinia look charming?"

Hearing this, Lavinia rolled her eyes at the duke, for she herself was wearing a dress of a similar green shade. Trent responded with a conspirational smile and greeted her with a kiss on the hand.

Emma saw the duke's intimate smile, though she didn't know its cause, and took heart. Trent had to feel something special for her sister if he could smile at her like *that*. She'd been watching the two of them with an eagle's eye for days, and she could find nothing to convince her that their affection of each other was developing. Alas, they seemed as fond of each other now as they were when they first met. But for the first time in a week, she had hope, thanks to his smile. It would be a happy marriage for both of them. And if she had to move to Scotland or Wales or some other such place in the wild to avoid seducing her brother-in-law, then so be it. Lavinia would never know about the two of them.

Sir Windbourne made up the third member of their little party, and he greeted Trent, heedless to the drama that was playing out before him. Emma had noticed Sir Waldo's obliviousness earlier in the week, and she laid this sin at his feet as she did a multiple of others. What gentleman wouldn't mind his affianced bride spending time with the most sought-after peer of the realm? Only a fool, concluded Emma, or a man so in love with his mistress that he wouldn't care if his wife were caught in flagrante delicto with the footman.

The orchestra struck up a quadrille, and even Emma wasn't brazen enough to send off Trent and her sister under Sir Waldo's beady eyes. She gave the duke a speaking look, making it very clear what she expected of him, and then she addressed a question to the baron to give the duke an opportunity to do it. "Tell me, Sir Windba—uh, Windbourne, what do you think of Jane Austen?"

"Jane Austen?" he asked, baffled by both the question and his fiancée's sister's sudden interest in him. "I've never met the girl. Why? What does she think of me?"

Everyone laughed at this sally, except its author, who hadn't meant to make it.

"Jane Austen is a lady author," explained Emma. "She writes works of fiction."

"A lady author, you say?" His posture straightened, and he raised his monocle to his eye, as if to spot any such animal as a lady author in the underbrush. "I don't approve of lady authors. It is my belief that women should not make spectacles by putting themselves forward in such a vulgar way—"

"Emma, why don't you and the duke join the quadrille? I don't believe they have started yet. Sir Waldo has many thoughts on this topic and his answer could take a great long while." Vinnie sent an apologetic smile to her betrothed. "Why don't you tell me what you think, and I'll give Emma the condensed version later."

Because Sir Waldo was much like a tree that fell in a forest—he made a sound whether one was there to hear or not—he approved of this plan.

"I feel awful," said Emma, casting one last lingering glance over her shoulder. "She shouldn't have to listen to that pedant tell her *again* why she mustn't write. I assure you, once is enough. I can't understand what she sees in him. Did you see the way she interrupted him? She knew a long-winded speech was coming and sought to save us. Why won't she save herself? Indeed, was it my imagination or did she even seem a little embarrassed? How can she marry a man who embarrasses her? She will have to spend the rest of her life apologizing for him. Take it from me, it's hard enough going through life apologizing for one's own behavior. I shudder to think what it's like to have to—" Feeling the cool air brush her arms, Emma ceased her senseless chatter and looked around her. The dance floor was not outside. "Where are we?"

"On the balcony. We need to talk," said the duke in an inflexible tone.

One did not use inflexibility with the Harlow Hoyden. "No, we do not," she said and spun around. The duke grabbed her hand and held her in place.

"If you return to the ballroom before I'm done talking, I will lift you up and carry you back outside," he threatened. "Now have a seat and do not make a spectacle of yourself."

Seething with anger, Emma sat down on the cold marble bench. She hotly resented his words. She would make a spectacle if she wanted, but she would not accept blame for a spectacle *he* created. "Very well," she conceded while giving thought to her options. Despite his black expression, she was convinced he was bluffing. There was no way the impeccable Duke of Trent would embarrass a lady and himself with such a brutish display. To do so would mean supplying the *ton* with a year's worth of scandal broth. She knew the duke well enough to realize that he would not relish being on the tip of every gossipmonger's tongue for a full twelve months. Having thought it through, Emma decided to stay and listen. If the interview became too disagreeable, she would simply walk away, reasonably sure that he wouldn't dare to follow.

Standing above her, the duke saw her calculating the odds. It was what he expected from her and one of the things he respected most.

"Lavinia was telling me about your ride through the park yesterday," Emma said, determined that if there were to be a conversation then she herself would direct it. "She informed me that you were joined by a Mr. Matthew Hardy. She said he's also a member of the horticultural society. Who is this Mr. Hardy?" she asked suspiciously.

"He is a friend," explained the duke.

"A friend? And why have we never heard of him before? Could it be, sir, that you seek to free yourself from your commitment to my sister by substituting him for you? Despite what you think, the Harlow sisters do not find the members of the horticultural society interchangeable."

This was not what the duke wanted to talk about, but he felt compelled to defend himself. "First of all, I do not have a commitment to your sister, I have a commitment to *you*. A commitment, I might add, that I have followed through with to little avail. Miss Harlow doesn't view me in any capacity other than friend and fellow gardener, which is a good thing since I will be mar—"

"Haven't you *kissed* her yet?" she demanded impatiently.

"Kissed her?" he repeated, horrified by the thought. He didn't want to kiss anyone but Emma, especially not his future sister-in-law. "Look, I don't want to talk about Lav—"

"You are a damnable fool, Trent," she said, cutting him off quite viciously. "All you need to do to make a female fall in line is kiss her."

The duke struggled to hold on to his temper. Somehow this conversation had gone terribly wrong. He wanted to talk of their marriage, not his and Lavinia's or Lavinia and Sir Waldo's. "After all that's happened between us, you still want me to kiss your sister?"

Emma's heart screamed in protest, but she'd never made a practice of listening to her heart. She recalled that smile he had directed at Lavinia when they'd first walked in. If it wasn't the smile of a man in love, it was at least an indication of caring and friendship. Emma knew that something as complicated as love did not happen overnight, but she was confident that given time, Lavinia and the duke would develop warmer feelings for each other. They would raise children and orchids and be very happy—as long as Emma didn't ruin it.

"Yes," she said in a soft voice after a very long pause, during which the duke held his breath, "after all that's happened between us, I still want you to kiss my sister."

The duke sighed, feeling the heart flow out of him. He was prepared to fight her willfulness and obstinacy and the sheer bullheadedness that he had come to love, but he had no words to overcome her indifference. The Duke of Trent was many things, but despite the Harlow Hoyden's opinion of him, he was not a fool. Only fools refused to see what was right in front of their eyes and only fools took up lost causes. If Emma had given any indication—a speaking glance or a sigh or even a moment of uncertainty—then he would have pursued the topic until he was lightheaded from speech. He would have indeed picked her bodily up off the dance floor and made sure she listened to him, regardless of the scandal it caused.

When he had arrived at the Northrups' earlier that evening, he'd believed that nothing could sway him from his course. He would leave with Emma as his betrothed or he would leave not at all. Indeed, he had amused himself with the image of him and Emma arguing on the balcony long after the other guests had departed. But now he had been struck with the truth and right between the eyes, at that. The episode in the carriage—the episode that had sustained him these many long days—meant nothing to her. The most deeply moving experience in his life, perhaps the fifteen happiest minutes of his entire existence, was mere experimentation for the Harlow Hoyden. She had warned him, of course, had told him straight out to his face that she believed women should experience other kisses. An outlandish idea, certainly, but one in keeping with her philosophy of freedom. Despite his disappointment, the duke could not cavil at her treatment of him. She had been honest. It was not her fault he hadn't listened.

"Very well," he said, suddenly realizing that she was

still sitting there. "I guess there's nothing else to say." He offered her an arm. "Shall I return you to your family?"

Emma blinked in surprise. "Is that really all?" she asked, suspicious of this easy capitulation. Pretending to give in was one of her favorite tactics, and she couldn't imagine anyone agreeing with her without an argument. But as she examined the discussion from other angles, she realized there was nothing to be gained by pretending to give in. The Duke of Trent was not trying to manipulate her or to get her to agree to something distasteful.

"Yes, unless there is another matter you'd like to discuss," he said.

Emma tried to think of a topic, but nothing came to mind. She didn't know why she was so reluctant to end their talk, but for some inexplicable reason she was. She recalled the heavy expression on his face when he was deep in contemplation moments before. What had he been thinking of to look so? She wanted to ask but knew that wouldn't be the thing. One does not tell a man that his beautiful kisses meant nothing one moment and then ask what was on his mind the next. She had that much sense at least.

"No, there's nothing I'd like to talk about," she said. "But I think I'd like to stay out here for a moment longer, if you don't mind."

It was on the tip of his tongue to tell her that he minded very much. It was not the thing for a young lady to be out on the balcony alone, where she was vulnerable to all sorts of bounders and cads. Anything could happen out there and no one be the wiser. In fact, anything just did. But the duke only nodded. The Harlow Hoyden's behavior was no longer his concern. The impulse to protect her from harm or scorn was still there, but he had no right to it. She was once again her parents' problem or her brother's or even Sarah's, but she was not his. The sooner he got used to that, the better.

Trent bowed and left Emma sitting there on the balcony with a confused look on her face. He'd known what she was thinking—it was all there on her face for anyone to read—and under different circumstances would have been amused by it. But now it only saddened him and all he wanted to do was get out of there. He returned to the ballroom long enough to say his good-byes and find Pearson. He had a bottle of very fine brandy at home waiting to be consumed.

Emma watched Trent walk away with an awful ache in the pit of her stomach. Although she couldn't quite put her finger on it, she had the strangest feeling that something momentous had just happened. Something momentous had just happened—and she missed it.

She knew her behavior had been for the best. Even if she had given in to her weakest feelings and admitted that their moment in the carriage had meant something—and it did mean something to her—no good would come of it. Emma would not find her own happiness at the expense of her sister's. And she wasn't convinced that happiness lay with Trent. He was dashing and charming and a wonderful, trustworthy friend, but he was also a man about town. His behavior and beliefs were commensurate with the behavior and beliefs of every other man who lived in London. It was acceptable for a man to be unfaithful. It is within his rights to keep a mistress. Emma knew she would chafe under such conditions. She couldn't maintain the comfortable fiction of ignorance, as she was expected to do, especially if she were to marry Trent. Her heart could not bear his betrayal and her self-respect would not allow it. She would have to divorce him or take him and his mistress to task in public or something equally scandalous that would have her family forever frowning on her with disapproval. No, it was better this way. It might hurt for a little while, but Emma was convinced that the pain would eventually go away. If he and Lavinia eventually made a match of it, then she would be happy for them. She was a grown woman who was in control of her life. She would not be done in by so meager a thing as love.

CHAPTER NINE

Although Emma never said anything to the contrary, Lavinia knew instantly that something disastrous had happened between her and Trent. She had seen them walk out onto the balcony together and return separately. When the duke had left she'd caught the defeated look on his face and tried to discover its cause. But try as she might to capture the duke's attention, he avoided her eyes with single-minded dedication. A few minutes later, he left the ball. He did not pause to say good-bye. Almost a half hour after this strange episode, Emma returned. For all intents and purposes, she looked exactly the same as she had earlier, but Vinnie could swear that something was different now. Emma had changed on some imperceptible level.

Vinnie didn't expect her to talk about Trent during the carriage ride home because Sir Waldo was with them, but as soon as he said good night, she prepared herself for a barrage of questions. It never came. Instead, Emma complimented the food and the music and the decorations. She had a nice thing to say about everything, except Trent. She had nothing to say about Trent. When Vinnie herself had tried to raise the issue, she was left high and dry. Upon hearing his name, Emma yawned widely and excused herself.

In the morning, Emma looked well rested and healthy. She partook voraciously of breakfast and chatted mindlessly through the entire meal. Vinnie didn't know what to make of this. She had expected listlessness and a chalky appearance like the last time. That Emma seemed so untroubled troubled her sister greatly, and she wrote to Trent requesting an interview. Vinnie knew better than to try to learn anything from her sister. The duke had been extremely helpful and good-humored on other occasions. She assumed he would be so now, but a note came back from his secretary informing her that his grace was out of town on business. She wrote back asking when his return was anticipated, but the unsatisfying reply was imprecise. He was expected back anytime in the next four weeks.

Now Lavinia felt deep concern. That her sister was acting oddly by not acting oddly was only to be expected but for the duke to behave in unusual ways was a twist that Vinnie had not foreseen, and it made her cross. She relied on him to be the sensible one. What could have sent him off for four weeks in the middle of the season? She considered the very real possibility that some great emergency had called him away but quickly dismissed it. The duke would not have left under those circumstance without a note. No, for him to disappear like this meant that Emma did something very stupid. Vinnie racked her brain for an answer. Again and again she came back to the Northrup ball and the defeated look on the duke's face. She recalled the determination with which the duke had tried to get an audience with Emma. The Northrup affair was the first chance he'd had to speak privately with her. Vinnie wondered what he'd wanted to talk to her about. Could it have been an offer of marriage? No, she dismissed, even Emma would not be such a fool to turn down an offer from a man like Trent.

Or could she?

Vinnie thought about her sister and how she had always been adamant about never marrying. Although

Vinnie respected Emma's convictions, she hadn't really expected her to stick to them, not when confronted with a prospect. It was one thing to toss away marriage as an abstract idea and quite another when a man was attached to the offer. *But this is Emma,* Vinnie reminded herself. *Emma, who never does things like other people.*

Having come to the conclusion that Emma must have rejected the duke, Vinnie turned her thoughts to Trent. She could understand her sister's behavior but what explanation could there be for his? The Duke of Trent was not the sort of man to run away without provocation. He was an experienced man of the world who had courted a great many experienced ladies. Surely he could overcome one green girl's fears? He knew her well enough to choose the right words, to assure her that when two people love each other marriage was a sort of freedom. Emma was a passionate creature and could never deny his heart. All he had to do was tell her what was in it. How could he have botched it so thoroughly?

Sitting at the escritoire, Vinnie made a vow to interfere one last time. If she had misread the situation and Emma and Trent were not fated, then so be it. But she must first hear it from the duke. He must convince her that he was *not* in love with Emma. She would gladly abandon the field under those conditions. But if there was some misunderstanding between them, she would not rest until it was sorted out. She couldn't let her two favorite people throw away their one chance at happiness. Happiness was too rare an animal to play fast and loose with.

She chose the wording of her letter carefully, assuring him it was a matter of great importance. She purposely kept the details vague, hoping that the duke's curiosity as much as his concern would bring him to her doorstep. And she was reasonably confident that he'd be turning up on her doorstep soon. Trent was too much of a gentleman to ignore a lady's cry for help and would respond instinctively. In a few days time, she would have him in the drawing room, and she would sit him down and tell him about Emma's fears of marriage. No doubt he would renew his suit.

Vinnie signed the letter, put it in the post and went about her daily business, confident that in a little while everything would be nicely sorted out.

Emma stayed close to home in the days following the Northrup ball. While Sarah and Vinnie were out shopping, she spent hours with Roger talking about the war in France and their childhood and favorite authors. Emma left her collection of Sir Walter Scott adventures for her brother, and when she observed that he hadn't touched them, she began reading them aloud. Although this was a new experience for Emma, she had a knack for it. She read long passages without ever once losing her place, and she had a variety of voices to call upon. Roger carelessly remarked that her talent would come in handy when she had children, and Emma chose that moment to excuse herself. Roger did not notice that anything was the matter.

As long as something did not remind her of Trent, Emma was as happy and content as she'd ever been. During those long hours by Roger's bedside, she had convinced herself that nothing had changed. But if something made her think of him—and this did not require much, for his name need not be mentioned—she would be overcome by an almost uncontrollable feeling of sadness. Sometimes it took all her strength to return to her room before the tears began slipping down her cheeks. Emma was not used to tears and only gave herself a further disgust by indulging them.

She knew the problem was inactivity, but she was trapped. It was the middle of the season and no one would countenance her returning to Hill Crest Park, where she could take her horse, Titan, on blistering rides through the fields. Never one to be idle in the best of times, Emma longed now for an occupation. She would no longer interfere with Vinnie's business—at least not for the time being. She would observe from a quiet distance her courtship with Trent, but she wouldn't do anything to further it. She admitted there was only so much a concerned sister could do, and she resolved to be more supportive of Vinnie's choices, assuming she made the right ones. If the plan with Trent did not work out, she would devise another one. But not for another few months yet. She would wait until they were back in the country, where things were clearer and less complicated. Once they were back at Hill Crest it would all make sense. They still had seven months until the wedding. Anything could happen in seven months.

Checking in on Roger now, Emma was disappointed to see that he was sleeping. She would have preferred company than to be alone with her thoughts, but she knew sleep was the best thing for him. His recovery had been going smoothly, and the doctor had just yesterday pronounced Roger healthy enough to get out of bed. He had spent much of the early morning downstairs in the dining room taking breakfast with his family. It had clearly worn him out.

She decided to go to the study, to read quietly by the fire. One was rarely disturbed in the study, and she chose a large wingback chair facing the window. It was an unusually sunny day in London, and she could hear the sound of birds chirping. She smiled, curled up in the chair and started to read.

Emma passed many undisturbed hours in this fashion and when she heard the door to the room open, she furrowed her brow in annoyance. She planned on doing the polite thing and announcing her presence immediately, but when she caught Sir Waldo's reflection in the glass window, she held her tongue. She was in no mood to be mistaken for Lavinia this afternoon. She curled up into a ball, so that Windbag wouldn't see her blond tresses from above the chair and waited for him to leave. Once he had assured himself that his fiancée was not here, he'd look elsewhere. Sir Windbag was not the sort of man who liked quiet introspective afternoons in deserted studies.

But the next sound Emma heard was not of a figure departing but of a drawer opening. Emma assumed he was looking for writing paper, and she wished he'd get on with it. Really, if it was writing paper he was looking for, he needn't have come so far. There were plenty of note cards in the escritoire in the drawing room. Impatient now, Emma silently shifted positions and curled her head around the side of the chair. She saw the baron flipping through a file and wondered what he was about. Her family's private documents were none of Windbag's business. When he took a document, folded it up and stuck it into his coat, she could barely choke down a shout of protest. Really, the gall of the man was insupportable. She herself had rifled through his private papers but had the decency not to take a thing.

The baron returned the folder to its drawer, and to Emma's amazement, he locked the cabinet. She stayed in her knotted position until she was sure that he was gone and would not return. Then she straightened her stiff arms and legs and ran to the drawer to try to open it herself. It was locked. *How dare he have our key?* she thought, irate at this development. *And how dare he steal from us!* The truly baffling thing for Miss Harlow was Windbag's motivation. Why would he be poking around in their things and what could they possibly have that he'd want? Her own late-night prowling had been spurred on by a desire to discredit him. Why would *he* want to discredit the Harlows? Even if he was searching for a reason to jilt Vinnie, she could not condone it. What right did that pompous jackanapes have to end an engagement with her far superior sister?

Emma decided there was only one course of action open to her. She would not know more until she had laid eyes on the paper he had stolen. There were two options. She could get her hands on the sheet now, while it was still in her house, or she could wait until Windbag brought it home and put it in his file cabinet. The latter approach was clearly the less attractive one: It required a greater amount of risk and offered no guarantee of success. There was no assuming that he'd file the document right away. It could remain in his jacket pocket for several days, and she was not foolhardy enough to try to invade his dressing room. There was nothing for it. She would have to look at the document today, right this minute. She could not take the chance of his leaving with it.

Straightening her hair and flattening the wrinkles from her dress, for Vinnie would never appear in public in a wrinkled dress, she left the study in search of Sir Waldo. She found him in the front parlor standing by a window.

He smiled in greeting. "Ah, there you are, " he said, coming to take her hands. Emma was confused by this show of affection, but she played along, grasping his sweaty palms without a word a complaint. "I was just about to take my leave. Ludlow said you were away from home."

"Ludlow was confused," she said. "I was visiting with Roger."

"Ah, yes, young Roger. I trust he's recovering well?"

"Very nicely," answered Emma, wondering if she'd have the courage to follow through with her hastily conceived plan. When she had entered the room, she'd had no thought as to how she would achieve her goal. Part of her had hoped that he'd taken off his jacket, thus making the task an easy one. But the room was cool and Windbag wasn't the sort to undress in another's parlor. However, the hand holding had given her an idea. "We expect he'll be participating in the social whirl again by the end of the month."

"Good. Very good," he said, squeezing her hands. "Well, I should be going then."

"Going, Sir Waldo? But I only just got here," she said with a pout.

If Sir Waldo had known either of the Harlow sisters better he would've been suspicious of a pout. However, he only laid a comforting hand on her cheek. "Lavinia, I know you're fond of me, but you mustn't be disappointed if I can't spend much time with you. I'm a man of business and have many commitments. And you are to be the wife of a politician.

If my career is to advance at all, we must both be ready to make sacrifices, you most of all because you are a woman and it is in your nature to sacrifice. Whereas I must always—"

Emma laid her lips on his and kissed him. She couldn't help herself. She would have done anything to avoid hearing yet another speech on the duties of a wife, even this repulsive chore. A shocked Windbag held himself stiff for a few seconds before relaxing. Then he began taking over the kiss, sticking his tongue so forcefully down Emma's throat that she thought she'd choke. But no matter. She managed to get her hands on the letter. Then she freed her lips and said, "Hug me, Sir Waldo, for you have been gone such a long time."

Too full of himself to question this strange speech, Windbag reached his pudgy arms around her and held her close. "There, there, Lavinia. You are an emotional child and given to freakish starts. I will cure you of that. The wife of a politician does not have the luxury of freakish starts..."

He went on in the same vein, but Emma was not listening; she was reading the purloined letter over his shoulder. It was on the same stationery as the other letters, the ones she'd found in his study. This message was equally cryptic, speaking of water temperatures and expected fog, but this time Emma wasn't taken in. She knew this was not some innocent communication of no importance. Although she didn't know what it was about and hadn't the least idea what Roger could possibly have to do with any of it, she felt positively that the message was coded. She did not know what it meant, but it was obvious to her that Windbag did. What was its importance?

She carefully returned the letter to his pocket, disguising her movements as an appreciative exploration of her future husband's arms. "You are so handsome, Sir Waldo," she said, batting her lashes at him so that he wouldn't see the disgust in her eyes.

"And you are just right, Lavinia. You are not too pretty to be a distraction and yet pretty enough to impress other men. You are a credit to me," he said, bringing his lips down on hers again.

Emma knew she was tougher than most men and women, but this was something she could not go through a second time. She turned her cheek and accepted a wet peck from him. "Didn't you say you were busy? I don't want to take you away from your commitments. The last thing I want to be is a distraction."

"Dear Lavinia, you couldn't if you tried, so don't worry yourself on that point," he said tenderly.

Emma simpered and preened and waved fondly when he looked back at her one last time. When the door to the drawing room was shut, she ran to the window and watched him climb into his carriage. She had to think fast. What should she do next? It occurred to her that the wisest thing would be to climb up those stairs and confront Roger. Whatever was going on, he was knee-deep in it, but she decided against it. His wound was still fresh, and Nurse and Sarah would not thank her for getting him riled up. And really, in his condition what could he do? He might try to ride to the rescue and harm himself further. No, she would leave Roger out of this.

She tossed on a pelisse and ran outside, assuring Ludlow that she didn't need the carriage. With Windbag about to turn the corner, she didn't have much time to lose. She followed on foot for two blocks, and then hailed a hackney when it became clear that foot power wasn't sufficient. "I want you to follow that coach there with the red-and-blue crest, but I don't want you to get too close. He mustn't know that we are following him."

"Ye suspect him of nasty doings, do ye?" said the driver with an understanding nod. "These 'usbands are all the same, untrustworthy as dogs. Don't ye worry. I'll keep 'im in me sights. Ye can count on John Smith."

Emma climbed into the cab, much relieved by this confident claim. She'd never tailed anyone before, and it seemed a rather complicated endeavor, keeping a delicate balance of close but not too close. As they drove through London streets, Emma reviewed the information gathered so far. She knew now that Sir Waldo Windbourne was indeed the villain she had been calling him all along. The messages he had stolen had to do with Roger, Roger who'd never done a secretive thing in his life. She thought of his visits to France. He had claimed he was looking after investments for their mother, but Mama had denied this assertion. Emma had concluded that Mama was behaving in her usual forgetful manner, but what if she was wrong? What if Mama had spoken the truth? Why then had Roger gone to France?

The coach stopped and Emma looked out the window, vexed to see that they were across the street from Sir Windbag's town house. Damn and blast! She had dashed out of the house, most likely frightening Ludlow with the haste of her departure, and all for naught. She sat in the coach for several minutes, fuming over this development. It was just like Sir Windbag to waste her time.

She was about to tell the coachman to return her to her house when he quieted her with a hand and pointed across the street. Windbag was on the move again. Dressed for travel in leather breeches and a greatcoat, he was carrying a large suitcase. He climbed into his coach and was again off.

They followed him down to the docks, to an unsavory taproom with raucous laughter emanating from it. It was the last place a gently bred lady should be, but that didn't stop the Harlow Hoyden.

"Miss, ye shouldn't go in there," John Smith warned. "That not be a place for a lady such as yeself."

"I appreciate your concern, but it's a matter of utmost importance," she said, reaching in to her reticule and extracting money to pay him. "How much do I owe you?"

The coachman jumped down and accosted Emma. "What can ye about, waving yer money around like that? Ye not on Bond Street now."

"Excellent point, my good man," she said, surreptitiously counting out change. "Here you go. I would appreciate it if you would wait here for my return, but I understand if you choose to leave. You will, of course, be amply compensated."

He put his hand to his mouth to shush her and looked around. "Ye don't say things like 'amply compensated' down here, lass. Will ye never learn?"

"You are right, Mr. Smith. I must learn quickly. Now, before I go inside, tell me, will you be here when I return?"

The driver had serious concerns of her ever returning, but he assured her that he wouldn't move until she came out.

"Excellent," she said. "This shouldn't take long."

No, thought the coachman, it would not take long for the men inside to eat her alive.

Unaware of the coachman's pessimistic thoughts, Emma drew the hood over her blond head and opened the doorway. Though it was the middle of a sunny day in London, the interior of the taproom was dark. An unpleasant smell of cigars and alcohol and male sweat accosted her as soon as she stepped inside. Her eyes swept the room quickly, finding no trace of Sir Windbag. He had been only a few minutes ahead of her. Where could he have gone?

Emma decided that the bartender was the best person to ask, since he seemed to be more sober than the other fellows. However, before she could get to the bar, an arm reached out and tugged her against a rough chest.

"Lookee, here," growled a man with repellent breath. "Jim's gone an' found himself an angel." He removed her hood and began running his fingers through her smooth curls. "She feels like one."

The other man laughed. "She looks like one."

"And she smells like one," said a third man.

"But is she a devil in bed?" called a fourth man.

Although all talk had ceased in the tavern and every eye was on her, Emma was not afraid. She had dealt with a dozen lascivious men before and she would do so again. Of course, she thought, looking at the room full of large, dirty men, she had never dealt with a dozen all at once. "Unhand me, sir," she said, wishing she'd had the sense to bring her pistols. She looked around for a weapon. There was a knife on the table. Perhaps she could reach it.

"The angel wants to me unhand her," said the man called Jim scornfully. "But I'm not ready to. What you gonna do bout it?"

Emma stomped on his foot as hard as she could and reached for the knife. In seconds she had it around his fat neck. If he wanted to he could wrench it free from her hand before she did any harm, but she hoped he was too stupid to figure that out. The only true ally in the time of crisis was a clear head, and few people kept one when knives were pressed against their throats. The room was silent and everyone waited to see what Jim's next move would be. No one was more interested than Emma.

"I'd let her go if I were you," said a cool, smooth voice from the back of the room. "That there is the Duke of Trent's lass, and even if she didn't have a knife to your throat, you'd still be in an untenable position. You don't want the duke coming down here and making trouble. They say he knows what to do with his fists."

Emma watched Jim digest this information. The ornery look was gone from his face, and he relaxed his grip. "Sorry, miss," he muttered. "Didn't realize."

"Not a problem, sir," she said, pocketing the knife, although she felt reasonably safe now. Then she walked over to the table of the man who had helped her. She offered her hand. "Mr. Squibbs, how lovely to see you again."

He shook her hand and insisted she take a seat. "I would love to sit and chat, Mr. Squibbs, but I don't have time. I came here following a gentleman and I'm fearful of losing him."

"Ah," he said, "a round man of medium height with a mole on his cheek?"

"Yes, that's he precisely. Where did he go?"

Squibbs gestured to the staircase to the right of the bar. "Went up there." Emma thanked him for his help and moved to stand, but he stopped her. "You can't go up there."

"But I must. It's a matter of utmost importance. Please do not stop me."

"But the duke will have my head if I let you."

"How do you know about the duke?" Emma asked, thinking that *ton* gossip would not reach this dirty corner of the city.

"He searched me out. He wanted me to promise to send him a message if ever I was to see you wandering the docks again."

"I should hope you told him no," she said, offended that the duke would conspire behind her back.

"Miss Harlow, when the Duke of Trent asks you to do something, you do it," he said, almost as if explaining a simple mathematical equation to a small child. "He's not a man one wants to make an enemy of."

Emma took exception to this line of reasoning but knew that to argue would be to waste more time. She shrugged, said excuse me and walked to the stairs. Mr. Squibbs followed, muttering under his breath. When she got to the top of the staircase, she was confronted with four doors. Blast it, she thought, why must there be four doors? She put her ear up to the first one but couldn't hear anything except muffled moans. Was someone getting hurt in there?

Mr. Squibbs pushed her aside, took out one of his special hearing devices and held it up to the door. "Not that one," he said, turning pink.

"Are you sure? I thought I heard—"

"Not that one," he insisted more forcefully and moved on to the second door. He listened for a few seconds and then handed the ear pieces to Emma.

She listened. It was indeed Sir Windbag's voice, only he didn't sound quite so pompous now.

"...the names of key English spies who have infiltrated the emperor's army. I will take this information to my contact, who will deliver it to the emperor's most trusted generals. Napoléon will be free and England will be conquered.

"This is helpful news, my friend. I'll go tell Devalier of what we have learned," answered a voice she'd never before heard, though she recognized the faint French accent. "You leave for the white cliffs?"

White cliffs? thought Emma, puzzling for only a moment. "Dover," she muttered under her breath.

"Good, good. Then I wish you God's speed," he said, walking toward the door.

Emma took off the listening device in a panic. Where were they to hide? She pulled Mr. Squibbs into the far corner and kissed him. A large, tall man, Mr. Squibbs hid her entirely from view. She heard Windbag snort in amusement at two people behaving so indecorously in a public hallway. Then he was gone.

"You must accept my apologies, Mr. Squibbs, for treating you so cavalierly," she said when she freed his lips. "I could think of no other way to disguise my presence."

"Not at all, miss," he said, putting her at ease, "only I'd prefer it if ye don't mention it to the duke."

Although Emma knew it was no business of the duke's whom she kissed, she assured him that she wouldn't say a word. "Now I must go. The future welfare of England depends upon it."

Squibbs looked at her oddly for a moment at this grandiose statement and then told her to stay put. "Let me make sure he's gone." He returned presently, informing her that his carriage just pulled away.

"Excellent. I shall take my leave." She handed his listening device to him and laid a soft kiss on the cheek in appreciation. "I thank you for your help, Mr. Squibbs, and England thanks you."

Squibbs blushed, said it had been nothing, really, and insisted on escorting her to her carriage. It wasn't a safe neighborhood for her to be walking around in.

John Smith was pleased to see her. "Glad ye okay, miss."

Emma climbed into the carriage and bid Mr. Squibbs

good day. "And I don't want you sending the duke a letter apprising him of my movements. First of all, it is none of his business. And second of all, I'm going directly there myself."

Squibbs thought this was precisely the sort of nonsensical statement only the quality were capable of and wished her well.

Because it had worked so well last time, Emma asked to speak with the dowager duchess. However, instead of being greeted in the drawing room by the duke, she was confronted with the great lady herself

Oh, what a bother, thought Emma, crossly. *This is what I get for observing the propriety on the eve of England's destruction.*

"Miss Harlow, to what do I owe the pleasure?" asked the duchess, polite as always but with a confused look on her face as she took in Emma's plain dress, not at all the thing one wore to pay social calls.

To what indeed? Emma's mind raced, searching for a convincing lie. "Mama sent me, to inquire after a scarf of hers, a blue silk scarf that she had with her when we visited here last month for your lovely tea party. And it was such a lovely tea party, your grace. Mama and I talk about it all the time, asking ourselves why can't all afternoon parties be as lovely as yours."

"Organization is the key to all good social affairs," she intoned wisely. "A lot of the young ladies of the *ton* do not take the time to organize, and their parties suffer for it. Here, let me order us some tea and ask after your scarf. Blue, you say? I wonder why it has taken Margaret so long to realize she left it. She is usually a very keen observer when it comes to her possessions. She once lost a gold bracelet when we were in school together. She realized it was gone within ten minutes of its falling off, and she had the entire dormitory looking for it. I do believe I was the one to find it."

"It is because of Roger, your grace," she explained. "He has been, among other things, a constant distraction for her." If only that were true, thought Emma. In reality,

Mama had only been distracted once since his return, on her way to a card party at Lord Firth's.

"Oh, poor Roger," the duchess said, shaking her head sympathetically. "How is your brother getting on?"

As Emma spoke of Roger's recovery, she looked at the clock on the wall. How long would she have to visit with the duchess before she could ask to see her son? That brought an even larger question to mind: *Could* she ask to see her son? Emma could very well imagine the duchess coolly bidding her good-bye. "And how is Philip adapting to London?" she asked, introducing the topic of male relations and preparing to bring the relationship closer to home. "I recall your mentioning him the last time I was here."

"Philip is well, my dear. How nice of you to remember. Trent and I are not accustomed to having youthful exuberance in our midst, but we're holding up admirably."

There, thought Emma, she said his name first. "And the duke, how is he?"

The duchess tsk-tsked. "He's as vexing to his mother as always, disappearing from London without a by-your-leave."

"Then he's not here?" asked Emma, faintly. It had never occurred to her that he wouldn't be in town and ready to help her save the country.

"No, he hasn't been here for three days. I don't know what happened—" She broke off as a servant opened the door and motioned to the duchess. "What is it, Budge?"

"We can't locate a blue scarf," answered the woman before bowing and closing the door behind her.

"Oh, well," said Emma, standing up. She had no more time to waste. Windbag was probably a mile out of town by now. "I'm very sorry to have bothered you about it, your grace. Perhaps Mama is confused and only thought she wore the blue scarf. I will go home and check her dressing room. It's probably there."

The duchess smiled agreeably. "No need to apologize. These things happen all the time."

"You're very kind," she said. "Good day to you."

Emma had let the hack go, thinking when she arrived that she would be departing in one of the duke's coaches. But since the duke was out of town and had been for the past three days, she needed to flag down another conveyance. She was walking to the corner when she heard Philip call out.

"I say, Miss Harlow," he said from the top of the carriage, "where are you going?"

"I'm on my way home," she said, thinking of what she'd do next. Going home, getting the curricle and racing to Dover seemed like the most sensible thing. But there was always the risk that the coach wouldn't be available or that Sarah would interfere. She hated to waste more time. Windbag already had an hour's lead on her.

"Please let me escort you," he said, with more manners that she thought him capable of.

Emma agreed. Hiring a hackney might take ten or more minutes, minutes that she didn't have to spare. "Thank you, Philip," she said, after she'd climbed up next to him. "The dowager was just telling me that Trent is out of town. Do you know where he went?"

Philip shook his head. "I ain't saying my cousin's given to queer starts, cause he ain't. He's top o' the trees, but I've never seen him behave so as he did on Sunday morning. He gathered his things, took his man and left without a word to anyone. Apparently, there is an emergency at one of the estates, but the duchess don't know about it. She says if there were a real emergency then someone would've alerted her. I don't know how true *that* is, since the duke's the duke now and it's his business to be worrying about the estates."

Although he couldn't have known she'd have use for him, Emma cursed the duke and the emergency that took him out of town at such an inconvenient time. Just when she needed a trusted ally. She would not despair, of course. Going after Windbag alone was her only option, though she knew that her family would disapprove of the impropriety of it. Really, sometimes there were things more important than propriety. She *would* stop Windbag from delivering his evil message. She would not rest until England was safe.

Miss Harlow?"

She looked at Philip in surprise. "Yes?"

"Are you all right? I've been talking to you for five minutes, but you haven't acknowledged a word I've said. You've just been staring through me, like I'm invisible. Is there something the matter?" he asked, sensing that the duke's absence was a great source of distress for her. "I know I'm not my cousin, but I will gladly stand in his stead, if there is anything you need."

"That is very kind of you, Philip," she said, laying a hand over his. "You are a dear boy."

"I'm not a boy," he said vehemently. "I know I'm still young and that I don't got town polish like my cousin, but I'm no longer a boy. If there is some matter you need help with, I do wish you'd tell me. I would be honored to serve you."

Emma thought this was a lovely speech and upon hearing it decided that she would confide all in Philip— confide all and take him with her. "I will tell you all directly but for the moment, make a right at that corner and change directions. We are heading toward Dover."

"What?" asked Philip, so shocked that he loosened up on the reins and missed the turn. "We're going to Dover?"

"We are only *heading* toward Dover," Emma said, pointing to the next turn. "We shouldn't have to go all the way. There are still several hours yet until dark. We will catch him by nightfall, Philip, and be back in time for dinner. Don't you worry. Nobody'll even notice we were gone. "

Philip wasn't worried about a thing. He had the sense to realize that the Harlow Hoyden was embarking on another escapade and that this time he had a front-row seat. Just wait until he told his friends about this. "Why are we heading to Dover?" he asked.

"To save England, my lad," she said, folding her hands in her lap and anticipating her next meeting with the insufferable, traitorous Sir Windbag. "To save England."

CHAPTER TEN

In the early hours following Lord Northrup's ball, when he was still deep into his cups, the duke took it into his head to leave London. He had no one to talk over his idea with—Pearson had left two hours before—and no one to dissuade him from taking this course of action. His valet had looked very concerned by this hasty decision, but as it was not a matter of dress or appearance, he kept his peace. He'd been with the duke for ten years now and knew the best way to hold on to his post was to tie an impeccable Windswept knot and to never question the master's decisions. He did manage, however, to deter Trent from driving the coach himself.

The duke dashed off an illegible note to his mama, telling her he'd gotten word of an emergency at Pembroke Hall, threw a few articles of clothing into a leather bag and left London. By that time the sun was starting to rise in the east.

The duke slept for the entire ride down to the hall, and when he got there he buried himself in his study, leaving a trail of confused servants behind him. They were eager, if a bit surprised, to serve him, and their willingness irritated Trent. He wished to be left alone. Although upon sobering, he regretted the impulse that had taken him away from London and Emma, he quickly realized that it was for the best. A few weeks away would give him a chance to get her out of his system. If he'd stayed, he would've no doubt given in to the desire to see her, a desire that was constant. Here he had the luxury of distance. Even if he was overwhelmed by desire, he could do nothing about it.

He had not been home for several months, and as always there were repairs to be made to the estate. There were no emergencies, of course, but there was certainly enough to keep him busy for a fortnight at least. He scribbled another note to his mother—legible this time—explaining his absence. He did not mention Emma, for the dowager didn't need to know about that, but he wrote of important work that needed to be done. He doubted that his mother would believe his excuse, but he also knew that she would never guess at the real reason. She would simply dismiss it as the strange behavior of a gentleman. No doubt his father had done something similar at least once in his life.

Lavinia's note arrived on the second day. Seeing the name of Harlow on the envelope, he'd thought for one beautiful fleeting moment that Emma had written to beg him to return to town. When he saw that it was from her sister, he curled it into a ball and threw it to the other side of the room. It lay there on the floor, a light blue piece of writing paper on a dark red carpet, for nearly the whole day. After dinner, Trent returned to the library and saw the letter exactly where he'd left it. "Damn servants," he muttered, picking it up.

He stared at it for several minutes before gently unfolding it. He read. "Dear Trent: I know whatever it is that has taken you from town must be very important to cause you to leave at this very moment. Something has happened with Emma that I wish very much to talk to you, my dear friend, about. She has done something extremely rash and, I think, ill conceived. It is my belief that you could help save her before it's too late. Fondly, Vinnie."

The duke lay his head back and sighed heavily. As

much as he wanted to tell Vinnie to go to the devil, he knew he could not ignore the summons, not when it had something to do with Emma. What mess had she gotten herself into this time? He thought of the words Vinnie applied to her behavior: *ill conceived* and *rash*. When had the Harlow Hoyden *not* done something ill conceived and rash? The blasted woman believed she was invincible, he thought, recalling some of her stunts. Fearing the worst, he looked outside and cursed the darkness. He would not return to London the way he left it: shabbily and without a care. He would wait till morning and depart Pembroke Hall then. Vinnie's tone had been forceful but not panicked, leading him to assume that the danger to Emma wasn't immediate. Whatever needed his attention could wait until the afternoon.

The duke was later in returning to London than he had expected. Thanks to a particularly deep pothole outside of Ashtonhurst, they had to pull into a posting house and fix a wheel. The duke passed a frustrating two hours trying to digest stale bread and read a three-day-old newspaper. Try as he might to distract them, his thoughts kept returning to Emma. He'd spent sixteen hours now with the news that something was wrong, and the nonchalant attitude he had felt upon first learning of it had deserted him. A sense of panic set in, as he pictured all sorts of horrible things, from her accepting a proposal from Carson to her murdering Sir Windbag. During the trip into London, the duke was forced to admit that his imagination was more vivid than he'd ever suspected.

He went straight to Emma's house, rather than waste time stopping at home to change. It was not quite the thing to make social calls in clothes covered with travel dust, but as far as the duke was concerned, he wasn't making a social call.

Ludlow let him in and directed him to the parlor to wait. The house was quiet and still in the late afternoon, and the duke wondered if Emma was near. Since it was too early to be out for the evening and too late to be making routine social calls or shopping, he assumed she was. Feeling calm for the first time that day, he called himself a bloody fool for being so smitten with a woman. Ah, but what a woman, he thought, recalling the episode in the carriage. Perhaps he had given up too easily. Emma might not be in love with him now, but he was the Duke of Trent, not some lovesick greenhead from the middle of nowhere. He would use his skill and experience to make her love him.

These thoughts cheered him considerably, and he was imagining his success when Vinnie came in. "Miss Harlow, how lovely it is—"

"Thank God you are come," she said, throwing herself into his arms and sobbing. "She has disappeared!"

He grabbed her by the arms and forced her to look at him. "Emma?" he asked, trying to push down the lump of fear that was rising in his throat.

"Emma," said Vinnie, wiping her eyes with an embroidered handkerchief. "Don't worry, I will get ahold of myself, your grace, for womanly hysterics serve no good. It was just that I was so overwhelmingly *relieved* to learn you are here. You're so dependable and resourceful, and you'd never let anything happen to Emma."

"No, I'd never let anything happen to her. Now tell me what has occurred," he demanded.

"I don't know what happened to her. Ludlow saw her leave the house around one this afternoon. She went by foot and didn't take an abigail. That was hours and hours ago, and she has yet to return," explained Vinnie. "Emma might be reckless and a little thoughtless, but she's never cruel. She would never have worried us like this unless something awful had happened." Fresh tears started to run down her cheeks. "She thinks she is invincible, Trent. She has always thought so. But she is not and just because nothing bad has ever happened to her, it doesn't mean that it never will. Oh,

I fear the scrape she has gotten herself into this time. What if she's hurt and lying helpless somewhere? Or what if she's been kidnapped?"

There was no catastrophe that Vinnie could list now that the duke himself hadn't listed hours before at the posting house. "We must stay calm and think this through. Our panicking will not help Emma. Now, where is Sarah?"

"She's upstairs with Roger. We thought it was best if we didn't tell him. Although his recovery is going well, we saw no reason to tell him since he couldn't help and might make himself sick with worry. Make *himself* sick with worry!" Vinnie laughed scornfully. "I can barely breathe I am so full of worry."

The duke knew exactly how she felt. "All right, Vinnie, I'm going to leave—" When she would have protested, he forestalled her. "No, let me finish. I haven't been home yet, and it's possible that she left word for me there." The duke knew it was a long shot, but he couldn't stop remembering how she'd called him her most trusted ally. On that occasion she hadn't taken a coach or an abigail. "If she didn't know I was out of town, then she might have been calling on me this afternoon. She has done so before."

For the first time in hours, Vinnie relaxed. "I don't think she knew you were gone. I certainly didn't tell her."

The duke nodded abruptly and gathered his things.

"What if she hasn't been there?"

He looked her squarely in the eyes. "Then we start asking questions. People do not disappear, Vinnie, they don't. If she left on foot, then she probably hired a hack. I will find that hack if I have to talk to every coachman in London. Do not fear, I will find her."

"I'm coming with you," she said, following him into the foyer, determined not to be left behind. "*We* will find her."

"Someone must stay here," he said reasonably, afraid that Emma's sister would slow him down. "What if she comes back?"

"Sarah is here." She put on her pelisse and gloves. "I'm going."

"Very well," he conceded because he didn't have time to argue. "Ludlow, tell Mrs. Harlow that Miss Harlow has gone for a drive with Lord Trent."

The drive to Trent's house was tense and quiet, both of the carriage's occupants wrapped up in their separate thoughts. Now that she had calmed down enough to think clearly, Vinnie wondered why it hadn't occurred to her to turn to Sir Waldo in her time of need. He was her fiancé, the man she had committed herself to for life. She didn't see him in a heroic way, of course, but he was steadfast and dependable. Weren't those two of his most valued traits, as he reminded her frequently? She could just hear the speech now. "Steadfast and dependable, Miss Harlow, that's what makes a successful politician. That and a wife who is also steadfast and dependable. A political life is not an easy one, and only we who are steadfast and dependable are suited to it."

He does repeat himself an awful lot, doesn't he? she thought, not for the first time. She'd been having lots of thoughts in the same vein about Sir Waldo and began to fear for the future of their relationship. The happy flush of romance was gone, leaving Vinnie with the awful feeling that she had made a terrible mistake. She now recognized his easygoing conversational style, which had first attracted her, for what it was: repetitive speeches about himself. She realized that the good work he wished to do was not for the benefit of the world but for himself. He did not see a wife as an equal; he saw her as an appendage—a not too pretty, not too ugly appendage. She was starting to suspect that he was intimidated by her brain power. Not only did he not want her to pursue interests outside of his, but he also did not want her to have original ideas. Original ideas seemed to frighten him, which only amused Vinnie and convinced her that they were not well suited. Surely a wife should not mock her husband.

But it was not only because of Sir Waldo that Vinnie was reconsidering. The last few weeks had been a revelation to her. She now realized that she had something to say that even the most glittering member of the *ton* was interested in, and she had the Duke of Trent to thank for that. He had made her realize that her ideas were good and worth listening to. Although their initial interaction had been sparked by Emma's devious scheme, their friendship had developed on its own. She now counted him among her favorite people.

The carriage pulled up to the duke's town house, and she was forced to cease her woolgathering. The duke helped her down and escorted her to the door. Although his return was unexpected, Caruthers greeted him with news of a visitor.

"Your grace, there is a…uh-hem…gentleman waiting to see you in the parlor, by the name of Squibbs. I told him you were away from home, but he insisted on waiting."

"Good job, Caruthers," the duke said, smiling. "Just the man I wanted to see." He took Vinnie's hand and squeezed it reassuringly. "Mr. Squibbs is an associate of your sister's. Good or bad, he'll know something."

Mr. Squibbs stood when he heard the door opening, and as soon as he saw Miss Harlow, he said defensively, "Now, miss, don't get angry at me. I told you I'd send word. I made a promise."

The duke approached the large, tall man with his arm extended and a wide smile on his face. "Don't worry, Squibbs, this is the other Miss Harlow. They are twins, you see."

"You mean there are two of them?" he asked, appalled by the very idea.

"Not quite," answered Vinnie. "We are alike only on the surface."

"What she means to say," explained the duke, "is that she doesn't go down to the docks to learn how to crack safes." At Vinnie's astonished look, Trent said, "I'll fill you in later. In the meantime, meet Mr. Archibald Squibbs. He is, as I said, an associate of your sister's. I made his acquaintance little more than a week ago, and at that time, he promised to let me know if your sister visited the docks again. I can only assume that his presence means she has. Have faith, Vinnie, we are about to learn what happened to Emma."

"She was at the docks again but alone this time. She didn't bring that hulking giant with her."

"Hulking giant?" asked Lavinia.

The duke flashed her a quick look. "Sylvester."

"Ah."

"Like I said, she came down alone. I think it was an unplanned visit, because she didn't have her pistol on her, and when one of the men grabbed her, she had to use the knife on the table to free herself."

"One of the men grabbed her?" the duke said in a deceptively calm voice.

Squibbs was not fooled. "Yeah, he did, but she handled herself like a regular goer. She had a knife at his throat quicker than you could say Johnny Jacksaw. I was damn proud of the lass. But anyway, she was there following a man and soon as the trouble was over, we went upstairs to find him. He and a confederate were in a room talking so I gave her one of my special listening devices and she eavesdropped on the conversation. I don't know what they were talking about but whatever it was, it got her all riled up. And when the man came out suddenly, she ki— She hid. Then she waited for him to leave and got back into her hired cab."

"Is that all? Think, man, did she say anything at all that revealed her plan?"

"Nothing, your grace. She thanked me and said that England thanked me, which made no sense. Then she was off. I came straight here to tell you. The man at the door tried to convince me you was out of town, but I knew better. Archibald Squibbs isn't taken in so easily."

"Thank God," said the duke, thinking that Archibald

Squibbs would be rewarded handsomely for his tenacity.

"This man she was following," said Lavinia. "Did you get a look at him?"

Squibbs nodded. "Medium height, round build, mole on his cheek."

"Beady eyes? Impossibly small lips?" she added.

"Yes, never seen a blighter with lips that small. How does he eat?"

She looked at Trent. "Sounds like Sir Waldo. It would make sense. She's convinced he's a villain."

Perhaps he is, thought the duke, recollecting Emma's thanks on behalf of the country. Could it be? "Are you positive she said nothing else—a destination perhaps? When she was listening at the door, did she say anything? Did she tell you what the conversation was about?"

"No, she didn't say— Wait, she muttered something when she was listening. What was it?" Squibbs closed his eyes and concentrated. It had sounded like clover. "She might have said Dover, your grace."

"Dover," he repeated, trying to make sense of this riddle. If what he suspected was true, then Dover would fit. But the idea was almost too ridiculous to consider. Sir Waldo Windbag a French spy? Trent tried to imagine the little round man conspiring against England, but the image was too amusing and he smiled. No, if anyone was up to no good it was Emma, who had come to the outrageous conclusion because she wanted to. Surely she had misunderstood what she heard from a willingness to believe the worst of her sister's fiancé. He had to admit that French spy was pretty good. If the man were rotting in Newgate then he would not be able to marry her sister.

"Dover?" said Lavinia. "Trent, what is she about?"

Trent decided to keep his thoughts about Windbourne to himself. "I think your sister is on the road to Dover."

"But how? She did not take the carriage. The horses are all in the stable. Oh, vexing girl. I bet she took the public stage or even went by post. She does like to travel by hack. Do you think she hired one to take—"

"No, my dear. No London hack would take one to Dover. She must have gone by stage." He returned his attention to Mr. Squibbs, who was nodding in agreement with this statement.

"Ye are right, your grace. She probably took the stage."

"Mr. Squibbs," the duke said, extracting a pile of notes from his purse, "do let me reimburse you for your trouble."

"No trouble, milord, but thank ye anyway."

"Well then, let me reward you for your help. Miss Harlow here was frantic with worry until moments ago. Surely that's worth something." He tried to hand over the money again.

"No reward is necessary. I'm as concerned about the lass as ye are and don't want to see 'er come to harm." Mr. Squibbs placed his hat on his head and bowed to the duke. "She's a spirited one, milord, and ye must keep a close eye on 'er if ye want to keep 'er safe."

The duke did not need a safecracker from the East End to tell him that. "You say that as if it's an easy thing, Squibbs. You have no idea what a challenge it is."

Squibbs bowed. "I suspect ye are up to it, milord duke, I suspect ye are up to it."

The duke accepted the praise without further comment. He suspected he was up to it as well, but it would mean nothing if he didn't acquire the right to keep her safe. Emma was not yet his. Indeed, it was only a few days ago that he'd tried to resign himself to the fact that she never would be. Recent events had changed his thinking drastically.

Vinnie regarded the tall, large man who was her sister's associate. He was a frightening man to behold, with a large bluish yellow bruise on his left cheek, but it had not taken two minutes for her to realize he was a gentle giant. No wonder her sister had turned to him for advice on how to crack a safe. That part made sense. It was why her sister needed to crack a safe in the first place that continued to baffle her. Realizing that Mr. Squibbs' visit had saved them hours of possibly fruitless searching, she thanked him profoundly for his help with a soft kiss to his scarred cheek.

Squibbs simpered and blushed and muttered a thanks. Then he was out the door with a request that the duke send word to him when the lass was safely returned to London.

"Now what?" asked Vinnie, watching the duke's guarded face. He had a plan in mind, that she could tell, but it was unclear whether it included her or not. It would have to include her.

"We give chase. She can't have gotten far."

"Can't have gotten far?" Vinnie was not as complacent as Trent. "You forget who we are talking about. The Harlow Hoyden went from London to Newmarket in under four hours."

"Yes, but we've already decided she's taken the stage," he reminded her. "They travel at considerably slower speeds than your sister."

Vinnie laughed, genuinely amused even though she was still terribly distressed. "Come, your grace, if you really believe they got past Hyde Park before Emma insisted that the coachman hand the reins over to her then you do not know her as well as I thought you did."

"Vinnie, you devil, I was trying to put a brave face on it. If your sister hasn't made it to Dover and crossed over to France by now then I should be very surprised."

This was not something that had occurred to Lavinia, and her face paled as she contemplated the possibility. "You don't think that even she would be foolish enough to cross into a foreign country."

Even seeing her white face, the duke could not lie to her. "I would hope not, but I can't say for certain. Considering how vehemently she feels about Sir Windba—uh, Windbourne, she would confront Napoléon himself if it would prove that he was a villain."

Vinnie's shoulders sagged. "I was afraid of that. We should be going, no? The sooner we leave, the sooner we shall find her."

"Yes, let us depart immediately. Don't worry, Vinnie," the duke said, patting her hand in comfort, "we will find her before it's too late. I have every interest in seeing her returned to us without harm, for I intend to thrash her within an inch of her life for worrying us so."

Contemplating his passionate words, Vinnie thought again how perfect he was for Emma. "I suspect that thrashing her is the last thing you want to do to my sister," she said, mischievously.

The duke smiled. "Well, not quite the *last* thing, but it certainly isn't the first. Come, there's no reason to delay. The horses are ready."

They were walking down the path to the street when a figure cloaked in a black cape approached the duke. "There you are, Trent, been looking all over for you. Keeping close to home, are you?" Pearson said, a glint of humor in his eye. "The clubs haven't been the same since you stopped coming by. Ealing is an interesting companion when he's sober, but get a few drinks in him and he becomes deadly dull. He has the devil's own luck when it comes to cards. It's awful enough losing your blunt to a sober man but losing to a man who is three sheets to the wind? Not at all amusing, Trent."

"Sorry, old man, I've been out of town on business," explained the duke, unwilling to linger longer than necessary. "If you'll excuse us, Miss Harlow and I have an important errand that cannot wait. Look for me tomorrow at White's."

"Which Miss Harlow are you?" he asked, examining Lavinia for some clue to her identity. "Are you the one who was out riding with Cousin Philip today or the other one?"

"The other one," said Vinnie, a dimple appearing despite her intentions. His question was rude, but the questioner had such a charming smile and a handsome face she was unable to resist. "But I suspect that doesn't help you with your identification."

"True," said Pearson, "and since you have not stepped into the void to introduce yourself, I will continue to call you the other—"

His speech was cut off abruptly as the Duke of Trent grabbed him by the arms. "Pearson, you saw Emma today out driving with Philip?"

"Yes," he answered, perplexed by this treatment.

"Around what time was it?"

"I don't know."

"Think! Was it after one o'clock?"

"Had to be. Took tea with my mama at one. I was there for an hour, perhaps two. I'd say I saw them sometime after three. I assumed they were going to the park, since the hour was fashionable. Now that I think about it, they were going in the wrong direction for the park."

Trent gave his friend a hearty pat on the back. "Excellent, Pearson, you do not know what a helpful friend you have been. Miss Harlow and I must go now, but could you do me a tremendous favor and look in on Mrs. Sarah Harlow? Tell her that Vinnie and I are going to Dover and all shall be well soon. This is all in strictest confidence, of course, but I know you're trustworthy." The duke could tell that his friend was extremely curious as to what was going on. In order to preempt further discussion, he said, "I promise to tell you the whole of it when we return. There is nothing havey-cavey going on, I can assure you of that."

Pearson bit down further questions and agreed to the duke's request. It was not often that Trent asked something of him and it was the least he could do. Perhaps Mrs. Harlow could be persuaded to tell him what was going on.

"Very well, Trent. I will see you when you return. And you, the other Miss Harlow."

As soon as they were in the carriage, Vinnie said, "At least now we know how she travels and that she is not alone."

The duke gave her a thin smile. "I take little comfort in her choice of traveling companions. I somehow feel that Cousin Philip's presence complicates the matter rather than simplifies it."

They were a few miles out of town when Emma insisted Philip stop the coach.

"What's wrong?" he asked, concerned. "Are you feeling ill? Take a deep breath. I often find that deep breaths calm a disturbed stomach."

"I am not suffering from a motion ailment like a frail miss," she insisted, disgusted by the very idea. "I've simply had enough of your driving. Give them here." She stuck out her hands.

"What?"

"You might as well give me your gloves as well. I was in a rush when I left the house and didn't plan for every contingency."

"My gloves?" He looked at his hands, large and masculine, and then at her small fingers. "They'll never fit."

"They'll fit well enough. Now give me the reins and your gloves."

Philip handed both over with great reluctance. It was one thing to have an adventure with the Harlow Hoyden but quite another thing to have a scrap of a girl criticize your driving.

"Now pay attention," Emma ordered as she took the reins from her hesitant companion. The gloves were large and her fingers were indeed swimming in them, but she made do. One of her best traits was the ease with which she made do with most things. "There's no reason why you can't learn a thing or two about driving a team. Now we only have two horses here so there's really nothing to it. See how I am holding the reins? My fingers are relaxed."

"My fingers were relaxed," he muttered under his breath.

"Your fingers were not," she corrected. "You were clutching the reins as if your life depended on it. That might work in the city, where one never achieves a respectable speed, but here on the open road you must trust your horses to know what's best. These are Trent's, are they not?" she asked, admiring his choice in horseflesh.

"Yes," he answered, reluctantly observing how much more control over the horses she had than he.

"He does know a thing or two, doesn't he?" she said sadly. Trent not only had his pick of prime horseflesh but females as well.

"Yes," he said again. "And awful showy about it, too. He is always telling one how to go about it. Philip, do this. Philip, don't do that. Philip, in civilized society we don't pick up our dinner rolls and eat with our hands."

"He can be quite monstrous at times, can't he?" she asked, taking comfort in this unattractive trait and delving for others. If she could just discover enough disagreeable things about him, then perhaps she could get over this uncomfortable episode. She didn't have to love him if she didn't want to.

"Yes, the way he calls me a young puppy and takes me to task for talking about frogs with your sister-in-law, Sarah. In Yorkshire, I went about as I pleased, talking about frogs without anyone protesting."

Emma had to admit that some of Trent's criticisms were not far off the mark. Philip did have the exuberance of a puppy, and while it might be charming in its own way, it was also exhausting and not at all the thing for society. Emma herself did not care a wit for what the *ton* thought of her, but she could understand why the duke would want his cousin to have its respect. Philip was a Keswick, after all.

"My cousin is a great showoff," he continued, warming to his topic. "He is always knocking Gentleman Jackson down. None of the other customers knock down the proprietor, nor do they expend the energy that my cousin does. He's the only one who works up a sweat. Honestly, Miss Harlow, if I worked up the sweat that he did, he would no doubt tell me that one only sweats in Yorkshire, not in London."

Miss Harlow was hardly listening to this last charge that he laid at Trent's feet. She was too distracted by the image of the duke's sweating muscles. She knew it was hardly the thing to do, but she indulged herself for a few moments. Although she had never seen his bare chest, she had felt enough of it to know it was impressive. And the muscles in his arms. How warm and soft they had been....

"Perhaps we should talk of something else?" she said, wanting to erase the distracting picture from her head.

"Like what?" he asked, reluctant to abandon a topic that had given him such satisfaction.

"We need a plan. What are we going to do when we catch up with Windbag?"

"That's simple," answered Philip. "We knock him on the head with a heavy object like a bottle or a chair; then we tie him up and call the constable."

Emma examined his plan as she directed the horses around a sharp bend. It was indeed simple, but she knew that sometimes simplicity was what the situation called for. But she could not like the idea of knocking him out and then calling the authorities, for what good would that do? Sir Windbag would only proclaim his innocence and without proof, who would they convince of his treachery? Such a course would slow him down, of course, but with Dover so close, the loss of a few hours—or even half a day—wouldn't make a difference in the long run. Sir Windbag's message must not get through, not with the lives of so many Englishmen at stake.

No, she refused to consider the idea of turning him over to a country constable, but knocking him unconscious and tying him up appealed to her. The most important thing was that he did not reach Dover. She and Philip could keep him hostage in their room at a posting house for days, or even a week if necessary. If they put a gag over his mouth to keep him quiet and explained to their host that a traveling companion had taken ill, then nobody would notice anything amiss. This had definite possibilities and would work in a jam, but Emma was more ambitious. It was her goal to bring about Sir Windbag's downfall. It was not enough that he fail in his evil mission but that he be publicly disgraced. The selling out of his country was a crime, surely, and deserved to be punished as the Crown saw fit. But courting the Harlow Hoyden's sister with the sole intention of stealing information from her brother was the worse sin by far, and Emma was determined to see him pay. Nobody toyed with her sister. Nobody.

"Do you have a pistol on you?" she asked Philip now, determined to keep her thoughts to herself. He was a useful companion and a goodhearted friend, but she was afraid that the duke's assessment of him was right. The boy was still a pup.

"A pistol?" He seemed disturbed by the notion. "Why would I take a pistol to Hyde Park, which was where I was going when I picked you up?"

"We must acquire one then. Windbag will surely be armed."

Philip accepted the truth of this statement and felt a glimmer of fresh excitement. He could hardly wait until Trent learned that he'd saved England from invasion—with the help of Miss Harlow, of course. She was a right 'un, and he would give her her due. "I don't have much experience with pistols, I'm afraid, but I've been hunting my whole life and am a decent shot with a rifle. Don't worry, Miss Harlow, I shall protect you."

Miss Harlow laughed, delighted. "I shall count on it, Philip. And I assure you that I will do my best to protect you. But I can only do that if I have a pistol. I've never hunted in my entire life, but I'm a decent shot with a pistol. And please call me Emma," she added. "We are hunting down a traitor to England together and that affords us a certain amount of intimacy, don't you think?"

Philip agreed to address her with such informality and then fell silent, preferring silent contemplation. In his mind, he was busy reviewing all the different manners in which his cousin could learn that he had saved the kingdom. The one he preferred most, of course, was the one in which he told him himself. That way he would see the look of complete shock give way to grudging respect. Still, having the Prince Regent call on Trent with the news that his cousin was a hero wasn't too shabby either. Really, there seemed to be no unacceptable way for it to happen.

Emma was glad for the quiet. She hadn't held the reins in ages, and it was a heady experience. She loved the wind in her hair, and she loved speed. Nothing else in the world was quite this exhilarating, nothing else gave her quite the same feeling of control. This was what she had been pining for, all those long hours in the house as she sought some occupation to take her mind off weighty matters. Reading to Roger had felt like a good substitute at the time, but now that she had the reins in her hands, she knew it had been a very poor one indeed. There was nothing to compare with this feeling of being alive. And this feeling of being alive made problems seem small and inconsequential.

After a few hours it started to get dark, and Emma considered pulling into an inn. Although it had been a clear day hours earlier, clouds now covered the fickle English sky. It would probably rain tonight and even if it didn't, clouds would surely obscure the moon. There would be no light to drive by and to attempt such a thing would only be foolhardy. Why, look what had happened to Roger. Besides, even if it weren't cloudy, the horses needed to rest. Emma was not a flat when it came to horses. She knew better than to drive them into the ground.

"We shall stop at the next inn," she said to Philip. "I thought we'd overtake them by now, but Windbag's lead was great. It seems that I underestimated him; I assumed a man of his size wouldn't travel with much speed. You are no doubt sorry you came. It was my promise that you'd be home for dinner."

"A fine Englishman I'd be if I let a slip of a girl go about saving the country on her own so I could sup by the fire! It makes no difference, Emma, I would have come regardless."

This fine speech pleased Emma greatly. "Excellent, my boy, but don't abandon hope of supping by the fire just yet. I have a similar wish."

They came upon the Spotted Eagle at twilight. Emma went in to bespeak two rooms for her and her brother, and she left Philip to stable the horses.

The landlady was suspicious of Emma and with good provocation. Respectable ladies did not arrive with complicated stories to explain the absence of luggage.

"So you see," said Emma, concluding her tale, "it's by the side of the road in Goudford, and although there are many things in it of value, my brother and I decided it was best not to let something like that slow us down. There is no telling how long Mama will hold on."

"Your brother, hmm?" Mrs. Biggley had the keys for two available rooms in her moist grip but wasn't convinced that something funny wasn't going afoot. A young woman with no luggage traveling with her brother? That didn't sound very respectable.

As the landlady was contemplating her next move, Philip came in and told Emma that the horses were right and tight for the evening. The lady had so many questions and criticisms for the young man that Mrs. Biggley concluded that they must be brother and sister. Nobody treated a lover with such careless disregard. She handed over the keys. "At the top of the stairs and to ye left. Will ye be wanting dinner?"

"Yes, by the fire in the private parlor, if you please," Emma said, surreptitiously wiping the damp keys on her dress and vowing to wash her hands thoroughly before coming down to dinner. "Do you happen to recall if a round man of so high came through here this afternoon?"

This question woke Mrs. Biggley's slumbering suspicions. "Why do ye want to know?"

"My good Mrs. Biggley, there is nothing amiss here," Emma assured her. "I only ask because our elder brother is before us on the road and we would like nothing better than to catch up with him. After all, he no doubt still has luggage and would make us look eminently more respectable. I am not used to traveling in such a ragtag manner, and it makes me uncomfortable."

The landlady was not impervious to Miss Harlow's dimples. "Aye, a man came by matching that description about two hours ago. I thought he was going to stay for the night, but he had something to eat and then went on his way."

"Excellent," she exclaimed. "No doubt we'll catch up with dear brother Waldo in the morn. I do so hope Mama is alive when we get home." Emma debated whether or not she should push her luck, but Mrs. Biggley had been so obliging she could not resist. "One more thing and then I will cease bothering you. Do you or any of your menfolk have a pistol I might purchase?"

"A pistol?"

"Yes, a pistol."

"What do ye need a pistol for?"

"Well, to avoid a repeat of our unfortunate incident." She leaned in as if confessing a great secret to the landlady. "I think things worked out for the best, our having to leave our luggage by the side of the road because we are traveling much faster without it and nobody got hurt, which is really the important thing. But Philip, dear brother Philip, had been bemoaning our helplessness for the last two dozen miles. I thought if perhaps we could make him a little less harmless, he will cease his complaining. You know how brothers are, don't you, Mrs. Biggley. A competent woman like you has to have dealt with a few irrational men in her time."

The landlady laughed. "The stories I could tell you! I think my Harry has a pistol. I'll get it to you after dinner."

"You are truly the most helpful woman I have ever met."

Mrs. Biggley almost turned pink with pleasure. "I'm sure ye just teasing me. You probably want to clean. I'll have Mindy bring up some water."

"Very well, I'll spare you your blushes," she said with great reluctance. "Do be sure to add the price of the pistol to our bill."

Emma walked to the stairs and indicated that Philip should follow. He had been a silent observer to the entire exchange, and he was fairly bursting with comments. He controlled himself until they entered one of the rented rooms.

"That was remarkable, Emma," he said, gushing, "the way you had her eating out of your hand. At first she looked like she wanted to toss us out of here on our duffs and now she is probably down in the kitchens baking us a cake. What skill! Can you teach me how to do that?"

"Do what?" she asked, wondering when the girl would bring up water so she could freshen up. The room was neat and small, and the duvet on the bed looked surprisingly clean.

"Make people do what you want them to do."

"Don't be ridiculous, Philip. I don't make people do what I want them to do. In my experience, all people want is a kind word and a smile. You'll do well to remember that." There was a knock on the door. "Now leave me for a moment. I want to clean some of the travel dust off. I believe she said dinner is in an hour. Shall I see you then?"

Their dinner of lamb, peas and potatoes was cold and bland, but since it was served by the fire and was the first thing Emma had had since breakfast, it tasted delicious. Chocolate cake still warm from the oven followed dinner, but there was no way of telling if it was made especially for them. Despite Philip's insistence that it was, Emma strongly doubted it.

The next morning the sun had barely come up before they were on the road again. Mrs. Biggley insisted on packing them a lunch, at no extra charge, and both Emma and Philip were very happy to see an extra-large slice of chocolate cake in their bags.

They drove fast, stopping at each posting house to ask after Sir Waldo. They found the one where he passed the night and discovered that he had left that morning only an hour before.

"We will catch him soon," said Emma, after climbing on top of the curricle. "He will have to stop for lunch."

Emma's prediction proved accurate and around noon they saw Windbag's red-and-blue insignia in front of an inn called the Hungry Lion.

"We've got him at last," she said, the excitement evident in her voice. "The only question is what will we do with him?"

"I thought we'd agreed on my plan," answered Philip.

"Yes, whacking him on the head and tying him up is a good place to start, but what if we call in the constable and the constable lets him go? We must gain evidence of his perfidy."

"Perhaps he has your brother's letter on him. Surely that can be used against him?" he asked impatiently. Philip didn't like all this talking. He wanted to get in there and save England as soon as possible.

Emma thought about this for long moments, which seemed endless to Philip. "No, not necessarily. He's engaged to my sister and runs tame in our house. He could simply say that he picked it up by mistake or something equally innocent. I'm afraid that bringing the constable into the situation is not the best idea."

"But we must do something now while the villain is in our sights. Tardy longer and we risk the chance of losing him. We'd have to give chase again." This was the last thing that Philip wanted. Giving chase was the most boring part of an adventure. He would not stand for it.

"That's not a bad idea, Philip. Perhaps if we follow him further he will lead us to his confederates. He may not be working alone. Other Englishmen could be involved in his evil plan." The more Emma thought about it, the more sense it made. Yes, it was important that they intervene before Sir Waldo passed on his secret information but there was no rush yet. They were still miles and miles from Dover. That would give them time to gather evidence against Windbag. "Yes, that is precisely what we'll—" Emma looked up. Philip was gone.

She turned around to see Philip disappearing into the Hungry Lion. "Damn that boy," she muttered, running after him. "The duke was right. He is an impertinent puppy. What's so wrong with taking things carefully and having a well-thought-out plan before jumping in harm's way?"

Emma went to the side of the building and pressed her face up against the glass. If it was at all possible, she wanted to avoid Windbag's seeing her. With a little luck she would intervene before Philip did anything drastic; then they could continue with her plan. The main room of the inn was empty save for a dog lying by the fire and a young lady wiping down tables with a wet cloth. Emma walked to the other side of the building and leaned against another window. Ah, there he was, in a small room eating a joint and reading the newspaper. Now, to stop Philip before he did something stupid.

But she was too late. She watched in horror as Philip opened the door and confronted Sir Waldo. The wretched boy hadn't even tried to use surprise to his advantage! He had a large wine bottle in his hand, and he had barely raised it threateningly before Sir Waldo had out a pistol and shot him.

Emma reacted instantly. Making sure she had her pistol, she ran into the Hungry Lion and burst through the door of the private parlor.

Philip was on the floor cradling his leg. He was trapped, and the look of terror on his face was commensurate with the situation. Sir Waldo was standing over him, his gun threatening. "Tell me who sent you and I might decide to let you live." He was so intent on his victim that he didn't notice Emma enter the room.

"Put down the gun," she said, her pistol trained on him, her arms steady as she held it in her grasp. "Put down the gun now!"

At first Sir Waldo seemed unable to digest what was happening. The look in his eyes was wild, and for one terrible moment Emma thought he might shoot Philip out of panic.

"If you're thinking of shooting him again," she said in her calmest voice, hoping to draw Windbag's attention to herself, "let me assure you that if he dies, you die. It's a very simple equation and one that even your little mind can grasp."

His eyes cleared and Emma saw him take in the situation. He was calculating the odds, trying to decide what he could get away with. She was eager to discover what his next move would be.

"Thank God you're here," he said, instilling a respectable amount of panic into his voice. "I was attacked by this madman and had no choice but to defend myself. Call the constable."

"I know that you know that I am not that gullible," she said, taking another step into the room. "Put the gun down."

"No, you're not the gullible one. It's your dear, sweet trusting sister who is gullible." He kept his pistol trained on Philip and his eyes on her. "How do you think she'll feel when she learns that her savage sister killed the man she loved? Do you think she will ever forgive you?"

Even if she had cause to worry, she could not. Philip's life was the most important thing here. "I'm her sister. She'll believe whatever I tell her, especially the truth."

"There are things that happen between a woman and the man she loves that cannot compare with the paltry love of a sister," he said, with a smug smile on his lips. "Her feelings are…shall we say, warmer, for me than you imagine. She will believe whatever I tell her to believe."

The fool, thought Emma, amazed, by his monumental presumption. *He is thinking of yesterday in the drawing room. He's basing his ludicrous supposition on a kiss that I gave him. The bloody fool thinks he has Vinnie wrapped around his finger.*

"I'll take my chances with Vinnie," she said, with a wry smile on her face. "Now drop the gun or I'll shoot."

Sir Waldo laughed with what seemed like genuine humor. "I will not bow to the will of a girl. Now I've humored you long enough. Leave us alone and you might live. Stay and death is a certainty. Come, I'm a very busy man and don't have time to play your silly little games."

Emma lined up her shot and pulled the trigger.

CHAPTER ELEVEN

Hoping to make up for lost time, Trent and Vinnie drove well into the night. Because the thin moonlight only popped out periodically between the clouds, the going was slow. Trent knew that it was far better to take their time and be cautious than to wind up overturned in a ditch. They were of no use to anybody in a ditch. Around eleven they pulled into a posting house.

The duke was very aware of the impropriety of the situation, and as soon as they stepped inside the inn, he realized that taking the girl with him was an act of madness. If anyone ever found out about tonight's work, Vinnie's reputation would surely be ruined and Emma would get her wish. He would be forced to offer for her.

Vinnie listened as he requested two rooms for the night. She saw the landlord balk at his story that they were brother and sister, but the duke's manner was so imposing that the man scurried away with his head down.

"Come," he said, leading her into another room, "I've gotten us a private parlor. I think it would be best if we ate quickly and then got some rest. I would like to start early tomorrow. Warm yourself by the fire. I expect the fare won't be what we're used to but we must eat something. It's been a long day."

Vinnie sat down and waited for the duke to take a seat before making an announcement. "If we run into any of your acquaintance, you must call me Emma."

"What?" He was in the process of opening his cloisonné snuffbox, and he froze at her words.

"You must call me Emma. We're identical twins, sir," she explained at his shocked look, "nobody would be any the wiser."

He put the snuffbox down and examined her by firelight. "I cannot believe you are serious."

"Reputations are all about perceptions; they have little grounding in reality," she explained. "We might be at an inn together unchaperoned, but we have done nothing wrong. I see no reason why anyone should suffer if someone should happen upon us."

"Emma would suffer," he said stiffly.

"I wouldn't call having a husband who loves her suffering," she said gently.

From the way his eyes narrowed, Vinnie knew he was about to give her a grand setdown. He'd had the same look on his face seconds before he treated the landlord like a troublesome fly.

"Don't, your grace, you will not convince me that you don't love her, and I'd rather not bestir myself for an argument," she said, fighting a yawn. "It has been a very long day."

"Very well," he conceded, wondering how and when he had given himself away, "but it's of little significance. She will not have me."

"Aha!" she exclaimed triumphantly. "I knew that was exactly the matter when I wrote to you."

"She told you then?" he asked, his heart lightened by the idea that Emma had talked about him. Perhaps she regretted her decision.

"Emma? You must be kidding, Trent. She is as closemouthed as an oyster. But I have eyes in my head and do not need to have everything spelled out."

He turned to study the fire. "I see no point in continuing this conversation."

"You are a sad disappointment to me, your grace."

His lips twitched as he recalled that Emma had once said the very same thing to him. "Am I?"

"Yes, I'd expect more from a hardened libertine such as yourself."

"What would you have me do, Vinnie?"

"Be patient with her; understand that she has a terrible fear of marriage; respect her freedom, which she values more than anything; love her unconditionally— you know, the usual things a suitor must do to court a reluctant woman."

Since these were the thoughts he himself had had when he first realized that he loved Emma, he waved a dismissive hand. "It's not something as innocuous as reluctance that I have to overcome. She's indifferent to me."

"She isn't indifferent. She's scared."

The duke laughed harshly. "The Harlow Hoyden isn't scared of anything."

"You're wrong, Trent, she's scared of one thing."

The duke was silent for long moments. It was only after the simple meal of chicken and potatoes had been laid out and the serving wench departed that he looked at Vinnie. "You think she cares?"

"Whenever your name is introduced into the conversation, she leaves the room. She gets an unfocused, sad look on her face when she thinks nobody is looking. Sometimes I hear her crying behind her bedroom door and when I knock she pretends she isn't there. Something is troubling her," she concluded, spreading soft butter on the bland boiled potatoes. "You are the most likely candidate. In fact, you are the only candidate. Please pass the salt. These potatoes have no taste whatsoever."

Feeling like a lovesick puppy, Trent fought the compulsion to ask for more reassurances. Only a greenhead could talk of nothing but the object of his affection. He passed the salt and hoped that Vinnie would volunteer more information without his having to request it.

She did not and the meal passed in comfortable silence. Vinnie was determined to give the duke time to digest what she had said. She would never forget the look in his eyes when he asked her if she thought Emma cared about him. It was the look of a man clinging to hope. He could scarcely let himself believe but neither could he bring himself *not* to believe. The emotions churning inside him—as well as the emotions churning inside Emma—had nothing in common with the tepid feelings she and Sir Waldo shared. Vinnie was no romantic fool and she would happily settle for less, but she could not settle for so much less. In the unfortunate case of her fiancé, familiarity did indeed breed contempt. As soon as she found him and assured herself that all was well with Emma, she would break the engagement. It would not do to earn the reputation of a jilt but it would also not do to shackle herself to a man she could not respect.

The duke was equally lost in his own thoughts. Hope was an insidious thing, and Vinnie's words had scarcely reached his ears before they lodged themselves in his heart. *She's scared of one thing.* He recalled the conversation he and Emma had had about marriage and could well believe that she was afraid of love. And with good cause, he thought, recalling the misery of the last couple of days. No one would willingly seek out something that could send one spiraling to such depths. But the heights, he reminded himself, thinking of Emma in his arms. The heights could be dizzying. Of course Emma wouldn't know that. She was a green girl with no experience with men. It was all new to her. She didn't know what pleasure could be found in the arms of a man. Indeed, he admitted that despite his vast experience, he was no expert on these matters either. He had never loved before.

The duke felt a great impatience and hurried through the meal, as if that would make the night pass more quickly.

He resented the dark sky and the miles that lay between him and Emma. He wanted her with him now. He wanted to look across the table and see her profile in candlelight. It was remarkable how Vinnie could look so much like the woman he loved and yet not affect him at all. He didn't look at those very same dimples and feel happy. He didn't stare into her identical blue eyes and feel desire. All those years of believing that only a woman's appearance mattered came down to this one moment in which he discovered that a woman's appearance didn't matter at all.

Vinnie suppressed another yawn. "I am thoroughly exhausted. Even if the bed upstairs is infested with bugs, I will fall asleep the second my head hits the pillow."

Trent smiled. "I trust there are no bugs, but you might want to check the sheets before climbing in. I judge this inn to be decent and well kempt, but then, as you've pointed out to me, all my judgments are not sound."

Swallowing the last of the tasteless potatoes, Vinnie stretched. "I vow, my muscles have never ached quite like this before. But then I have never spent quite so many hours in a curricle before. Do you think tomorrow promises more of the same?"

"No, I expect to catch up to Emma by midday. We will leave early, about an hour before daybreak, to catch the first glimmer of light."

"In that case, I shall take myself off to bed right now," she said, standing. "It's almost midnight and an hour before daybreak sounds frighteningly soon."

It was not soon enough for the duke. His mind was racing with such flights of fancy that he feared he wouldn't sleep a wink. Thoughts of Emma consumed him. "I think I shall stay here and have a glass of port before retiring."

"Good night, your grace. You will instruct the servants to pound good and hard on my door at the desired hour? I fear I will not wake otherwise."

***

Vinnie's concerns proved justified, and it required extended knocking on the door to wake her. She climbed out of bed, feeling every muscle in her body ache, and went about her morning toilette. One could not feel refreshed after putting on the clothes one wore the day before, but at least her eyes were open. She found Trent in the parlor drinking tea and ordered a cup for herself. They did not linger long, and within a few minutes they were on the road again.

They drove for an hour before they came to a posting house. The duke told Vinnie to stay put for he would only be a minute, but she insisted on climbing down. "Your conveyance is well appointed to be sure, but the seat grows harder with each passing mile," she explained.

Trent laughed, gave her his arm and led her into the inn.

"What? Back so soon? Did you forget something, missy?" asked Mrs. Biggley as soon as she saw her. She had a load of firewood in her arms.

Vinnie felt the duke stiffen beside her. "I was not here before. You have me confused with my sister. We look very much alike."

"Very much?" repeated the landlady. "Forgive my language but you're a damn near matched set. Are you going to see your mother, too? Makes no sense to me, a train of siblings traveling to see your ailing mother one after the other. What, can't you stand each other enough to travel together?"

"A train of siblings?" asked the duke. "There were others?"

"Who are you?" She crinkled her eyes suspiciously. "Another brother, I suppose. I knew something was havey-cavey about the whole business. A sister and a brother traveling together without any luggage, going to see their dying mother, following two hours behind their older brother. No, not the goings-on of respectable people. And she asking for a pistol." She put the firewood down in the taproom and returned, her cheeks flushed from the exertion. "Yep, the whole business was havey-cavey."

"She asked for a pistol? Did you give her one?" The

thought of Emma driving around the countryside armed with a deadly weapon horrified him.

"Sold her my son Harry's for a pretty penny." Misinterpreting the duke's look, she said defensively. "Well, I had to sell it for a profit, didn't I? It was me son's only pistol and I have to buy a new one now."

"Did she say why she needed a pistol?" asked Vinnie, more curious than worried. She knew Emma was a perfect shot and would never hurt herself or anyone else by mistake.

"Wanted it for protection. She and her brother were held up by highwaymen miles back. Lost the luggage in the scrape. Or so she said. I believed her at the time. Now that there are two of you, I'm not so sure."

"When did they leave?" the duke asked, impatient now to be gone. Emma had a pistol. The very idea terrified him to the bone.

"Ye just missed them," she answered and watched the fine gentleman turn on his heels and march out. "Maybe a half hour ago," she called to his departing back.

Vinnie ran after Trent and sensing his concern, she said, "It's all right. Emma is a sure shot. She won't accidentally shoot Philip."

The duke helped her into the vehicle. "I'm not concerned about Philip." He grabbed the reins in his tense fingers and set the horses in motion.

"She will not hurt herself either."

"It's not Emma's life I am concerned about. It's Sir Waldo's," he said tersely, urging the horses on. They were only a half hour behind!

"Sir Waldo's? I know Emma has no affection for the man and would greatly like to see him out of my life, but my sister is no murderer, sir!" she protested, offended on her sister's behalf. "How dare you even think it!"

"Vinnie, I love your sister with all my heart, but I fear she isn't in her right mind at the moment. You know she isn't logical in her hatred for your fiancé. She's so convinced that he is a villain that she can't think straight. Remember

Mr. Squibbs? Your sister befriended him so she could learn how to crack safes but not just any safe—Sir Waldo's," he said, looking at her to monitor her reaction.

She paled. "What?"

"She and I broke into your fiancé's house looking for proof of his wickedness. I knew her plan was a dangerous waste of time, but I couldn't let her go on her own, as she threatened to." He returned his eyes to the road, especially careful to avoid all potholes since time was now of the essence. Who knew how close on Waldo's heels Emma was. "It is my fear that Emma wants to believe so badly that Windbourne is a villain that she has convinced herself that he's a traitor to his country."

"What?"

"You heard what Squibbs said. Emma thanked him on behalf of our country after listening to Windbourne's conversation. Who knows what she overheard, probably Windbourne talking about some investments he made in France, but she must have misunderstood."

"Emma is not a fool."

"Then you believe Windbourne is a spy?"

Vinnie found that impossible to credit. "There must be some misunderstanding here, on her part *and* ours."

"Very well. But your sister is chasing after a man whom she believes is a traitor to his country and she has a gun. I am terrified of what might happen. Not for Sir Waldo's sake, Vinnie, though I am sorry to say it for I know he is to be your husband, but for Emma's. She must not kill an innocent man," he said in a hard voice. "She must not have that on her conscience."

Vinnie didn't know what to say so she held her tongue. Despite the conviction with which he spoke, Trent had not managed to convince her that Emma's mind was unbalanced. There was something here that they were missing but what?

The drive was long and tense, and the duke did not stop for anything. At one intersection, Vinnie feared that they would hit another carriage racing at breakneck speed but rather than slow down, Trent sped up, avoiding a collision by mere inches. Vinnie turned in her seat and saw an irate coachman raising a fist at them. She straightened in her seat and held on for dear life. Although her thoughts weren't quite as tortured as the duke's—he was busy trying to decide where in Italy they would choose for their home in exile—she was extremely concerned about her sister's welfare and her fiancé's. But she knew now that breaking the engagement was the right thing to do. She had listened to the duke consign Sir Waldo to an early grave and felt nothing in particular. Of course she didn't want him to die, but then again she didn't want anyone to die. A wife should care particularly about the welfare of one's husband. Though she had no experience with marriage, she knew that much to be true.

After a while Trent brought the carriage to an abrupt halt, which sent Vinnie flying forward in her seat. She expected the duke to apologize, but when she regained her balance she saw that he was already on the ground. A quick survey of the area revealed an inn and two carriages, one of which she positively identified as Sir Waldo's. Her heart racing, she climbed down and followed Trent.

The panic Vinnie felt was nothing compared with the duke's. He tore open the door and quickly swept the taproom with his eyes. It was empty. Only a gray dog whose tail thumped in expectation lay by the fire. He looked to the left. There was a door to a private parlor. He ran to it and threw it open. The scene that met his eyes was the one that had tortured him over and over again during the carriage ride. Emma was pointing a pistol at Sir Waldo. All he could see was Emma and the pistol in her hand and her finger on the trigger. Some words were exchanged, but he couldn't make sense of it. Only the trigger and Emma's finger existed for him. He saw her lift the gun a fraction of an inch. He saw the trigger finger move.

Without thinking he dove into the room and pulled Emma down with him. The gun discharged but the bullet—

thank the Lord—missed its mark. It was impossible to tell who was more dumbfounded: his beloved or her victim.

Sir Waldo moved first. The events of the last few minutes, from the second the boy had barged in on him with the bottle of wine to this last incomprehensible turn, made no sense to him. He didn't doubt that Emma was on to him. Exactly how much she knew worried him. *How* she could know so much mystified him. He admitted then that he had always grossly underestimated her. That she was wild and a nuisance and a bad influence on his fiancée he knew. That she was clever and dangerous was a revelation.

Since Emma and the duke had yet to regain their feet, he knew that the advantage was temporarily his. The boy cowering in the corner did not bother him. He doubted that anyone would take that callow youth's word over his own. It was the Duke of Trent who caused him genuine concern. The duke's word would be accepted without question. Waldo had not planned to cut his ties with England quite so soon, but there was nothing for it save to kill the peer. Though his involvement in the spy game was deep, he hadn't killed any of the upper ten thousand yet—at least not by his own hand. That some of the sons of England's finest families died on battlefields during the war, thanks to information he'd provided he couldn't help, but up until then he had limited himself to killing footpads and lackeys. He raised his gun.

Emma fought violently to extricate herself from the duke. She was angry—she had never been this angry in her entire life—but she pushed it away. She didn't have time for anger. Now was the time for the clear head she was famous for. She pulled her torso out from underneath Trent just in time to see Windbag take aim at the duke's head.

"No," she screamed, kicking the legs out from underneath Sir Waldo. The gun discharged harmlessly toward the ceiling. Waldo toppled a table as he fell. The loud crashing sound roused the dog in the next room, and he started to bark.

Emma struggled to get to her feet before Waldo recovered his balance. She didn't have her gun—she had lost that when Trent tackled her—but she had her fists and her righteous anger. How *dare* he try to harm the duke? Why, that worthless little traitorous toad!

"Of all the gall," she mumbled, jumping on Waldo and sending him back to the ground. She punched with more enthusiasm than accuracy, but she managed to get one right in the groin. While Waldo was distracted by pain, she tried unsuccessfully to grab his gun. He held on to it with force and vigor and before a few seconds had passed he had it pressed against Miss Emma Harlow's head.

The entire episode passed in less than thirty seconds, and by the time Vinnie got to the door, the major struggle was over. "Oh, my God," she gasped, horrified by the sight of her fiancé holding a gun to her sister's temple. "Oh, my God."

She looked at the duke, who was standing across from Waldo and her sister with brown eyes blazing with murderous intent. It was the most awful expression she'd ever seen in her life, and she felt a tingle of fear, even though it was not directed at her. Sir Waldo might be holding all the cards now, but in a few seconds or a few minutes or even a few hours he would be at the duke's mercy. It seemed to her a terrible place to be.

"Let her go," the duke growled in a low voice. It hardly sounded like him.

"You must be joking, your grace. Let my ticket out of here go because you said so? Really, what kind of a player would I be if I handed over my ace in the hole?" he asked, as his breathing returned to normal.

Emma tried to move her head a fraction of an inch, not so much to escape the gun as to get away from Sir Waldo's hot breath, which was brushing her cheek. "See, Vinnie," she said, trying to sound normal, "I don't want to gloat, but I did tell you he was a villain. My instincts about these things are never wrong."

"Sir Waldo," said Vinnie mimicking her sister's calm demeanor, "I must end our engagement. It's not because you have a gun pointed at my sister's head—although that's of course a factor—but because I don't think we'll suit." She took off her diamond engagement ring and tossed it at him.

The Harlow sisters' conversation, more in line with the drawing room than a hostage situation, made Sir Waldo nervous. Why weren't they more afraid? What did they know that he didn't? He looked out the window. Was there a legion of Runners outside waiting to overtake him? He cocked his gun. That would not happen.

"One false step and she's dead, do you understand?" he said, his attention entirely on the duke. "One false step."

Emma could tell that her relaxed attitude rattled Windbag, and she decided she wanted him rattled. "Vinnie, I don't know how you stayed engaged to this man for so long. His breath is horrid."

"I encouraged the eating of mint leaves, my dear. It's known to help some."

"Shut up," shouted Waldo, the sweat beginning to trickle down the side of his face. "The two of you just shut up and let me think."

"Mint leaves? Do you grow those in the conservatory?"

Sir Waldo pulled on Emma's hair and tugged her head back hard. "I said shut up!"

"Emma, for God's sake!" exclaimed the duke, who had been listening to the interchange between Emma and her sister with astonishment. She really was amazing, his darling. A gun at her temple and not a trace of fear.

"Don't worry, Trent. He's not going to kill me just yet. He still has work to do, and he needs a hostage to ensure it gets done. He knows that if he shoots me here and now, you will tear him limb from limb with your bare hands. It's all over his face, isn't it, Windbag?" she asked. "He's wearing one of those hunt-you-down-and-kill-you expressions that I've never actually seen before. Look at those eyes. I don't think I've ever seen anything quite so black in my entire life. Have you, Windbag? I'm sure you don't take comfort in it, but I do. Even if we walk out that door and you kill me, it's all right because I know that the duke here won't rest until you are as dead and buried as I am. Or perhaps not. I'm not very good at reading these terrifying expressions. Perhaps he doesn't intend to see you buried. He might leave your corpse out to be picked over by vultures. So you might want to think carefully, Windbag, before you make your next move. You might even want to leave me here and run for your life. I won't follow you, I promise. All I wanted was for my sister to break her engagement to you and voilà, it's done. My hard feelings toward you end right here. I hold no grudges."

Emma didn't think that her reasonable speech would bear fruit, but it did give her an opportunity to get one long last look at Alexander Keswick, Duke of Trent. She had never seen a more magnificent sight than he there with his eyes blazing and his jaw firm. She would get out of this if for no other reason than to feel his hot, sweet lips on hers again.

"Now Miss Harlow and I are going to leave out the front door. Lavinia, come here." She was still standing by the doorway and stepped inside the room at his command. "Stand next to the boy on the floor. You too, duke, over there where I can see you. Drop the gun and keep your hands in plain sight."

The duke complied, never taking his eyes off Emma. From the moment he had risen from the floor to see the gun at her temple, he had not taken his eyes off her.

"Very good, duke," Waldo said from the doorway. "I'm pleased to see that a man of your rank can take orders. Here's another one. Stay where you are. You are to remain at this inn for at least twenty-four hours. If I even hear horses' hooves approaching then she's done for. Do you understand?

The duke nodded abruptly.

"Very good. I won't say it was a pleasure, but it

wasn't all bad." He nodded and pulled Emma through the door and out of sight.

The duke kneeled at Philip's side. "Are you all right?" he asked, his tone brusque.

"I'm fine. Emma saved me, but this is all my fault," said Philip, the shame and fear equal in his voice. "She wanted to move cautiously, but I jumped right in and got myself shot."

"No," corrected his top-of-the-trees cousin, "I am to blame. Emma had everything under control until I burst in. Tell me quickly, is it all true. Is Windbourne a spy?"

"Yes, he's meeting someone near Dover to reveal the names of English spies who have infiltrated the French army. If he succeeds, Napoléon could escape and France attack."

The duke shook his head, almost incapable of digesting it all. "I am a fool," he muttered, "a damnable fool." He stood and took Vinnie's hands in his own. "Please forgive me, my dear, for putting your sister's life at risk."

The regret was etched on his face, and Vinnie could not bear to look on it. "There is nothing to forgive," she said, running a comforting hand down the side of his cheek. "You thought to save her soul, Alex."

Trent laughed harshly. "Save her soul? But who will save mine if she dies?" He shook off the mood and strode to the door. "You will look after things here while I'm gone? Send for a local doctor and get a room. Philip's wound is a clean one and should heal with little trouble. I will return in a day or two." He stuck the gun into his pocket and strolled out.

Vinnie raced after him. "What of his threats? He will hear you approach and kill her."

"Then I shall be silent and he'll never hear a thing." At Vinnie's unconvinced look, he said, "Don't worry, I will return her safely. I promise you that. I am a skilled huntsman and know what I am doing. I will not lose her, Vinnie, not now."

CHAPTER TWELVE

As soon as they left the inn, Windbourne adjusted the position of the gun so that it was no longer pointing directly at Emma's temple and was now aimed in the vicinity of her kidney. He walked closely to her, holding one arm as a gentleman would and hiding the pistol in the folds of her skirt.

Windbourne's coachman noticed nothing odd about the arrangement, which must have surely looked bizarre. His employee had arrived alone and was now leaving with a beautiful young woman on his arm. Emma had hoped to find an ally there but the coachman's ready acceptance tempered her optimism. She was on her own.

Emma did not have a plan, but she wasn't worried about that yet. She had been a hostage for only ten minutes, and that hardly seemed enough time to grasp the situation let alone devise a way out of it. Windbourne sat next to her with his gun pressed to her side, which was a small relief. At least she didn't have to stare at his beady little eyes and tiny features. Windbourne was nervous, she could tell from the way the gun shook and the way he kept looking outside to make sure that Trent wasn't following them.

Although he had no reasonable expectation of seeing the duke two paces behind, Windbourne could not help but check and double-check. His threat had been genuine, he did intend to shoot her if he caught wind of a chase, but he was beginning to realize that all pursuits were not preceded by thundering hooves. Emma's speech had not been all exaggeration. The look in the duke's eyes had been deadly; it had indeed been of the hunt-you-down-and-kill-you variety. In those few seconds, Windbourne's plans had changed radically. He would not be able to return to England until the French won the war. Then he would once again walk the streets of London, as a victor this time and not a lowly impoverished baronet. The French would need people like him, willing, educated Englishmen, to help the transition to go smoothly. He was not playing a part when he talked to Vinnie at length of his political ambitions. He planned to rise either in his own government or another's. And he would need a wife, a gentlewoman who would devote her career to the advancement of his. He had been willing to take Miss Harlow with all her faults, but that was not to be. After the war, he would have to find another woman to marry.

The long ride passed in silence. Emma was done taunting the man and couldn't stomach the thought of conversation with the toad, even if it meant learning more of his plan. She had little respect for Windbag's intelligence, but she doubted even he would be stupid enough to reveal anything. For that reason, she was determined to wait him out. He would make a mistake at some point. People like he always did, and when the slip came she would be ready. In the meantime, she kept her eyes trained on the passing scenery. She wanted to know where they were at all times. When they turned off the main road, she made note of the tall maple tree with the knotted trunk that marked the intersection. She wished there were some way she could leave an indication of their direction for Trent to follow. He was on their trail, she knew that. What she didn't know was how long he would remain so if they continued taking right turns and lefts.

They stopped once to rest the horses, but it wasn't at a posting house. Windbourne didn't let Emma get out of the carriage, but she saw through the window that they'd stopped at a large cottage with a thatched roof. Smoke was pouring out of the chimney, and the scent of fresh bread was in the air. Her stomach grumbled, reminding her that she'd never partaken of the packaged lunch Mrs. Biggley had given her hours before. It was probably still lying on the floor of the curricle in a brown woven bag. As much as it pained her, she knew she'd have to ask Windbag for food. Hunger was a distraction she couldn't afford. She must remain focused on her goal: escape. If Trent didn't find her, then she'd get out of this unpleasant situation on her own. It would be easier with his help, of course, but she was capable and intelligent and constantly extricating herself from scrapes. And really, what was being taken hostage except a rather large inconvenient scrape?

Emma watched Windbourne carefully, wondering what he was going to do. He had made no move to leave the carriage and enter the cottage. Wasn't he hungry? After all, she and Philip had interrupted his lunch in an extreme fashion. His roast had been one of the first things to topple in the struggle.

What would he do if he left me? she thought, searching the landscape for more thatched roofs and smoking chimneys. *Would he have the coachman keep an eye on me? Would the coachman have a gun? Would he be inclined to shoot and kill a gently bred young lady simply because his employer asked him to?* The answers to these question, she realized, depended on how deeply involved in Sir Waldo's treacherous scheme the man was. If he was benefiting in some monetary way, then he would follow Windbag's commands to the letter. But what if he was not? Why run the risk of Newgate and possible hanging just to satisfy an employer's wishes?

Emma decided she would like to have a moment alone

with the driver, to get a feel for what his game was. Therefore, she looked at Sir Waldo and tried to assume a defeated pose. "May I please have something to eat?" she asked quietly, hoping she sounded faint. "I'm so very hungry."

"You'll eat when we get there," he said, without even looking at her.

"Get where?" she asked.

"To a little place near Dover where I'm to meet with a confederate. After that it's off to France for me."

"And what happens to me?" she asked angrily, no longer looking defeated or sounding faint.

Windbourne shrugged and looked at her, his tiny lips curled in a sneer. "I don't know what happens to you. I might shoot you before departing or I might leave you as a present for my French associates. They do so love English women."

Although the idea of being so ill used by any man— not just her country's enemy—horrified and repulsed Emma, there was nothing in her expression that revealed the true state of her emotions. In fact, she smiled to let him know how little she thought of his threats.

This sort of behavior annoyed Windbourne greatly, and he turned away from her with a queer squeak that sounded like the high-pitched bark of a little dog. Emma smiled again, this time with genuine humor.

They resumed their drive shortly thereafter and arrived at another cottage just as the sun was going down. Here Emma was brought inside. The dwelling was small and dark with shabby furniture and a low ceiling. She had barely entered the first floor before she was dragged up to the second. It was drearier than the other, with a bed in one corner and a table and a chair in another. The floorboards were old and worn and seemed to be home to a prosperous family of mice. Emma tried not to be squeamish and bit down a cry of alarm when a mouse ran across her foot.

Windbag tossed her onto the bed and pushed her shoulders back. For one fleeting moment Emma felt terror, the sort she'd never before known. Surely he wasn't going to—

He took out a long cable of rope and tied her hands to the wrought-iron headboard. Then he tied her ankles together. The rough rope cut into her wrists, but for the moment she didn't mind the pain. She didn't even feel it, so great was her relief. The ropes were tight and she had no experience in extricating herself from situations like this, but they provided her with an objective, with something to focus all her attention on. She would wriggle free of the ropes. She would. There was no doubt in her mind. All it would take was patience, stubbornness and a refusal to give in to pain. She had these qualities, although patience in less quantities than the others, and already she could feel the ropes loosening. Or was that just wishful thinking? she wondered.

When Windbourne was done securing the ropes around her ankles, he straightened up. "That should hold you for a very long while." Taking the room's only light with him, he crossed the rotted floorboards to the stairs.

"Where are you going?" Emma asked.

"Nowhere, my dear. I will be downstairs the whole time should you try to escape. Be warned; both I and my driver are armed and we both shoot to kill," he said, before disappearing down the stairs.

Left alone, Emma applied herself to the ropes with unprecedented vigor. The Harlow Hoyden had devoted her energies to many cherished goals in her lifetime, but nothing had ever mattered as much as this. It was not only that she didn't want to die in a mouse-infested hovel outside of Dover, but that she also wanted—nay, *needed*— the satisfaction of thwarting Windbag. She wanted to see him rot in prison. If he was sent to Newgate, then she would visit him once a month just to gloat.

The metal frame of the bed was not of good quality, and to Emma's profound relief she found a rough edge. She discovered it quite by accident when she cut her hand on it, and although she could feel the blood trickling down her forearm, she didn't care. Here was something that would save her life.

After a while Emma heard the sound of approaching horses and her heart stopped in her chest. Could it be Trent? She fought even harder to free herself from the ropes, because that was the only thing she could do to help him save her. But it wasn't the duke. Through the window by the bed she could see a carriage pull up. She watched Windbag go outside to greet it. He had a candle in his hand, which momentarily illuminated the face of the visitor. The man had a well-kempt black beard, thin lips, heavy lidded eyes and firm chin. He would have been handsome save for the malevolent scar that ran across his cheek from ear to lip. Then the two men went inside. Emma could hear the sounds of scraping as they entered the large room. The walls of the little house were thin but not thin enough. Try as she might she could not make out any words and quickly gave up the effort. She had more important things to do.

Progress with the ropes was slow but steady. She could feel the strands snapping one by one against the rough edge. The bands were loosening, and she could move her hands more freely now, which made the endeavor easier. The man stayed only a half hour, and by the time Sir Waldo escorted him to his carriage, Emma's hands were unfettered and all that was left was for her to untie the ropes that bound her legs. In an instant she was free, but she knew that she had to plan her next move very carefully. She could not behave rashly and risk the country's security further.

The carriage drove away in the near total darkness, and Emma wondered how far she would get on foot in unfamiliar territory. A horse would help. Yes, she thought, a horse would improve matters greatly. She was an excellent rider, and even though it was dark, there was a very good chance that she might reach Dover before midnight. She would have to steal one of Windbourne's mounts. Where was the coachman? Was he watching the horses? She didn't think he had cause to. Windbag had seemed confident in his knot-tying abilities. As far as he was concerned, she was settled in for the night. Very well, she would steal a horse.

But running away went against the grain for Emma. She had plans for Windbag, big plans that did not include his sneaking away to France under the cover of darkness. How could she bring him to justice if he escaped? *I have nothing*, she reminded herself, *no gun, no knife, no bow and arrow. I must save myself first and then worry about Windbag later. As soon as I get to town and warn the constable what's amiss, I will come back here with a pistol. That is the best you can do. Accept it.*

Emma opened the window and considered her options. There was a very frail tree to the right of the window, which may or may not hold her weight. The second floor wasn't particularly high, and she decided that hanging down and jumping offered the least chance of injury. It was only a fall of ten or so feet. This portion of her plan went without a hitch, and she crept silently around the house, quickly locating the horses and carriage.

"Bloody hell," she muttered when her eyes met the back of the coachman. He was brushing down the horses and singing an off-colored ballad to the tune of "God Save the King." He seemed to be very involved in his work.

Curse it! Emma thought, *now the onerous task of finding something heavy and hitting him over the head with it falls to me.*

She began looking around for something useful in the moonlight. There was a pile of junk behind the cottage, and as quietly as possible she dug through it. There were empty wine bottles, which she set aside in case she couldn't find something better. The pile was made up of mostly useless items such as broken carriage wheels and old chairs. She had just resigned herself to the wine bottle when she discovered a rusted shovel. It was perfect.

From the coachman's enthusiastic and off-key singing, she knew he was still hard at work. She crept up behind him silently. Although she saw one of the horses' ears twitch, it was silent enough for the man whose attention was focused exclusively elsewhere. He never knew it was coming, and he obligingly fell to the floor after one hit. Emma was relieved; she didn't know if she would be able to do it again. The shovel was heavy, the man was tall, and it took all her strength to bring him down. Recalling Windbag's claim, she rooted through the man's pockets, looking for firearms. He had nothing on him.

Sensing something was wrong, the two horses fidgeted uneasily. Emma knew it was better to waste precious minutes calming them down than to hop on without a care. Horses were high-strung creatures who behaved erratically when upset. Her life depended now on their constancy.

But as Emma was cooing sweet nothings into their ears, she began to rethink her plan. Circumstances had changed now. She was no longer defenseless, and Windbag certainly wasn't expecting her to waltz inside with a shovel at the ready. As far as he was concerned, she was tied to a bed in the attic. The element of surprise was one of the most important components of a successful campaign. It would certainly be more satisfying if she could knock him out, rather than scurry off to safety like a frightened child. She was afraid, of course—their last encounter had not ended in her favor. But when had Miss Emma Harlow ever run from a challenge?

Having decided on a course of action, there was nothing to do but follow it through. She picked up the shovel and crept to a window. The curtains were closed, but through a tiny corner she could see Windbag at a table eating his dinner. *The bastard! He knew I was hungry.*

She went to the front door and opened it slowly. It did not make a sound, but the cold air rushed by and alerted Windbag to her movements.

"Smithers," he said, without turning around, "fetch me another tankard of ale."

Emma moved quickly, crossing the floor in a matter of

seconds and raising her shovel. Just as she was about to strike, Windbourne turned to see why Smithers had not answered him. She connected with his collarbone, which dazed him for a second, but just as she was about to lift the shovel again, Sir Waldo's hand came out and reached for it. He gave the handle a violent tug with both his hands, but he could not break her ironlike grip. Then he tried another tactic, pushing her backward against the table. He was stronger and heavier than Emma, and with all his weight on top of her, her legs gave out and she found herself lying flat on the table. The handle of the shovel was pressing against her jugular now, and although she used all the strength in her arms, she was unable to dislodge it. She could see the bright light of triumph in Sir Windbag's eyes, and she turned her head to avoid it. If she was going to die now and like this, then the last thing she saw would not be his smug beady little eyes. It was getting harder and harder to draw breath, but the fight had not gone out of her yet and she flailed her legs about, trying to make contact with his groin. Her actions only angered him, and he pressed down harder, so hard that Emma felt for sure her neck would snap. Any second she expected to hear a crack.

Then Waldo was off her and was sailing across the room. His thick body landed against the wall with a dull thud. He returned quickly to his feet and dug into his pocket for his pistol, but the Duke of Trent was too fast for him. Another swing of the duke's powerful arms and he was down again. The duke was on top of him, this time before he could rise. He didn't even try to retrieve his gun. All he could do was protect himself from the duke's powerful punches, which was an ineffectual tactic against so potent a force. The last thing Windbourne saw before he blacked out was the Duke of Trent's blazing hunt-you-down-and-kill-you eyes.

Trent slapped Windbourne once to make sure he was out, then stood. As soon as he regained his feet he was almost toppled again by Emma. She was in his arms in a second and being devoured by him another second later. His lips came down on hers with such power that he feared hurting her, but she returned the kiss with equal intensity. She seemed no more capable of treating him gently than he was her at that moment. For the last seven hours he'd had no thought that hadn't centered around her, had passed no minute that wasn't consumed completely by worry for her. Some part of him—the only sane part left—knew that this was folly. The enemy might be down, but they had no idea for how long. Their passionate reunion could wait until they were safe, completely safe. But instead of pushing her away, he pulled her closer. Instead of thinking clearly, he immersed himself in sensation. When Emma groaned, he lifted her up and wrapped her legs around his waist. He ran his fingers through her hair, along her back, under her dress, his lips never breaking contact with hers. The kiss lasted five minutes.

Emma drew back first. "Your grace," she said, gasping for breath, "we must warn the authorities—"

Trent wasn't ready to talk yet and covered her lips again with his own. Since thought had returned, he was gentle this time. He brushed sweet kisses against her top lip and ran his tongue along her bottom lip. He lowered her tenderly to the ground, sliding her against his body so she could feel his desire. Despite her concern for the future of England, Emma found herself being drawn deeper and deeper in his all-consuming web. She could not resist this man. She had no idea why she ever thought she could.

"Trent," she said, her voice husky, "we must talk."

"I know," he said, tucking her head against his shoulder and hugging her with all his strength. "I know we must talk."

"The authorities must be alerted, and we must capture the awful man with the scar, for he is a spy, too. And Philip, how is Philip?" she said, all in a great rush. Her heart was still racing and her breath was still short, but she knew someone here had to be sensible.

"Philip is well, at least he was when I left, which was not two minutes after you," he answered, his breath a soft breeze against her neck. He knew that they had to see to Windbag and the unconscious man near the horses, but there was something he needed to do first. He could not live another minute without apologizing. "Emma, dear darling Emma, I'm sorry, so sorry."

Surprised by the abject remorse in his voice, she pulled away. "As well you should be, sir. Do you see what sort of trouble you've made? When you burst into that room and tackled me, I thought I'd never forgive you."

The duke nodded. He expected nothing less from Emma. He'd behaved foolishly and put her life at risk. Not only that but because of him she'd suffered through a terrifying ordeal. He did not know the events that led up to this evening's brawl, but he didn't need to. Her life had been within seconds of ending. Had he been a minute later it would have all been over. He didn't know if he could forgive himself. He lowered his arms, stepped away from her and looked at Windbourne. Something had to be done with him.

"Not so fast," Emma said, catching an arm and tugging her toward him. "Although nobody credits me with any sense, I happen to have a great deal of it. You entered a room and saw the Harlow Hoyden pointing a gun at the man she detests. I loathe the conclusion, but I understand why you drew it. Most men would have thought the same thing."

Although her words were meant to make the duke feel better, they in fact did the opposite. Yes, most men would have thought the same thing, but Trent did not think of himself as most men. He loved her, and the damnable thing was that he should have believed in her. He knew Emma better than anyone, except perhaps Vinnie, and he should have trusted her to behave in a rational manner. His conclusion had been the logical one, but a man in love wasn't supposed to be logical. He was supposed to have faith.

"I think I'd prefer your ire to your understanding," he

admitted ruefully. "When one has made such an egregious error as I, one wants to be cursed and raged at. Your easy forgiveness leaves me feeling worse."

"Please, your grace, you think I don't know that?" She smiled, revealing a dimple. "I did warn you that I have a great deal of sense."

Trent was unable to resist her dimples and brought his head down for yet another kiss. It was short-lived this time, and the duke retained a clear head. It would not do to lose control again. "Enough of that. We have much to do before we rest. Come, let's tie up Sir Windbag and the man outside. Then you will tell me all that has occurred since the last time I saw you."

Emma walked over to Windbourne and relieved him of his pistol. She also found extra rope in his front pocket. "There is not much to tell. I've had a very tedious day. All I did was sit in the carriage and plan my escape." She wrapped the cord tightly around his wrists several times, sighing in satisfaction. There were no rough metal bed frames to aid him in his escape.

"No, I do not mean all that has happened today, although I am particularly interested in the events leading up to the scene I interrupted, but all that has happened since Lord Northrup's ball." He watched her tie a sailors knot with ease and wondered at her skill. "It seems you have been busy."

"Not really, sir. It has only been the last two days." She cut the rope with a knife that had been lying on the table and handed the rest to Trent. "For the man outside. If you wouldn't mind? I'd rather keep my eye on Windbourne in case he wakes up. We need to find out more about the scarred gentleman."

Trent did mind, of course. He didn't relish the idea of leaving her alone with Windbourne, albeit a trussed-up, unconscious one. He would never forget the terror he felt upon coming through the door and seeing that round man on top of Emma. He had realized instantly that she was still alive from the frantic kicking of her legs, but from the almost purple color of her face he knew she couldn't hold on much longer. Luckily she didn't have to. "I'll be right back," he said, walking out but leaving the door open so that he might hear her if she called out.

Emma stared at Windbourne, wondering when he was going to wake up. It was just like him to be so disagreeable. Now that she was ready to talk, he was out cold. Emma lamented the lack of smelling salts at her disposal and decided to toss a pitcher of water on his face. That sometimes worked.

Windbourne was sputtering and cursing when the duke returned. "Just in time, Trent," said Emma, well satisfied that her trick worked, "Sir Windbag and I are about to have a little talk. He was going to tell me all about his spying, and I was going to tell him all about Newgate. It seems like an even trade of information. And if he is shy, I thought I might peel off his fingernails one by one."

"Peel off his fingernails one by one?" asked the duke. "Where does a gently bred lady such as yourself learn about such things?"

"I don't recall where specifically, but I must have read it in a book. Perhaps *The Mysteries of Udolpho* or *The Castle of Otranto*."

"Such useful information to be had from gothics, and they say reading corrupts the female mind," observed Trent with twitching lips.

"You can't let her do this, your grace," said Windbourne, his face pale. "You are a gentleman and cannot condone such brutish behavior."

"Funny you should say that, Sir Waldo," said the duke with careless amusement. "Before this afternoon's incident, I would have agreed with you. But there's something about the memory of your gun to Miss Harlow's head that makes me feel brutish." He turned to Emma and raised an eyebrow. "My dear, would you start with the left hand or the right?"

"I suppose the right because that is the hand most people use to hold a quill. That would be the most inconvenient, don't you think?"

Windbourne blanched, and before Emma even got to ask a single question, he confessed all. "The man who was here earlier is René Le Penn. He poses as a dispossessed count and has entrée to all the local soirees, but he's a French spy. He will take the information I gave him and bring it to France. I have been operating as a spy for two years. I need the money to pay off my gambling debts or else the moneylenders will repossess my home, which has been in my family for 300 years. I was recruited by an Englishman, one who is very high up in the government. It was he who gave me your brother's name and told me to watch for the communiqués, which would arrive in the form of harmless weather reports. The idea to court your sister was his, but I had always intended to do the honorable thing toward her," he said earnestly, as if this would redeem him a little in Emma's eyes. "I did not want to harm your brother, but he was in danger of passing along vital information that would have hurt the French cause."

"Roger's accident was your doing?" Emma asked in a low, soft voice.

"Did I say that? I didn't mean to say that," babbled Windbourne as sweat trickled down his cheek. From the chit's expression at this news, he feared once again for his fingernails.

"You are lucky that Roger didn't die," she said, "or you surely would now in this mouse-infested hovel outside of Dover. As it is, you will spend the rest of your worthless life rotting in Newgate, if they don't decide to hang you first. Come, Trent, we must warn the troops and capture this Le Penn. Shall you drag the prisoner or shall I?"

"I'll take him," said the duke, pulling the injured man to his feet. "We'll put him in the carriage with the other man. By the way, that's quite a fierce bump you've given him. I don't expect he'll wake up for hours."

"Really, Trent?" she asked, flushing with pleasure. "I did fear that I had barely knocked him over. The shovel was so heavy and he so tall."

"Never doubt yourself, my love. You are an Amazon."

They were outside now, and Trent considered the problem of seating arrangements. He did not want to put her in the carriage with two dangerous traitors, even with shackles and a pistol, but neither did he relish the idea of her driving the coach in the dark. Deciding that the latter was the least of all evils, he handed his gloves to Emma. "Take it slowly and be careful to avoid potholes. We are in no rush."

Emma was very much inclined to differ, but she restrained herself for the duke's sake. They were indeed in a hurry, and once she had the horses in hand, she would waste no time in getting to Dover. But for the moment she just nodded, to the duke's great relief. Of course, she didn't blame him for his nerves. Few people were as good with the reins as she.

Since the moon was bright, the ride to Dover was swift. Emma negotiated the road with little trouble, and, except for one instance, an aberration, really, in which she took a sharp corner a shade too quickly, without incident. Once they entered the city limits of Dover, Trent instructed her to stop at the first respectable hotel they passed. Emma was instantly suspicious of this request, but since she could not imagine where else to go—how did one find the commanding general of the army barracks if one did not ask at a hotel?—she complied.

The duke disappeared inside the hotel for a minute and reappeared with a heavy-set man in tow. "Emma, you can come down from there now," he said, offering her a hand. "Mr. Jones is going to drive us to Colonel Rivington's house." He helped her into the carriage, where Smithers was still unconscious and Windbourne was tied to the door. Trent had put a handkerchief in the man's mouth so that he couldn't cry out for help.

When they arrived at the colonel's house, they discovered

that he and his wife were hosting a route. The duke seemed disturbed by this, but Emma thought it was exactly the sort of thing one should expect when one showed up on a colonel's doorstep with two prisoners. They used the back entrance so as not to frighten any guests with Smithers' unconscious form, which Mr. Jones obligingly carried. They were shown to the study and instructed to wait. The duke took one look at Emma's pale face and requested that a plate be made up. The servant returned almost instantly with a repast of lamb, chicken and fish.

As soon as the housemaid had left, Emma fell on the plate. She was ravenously hungry and didn't care that her manners were unladylike. Windbourne was a traitor, Smithers was out cold, Mr. Jones was a stranger to her, and Trent already knew she had no manners. What use was there in pretending? After several savory bites, she recalled that Trent had also been on the road all day and offered to share her dinner. He accepted with a pleased smile and that was how the colonel found them, sitting at a table by the fire eating supper.

The interview with the colonel did not go smoothly. He was skeptical of their story and asked the same questions over and over again, as if expecting the details to change. It was clear to her that the only reason he listened to them at all was out of respect for the seventh Duke of Trent. She realized then that had she shown up there alone, she would have been denied entrance and England's safety would have been breached. She was very thankful for the duke's presence.

"Are you absolutely sure about Le Penn?" the colonel asked for the second time. "He is a most respected member of Dover society. My wife and I have played host to him many times, and if it were not for his mother, who had taken ill this afternoon, he would be here tonight. Can we trust this spy to tell us the truth? He is a man without honor."

"Does Le Penn have a long scar that runs from his ear to the corner of his cheek?" queried Emma, speaking for the first time since his entrance.

Rivington turned to her in surprise. During the last forty minutes she had been silent and he had forgotten her presence. "Yes, he does."

"Then we're absolutely sure. I saw him myself. Perhaps you should send a man to his house to inquire after his mother?" Emma suggested. "If he's there keeping vigil by her side, then he will be very pleased by your concern. But you will not find him there. He's on his way to France—or will be, as soon as the tide favors him."

"It's a sound idea," said the duke, hoping to draw the colonel's attention away from Emma. The entire affair had been unconventional, and he didn't want the man speculating about her involvement. Even though the nation's security had rested in the balance and even though they were to be married as soon as the bans were posted, this adventure would not enhance the Harlow Hoyden's reputation. Society loved its heroes, but only when they were male. "I have no doubt of the outcome, but it would put your mind to rest."

The colonel nodded and sent a servant to fetch a soldier. "I'll send a man to his house and several to the docks. There's no point in taking chances. Your grace," he said, bowing. "I can't thank you enough for this night's work. You too, Miss Harlow. I will be going now to see to official business, but my wife will continue as hostess. You're invited to stay and enjoy the party."

"Thank you but no. It has been a rather long day. If you will excuse us?" The duke was eager to get Emma to the hotel. Although he knew she would never admit it, she seemed as though she would fall asleep on her feet.

"Of course, of course. Be sure, the Home Office will hear of your patriotic deed."

They left Windbourne and the coachman in Rivington's study and took their leave, driving back to the hotel quickly and silently. As to be expected, the host at the Dover Inn looked at them askance at their lack of baggage. Before Emma had a chance to, Trent made up some story about incompetent servants and luggage that was two towns behind.

The host was well pleased to show the duke and his lovely wife to his finest room, the commodore suite.

"Please ask one of the servants to bring up some brandy. And my wife will need a fresh change of clothing," the duke said, inspecting the room. It was large and had a dressing area, which would serve well enough as a second bedroom. "And some extra blankets; the air has a definite chill."

"Of course, your grace, of course. My daughter is just the size of your lovely wife. I will bring you some of her finest dresses. She will be very happy to help the duchess." He smiled at Emma, who blushed. She was not a duchess and could not like being called one. "Would your graces like a tub of hot water to be brought up as well?"

Emma would have loved nothing better than to soak in a tub, but the thought of bathing with the duke nearby threw her thoughts into a frenzy. She was about to decline when the duke answered.

"An excellent idea," he said, before closing the door. He turned to Emma, whose face was now an unnatural shade of red. "Do not look so. I will take myself off and give you some privacy. The room downstairs seemed like a decent place to have a drink."

"And what of you, sir? Shall I go downstairs to let you bathe?" she asked in all seriousness. It sounded like a logical plan to her.

The duke smiled and demurred. "That is not necessary. I trust you to respect my modesty."

"And I trust you," she answered.

"How odd," he said, his voice suddenly deep and husky, "for I do not trust myself."

At these words, Emma's heart jumped. The memory of his breathtaking kiss was still on her lips, and she felt the color rise again in her cheeks. She had to turn her head away because she could not stand to gaze into his eyes any longer. The expression in them was intense and fierce, and she could well understand his attraction for the women of the *ton*. If he

227

stared at them all like that, then his claim to be a libertine was true. No woman could resist such a searing look. "It will be good to change clothes. I have been wearing this dress since yesterday morning and cannot wait to burn it in the fire, it is so dirty. There's even a splatter of blood on it somewhere."

Trent knew why she turned away and was glad for it. He had been through an awesome spectrum of emotions in the last forty-eight hours, and his grip on his control was tenuous at best. He had spoken the truth earlier. Were Emma to take a bath in his presence he would not be able to stop himself. He would strip off his clothes and be in the tub with her before she had even taken the soap in hand. But that must wait until after the wedding. He wouldn't disgrace now, nor show her so little respect, not when she was the person he respected most in the world.

A knock on the door announced the servants. They brought brandy and a pile of clothes and buckets of water to fill the tub. When they were done arranging it all, the duke excused himself to go have a drink alone.

"I shan't be long," said Emma, reluctant to see him go, though she understood the necessity. "Perhaps only thirty minutes."

"Don't rush on my account," he told her before shutting the door behind him.

Emma undid the buttons on her dress, which was a challenge since they were in the back. Then she slid it off her shoulders and took off her underthings. The dress smelled, but she resisted the urge to throw it right into the fire. First she would make sure that the landlord's daughter was really her size.

She stepped into the bath. The water was hot and wonderful, and for several minutes Emma rested her head against the edge, luxuriating in the feel. She was even tempted to close her eyes, but fear of falling asleep and being discovered by the duke kept them open. Picking up the pink rose-scented soap, she began scrubbing her arms and legs. After she washed her face, she ran the washcloth over her neck and noticed for the first time the soreness. It made sense, of course, considering how close Windbourne had come to choking the life out of her, but she was still surprised and wondered if there would be bruises there. If so, she could only wear high-necked gowns until they healed. Even the Harlow Hoyden wasn't bold enough to go walking down Piccadilly with disfiguring welts on her neck.

Emma washed her hair, climbed out of bath and put on the nightgown supplied by the landlord. Aside from being three inches too short, it fit. He had also been kind enough to provide a dressing gown, and she put that on as well. When the duke returned some forty-five minutes later, she was sitting at the mirror brushing her wet hair.

The duke stood in the doorway for a few seconds, transfixed by the sight of her. In the blue cotton nightgown with her hair glimmering in the firelight, she was irresistible. He walked over to her and took the brush out of her hand. "May I?" he asked, although he did not wait for a response. The need to touch her was overwhelming, and if he had to settle for this innocent maidlike task, then so be it. He would take what he could get.

"It's full of knots," she said softly, watching him in the mirror.

"I'll be gentle."

"Yes, I know you will."

At that, the duke raised his eyes and met hers in the mirror. His expression was as intense as earlier, but she kept her gaze steady, refusing to turn away. "I'm afraid you are in for a rude surprise, your grace," she said, floundering for a topic. "By now the water is cold."

"I assure you, cold water will not bother me in the least."

Something in his voice made her flush, and she could not maintain eye contact anymore. She shifted her position and took the brush from his hands. "How inconsiderate of me. No doubt you would like to bathe now. I will climb into bed and keep my eyes trained on the wall. How does that sound?"

The thought of Emma climbing into a bed whilst he was in the room sounded like heaven to him, but he tried to keep his voice level as he answered. "I thought perhaps you would like some brandy before going to sleep. I can bathe later."

"Pooh," dismissed Miss Harlow, "I'm wide awake and we can drink the brandy together after your bath. You won't take long, will you, sir?"

"No, of course not."

"Good." Emma stood up and walked over to the bed. The linens were fresh and soft, and she almost purred in satisfaction as she lay down on them. With her back toward him she said, "This bed is divine. Last night's bed was awful. Oh, do you mind if I talk?"

The duke was in the process of removing his shirt when she asked this question. Although bathing with her in the room would be easier if he could close his eyes and forget her presence, he would not deny himself the pleasure of her company. "No, I don't mind."

"Good. Anyway, last night's bed was awful. The linens were coarse and whatever detergent they use smells like a stagnant pond. And the bed was lumpy. Philip said he slept all right, but I don't know how he could on such a lumpy mattress."

Trent halted his movement and tried to control the sudden rage that overtook him. How dare that insolent puppy sleep in the same bed with Emma! Even though he was raised in the wilds of Yorkshire, he should know such behavior was not proper. Not proper and not forgivable, at least not as far as the duke was concerned. "You shared a bed with Philip?" He tried to keep his voice neutral.

Emma laughed and the duke could well imagine the dimples. "Of course not. Philip was the perfect gentleman and gave me first choice in the picking of beds. I tried them both out and chose the one with the least amount of lumps."

He let out the breath he had been holding and stepped into the tub, his back toward Emma. The water had chilled, but it was nothing to make a face at and it went only a small way in cooling his libido. He was not surprised, of course. He wanted her as he had never wanted another woman before and was even now imagining all the things he'd love to do to her. The softness of her hair, the sweetness of her scent, the gentleness of her voice—all these things conspired to drive him mad. If he were a wise man, he would never have gotten himself into this mess in the first place. Only a man crazy with desire took a bath with a temptress five feet away. And only a crazy man would share a room with her, pretending to be man and wife. He should have gotten two rooms, damn the proprieties. So what if it looked suspicious? As soon as he was done with his bath he would return to the taproom, where he would pass many long hours, returning only when he was sure she was asleep.

"I suppose tomorrow night we will have to stay at the Hungry Lion," she said, continuing her discussion. "I didn't have a chance to form much of an impression, since my visit was so short. That's where Vinnie and Philip are?"

Trent did not answer.

Emma repeated the question and waited. "I say, you haven't drowned over there, have you?"

"What?" said Trent, realizing belatedly that Emma spoke. "Uh, no."

The duke sounded so strange that Emma forgot herself for a second and turned around. Her eyes met his smooth, tanned back and her mouth went dry. She knew she should turn back—after all, the duke had trusted her and she was now betraying that trust—but she couldn't bring herself to move. Her mind sent out commands, but her limbs would not respond. All she could do was stare at his beautiful body. Those muscles in the shoulders that she had run her hands over, so that was how they looked. She had seen drawings and sculptures of unclothed men, but none of them had looked like this.

She must have made a noise because the duke turned around, concerned. To her surprise, she wasn't embarrassed to be caught behaving so improperly.

"Emma," he said, his voice an agonized, strangled whisper.

She could see the desire blazing in his eyes, and she could no more halt her next actions than she could stop her next breath. She rolled off the bed and walked slowly over to the bathtub. Then she lowered herself into the duke's lap, wrapped her arms around his neck and brought his head down for a kiss. The kiss was hot, and Emma scarce felt the temperature of the water. She was burning up with a fever she had never before felt. Her body demanded things she could not name, but she could tell from the look in the duke's eyes when she pulled back that he knew very much what she wanted.

"We mustn't," he whispered as he pulled the dressing gown from her shoulders. "We really mustn't."

He tossed the soggy robe onto the floor near the fire, and it landed with a quiet thud. Emma laughed, feeling happier than ever before in her life. "Oh, but we must, your grace. We really, really must." She laid kisses along his chest, soaking in the pleasure of having him there and knowing they would be not be interrupted. They were not in a carriage that would pull up to her town house at any minute.

"Alex," he said, his voice low and husky. Her tongue was driving him wild, and he could scarcely complete the thought. "I told you to call me Alex."

Emma did not acknowledge his command but continued to explore his magnificent body at her leisure. She adjusted her position, sending water over the side of the tub, and ran her fingers over his stomach.

The duke knew that everything she was experiencing was new for her, and he tried to keep a tight rein on his passion in order to let her explore freely. But the provocation she offered was too much, and after a few long moments of her fingers caressing his manhood he could stand it no more. He pulled her toward him and brought his head down to hers with force, capturing her lips in a rapturous kiss. The thin cotton that separated her skin from his was unbearable to him and he undid the three buttons in the back with deft hands. Since the fabric was wet, it would not slide easily over Emma's head, and Trent chose the only recourse that would remove the unwanted barrier quickly and efficiently. He tore it in half. The offending garment joined the robe on the floor.

It was the first time the duke had seen Emma's body in the light, and he let out a haggard sigh at the breathtaking sight of her creamy white, beautiful breasts. With the lightest touch, he ran his hands over them, thanking God that this precious, wonderful woman was his tonight and always. He heard her laugh softly. He raised his head. "Do I amuse you, Emma?" he asked, his tone light and teasing.

"That was a borrowed gown, Alex. I am loath to imagine what the landlord will think when he sees it," she explained, wishing he hadn't distracted her with his wicked touch. She had never before seen a man naked—let along a naked man aroused—and she was very curious about every part of him. His manhood had been so smooth.

"Then the landlord will never see it." He brushed a lock of hair behind her ear and laid a soft kiss on her forehead. "I will tell him my darling wife could not bear to part with it and reimburse him for the cost."

Emma smiled, though these sweet words also saddened her. There were things other than the nightgown that she could not bear to part with. But she would not think of that now. Tonight was for her, for him, for them, for the chance to experience something perfect and wild that would never happen again. She kissed him gently on the lips and felt him respond ardently.

"I cannot do what I want in this tub," Trent said between long, luxurious kisses.

"All right," she said, her voice a soft whisper and she climbed out. Feeling his eyes on her bare back, she suddenly felt awkward in her nakedness and grabbed a towel that was folded on a chair. She held it up. "Come, I will dry you off."

Trent stood in the tub, pausing a moment to let the water run off his body before stepping on to the wooden floor. He waited expectantly for Emma to dry him off, but after a minute she still had not moved. "The towel, my dear?"

"Oh, yes," she said, pulling herself out of a trancelike state. The sight of his body—those powerful thighs, those glistening shoulders, that muscled stomach—had stolen her thoughts, and she could do nothing more than stare like a schoolgirl. She had not known that his clothes had hidden *such* treasures. She applied the towel vigorously to his shoulder, then his torso, buttocks and legs. "You are beautiful, Alex."

He took the towel from her grip, threw it onto the floor and lifted her into his arms. Then he carried her to the bed and gently laid her down on cool sheets. "I am not the beautiful one here," he said, perusing her body with his eyes.

Emma felt exposed and fought the instinct to cover up. For one night only she would be the brazen hussy the whole world already thought her to be. When the duke suckled her breasts, she arched back, bringing her body even closer to his, and when he laid intimate kisses along her thighs, she opened her legs to allow him better access.

The duke carefully raised a finger to the most intimate part of her, and he heard Emma gasp in shock and pleasure. Delighted with her response, he ran a finger along the moist folds, until he found her sensitive nub. He rubbed it gently.

"Alex," she said, almost panting with the need that seemed to grow within her every second. "Alex."

"Shh, my love, it's all right," he assured her, increasing the pressure.

Emma closed her eyes and focused on the pleasurable feelings. She knew she could trust Trent, and she moaned his name once again as she was overcome by wave after wave of sensation. For fleeting seconds she lost control of all her muscles. It was truly wonderful.

She felt Trent's lips on her neck, but she refused to open her eyes. "That was very good, your grace," she said, unable not to tease him. "You have most skilled fingers."

"There's more, Emma." He kissed her ear and felt her tremble in response. "I will be gentle."

"Yes, I know you will," she answered, her eyes still closed.

The duke had never lain with any woman as innocent as Emma, and he was fearful of not being gentle enough. He positioned himself at the entrance of her womanhood and carefully slid inside. His movements were slow and deliberate and when he had pushed himself all the way in, he rested his weight on his elbows and looked at Emma.

"Open your eyes," he said, trailing hot kisses down her cheek. "Open your eyes and look at me."

Emma complied.

"Do you feel any pain?" he asked, almost afraid of the answer. He knew this initiation could not happen otherwise, but still he was loathe to hurt this precious creature in any way.

"A small amount, Alex, but nothing worse than usual," she answered honestly. "One does not get to be the Harlow Hoyden without a few scrapes and bruises."

He laughed softly and began to move within her, slowly at first. He tried to keep his weight on his elbows so as not to crush her with his body, but Emma had other ideas. She threw her arms around him and pulled him close.

"I want to feel your body against mine, your grace," she whispered in his ear. "You feel so wonderful."

"God, you feel wonderful, too."

The duke increased his pace, keeping his eyes on Emma's face so that he could gauge her every reaction. He had spoken the truth when he said she felt wonderful. Indeed, no woman had ever felt so good in his entire life, but he held on to his control. The experience must be perfect for Emma. Not just because she was to be his wife or because it was her first time but because he loved her and she must get as much pleasure out of his body as he did of hers. His pride would accept nothing less.

He could tell from her heavy breathing that she was getting close, and when he felt her body tense in his arms, he let himself go, driving harder and harder into her soft body. His climax came fast, drenching him in a sea of sensation. It was overwhelming and all-consuming, and it wiped out everything that had come before it. There was and had always been only Emma. And from that moment on she would be all that he knew.

The fire crackled as Emma watched the duke pour brandy into a snifter. "That's enough," she said, when he had filled the glass halfway. "I'm already intoxicated by you and do not need the nectar of brandy to help me along."

"Intoxicated by me?" he said, handing her the glass. She was sitting by the fire in a large armchair, her hair, still partially wet, flowing freely down her back. Since self-consciousness had gotten the best of her, Emma wore a sheet draped around her body. The duke thought she made a charming Roman and had said so as soon as she had donned the improvised garment. He himself felt no need to cover up his nakedness. He was in the garden of Eden and had no desire for clothes—at least at the moment. "I did not expect romantic drivel to drop from Miss Harlow's lips."

She laughed. "I imagine lots of things have happened tonight that you did not expect."

Taking the seat across from her, he admitted the truth of the statement. Indeed, he still found it hard to believe what had transpired in that room. "Point well taken, my love. Although my ire at your rash behavior was such that I did envision some physical contact between us, it was certainly not of a sensual nature."

His voice was low and husky, and Emma felt tingles run up her spine. She had just made love with the man not an hour before and already she wanted him again. It was a sorry state of affairs and one that she would examine in more depth on the morrow. Until then, she would enjoy everything that happened. "I object to your characterization of my behavior as rash. The fate of England hung in the balance, and I acted as any patriot would. What would you've had me do?"

"Seek help," he answered.

"I did, your grace," she reminded him, "but as you were away from home, I had to make do with Philip. I have not asked if everything is all right. Surely only a very important emergency could have taken you from London in the middle of the season and without a word to Vinnie. You and she have become great friends in the past weeks, haven't you?"

He did not relish the introduction of her sister into the conversation, for mentions of Vinnie were usually followed by exhortations to kiss her. He answered honestly but with caution. "I consider her a great *friend*, yes."

But for once Emma's mind was clear of schemes. "Tell me how things are with you. Your estates are in good order?"

"The emergency turned out to be a tempest in a teapot," he said. When he had gone scurrying off to Kemsley, he'd been convinced that it was over between them. Now she was wrapped in a sheet drinking brandy in a hotel room with him. Life—and Emma—were unpredictable.

"Excellent," she said, taking a sip of brandy. It was smooth and made her throat tingle.

"You have still not told me of your adventure. How did you discover that Sir Windbourne is a spy?"

"He is a very stupid spy who doesn't check a room thoroughly to make sure no one is there," she said, before going into details of what had occurred during the last two days. "And how did you track me so quickly? As of yesterday afternoon, you were still out of town."

Not wanting to explain about Vinnie's note, he said, "Since the emergency had proved to be only a small matter, I resolved to return to town as quickly as possible. There was a note from Vinnie waiting for me. She was concerned about your disappearance. The next time you dash off to chase after a villain, you must send word to her. She was most overwrought in her concern for your welfare. We would have been quite in the dark had Mr. Squibbs not kept his word to me."

"Ah, yes, Mr. Squibbs. I was meaning to ask you, your grace, what right you have to keep tabs on me through my associates?" She found it hard to look suitably outraged in a makeshift toga.

"I have a vested interest in keeping that beautiful body of yours safe, especially now that I know it can bring me such bliss," he answered, his eyes steady as they gazed at hers. He saw a gentle blush move up her cheeks and marveled at his reaction. He wanted her again. "And a good thing I did, too. If Squibbs hadn't paid me a visit, I wouldn't have learned what had transpired."

"I can't believe Mr. Squibbs went to you after I'd assured him I'd be seeking you out myself."

"Don't be angry. He was only keeping his word to me," the duke said, sipping his brandy. "And thank God. Who knows what would have happened if he had not told us your direction."

"Very likely I would have returned to London with a captured Sir Windbag in tow and we would have missed out on a delightful hostage episode," she said mercilessly. "Yes, it was a very good thing you found me when you did."

"Although I regret my hasty actions, I do not think the situation would have resolved itself quite so easily as you say. Sir Waldo wouldn't have gone tamely with you, and Philip could have been seriously injured in the process. If I recall correctly, Windbourne's gun was aimed at him."

Remembering Philip, Emma was instantly remorseful. "How is the dear boy? I take full responsibility for his misadventure. I should have known better than to bring a green boy on a such a dangerous enterprise. 'Twas only that he had spoken so passionately about being of help to me, and you were gone."

"Since I did not linger long after you, I didn't get a clear look at his wound, but it seemed to be minor. He'll need a cane for a few months and all the young misses will swoon at the romantic figure he'll cut, but then he will be back to normal in no time—and back to Yorkshire, I hope. I find him a tiresome boy."

"Never say so, Trent!" she protested. "He admires you so much and you'll just have to learn to be more patient. And perhaps take a dive every so often at Gentleman Jackson's. All the young gallants think it's rude for you to be so invulnerable."

The duke laughed. "They would not thank me for going easy on them as a favor to a female."

Emma acknowledged the truth of this statement and changed the topic. "Now you must tell me how you found me in that awful little house. You were not behind us, for I kept my eyes peeled to the road in hope—and in fear—of catching sight of you."

"I only took one horse and stayed off the main road. It was not hard to navigate the forest by the side of the road and when we came to a clearing I held back. I would like to say you were in my sights the entire time, but you were not. Still, I always had a fair sense of your direction, except when you turned off the main road that second time," he added. "I had to do a fair amount of backtracking to find you then."

"Have I thanked you yet for your perfect timing? A few more seconds and it would have been too late," she said softly, remembering the feel of that horrible, unforgiving handle pressed against her neck and shuddering, despite the warmth of the fire.

The duke stood up and walked over to Emma. He placed kisses along her bruised neck. "If it's any consolation, I don't think Windbourne will escape with his neck unscathed."

"I should hope not. The man is a—"

But the duke had had enough talk of Windbourne and he covered her mouth with his own. He had meant to silence her for only a moment but once his lips met hers, there was no further thought of letting go. He ran his hands down her back and felt her instant response. He picked her up and carried her to the disheveled bed, leaving the sheet on the floor by the fire.

CHAPTER THIRTEEN

The next morning, Emma was awakened by the noise in the hallway, but she resisted the impulse to open her eyes. The duke's arms were around her stomach, his warm breath brushing her neck. She would not be the one to bring this beautiful night to an end.

Several minutes later she felt the duke stir. He placed a kiss on her ear, sending shivers down her spine.

"I know you're awake, so there's no use in pretending," he said, turning her onto her back and observing her shut eyes.

"If you're here, then I'm still dreaming," she said softly as the people above them pounded on the floorboards.

"There you go again with that drivel," the duke said, well satisfied with her turn of phrase. "That you are so romantic pleases me."

"Does it, your grace? Is that the only thing about me that does?" she asked, playing with the hair on his chest.

"Alex," he corrected. "And no, there are one or two other things as well."

She kissed his chest. "Would you care to name them?"

"Your lips, for one. They are—" He broke off as she lavished attention on his nipple.

She looked at him with an impish smile. "You were saying, Alex, about my lips?"

"Your lips are magical," he whispered before covering them with his own. For a few long moments he lost himself in the sensation of her but then he fought the burgeoning desire. He pulled away. "We must ready ourselves for departure. The hour grows late."

Emma didn't care to talk about the hour. "Please, Alex," she purred, pressing her body sensuously against his, "an extra half hour won't hurt. Please, just one last time."

Trent tried to resist the arousing lure of her body. "Vinnie is probably out of her head with worry by now. When we are married, I promise we will do nothing but make love all the time."

Emma froze. "Married?" she asked.

"Yes, of course. Two people cannot behave as we have and not get married," he said, laying a whimsical kiss on her nose. "It's just not done."

"That's not a reason to get married," she protested, giving him an opportunity to provide a better one.

The duke looked down at her in surprise. "I'm a gentleman, Emma. I do not make love with innocents and then desert them."

Emma listened to his answer with a growing sense of alarm. If he had given any indication of his regard, had hinted in the most meager way that he loved her, she would accept his offer with zeal. But she would not accept this, this customary sense of obligation. She would not—indeed, could not—marry a man who didn't share her feelings. That way lay disaster. The Harlow Hoyden could not take a husband who'd come to her from the arms of a dancer in Chelsea, especially now that she knew what women and men did alone together in bed. What she had done with Trent was sacred, and she would not let him devalue it—and her—with his marriage of obligation. "Thank you for your…flattering offer, your grace, but I have no wish to get married. You have done your duty by asking, so let there be no more talk of desertion. Really, we should get dressed. The hour grows late." She moved to get out of the bed, but the duke held on to her arm.

"What madness is this, Emma?" he asked, trying to understand how her demeanor could change so swiftly from lover to stranger.

"No madness. Please let me go. No doubt Vinnie is out of her head with worry by now."

But he did not let her go. He could scarcely believe that only a few minutes earlier he had woken without a care in the world. Never in his life had he been happier. "How can you talk so coldly after what we've just done?"

"What we've just done?" she asked, her voice almost harsh in her disappointment. "Is it not what you do with dancers in Chelsea and widows and any willing female who crosses your path? Isn't that what you libertines do? Come now, your grace, there is no need to get maudlin on me. We have passed a pleasurable evening. There's no reason for you to ruin it with unreasonable demands."

At these words, the duke felt the most overwhelming anger of his entire life. He let Emma go, stood up and disappeared into the dressing room. He wanted to argue with her, rail at her, but he was afraid of what he might do. His emotions now were unpredictable, and he could not be relied on for rational behavior. How dare she dismiss what they'd shared as "a pleasurable evening" only! And to call his offer of marriage an unreasonable demand! To think that when he opened his eyes not ten minutes before he'd believed he was holding the future in his arms, to think that he had foolishly assumed it was all sorted out. No woman had ever responded so passionately as Emma. No woman had ever loved him as Emma had. Why wouldn't she want to marry him? And to be told that it was all meaningless—nothing had ever crushed the duke so. He could not risk being in her presence any longer, so fearful was he of causing her harm.

It was for the best, he decided, that he hadn't admitted his love. It had been on the tip of his tongue, but for some reason—some half-formed fear of being rejected—he'd held back. He'd wanted her consent first. But it was good that she didn't know the truth, that his heart was hers to do with as she wished, for no doubt she would trounce on it without a thought. He had been warned about the Harlow Hoyden, but he'd let infatuation override good sense. Poor Vinnie. She had no idea what a soulless creature her sister was.

Dressed, the duke entered the bedroom. He carried his greatcoat over one arm. Without looking at her, he said, "We leave in fifteen minutes. I will meet you at the coach."

From the bed, Emma watched him leave. As soon as the door shut, she surrendered to the storm of tears that had been lodged in her throat. He had not denied it! She'd given him a chance to say that what they'd done was not at all like what he'd done with the widow Enderling and the dancer in Chelsea. She hadn't expected him to, of course, but she had hoped nonetheless. God, had she'd hoped. But the fire that had blazed in his eyes when he'd beheld Windbourne holding a gun to her temple had been extinguished by the mundanity of regular life. Sanity had returned and with it the realization that an indulged mutual attraction wasn't reason enough to get married. He'd thankfully made his escape while his bachelorhood was still intact.

Determined not to give away the true status of her emotions, she splashed her face with water. Then she looked into the mirror. Her eyes were still red and puffy from tears. She dressed herself in the landlord's daughter's gown. Its cut was simple, but the color, a light mint green, was unflattering and made her complexion look sickly.

"Well, I feel sickly, don't I?" she muttered, putting on a bonnet that the landlord was kind enough to provide. *If only I wore spectacles,* she thought, trying to cover up her eyes with the bonnet.

She made her way downstairs and was relieved to see no sign of Trent. The landlady offered her a cup of tea, and she accepted it along with an offer of toast. Although she had awoken ravenously hungry, now in the presence of food, her appetite deserted her completely. She could not bring herself to touch the toast; she could only stare at it and the cup of tea, distracted by thoughts of the duke. Last night had been so perfect. If only this morning he hadn't uttered that fateful word: *marriage.* Or having muttered it, accompanied it with talk of love.

I will not be bothered by this, she resolved, picking up a slice of toast and taking a bite. The piece was soggy and soaked with butter, and it slid down her throat easily. Still, she couldn't bear another taste. Food was not what she needed now. Now she needed a plan, some way to deal with the duke during the next few hours and the days that followed. She would still see him around town, at social functions that could not be avoided, with the widow Enderling, perhaps, or another woman. Then a horrible thought struck her. What if he was enamored with Vinnie? Oh, God, what if he wanted to marry her?

The thought was too distressing to contemplate for even a minute, and she forced her mind on to other matters. She wondered how Sir Windbag was faring in a dank Dover prison. That made her smile. If matters between her and Trent had been anything than what they were, she'd have requested a short stop to gloat. It was not often that one witnessed the crushing defeat of an archenemy.

A clock in the parlor chimed the hour, and Emma realized that the inevitable could not be put off any longer. Taking several deep breaths, she got to her feet, thanked the landlord for his hospitality and walked outside into the blinding sunlight. Although still very early in the day, the temperature was already warm and the scent of spring was in the air. It was the sort of day that made young romantic hearts giddy. Emma cursed the blue sky and walked over to the carriage. The duke had the horses in hand and was only waiting for her to begin the journey.

He acknowledged her presence with a nod but didn't look at her. The duke wasn't quite ready to gaze upon her yet. Although his anger had cooled somewhat during the intervening half hour, he feared the sight of her would ignite the flames again. He'd struggled hard to retain his dignity, to not burst into the parlor and beg her to marry him, and he refused to lose it now that the end of their adventure was so near. He need only return to the Hungry Lion; then he'd be free of her. Well, perhaps not free of her, but he would never have to be alone with her again. The source of temptation would be removed, and he could begin to recover from this fleeting madness one called love.

He tugged on the reins, indicating to the horses that it was time to depart. There had been a coachman available for hire at the inn, but Trent decided driving was the best way to avoid being trapped for long hours with Miss Harlow in the small compartment of the conveyance. He preferred fresh air and physical distance, however meager, and the distraction of something to do other than stare at her beautiful features and pine for what could never be.

Emma was relieved by his decision, for many of the same reasons, but she bitterly resented a society that left men free to make choices. She would have preferred to drive the horses herself and end this interminable boredom. The last thing she needed now was to be alone with her thoughts, her traitorous, torturous thoughts. All she could do was replay this morning's scene over and over again in her head, from the moment she woke up feeling glorious to the second Trent had uttered the words that crushed her heart. And no good could come of that. There was nothing she could have done differently, nothing save accept his proposal. The very idea was preposterous. Other ladies might marry to appease a gentleman's misplaced notion of honor but not she. Miss Emma Harlow had too much pride and too much self-respect and far too much sense. Such a union would end in disaster, and it was better to nip the whole thing in the bud than to let it flower into inevitable public disgrace.

When they returned to London, she would insist on accompanying Roger to the country, where he could recuperate properly. London was a bustling, dirty metropolis and not at all the sort of place a recovering amputee should pass his days. He needed green rolling hills and sweet

Derbyshire air and children's laughter. Surrounded by familiar things, he would grow strong again. He would grow strong again and forget this wretched affair entirely.

Settling her immediate future made Emma feel a little better, but it did nothing to rush the carriage to its destination. She could scarcely believe they were retracing their steps from yesterday. Had the journey really taken this long? She looked out the window and examined the passing landscape. It all looked vaguely familiar in that country-scenery sort of way, but the details she'd tried to commit to memory to aid in her escape eluded her completely.

Finally she saw the Hungry Lion. The instant the carriage came to a complete stop, Emma jumped down and ran to the front door. She found her sister inside the private parlor. Lavinia was sitting near to the fire, reading a book.

"Vinnie darling," she called as she dashed into the room.

Her sister leaped to her feet in time to catch her sister in a hug. "You are safe," she said, the relief apparent in her voice.

"Of course I'm safe," said Emma, tightening her arms around Vinnie. It was so good to be with someone who loved her. She felt teardrops forming in the corners of her eyes and could not fight them.

"There is no 'of course' about it. You left here in the care of a madman." Vinnie pulled away and looked at Emma. "A madman whom I almost married. Can you ever forgive me?" she asked.

Emma wiped away a tear with a cold finger and stared at her sister uncomprehendingly. "Forgive you? Whatever for?"

"You are very gracious, my dear, but the atrocities that Sir Waldo visited upon my family are entirely my fault," she explained, her bottom lip quivering. "You could have been killed—and Roger, too." At Emma's look, she said bitterly, "Yes, I reasoned that out for myself. Our brother's accident was anything but." The tremendous fear she'd been living with for the last twenty-four hours overcame her, and she started to cry in earnest. "I don't know what I'd have done if anything had happened to you."

Emma pulled her sister into her arms again and chastised her for being so absurd. "Nothing did happen to me, silly. And Windbourne's sins cannot be laid at your feet. He is a traitor to England and has tricked everyone, even the prime minister. As for Roger… Well, if that nincompoop had been killed, then he'd have no one to blame for it but himself. How dare he go around playing spy and not tell a soul? We are his family and should be the first to know if he's undertaken a secret mission to save the empire."

Vinnie laughed softly at this statement. Emma was always so bracing—and so ridiculous. Her view of the world might be skewed, but it was refreshing and just the sort of thing a worried sister sometimes needed. "You were not taken in," she observed.

"But I'm unusually perceptive," she said, making light of the whole situation until she noticed her sister's sincere distress. "Really, Vinnie, I didn't know he was a genuine villain. A puffed-up, pompous bore with more hair than wit, certainly, but never a scoundrel who would sell his country for a few farthings. Indeed, my dislike of him was entirely personal, and I will now admit that perhaps I was a teensy bit afraid of how your marriage would affect our friendship. I have only one sister, and I might have been fearful of losing her."

Vinnie blew her nose into a crisp white handkerchief and tried to compose herself. Emma had been through an ordeal and needed to receive comfort, not give it. "Tell me of your daring escape. Did Trent catch up to you? He left here with the devil—" She broke off when she felt her sister stiffen. "What's the matter?"

Emma extricated herself from Vinnie's arms and pasted on a wide smile that seemed to crack her face in half. "Nothing at all is the matter. Why do you ask? Trent is here. He arrived last night just in the nick of time, as they say. He was right behind me. Perhaps he is still stabling the horses. Where is Philip? The duke assured me he's fine, but I want to check for myself."

The immense change in Emma's demeanor indicated to Vinnie that something else had gone wrong between Emma and the duke. *Oh, pooh, what has happened now?* She realized that the path of true love rarely ran smoothly, but these two seemed particularly blighted. She considered pressing the issue with Emma but decided to have a talk with Trent instead. He was the much more forthcoming one.

"Philip's upstairs. He's in the first room on the right. You will probably find Lucy, the landlord's daughter, hovering by the door. She's a silly chit, and Philip has been playing the wounded hero of the empire to the hilt." Vinnie smiled. "This morning she was wrapping bandages and practicing her French. She's all prepared for an invasion, and I think she'll be disappointed when it doesn't come." She cocked her head. "I trust it is not coming?"

"We have much to talk about, dear, but no, for the moment England is safe from invasion." She crossed to the door. "I'll check in on Philip, and then I'll tell you all about my adventure."

Emma had scarcely left the room before the Duke of Trent entered. Although Vinnie knew it was not at all the thing for an unmarried woman to accost a duke, she hurled herself into his arms with a cry of thanks. "Oh, you dear, dear man. She is safe, just as you said she would be. Safe and unharmed, thanks to you. How can we ever repay you?"

The duke wrapped his arms around her for a moment only before releasing her and standing a good distance away. "There's no need for repayment. She would not have been in such a predicament had I not interfered. We are even," he said, abruptly turning to leave the room.

The duke looked tired and withdrawn, and Vinnie decided she could not wait to interfere. "Please sit down," she said to his departing back, "and tell me what has transpired between you and Emma."

Her words halted his movements, but they could not draw him to a seat by the fire. "I found her in a hovel outside Dover. She'd already escaped her restraints and knocked out

Windbourne's confederate by the time I arrived," he explained matter-of-factly. "All that remained for me to do was to help her overcome Windbourne's superior strength. We then brought him to Colonel Rivington, who has assured us he will take care of the matter."

"Bah, I don't care about any of that," she dismissed with a cry. "I want to know what has the both of you acting so oddly."

"I don't know what you mean," he said coldly.

"You are acting all stiff and ducal, as if you are about to give me a crushing setdown. And Emma is behaving erratically again, tensing up at the mere mention of your name. What has happened to make it so?"

"Forgive me if I act ducal, Miss Harlow, but I am a duke."

"Miss Harlow?" she echoed. "Oh, it must be really, really terrible if I am Miss Harlow again. Do tell me what happened, so I can help make it better."

"I don't know what you mean," he said again. "Now, if you'll excuse me, I must talk to the landlord about a room."

Vinnie watched him go, a feeling of helplessness overcoming her. The duke had always been candid and aboveboard with her from the very moment she'd confronted him about Emma's scheme. If he would not tell her what happened, then it must be worse than she imagined. Very well, there was nothing for it but to drag the truth out of Emma.

She found her answering Philip's absurd questions.

"No, I don't know if they'll give us medals," she confessed, "but most likely we'll be called upon to provide testimony against him. At least I hope we'll be called on to provide testimony. I, for one, am looking forward to it."

"Do you think there will be a trial then?" asked Vinnie, entering the room. It hadn't occurred to her that Sir Windbourne's exploits would be published throughout the kingdom. For years she had tried to live a circumspect life and draw little attention to herself. She would not like looking the fool and having her name bandied about by members of the *ton*. There it was—another reason to despise Sir Waldo, as if there weren't enough already.

"Of course there'll be a trial," insisted Philip from the bed. "There will be a great big trial that will cause a sensation. Nothing else will be talked about for months."

Emma noticed her sister's discomfort. "He's just a boy from Yorkshire and knows not of what he speaks. It will be a nine days' wonder and a mere footnote in the annals of history. A traitorous spy among the upper ten thousand is nothing compared with what Lady Caroline Lamb might do in her pursuit of Lord Byron."

"I suppose it's possible," Vinnie allowed, although she wasn't at all convinced. "But come, you should not be offering me comfort. You have just returned from an awful experience. Let's let Philip rest. I suppose it's been days since you've had a decent meal," she said, ushering her sister out into the hall. "And you must tell me where you got that horrid dress. As if the color weren't bad enough, those sleeves are five years out of fashion."

Emma followed Vinnie into her room and took a seat on the bed. The truth be told, she was very tired. Neither she nor the duke had gotten much sleep. Images of how she passed the night before flashed through her mind, making her feel embarrassed and wretched all at once. How long would these memories linger?

Vinnie watched her sister very carefully, noticing the blush that covered her cheeks and wondering at its cause. "I wish I had a change of clothes to offer you," she said, "but I left the house with nothing but the clothes on my back, as you did."

"Please don't apologize," Emma insisted. "I have suffered worse atrocities these last two days than an awful mint-green gown with unfashionable sleeves."

"Have you?" Vinnie asked consideringly. "Perhaps you should tell me about them."

"They are nothing, really. I won't say that Sir Windbag

was a perfect gentleman, for we both know that would be a lie, but he didn't harm me in any way, aside from a few bruises and scratches." Her neck was still very tender, but she chose not to linger on that, because doing so only reminded her of the soft kisses Trent had laid there.

"And Trent?"

Emma stiffened and fixed her eyes on the door. "He's also unharmed."

Observing Emma's reaction, Vinnie positioned herself with deceptive casualness in front of the door. "I want to know what happened between you and Trent."

Emma stood. "Now that I think upon it, I can't like the way the doctor has bandaged Philip's wound. It was wrapped too tightly and might cut off circulation to the boy's foot. That would be unfortunate. I must check on it right away to put my mind at ease."

"Tell me first what happened between you and Trent."

"There is nothing to tell. Now, please, step aside so that I may tend to Philip."

"No," Vinnie said, her voice unusually authoritative.

"No?"

"No, we are not leaving this room until you tell me the truth." She leaned against the door and made herself comfortable. "Not five minutes before I was all but given the cut direct from Trent. You have done something to upset him. What is it?"

"Why must it be I who has upset him?" Emma asked angrily.

"All right, tell me what he has done to upset you," Vinnie said agreeably.

"Nothing has occurred. Now do let me leave. Philip's leg might be gangrenous and fall off at any moment. Can you live with that on your conscience?"

"Dear Emma, I have spent the last twenty-four hours with that boy and he has given no indication of discomfort. And since I was here when the doctor put the dressing on, I'm confident that it has been applied correctly."

For the first time in her life, Emma felt like a trapped rabbit. She had never seen Vinnie stiff with resolve before. "You're being completely ridiculous, Vinnie. I have nothing to say on the matter." She sat down on the bed, her posture rigid. "I will remain here all afternoon if that's your desire, but I won't say a word about the Duke of Trent." Her eyes swept the room. "My, what a lovely day it is. I daresay it will rain tomorrow."

"No, we'll not talk of the weather, you vexing child!" Vinnie said frustrated. "We will talk about Trent and Trent only."

"There is nothing to talk about."

"That man is in love with you, Emma, completely and totally in love with you."

Emma turned her eyes away, fearful that Vinnie would see the tears that were starting to form again. Who could have guessed that just hearing those beautiful, impossible words could send spikes hurling through her heart? "Don't interfere," she said, when she felt in control again. "You know nothing about the situation, so don't interfere."

"You're allowed to interfere in my life to your heart's content but I can't reciprocate?"

"I have never interfered in your life," she said, the denial sounding hollow even to her own ears.

"Really, then what would you call your scheme to break up my engagement? Sending a libertine to seduce me was not interfering? Because it certainly felt like interference to me when Trent was plying me with unnecessary compliments."

"The compliments were not unnecessary!" she denied hotly before the truth of the matter hit her. "You know about that?" Emma asked softly. The possibility of Vinnie's discovering all was not something that had previously occurred to her.

"Yes. I've known about it for ages, and the only reason I played along was because I had a scheme of my own," she replied.

"What sort of scheme?" Emma narrowed her eyes

suspiciously.

"I hoped to bring you and Trent together by not only giving you a reason to meet with him but also by making you jealous. And it worked."

"It did not."

"Don't try to cozen me, Emma. We are twins, and I know your thoughts as clearly as I know my own. You have been pining for the duke for weeks now."

"I have not been pining."

"You've been pining and without cause. The man is infatuated. He has told me so himself." Vinnie walked over to the bed and took her sister's hands in her own. She was reasonably confident that Emma wouldn't try to run away now. The look on her face revealed that she was too shocked to do anything. "Now tell me what has happened to make you both so cross, and we'll sort it out. It cannot be an insurmountable problem, for I'm convinced that the two of you were made for each other. I have never seen a pair so well suited."

As much as it caused her pain, Emma loved hearing these words, and if she were of a weaker disposition, she'd have begged her sister to say more. "He asked me to marry him, and I turned him down," she explained matter-of-factly. "Let's please leave it at that."

"You silly girl, why would you ever turn down a man like him?" Vinnie asked, running her hand over her sister's disheveled hair. "You'll never find a better match."

"He doesn't love me."

"He does."

"No, Vinnie, you're just seeing what you want to see. Take off those rose-colored glasses and for once see the world for what it really is. The Duke of Trent desires me," she said, hoping to shock her sister. "I know for a fact that he desires me greatly. But desire is not love and I will not shackle myself to a man who doesn't love me. I will not put a brave face on it and stand by as my husband frequents opera dancers and Drury Lane actresses. You know me, Vinnie. I'm careless and sometimes foolish and I often do things without thinking them through first but not this. I am not such a fool that I would rush headlong into marriage with a man like Trent. And I won't let him do it either, not out of some misplaced sense of obligation. We would both be miserable."

Vinnie listened to this heartbreaking little speech and marveled at how her sister could have so thoroughly misread the situation. "But he does love you, Em. I know he does."

Emma closed her eyes to pray for strength, but all that did was bring the image of Trent, always near, to the fore of her mind. She could see him as he was the night before in the candlelight, gentle and tender, brushing the hair out of her eyes as he joined his body with hers. If a man loved you, surely that was the time to mention it. Then or afterward when he held you in his arms or even later, when he kissed brandy off your lips. "You are wrong. Now please let me get some rest. I'm suddenly exhausted."

Although it went against her instincts, Vinnie decided to leave her alone. Closing the door quietly behind her, she admitted that the situation was very serious indeed. She'd never seen Emma so distressed before, nor her face so pale. *She must really be exhausted,* thought Vinnie. *It's not just an excuse to get rid of me.*

Vinnie decided it was time to straighten this mess out once and for all. She couldn't imagine what the duke was about, asking Emma to marry him without uttering any words of love. He was supposed to be an accomplished flirt, and yet when it came to this most basic rule of courtship he was but a green lad.

She found him sitting next to Philip's bed. She inquired after Philip's health and then focused her gaze on the duke. "Your grace, may we have a private moment in the parlor?"

Although good manners bade that the duke stand upon her arrival, they could not get him to agree to her suggestion. "Now is not the right time. Perhaps later?"

Vinnie knew later would never come. He would put her off all night and in the morning he would be gone before any of them awoke. "We have something very important to discuss and it cannot wait. I must insist that you come now."

He resisted her command. "I couldn't possibly devote myself to an important discussion until I assured myself of my cousin's well-being."

"What, me?" asked Philip, surprised by the duke's words. "I already told you I'm—"

"You are looking a bit flushed," said the duke, laying a hand on his cousin's forehead. Although he had no experience in the sick room, laying a hand on someone's forehead seemed like just the way to treat an invalid. "You might be running a fever. I will stay here with you just to make sure."

Vinnie arched an eyebrow at this little pantomime but refused to be deterred from her goal. She felt Philip's forehead for herself. "He's as cool as a cucumber. There's nothing to worry about."

"Since he was warm but a few seconds ago, I'd say there is much to worry about. A rapidly fluctuating body temperature could be a sign of infection. Perhaps you should fetch the doctor."

"I ain't got an infection," said Philip, who hadn't a clue as to why Miss Harlow and his cousin were acting so strangely, "and I don't need the doctor. My leg hardly hurts. Where is Emma? We weren't finished talking."

"She's resting," explained Vinnie, "and is not to be disturbed. If you're feeling strong enough, you can come down for dinner and talk to her then."

"I feel fine," he said eagerly, with a sideways glance at Trent. He hoped the duke would not contradict him again. "I haven't gotten all the details out of Emma yet. She still hasn't told me how she came by the bruises on her neck."

"Nor I, Philip. But perhaps Trent can fill us in on the story," she said, changing tactics. If she couldn't talk with the duke alone, then she'd talk to him with company present. Vinnie took a seat opposite the sickbed and made herself comfortable. "No doubt he was also present. I'm loath to ask Emma for details; she is so pale. I've never seen her appear so fragile before. She seems almost broken in some way. Clearly, something very traumatic has occurred. Do tell us what."

Trent coughed awkwardly and evaded Vinnie's direct gaze. "She had a tussle with Windbourne. When I arrived he was applying a shovel to her throat and pressing the life out of her."

"That is all?" asked Vinnie.

The duke's eyes blazed as he vividly recalled the scene. "Surely almost dying is enough."

"Pooh, Emma has gotten herself into scrapes worse than that. She's forever running in where fools fear to tread. Why, one of my earliest memories is of Emma sitting blue-lipped in front of the fire trying to warm up after taking a dip in the frozen pond," she recalled almost fondly. "We were little girls, not yet five years old, and the pond in the park had just frozen over. Emma came barreling out of the house with her ice skates over her shoulder, only to be stopped by Roger, who said the ice wasn't hard enough yet. Well, Emma being Emma, she disregarded him completely and the second he turned his back, she was skating. The ice, of course, was too thin and she fell under almost instantly. No one was there to help her, but she pulled herself out of the freezing water easily enough and walked back to the house. We only learned of her adventure because she left a muddy trail. It took our housekeeper, Mrs. Pilson, hours to thaw her."

"She's got gumption," said Philip, "gumption and courage."

"Courage is meaningless unless accompanied by good sense," intoned the duke, easily picturing the scene at the pond. How Emma had lived to the ripe, old age of three and twenty amazed him. It was just as well that they were not to make a match of it, he thought, imagining the headstrong foolish offspring she would no doubt produce.

But the relief he felt at not having to fish his daughters out of a frigid pond was short-lived, for the image of a little replica of Emma, four years old, caused a sharp pang.

Vinnie watched the duke carefully, looking for a reaction, any reaction, and was pleased to see him flinch. "Yes, courage is meaningless without sense, which is why we are fortunate that Emma has such a good head on her shoulders."

"Emma?" Trent asked.

"Yes, she has always been very sensible."

Although Trent wanted to change the subject, he could not let this statement go unchallenged. "I have never seen evidence of it. What do you call attacking Windbourne with nothing but a shovel?"

"Patriotism."

The duke snorted.

"You're wrong to be so dismissive," Vinnie said, deciding that now was the time to end this problem-wrought courtship. "Only a woman of good sense turns down a proposal from a man who does not love her. Only a woman of good sense does not enter into a marriage where the love is only on one side. Only a woman of very good sense would break her own heart rather than ruin the life of the man she loves."

"Vinnie?" he said, his voice low and his eyes unusually bright.

She smiled kindly. "You never said it, your grace. How would she know?"

"Know what?" asked Philip, confused by the change in the conversation's direction. Minutes ago they were talking of daring rescues and villains and now the topic was love—insipid, maudlin love. How did that happen?

The duke wasn't inclined to answer Philip. He needed to see Emma and talk to her, and he needed to hold her. Now, desperately, before another second had passed. He left the room without excusing himself but returned seconds later. He looked at Vinnie, and before he could formulate the question, she answered it.

"Third door on your left," she said, laughing happily at his eager expression. She had never in her life seen such a change come over a person. In a split second his demeanor had gone from cautious and sad to exhilarated and impatient.

He knocked softly on the door and waited with a jittery heart for Emma to answer. When she did not, he opened it slowly. Despite the traces of daylight creeping in through the edges of the curtains, the room was dark. Emma was lying on top of the covers, her hand under her cheek. The duke crept quietly to her side and rested on his knees by the bed. He ran a gentle hand through her hair, marveling that this spirited, courageous woman loved him. In the thin light he watched as her eyelids fluttered and opened.

The duke tensed, expecting her to jump out of bed and spit fire at him, but instead she just stared at him for a moment. Then she smiled, not fully awake. Her eyes were unfocused and soft, just the way they had been when he'd awakened that morning, and he decided to say now what he should have said then.

"I love you," he whispered, pressing a kiss against her soft cheek.

"I love you, too," she murmured, almost as if she were talking in her sleep. Then she closed her eyes again.

This was not quite the reaction the duke had anticipated. He'd expected lavish kisses and detailed explanations and giddy arguments over what they would name their children. It had never occurred to him that the first time he declared his feelings to a woman that it would put her to sleep. Still, he was well satisfied with her answer. All a man could wish for was that when he told a woman he loved her she promptly said it back.

He kissed her cheek again and, hearing her sigh, decided it was better to quit the room. The events of the last few days had exhausted her, and God knew he hadn't let her get much sleep the night before. He'd let her sleep now, though. Leaving her was the last thing he wanted to do, but he was a sensible man. They had the rest of their lives together; he could spare the two hours before dinner. He'd be back at seven, of course, to wake her up. Perhaps then they could talk about the future.

With much regret, the duke got to his feet. He didn't know how he was going to pass the next two hours. He would probably station himself outside her door so that he could be near her without waking her up. No, he decided, he wasn't that much of a besotted fool. He'd return to Philip's room, which, being just down the hall, was close but not too close. Perhaps they could play cards. Surely the landlord had a deck on hand.

At first Emma's sleep-addled mind dismissed the duke's declaration as a dream. It was what she wanted to hear, had indeed wished to hear, and it seemed just the sort of thing that a smitten woman's mind would fabricate. But something about it simply wasn't right. What was it? *My eyes were open.*

Emma awoke instantly, just in time to see the duke's hand reach for the doorknob. "Wait," she called to him as she scrambled off the bed, "wait a second." He turned around and even in the darkened room she could see the delight in his eyes. "You cannot make a confession and walk away," she said, throwing herself into his arms.

"Why not?" he asked with a laugh. "You made a confession and then fell asl—"

The Harlow Hoyden silenced him with her lips. It was a searing kiss, and the duke responded enthusiastically, tightening his arms around her. It lasted for several long moments; then the duke raised his head. "I love you."

"Good," she said, her dimples out in full force.

"Thank you for staying awake this time. I'm relieved that all my declarations will not put you into a state of repose."

"I don't know about that. I certainly want to be in that bed right now."

Trent laughed and lifted her into his arms. "You are wicked, Miss Harlow, seducing me in my bath last night

259

before I could gather my wits about me."

"What are you saying? If you had your wits, then we would not have had last night?"

"No," he said, sitting on the bed, "I'm saying that had I not been overcome with lust, I would have told you how I felt last night. It's a great shame that you are so skilled at igniting a man's passion, otherwise we wouldn't have passed such a miserable day."

Although the day had been the worst of her entire life, Emma could laugh easily at it now. "Surely it's not a *great* shame that I am so skilled at igniting your passions, your grace," she whispered into his ear before nibbling on the lobe.

The duke shuddered in response. "Really, Emma, when you use the words *ignite* and *passion* in the same sentence, you should address me by my given name. Perhaps you should practice saying it."

"I love you, Alex."

This employment so moved the duke that neither one of them was able to speak for a very long time. "We should stop," muttered the duke, as he undid the buttons on the back of her ugly mint-green dress.

"All right," she breathed, paying similar attention to his shirt.

He moved the fabric aside and kissed the tops of her breasts. "In a moment then."

She sighed luxuriously and pulled his shirt free of the breeches. "In a long moment."

He lifted his head and removed the unwanted barrier of his shirt entirely. "A *very* long moment."

Emma indulged a deep, throaty laugh and pushed the duke back against the pillows. Her loose blond hair brushed his shoulders as she leaned down to kiss him.

Suddenly there was a knock on the door.

"Emma darling, are you awake?"

Both Emma and the duke froze, but only she had to fight down an unexpected bout of giggles. "It's Vinnie," she whispered into her beloved's ear.

"I know," answered the duke.

"What should I say?"

"That you are awake?"

Still straddling the duke, Emma said, "I'm awake."

"Good, and is the duke with you?"

Emma looked at him and saw him nod in the faint light. My God, was he with her! "Yes."

"Very good, then do tell him to present himself to me within the next fifteen minutes to ask for your hand."

"All right, dear," Emma said, her face pressed against Trent's warm flesh, and she gave in to the fit of laughter that had almost overtaken her during her exchange with Vinnie. Then she raised her head and said, "You know more of these matters than I do, Alex. Is fifteen minutes enough time?"

"Well," he answered consideringly, "it's now only thirteen minutes, since you wasted two laughing. And although there are some gentlemen who can not only complete the task in thirteen minutes but also take pride in that fact, I am not one of them. We will do this right or not at all. Now hand me my shirt so I can go present myself to Vinnie. Do you suppose she has the authority to give me your hand?"

Emma climbed off him reluctantly. "Possibly. She *is* six minutes older."

"I will of course send word to your father as soon as we return to town." He pulled one arm through the cotton sleeve. "We'll wed by special license as soon as I can get everything arranged."

"Excellent," she said, lying on the bed with her dress still undone.

Trent buttoned up his shirt and turned his attention to Emma. She let him make her respectable and presentable again and then kissed him with such passion that he nearly undid all his good work. He pulled himself away and opened the door. "You may as well come along. Vinnie will have more fun gloating if both of us are there."

"Vinnie doesn't gloat," Emma insisted, taking his hand.

They found her sister in the private parlor with a book on her lap. She wasn't reading but rather staring out the window at the setting sun. "Three minutes to spare," she said, turning her head when she caught their reflection in the window.

"I've learned by now not to flaunt the dictates of either of the Misses Harlow," he explained with a smile. Then he walked over to Vinnie, took her hands in his and pulled her into his arms for a hug. "Thank you, my dear friend."

"No, thank you two for finally sorting out all the misunderstandings," she said, brusquely. "I assure you I didn't have the energy to go another round with either one of you."

Emma laughed. "Vinnie, I don't know how you did it but thank you. You're the best sister in the world, and I love you dearly."

These heartfelt words brought tears to Vinnie's eyes. "Ironic as it is, you owe Windbourne your thanks more than me," she said, trying to lighten the moment. "If he hadn't been such a scoundrel, Emma would never have stolen that orchid and the two of you would not have met."

The duke was unwilling to give Windbourne any credit. "We would have met, I'm sure of it."

"Well, I'm glad that's all over. The lovers are reunited, and the villain is vanquished. A very satisfactory ending, no? Now, where's the landlord? I wanted to request lamb chops for dinner."

Emma laughed. It was so like Vinnie to go from the poetic to the prosaic in one breath. "It is not *all* over."

Vinnie halted her movements, not liking her sister's tone. "How so?"

"We still have to catch the villain in the Home Office. Windbourne said that someone was feeding him information," she explained. "We can't let that man go free, not when the safety of the country rests on it."

"She's right," Trent said. "He will have to be caught, but we do not have to do it. We will tell the proper authorities and they will apprehend him."

"But who should we trust with the information? Nobody save the prime minister is above suspicion," Emma pointed out.

"We'll tell the prime minister then," he said reasonably.

"But he'll have the very same problem. No, it seems clear to me that the only thing for it is for us to set a trap and catch the villain ourselves. It won't be very hard, I'm sure. We'll have Roger spread some false information such as Windbourne told me the name of his informant. That alone should suffice."

"Suffice in provoking someone to murder you," Trent growled.

"Exactly, that's when we'll catch him."

"You can't be serious," said Vinnie, horrified by this plan.

"Why not?" Emma was wide-eyed with surprise.

"You could be killed."

"Pooh," she said, waving a dismissive hand.

Trent raised an eyebrow at Vinnie. "Courageous *and* sensible, I believe you said."

Vinnie made a moue of disgust. "That was for your benefit, and it was an outright lie."

"It's a sensible plan," insisted Emma, "and I challenge either of you to come up with a better one."

"We'll say that Windbourne told *me* who his informant is," said the duke.

"But Windbourne never had a chance," said Emma.

Although Vinnie didn't want Roger to put it about that Windbourne had told any of her family the name of the traitor, she much preferred that Trent be the bait than Emma. He was less impulsive. "The informant wouldn't know that."

Emma sent her sister an annoyed look. "It doesn't matter. Trent will never do. He is too worthy an opponent for anyone to willingly take on. No, it must be a seemingly weak and helpless female; we are continually underestimated by the other sex. We can use that to our advantage."

Because there was truth in this statement, the duke said, "We will talk about this later."

"Trent, you must stop her," ordered Vinnie.

"I cannot stop her, Vinnie, no one can. Surely you know that by now. But I can be at her side and protect her."

"Bravo," cheered the Harlow Hoyden, "that's just the sort of speech a bride longs to hear her groom make."

Vinnie rolled her eyes in disgust. "I wash my hands of the lot of you."

Emma didn't laugh until her sister's stiff figure was out of sight. "She can be very dramatic sometimes."

"Emma, I love you."

She stopped laughing. It was amazing how those words, still so shiny and new, could make her heart leap. "I know and it's very kind of you to say so."

"I want to make you happy as my wife."

"Never visit dancers in Chelsea and let me drive the curricle and you'll succeed to that end beautifully."

"Dancers in Chelsea?" he asked, trying to discover the relevance of this statement.

"When you were listing your qualifications as a libertine, you told me you kept a dancer in Chelsea. Or was it an opera singer in Mayfair?" she said, making light of something that had tortured her for so long. "No matter, as long as there are no performance artists in your life, I'll be quite happy."

"You have no need to worry on that score, Emma. I ended that alliance weeks ago. I have been unable to think of anyone but you."

"Not even the widow Enderling?"

"My God, don't tell me that's the reason you said no to my proposal this morning!"

"What?" Emma asked, confused.

"You really do believe I'm a libertine."

"Bah! Despite your best efforts, you never managed to convince me."

The duke ignored her feeble protestation, recalling instead the words she had coldly hurled at him when they'd first woken up. *What we've just done? Is it not what you do with dancers in Chelsea and widows and any willing female who crosses your path? Isn't that what you libertines do?*

Now, of course, in retrospect it was all so clear. He could even pinpoint the exact moment when everything went disastrously wrong. Instead of stalking off like a wounded tiger, he should have taken Emma into his arms and sworn to her that what they'd just done was nothing like what he did with a mistress. Emma had needed reassurances, and he left the room to nurse his bruised ego. "Emma, I won't pretend that I haven't had my share of encounters, but I've never experienced anything that even comes close to last night. And if I were a libertine, which I am not, by the way, my share being considerably less than, say, Carson's, I would repent and change my ways for the chance to spend just one more night in your arms. You make me extraordinarily happy, imp, and you make me feel things I didn't know were possible."

"A very pretty speech, sir," Emma said, pleased of course but also disconcerted by the intensity with which he spoke. She lowered her eyes.

Trent placed a finger under her chin and raised her head until her eyes met his. "It's only the truth, Emma. I'm sorry I didn't say it sooner." He stared at her steadily until she gave some indication of understanding and then kissed her gently on the lips. "And as I was trying to say earlier, I want you to be happy as my wife, for I know you have no love of marriage—"

"It is not marriage I mind so much as husbands, Alex," she rushed to explain. "As you yourself pointed out, Windbag's desire to have Vinnie do nothing but raise his children and see to his comfort made him a husband, not a villain."

"*A* husband, yes, but not *your* husband," he corrected. "I am not a fool, Emma. I expect you to have interests outside of our marriage. I only ask that you try to avoid danger, and if you cannot then that you take me with you. There will be no more solitary trips down to the docks."

"Well of course I'll take you with me. For one, you are my most trusted ally and for another, you're great fun to have around."

"Thank you, my dear, I don't know when I've been paid a higher compliment."

Emma smiled, beginning to see the advantages of having a husband. No one in society cared what boring, old married ladies did, nor did they expect them to behave with the *utmost* propriety. Perhaps this was where true freedom lay. "Alex, when we are married, will you mind very much if I race to Newmarket alone to try to beat my own record? It was the very devil having to take Roger with me for the sake of my reputation."

Her husband-to-be laughed. "Not at all, my dear. Indeed, I think I shall take a crack at it myself."

CHAPTER FOURTEEN

They had barely pulled the carriages up to the town house before Sarah was running toward them. She saw Emma first.

"Oh, you poor dear," she said, holding her sister-in-law tightly in her arms. "We have been so worried. You must never do that to us again, you wicked girl. The next time you run off, you must leave a note."

Emma laughed delightedly at Sarah's censorious tone. "I didn't mean to cause trouble, my love. The situation called for immediate action. Once we are inside, we'll tell you all about it and I'm sure you'll agree that I behaved in the best way possible."

Sarah doubted that she'd ever agree to such an outlandish claim, but before she got a chance to say anything, Vinnie stepped out of the carriage. Releasing Emma, she walked over to Vinnie and put her hands on her shoulders. "Ah, the sensible twin! Vinnie, what am I to do if I cannot rely on your good judgment?"

Vinnie donned a penitent looked that was belied by the twinkle in her eye. "Sarah, trust me, the situation was so unlikely, no one's judgment could be relied upon to be wholly sensible."

Sarah, whose interest in what had happened during the last few days was already acute, became, impossibly, even more curious. Correctly reading her expression, Vinnie said, "Emma is right. Let's not have a talk on the front walk of the house. We will be inside soon enough."

Sarah agreed with this statement and devoted her energies to moving the party indoors. The trouble seemed to be Philip, who was trying to get out of the carriage.

"No, I think I should take you right home," said the duke, stopping his cousin's attempt to hop down on one leg. "The long ride couldn't have been good for your wound."

"Don't be such a flat, Trent. I ain't going home to lie in bed while the rest of you plot how to catch the master spy," he protested. "Tell him, Miss Harlow, how I have as much a right as anyone to be here."

"He's right, Alex," said Emma, responding promptly to this plea for help. "He did take a bullet. Besides, the drive wasn't that rackety. I missed all but the smallest potholes."

"Alex?" echoed Sarah. "Since when do you call the duke Al—" Then she digested the rest of the sentence and paled. "Bullet? How did Mr. Keswick get struck by a bullet?"

Emma laid a comforting hand on Sarah's shoulder. "We'll tell you all about it in a minute, dearest. Just let us get Philip comfortably settled in the drawing room. And perhaps we could get something to eat. We hardly stopped on the way, for we knew you and Roger must be beside yourselves with worry. How is my dear brother?"

"He is well."

"Good. Why don't you go into the house and see about food? And if Roger is awake he should join us for our discussion. This concerns him, too."

Realizing that to stay and argue would only waste time, Sarah agreed. She returned to the house, told Ludlow to help Roger to the drawing room and disappeared into the kitchen to see about a light collation for the group of weary travelers.

Although her interest in the events were keen, all such thoughts deserted her when she saw the duke sitting so close to Emma on the settee. Was he holding her hand?

"Emma, are you and the duke…" Before she could

finish the sentence, Emma was nodding happily. Sarah felt a lump form in her throat and fought the surge of emotion. Imagine! Emma a duchess. "That is above all things wonderful, my dear. Come, let me give you a hug."

Emma willingly complied and then stood back as her sister-in-law subjected Trent to similar treatment. "Your brother will be very pleased. Where is he? I sent Ludlow up fifteen minutes ago." Sarah sat down in a large armchair by the fire. "This is such a lovely surprise. I had given up on either one of you girls getting married and now both of you are betrothed."

Vinnie blushed. "Ah, not exactly, Sarah."

Sarah turned to Vinnie. "What do you mean?"

"I've broken off my engagement with Sir Windbourne."

"But why?"

Vinnie looked so abashed by this question that Trent stepped in to answer. "That's what we are here to discuss. As soon as—" The doors opened and admitted Roger, who was strong enough now to climb down the stairs on his own. "Ah, there you, my good fellow. We were just about to start telling our tale."

Roger accepted Trent's hand, greeted his sisters with surprisingly strong embraces, inquired after Philip's health and took a seat. "Well, you are an unlikely party. Emma, wherever did you get that horrid dress?"

"Roger!" admonished his wife, who thought that Roger should not point out how awful Emma looked on the off chance that her betrothed had not yet noticed.

Roger sent Sarah a confused look.

Emma laughed. "The dress is a cautionary tale of what happens when you leave town without luggage."

"Yes," said Sarah, "do tell us why you had to leave town without luggage, without a companion and without advising your family."

"It's not a pretty story," stated Emma. "It starts with Roger."

"With Roger?" repeated Sarah.

"Me?"

"Yes, you," she told her brother. "Does Sarah know about your work for the government?"

"How do you know—" He coughed. "I mean, what work for the government?"

Emma smiled thinly. "It is too late now, Roger. The cat's out of the bag. We all know, as did Sir Waldo."

"What work?" asked Sarah.

Roger looked distinctly uncomfortable. Emma felt little sympathy for him. When one lied to one's wife and put oneself in danger, one must be prepared to suffer the consequences. "Should you tell her or I?" she asked.

He straightened his shoulders and turned to his wife. "I've been doing a little work for the government. Nothing very important, really, just passing along information from the Home Office to some of our operatives in the field, here and in France."

"But why?" Sarah asked, hardly able to digest this information. "The war is over, is it not?" Reading Sarah's expression, Emma knew that Roger would have to give a more thorough account of himself when they were alone.

Roger shook his head sadly. "We know that Napoléon is planning to escape St. Helena, but we don't know when or how. His most trusted generals have gathered in Corsica and are even now scheming to invade England." He looked at each of their shocked faces. "This is top-secret information, you understand. It doesn't leave this room."

Emma nodded. "Your messages were being intercepted by Windbag."

"Impossible!"

"Not quite," said Vinnie with wry humor. "He had a key to your private drawer, and as my fiancé, he had free run of the house. Indeed, it was rather easy for him. Emma caught him in the act."

Roger looked at Emma for confirmation. She nodded.

Still, he could scarcely credit it. "But how did he know?"

"Someone in the Home Office betrayed you," Emma said.

"Who?" he asked, his voice low and dangerous.

"We don't know that yet," answered Trent, "but we have a plan."

"A stupid plan," muttered Vinnie.

"I think it's a fine plan," said Philip, who had been quiet until now. "Emma's the best choice. I'd do it myself, only I ain't so agile with this cane. And no one in his right mind would go after Trent. Everyone knows he's a master shot and good with his fists."

"What's this plan?" Roger asked, a suspicion already forming.

Before explaining her plan, Emma went back to the beginning, to the afternoon in the study when Windbourne came in to do his dastardly business. The telling took a while, for everyone broke in with different remembrances, and Emma, fed up with the interruptions, insisted that Trent finish the story.

Roger didn't like the plan any better than Vinnie, but he reluctantly admitted that telling his superiors that Emma knew the name of his betrayer was the surest way to learn his identity.

"I do not like it," said Sarah.

"None of us like it," said Trent.

"But she has already been through so much horror."

"Pooh," dismissed Emma, glad that her sister-in-law could not see the awful-looking bruises on her neck. "What I have been through can only be categorized as discomfort. And with our country's safety at stake, how can I cavil at a few more moments of discomfort?"

Sarah knew it wasn't that simple. "But your life will be at stake!"

"Trent will protect me, and besides, as I've demonstrated in the past, I can take care of myself."

"Fending off a few overeager suitors is not the same

as confronting a murderer," Sarah said, making what she thought was a very good point.

"We do not know that he's a murderer," Emma reasoned. "He might only be a traitor."

Sarah was unimpressed by this argument. "A man who would betray his country is without conscience."

Emma threw up her hands. She'd never known Sarah to be so difficult. "All right, then provide us with another plan and we will happily abandon our imperfect one."

Sarah had several ideas that she thought were quite good, but either Roger or Trent or Emma—or all of them together—shot each of them down. It seemed that anything they did put someone's life at risk. She finally agreed.

"Excellent," said Emma. "So first thing in the morning Roger will visit the Home Office and make them aware that Windbourne told me the name of his informant. However, to everyone's dismay, I passed out from a head wound before I could reveal the name but the doctor believes I should wake up within the next twenty-four hours."

Roger nodded. "A specified amount of time will ensure that the villain will move swiftly."

"And be sure to mention the part where I am lying in bed unattended in a largely deserted house," Emma added.

"Good," said Trent standing up. "I think I should get Philip home. No doubt my family is wondering what happened to us, and I'm sure that Emma and Vinnie haven't had much rest since their adventure began."

Emma fought a blush as images from her night with Trent played in her mind. She seemed to have developed the habit of recalling her fiancé's naked body at the most inopportune times. She faked a yawn to hide her embarrassment. "Yes, I'm thoroughly exhausted. And I'm longing to get out of this awful dress."

Now Trent's eyes blazed as he recalled how close he himself had come to getting her out of that awful dress. He cocked his head to the side, indicating that he wanted a quiet word with Emma. They stood in the corner of the elegantly appointed room surrounded by her family.

He lowered his head and said softly, "I'll hardly be able to sleep tonight without you in my bed."

Her color rose. "Alex," she said, wanting him to stop and continue at the same time.

He smiled, pleased by her charming response. "I will be back here tomorrow before Roger leaves. I do not want to take any chances."

"Excellent, then we'll spend hours and hours in my bed chamber. Whatever will we do to pass the time?" she asked innocently.

"Nothing distracting, imp, and I don't think we'll be alone, so abandon your lascivious thoughts. I suspect Roger will be taking a pistol and hiding behind a curtain, too."

"Oh, well, a girl can dream, can't she?"

"Yes, and I hope she does—of me."

His betrothed thought this was rather likely.

Emma tied her dressing gown around her waist, luxuriating in the feel of her own clean clothing against her skin, and knocked on her sister's door.

Vinnie's maid opened the door to reveal Vinnie sitting in front of the mirror brushing her hair. "That will be all, Emily. Thank you for your help."

"'Tis luvely to have ye back, miss," said the soft-spoken girl. She smiled thinly at Emma. "Ye too, miss."

When the maid had closed the door Emma said, "Liar."

"What's that?" Vinnie put down the brush.

"I was calling into question the veracity of your maid," she said, sitting down on the edge of the pink-covered bed. "I know for a fact she isn't happy I'm back."

"What ridiculousness."

"Lucy says Emily hates doing the mending and that there's always twice as much when I'm in residence."

"Well, you won't be here for long." Vinnie fluffed a pillow against the headboard and sat down across from

Emma. "I get the feeling from Trent that you'll be bothering other servants with your torn dresses before the week is out."

"Yes, he does seem eager to leg-shackle himself to the infamous Harlow Hoyden. You'd think a man of his age and experience would know better."

"He does, which is why he is so determined to see it done right and proper as fast as humanly possible." Vinnie sighed and fell silent for a moment, suddenly reflective. "It's funny, isn't it?"

"What?" asked Emma, lying back on the bed and turning her head to face her sister.

"Well, here you are getting married, after you swore up and down that you never would, and I, who always longed for children, am suddenly thinking that the role of spinster aunt might suit me fine."

Emma sat up and took her sister's hand. "Vinnie, just because your first fiancé turned out to be a villainous traitor doesn't mean that you won't find someone else. You mustn't start thinking again that you'll wind up on the shelf. You won't, Vinnie. You're smart and interesting and passably pretty and funny and you can have any man you want."

Vinnie laughed and extricated her hand. "Not quite any man I want but I will agree that I stand a reasonable chance of catching a husband if I want one. See," she said, a hint of pride in her voice, "I'm not quite as insecure now as I was before I met Windbourne. But I've realized that my flowers are so much more than a hobby, and I can't give them up. Trent suggested that I write some pamphlets for the—"

"Trent suggested it?" she asked.

"Yes. They'd be just for the Horticultural Society and the topic would be boring drainage systems," she rushed to explain, "but it was very flattering to be asked, don't you think?"

"Yes, very flattering indeed."

After a long pause, Vinnie said, "I've been thinking of writing a book on how to grow orchids."

"You have?" She turned away so that her sister wouldn't see the tears in her eyes. Vinnie would only ask what was wrong, and she'd be at a loss to explain. Indeed, she didn't know why she was crying. Perhaps it was because Trent was so good or because her sister was finally realizing her own worth.

"Yes, I even have a few chapters already done. I'd be honored if you'd read them. One or two pages are a little scorched. Sir Waldo dropped them into the fire by mistake."

She wiped away a tear. "Of course, although I'm sure I won't understand half of it."

"Oh, but you should. I've written it with people like you in mind."

"Simpletons who don't know a trowel from a rhizome?"

"Beginners. Really, Emma, you are attaching yourself to the finest orchid grower in the country. I don't think you'll stay disinterested for long."

"I'm not so sure about that," said Emma, thinking how dreadfully dull it must be to watch plants grow. "And you have it the wrong way around, my dear. It is Trent who is attaching himself to the finest orchid grower in the country."

"And *I'm* not so sure about that. But no matter, I will devote myself to my flowers for a few years, and if I happen to meet a man who sets my head spinning the way Trent does yours, then I'll consider the prospect. Until then…."

"Trent does not set my head spinning!" she protested. "What a perfectly ridiculous phrase."

"Really? Only a girl whose head isn't on straight goes down to the wine cellar in order to escape hearing about her sister's ride through the park." Vinnie giggled.

A thought struck Emma. "You did it on purpose!"

"If you can't torment your lovesick sister, then who can you torment?"

Emma couldn't quite raise the proper amount of outrage. It had been she who cast the first stone when she'd formulated her plan to have Trent seduce Vinnie. The clock on the wall struck ten and Emma rolled off the bed. "I'm thoroughly exhausted, my dear, and want nothing more than to sleep for hours and hours." She kissed her still laughing sister on the forehead. "I will see you tomorrow, and we'll talk more about this torment you imposed on me. I'm suddenly suspicious of a whole host of incidents."

"As well you should be," Vinnie called after her.

Barely able to keep her eyes open, Emma climbed into bed, blew out the candle and was asleep mere moments after her head hit the pillow.

Emma thought she was reliving the nightmarish moments when Windbag almost ended her life in that little hovel in Dover, but when she tried to wake herself up from the dream she realized with terror that she was no longer asleep. The hands around her neck were very real. The room was completely dark, and she could barely see the outline of the figure standing above her trying to squeeze the life out of her body.

She tried to scream for help, but when no sound issued forth she realized she would have to alert her family to danger another way. Struggling to free herself of his hold, she reached blindly to the side of the bed. Surely there had to be an object there that when thrown against the wall would shatter loudly. Her hand connected with something cool and hard. A silver candlestick.

She clutched the candlestick in her grasp and struck her attacker on the back of his head. The blow was not delivered with enough force to dislodge the assailant, but it did surprise him. He loosened his grip for a fleeting moment and Emma eagerly swallowed. Feeling considerably stronger, she thrashed him again.

He muttered angry curses and in a fit of temper slapped her hard across the cheek. The pain tore through Emma, but she took no notice. His rage had given her the advantage, and as soon as he removed his hands from her throat, she screamed as loudly as she could. He realized his mistake instantly and put a muffling, sweaty hand over her mouth. She bit his palm. He pulled away his bleeding hand and tried to regain his grip on her throat but could not. Emma bashed him with the candlestick for a third time. The strike fazed him for a moment. She screamed again. Where was help? Vinnie's room was right across the hall and Roger's was only five doors down. Surely they didn't all sleep *that* soundly!

Emma was about to raise the candlestick again when she felt something cold and sharp at her throat. It was a knife.

"Don't move," her attacker said, revealing his identity for the first time, "or I shall slice you from ear to ear."

It was too dark to see his features, but she knew it was Windbourne. "How?" she asked, unable to understand his presence in her bedchamber. Why wasn't he locked up in a Dover gaol?

He laughed, an awful sneering, mocking sound with little humor. "Colonel Rivington is a fool. After you left, Le Penn convinced him that you and Trent were impostors who work for the French. It wasn't very hard. Le Penn wasn't home when the soldier got there, but his mother had the presence of mind to be lying in bed sick. And the soldier whom the colonel sent to the docks was a man Le Penn often paid to do chores for him. He alerted him to the troubles, giving Le Penn the chance to find a doctor and return to his home. Rivington was inclined not to trust either of you. He thought your story was rather suspicious. Once Rivington was assured that Le Penn and I were patriots, he let us go."

"You're very stupid, Windbourne," she said, wishing the room weren't quite so dark. If only there was some moonlight to see by. "You were free and yet came to London to enact petty revenge. You will hang at Whitechapel when you could have been safe in France."

"The revenge, which is in no way petty, I assure you, my dear, is merely a convenient aside to a more complicated, more encompassing plan. Le Penn and I were returning to London regardless."

"Le Penn is with you? Then he hasn't passed along the information yet? The French do not know the names of the English spies?" Emma laughed hysterically. "You are stupid *and* a bad operative."

"France will get the information as soon as we settle a debt with McEnvoy. He made certain promises that we're going to give him a chance to deliver on a little earlier than planned. And if he doesn't…."

"And if he doesn't?" she asked, though she could well imagine that he, too, would feel the cold steel of Sir Waldo's knife.

"That's no concern of yours. Indeed, I'm very happy to report that in a moment you'll never have another concern ever again, you interfering bi—"

"That pressure you're feeling on the small of your back is the barrel of my pistol," Vinnie said calmly. "It's silver with a faintly pink-tinted mother-of-pearl handle. I give you a detailed description lest you think I'm holding something harmless like a candlestick or butter knife."

Emma's shock, which was considerable indeed—who knew Vinnie could move with such stealth—was nothing compared with Windbourne's. He began to sputter, a rather ridiculous sound that unaccountably made Emma want to giggle. She controlled herself. She wouldn't do anything that might possibly disturb Vinnie's concentration.

"Now, if you don't release Emma, I'm going to shoot you with my silver pistol with the lovely mother-of-pearl handle." In the almost complete darkness of the room, Emma could barely make out the figure of her sister. "Although I don't have much experience with guns, I have taken one or two shots in my lifetime and know very well that I'm quite accomplished at pulling a trigger, especially one like this, which easily gives way under the slightest pressure. Do you understand me, Sir Waldo?"

"Vinnie, my darling, you don't understand what—"

"Waldo, my dearest, I understand very well. Now, tell me, do I shoot you? It will make a bloody mess, but I don't suppose Dobson will mind very much. We're not an impoverished family and can afford the purchase of new blankets."

The cold way in which her sister spoke gave Emma chills. She never suspected that dear, sweet Vinnie could face a murderer with such steel in her shoulders.

"I'm putting the knife down," he said bitterly. "Don't shoot."

Windbourne lowered the knife, and Emma let out a breath she had been holding for an intolerably long time. Now that the fight was over, her heart was pounding with painful swiftness and her knees felt weak. But she knew she had to remain strong. Until she beheld him for herself behind bars in Newgate, she would consider him a threat.

She was about to get to her feet when she saw him move with sudden speed in her sister's direction, the outline of the knife horrifyingly distinct. "*Vinnie!*" she screamed a split second before she heard the gun discharge.

Emma lit a candle. In the gentle glow, she could see Windbourne's lifeless eyes staring up at her. Vinnie, pale and shaking like a leaf, was staring down at him. Tears pouring down her face, Emma ran to her side and pulled her into her arms. "Don't look, dear," she said, pressing Vinnie's face against her shoulder. "Just don't look."

Vinnie held on to her with all her strength and although her body was trembling, her voice was steady. "It's all right, Emma. I'm here and everything's going to be all right."

Emma laughed hoarsely. "I'm supposed to be comforting you."

Just then Sarah came running into the room, followed closely by Roger. Upon seeing Windbourne's corpse on Emma's bed, Sarah screamed. Roger soberly covered the body with an already bloody blanket and suggested in his calm, even voice that they let Ludlow handle the cleanup.

Emma and Vinnie agreed with alacrity, and they followed Sarah and Roger into the drawing room, where soothing tea was ordered.

Roger called for an explanation, and Emma had barely started her recitation when a loud pounding sounded at the door. Everyone froze. Roger told his family to remain where they were and went into the foyer to answer it. He looked through the peephole and said, "Good God, it's Trent."

Emma jumped to her feet and ran to the door, pushing Roger aside. There stood Trent on the doorstep, a wild and uncharacteristic look in his eyes. He stared at her for a moment as if not seeing her. Then with a strangled cry he dragged her into his arms and held her so tightly she couldn't breathe.

"I'm all right," she whispered over and over again, running her hands through his soft hair.

After a while, Trent nodded and kissed her neck. He took a deep breath and tried to steady himself. "He told me you were dead."

"Le Penn?"

"Yes, he told me you were already dead, that there was nothing I could do. He said he came here first and made short work of you." He pulled back and stared into her beautiful eyes. "I couldn't believe it."

"Of course not," she said, running a comforting hand down his cheek. "Nobody makes short work of me, Alex."

"God, no!" he said, brushing his lips gently against hers before kissing her passionately. They would have stayed like that for a great many minutes if Sarah had not coughed discreetly over their shoulders.

"It's not that I don't think the actions are warranted," she explained, "it's just that it's not quite the thing to behave so on the front doorstep. Shall we take it into the drawing room?'

Emma laughed, recalling that they were indeed outside. However, the late hour ensured that few passersby would witness their improper behavior. Still, she took Trent's hand and led him inside.

"We've had an eventful evening," said Roger, "as it appears you have as well." The duke's presentation was not impeccably flawless as usual. His jacket was torn, his hair thoroughly disheveled, and there seemed to be dried blood on his lip. "Why don't you tell us what happened to you, and then we'll return the favor."

Although this plan had merit, the duke would rather have talked first about Emma. He could not miss the swollen red bruise on her cheek. "I was attacked by Le Penn, who is, as you know, Windbourne's associate from Dover. He came upon me in my bedchamber with a gun, and had I not been still awake, he surely would've killed me without my ever being the wiser. Fortunately, sleep had eluded me and I was able to dodge the shot. A fight ensued. Rest assured, Le Penn will not be bothering us in the future."

"He is dead then?" asked Roger.

"No, he's not dead, but I will make sure that this time he doesn't escape, even if I have to guard the prison gates myself."

"He never went to prison," Emma said, launching into an explanation of what had happened to her.

When she was done, the duke turned to Vinnie. "My dearest friend, I can never thank you enough."

"Pooh," she said, dimples in both cheeks. "Just hand over a cutting of your *Quisqueya fuertesii* and we shall call it even."

The duke laughed. "My conservatory is at your disposal. In fact, the entire conservatory is yours. Do with it what you will."

"I'm not so gullible, your grace. I'll install one of my useful drainage systems and then you'll suddenly reclaim it. No, I will content myself with a *Quisqueya fuertesii*. And perhaps a *Restrepia guttulata* as well."

Roger stood up. "I should see how Ludlow is getting on. In a few hours I will send a note to Garrison, my boss at the Home Office. He will know what to do about McEnvoy."

"Is he very high up?" Emma asked.

"He is a midlevel secretary who has access to many

privileged documents. I expect with a little convincing Le Penn will be willing to inform against him so that it won't just be your word against McEnvoy. In my experience, these spies never have much fortitude when confronted by determined English soldiers," Roger said. "Now, if you'll excuse me, I should help Ludlow. No, Trent, you should stay with the ladies. They've had a troubling evening and could use the company."

"Actually," said Vinnie, stifling a yawn, "what I could use is sleep. Do you mind, Emma, if I turn in?"

"Of course not, dear, only are you sure you're all right?" Emma asked, fearful that the events of the last hour might be overwhelming to Vinnie. It was still hard for Emma to believe that of the two Harlow misses, Vinnie was the one who had actually shot and killed a man. She seemed remarkably unfazed by it.

"Yes, I'm quite positive," she assured her. "Indeed, I'm more worried that you'll have nightmares. I'm not the one who woke with a man's fingers around my throat." On that note, she left the drawing room, indicating to Sarah with a speaking glance that she should do the same.

"Oh," Sarah said, because the idea of giving the two lovers a moment alone had not occurred to her, "I suppose I ought to see about having a spare room made up for you, Emma. You can't possibly stay in your own chamber tonight—or ever again, for that matter. Trent, I trust you won't stay too long. The extraordinary circumstances allow for leniency but in the end propriety must be observed," Sarah said, giving Emma a soft kiss on the forehead.

When they were alone, the duke pulled Emma into his arms and kissed her gently. He meant only to tease her lips with his own before bidding her good night, but once he tasted her, he couldn't draw back. He drank her in, savoring the life that beat so forcefully within her. His hand grazed her breast, and feeling her nipple harden beneath the soft fabric, he moaned.

"You're everything to me," he whispered, running a

hand under her dressing gown. He could feel her heart beating under the smooth, warm flesh. She was so startlingly alive.

"I'm rather fond of you myself," she said, her voice low with desire. She knew it wasn't at all the thing, but she wanted him, here in the drawing room by the fire. Tonight they had both come very close to dying, and she could think of no better way to celebrate life than to make love in the drawing room. So what if they were not yet married? That was a condition easily rectified.

She extricated herself from Trent's grasp, walked over to the doors and turned the latch. "There," she said, a mischievous smile on her lips, "now we shan't be disturbed."

Trent felt the blood pounding in his ears—and elsewhere. "Sarah said I shouldn't stay long," he protested, trying to do the right thing. Under normal circumstances they would have never been left alone in a deserted drawing room in the early hours of the morning.

Emma took off her nightdress and threw it on the floor. She stood before him, her golden skin glowing in the firelight. "Then we won't take long."

Trent groaned. "But propriety, my love."

Emma laughed. "I'm the Harlow Hoyden, Alex. The last thing anyone expects from me is propriety."

ABOUT THE AUTHOR

Lynn Messina is the author of nine novels, including the best-selling *Fashionistas,* which has been translated into 16 languages. Her essays have appeared in *Self, American Baby* and the Modern Love column in the *New York Times,* and she's a regular contributor to the *Times* Motherlode blog. She lives in New York City with her husband and sons.

Made in the USA
Columbia, SC
17 January 2020

86895467R00171